I0763604

Creed of Legends

Book One of the Tales of Fear & Fortitude

A.K. Kubica

Twin Swords Press

For rights and permissions, please contact:

A.K. Kubica
contact@akkubica.com

Twin Swords Press
Visit our website at www.TwinSwordsPress.com

Illustrations by Serge Victor, Jamie Koala, and Pablo Martinez

2nd edition

Hardcover ISBN-13: 979-8-9923623-2-9
Paperback ISBN-13: 979-8-9923623-0-5
eBook ISBN-13: 979-8-9923623-3-6

Published in 2025

To all my loved ones who knew I could succeed
well before it was made apparent to me.
Your words of encouragement helped me
believe in myself and I will be forever grateful.

Sapphire Isles
Diamond Isles
Lolaith
Zethland
Bay of Gems
Bay of the Blessed
Bentixt
Phesius
Hyglen
Nesliaxe
Kresha
Sea of
Kissing
Stones
Geldivin
Fayn Forest
Falla Bay
Gwendalir
Jaguar Hills
The Great
Salt
Sea
Sycil
Krashkin
Turivaun
The Lady &
the Moon
Creet
Kevilly
Dakriarc Bay
Hoefke
Sceryl
Zevida Bay

PRONUNCIATION GUIDE

Ælon - Ā (as in 'cat') - lawn

Ahnvil – AHN-vill

Aiylus - EYE-luss

Auphier - AWE-feer

Bentixt - BEN-ticks

Brudais - brew-DAY-us

Dania - DAY-nee-ah

Eldeva - EL-dev-ah

Estriella – ez-ree-ELL-ah

Eusol - yew-SOL

Ithiador - ITH-ee-ah-door

Jandros - JAWN (as in 'shawn') - drose

Kevilly - kev-ill-EE

Hyglen - HIGH-glen

Lolaith - LOW-layth

Loya - loy-AH

Madidus – mah-did-US

Masiya – meh-SIGH-ah

Mayora - may-OR-ah

Morvian - MOR-vee-an

Omaiya - oh-MY-ah

Pallina - pah-LEE-nah

Pexix - PEX-icks

Phesius - FEY-see-uss

Recluos - REK-low'ss

Rydril - reh-DRILL

Staliva - stah-LEE-vah

Sycil - SIGH-sill

Turivaun - TOUR-ih-vawn

Vorsai - VORE-sigh

V'pnor – VEP-noor

Xenia - ZEN-ee-ah

PROLOGUE

XENIA

The eyes never lie even when the mouth will oblige.

Xenia watched as the little bastard's pale eyes darkened as they rested on her son's face. Clenching her fists, she inhaled sharply. Her husband stood next to her, instinct, no doubt, telling him to calm her. His uniform brushed against the bare skin of her arm while his hand slid into her own. The nails of her other hand dug into her palm, nearly drawing blood. Leifius was the only one who could have soothed her in that moment, but even his presence didn't seem enough to quell the desire to tear the king of Creet's face to shreds.

Leifius' hand gave hers a sharp squeeze which jarred Xenia from her thoughts, and she suddenly came back to herself. She took in the brightly colored tapestries that hung from ceiling to floor as if they were attempting to hide the ancient stone masonry—tapestries which used to mute the cold, desolate feeling but now simply seemed saturated by it. She had never liked the haunted aura of Castle Doriell. The Order had taught her to read the magick that coursed through a structure, understand its past… Xenia did not like what she read within these walls.

She shut her eyes tight as the memories began to wash over her in unbroken waves—memories of blood-red execution and murder, back-stabbing and treason, despoilment, and abuse. Xenia blanched at the vivid imagery as it coiled around her, tightening like a serpent. Steadying her breathing as she had been taught, the coils loosened and the magick slowly melted away from her, leaving only the overpowering stench of fear. It was her own fault, she admitted, for keeping the floodgates open with her raw emotion.

Squaring her shoulders, she opened her eyes to scan her surroundings. Her eyes first focused on the redwood tables that lined the room, as their crimson hue mirrored the murder that had passed before her Inner Eye only moments before. They were adorned with bejeweled silver goblets and pitchers, rich mahogany trenchers, and linen napkins which hung off the tables to flaunt the beautiful embroidered royal crest of the House of Linyeus, golden hammer crossed with silver saber and adorned with a bright six-pointed star.

Xenia had forgotten where she was in all that had transpired within her own mind, and her heart gave a sudden jolt of fright when she remembered what had been the cause. Her eyes darted from face to face until she found her son, eager to see Brudais well and whole, standing beside his father. He was garbed in a linen toga draped tightly across his shoulder, his posture erect, and half his straggly hair pulled back into a loose bun. He nodded respectfully at each remark and his bright blue eyes followed the flow of the conversation as it made its way between those who were assembled.

Leifius stood to his left, a carefully concocted mask of polite indifference shown across his handsome features. His tall, muscular frame complimented his military uniform strikingly; whether it was his fame that made him seem larger than life or his demeanor, she could not tell. His reputation as hero of the Crescent Moon Wars had earned him her hand in marriage, but even after knowing the man for twenty years, she was still in awe of him, as was the rest of Creet. When one walks amongst legends, one is doomed to live in eternal fascination.

Across from Leifius stood Regent Cavison, uncle to the king. His face was pale and weathered and his chestnut hair hung limply about his shoulders. He seemed older than his years could boast. Taking the regency upon his brother's passing had been an affliction to his youth, as had raising the hellion, Tarison. The boy-king, as he was known, stood on Cavison's right. Xenia studied Tarison's features intently: the way his mouth was set in a perturbed frown, his brown hair slicked carefully back, the hint of stubble that graced his chin. She avoided his eyes as she examined him this time. She did not want to act on the anger that had so recently been quelled.

As she shifted her attention back to the conversation, her eyes met the regent's, and she smiled demurely. He returned the smile, undoubtedly assuming her expression was directed at something he said, rather than to reassure him that she'd been listening at all.

"We are delighted that your family was able to attend, Commander," Regent Cavison said to Leifius, a hand placed on her husband's shoulder. "I might ask that they come to court more often."

"We would be more than happy to oblige," he replied, glancing over at Xenia as she tightened her grip warningly on his hand, "but we prefer the peaceful countryside to the bustle of the city streets, and the beautiful villa we've been granted by the crown should not go to waste."

"Yes, of course! But an occasional dinner wouldn't be too bothersome, I'm sure."

"On the contrary, Your Highness; it would be an honor."

Tarison began tapping his foot impatiently. The lustrous purple silk which covered his thin linen tunic gave him the appearance of royalty, but his demeanor did nothing to complement it. Cavison whispered something in the boy-king's ear, and Tarison walked away with a curt bow and an, "Excuse me."

When he was out of earshot, Cavison heaved his shoulders with an exaggerated sigh. "I apologize for the king's behavior; he is a restless boy… but perhaps your young Brudais here would make a fine influence." Moving his gaze to her son, his smile returned. "I've noticed your own restlessness has not impeded your ability to make polite conversation and remember protocol."

Brudais smiled easily back and inclined his head in a way that mimicked his father almost identically. "I am your humble servant, Your Highness."

Cavison's smile brightened, though from Xenia's experience, it was an easy feat to accomplish, particularly with flattery. "What manners, indeed!" Returning his gaze to her husband, he said, "I wonder how they would get along. My nephew could benefit from having such esteemed friends."

Xenia looked over at her son, whose stance stiffened at the suggestion. Friends with the king would be a true honor, of course, and one for which any boy his age would happily jump to task. Except that Tarison wished her son ill, she was sure of it. There was only one way to know if her intuition spoke true.

Xenia picked up the wooden rod and stirred the cauldron in slow and measured movements. As she did, little flecks of the liquid within splashed onto the stone floor, bubbling up and then sizzling into wisps of steam.

She sat in the center of the solar, the windows shuttered so that no light might disturb her. A collection of odd-shaped bottles surrounded her, while a cauldron sat in a bed of hot coals before her. The solar was her sanctuary when she needed a moment from her family, her workplace when it became necessary. She had not called this kind of magick to her in some years. It was old spellverse which she had learned from her tutelage in the Order of Estol, so she read carefully from the worn piece of parchment at her feet.

Her gaze shifted from parchment to cauldron, waiting impatiently for the liquid to cool as the instructions dictated.

The eyes never lie. It was a phrase that kept rolling through Xenia's mind like quiet thunder—a warning. All her thoughts came back to Tarison's cold, dark gaze. It only made her more impatient for her potion to cool to the proper degree, but magick was not something that a Human trifled with idly. If one toyed with it, it would pay them back tenfold.

She dipped the ladle into the cauldron, a messy trickle of dark liquid streaming down its length as she brought it up to touch it to her lips. She knew it was too early to drink it, but... Xenia tipped it back and gulped down the entire ladle of potion.

Xenia grasped at her neck, a rasping moan escaping her, as the hot liquid coated the length of her throat, burning in its descent.

Choking and spluttering, she cursed her own impatience. Perhaps it had only needed a few more—

Her vision swerved and spun, and she felt the painful heat that had filled her throat now filling her skull. For several moments, Xenia was completely at the mercy of the magick within her, and she fought against the madness it threatened to unleash before she was consumed by it.

The spinning came to an abrupt halt, and Xenia was trapped within her own mind. She stopped trying to get out; this was exactly where she needed to be.

She felt the heat dissipate from her head as a gentle warmth glided gracefully up from her toes, enveloping her extremities before it rose to the base of her skull. There it sat, the magick she had called, poised and waiting to bring her on the journey to another time. Catching her intention, Xenia's mind began to spin again, but this time it wasn't fast or painful. It simply *was*.

Fragments of tangibility could be discerned in images, sounds and emotions as she began to drift slowly through the lands of the imminent. A child plummeting from a height, a horse refusing to budge, laughter echoing against a stone passage. None of it meant anything to Xenia. She needed to know *why*; she needed to know *when*. The magick was indignant to her irritation and continued to guide her wistfully through obscurities without any aim, it seemed, except to irritate her further.

She was about to release the magick out of pure frustration when a small light bobbed in front of her. Knowing that this must be what she sought, she grabbed for it. The visions revealed themselves like a waterfall, bracingly cold and powerful.

Her son, now a man grown, knelt humbly before Regent Cavison, whose smile was bright as he passed Brudais the ceremonial staff of office, dubbing him the Commander of the Royal Military. Tarison sat the throne clapping idly with the rest of the assemblage, but his eyes were narrowed slits of abhorrence.

The image blurred like a new painting under the flow of a water current, and a different scene emerged.

Brudais knelt in a pool of Cavison's blood, his hands on the regent's chest as he lay still and cold on the floor of his bedchambers. His cry was muted, but his face distorted in agony. Tarison stood behind them in the door frame with a grim frown, waving in the mender. His eyes, though, held a light of mirth about them while he watched Brudais struggle to his feet, yet his brows were drawn together in sorrow.

The canvas swam again, the colors fading in a blur.

In full military dress, Brudais knelt before the throne of Creet, his fists tight at his sides and a bitter cringe on his face, as if it were taking all his might to perform this simple act. Tarison sat poised, looking almost bored as he sent the Commander away with a flippant wave of his hand. The king may have appeared unconcerned, but his rapturous eyes were taking in every moment of Brudais' torment.

The colors blurred suddenly to a violent crimson, and Xenia clutched the shawl she wore, balling it up into her fist as she braced herself for what came next.

In a vast battlefield, surrounded by dead soldiers, Brudais knelt before the king, sword held loosely at his side in one hand while the other grasped feebly for the wound in his neck. Blood poured down the side of his throat, staining his tunic a bright shade of red from neck to knees. Tarison grabbed the back of her son's head to watch him take his last breaths, his eyes swimming in ecstasy.

Xenia cried out in horror and found that she was not alone. She Saw her son standing over her, but not the young son she knew. The vision before her was of a man with sandy blonde hair that hung to his shoulders and sharp blue eyes. He wore the standard military uniform, with a muscled bronze cuirass and light tunic cut off at the shoulders with a set of leather greaves and bracers tied at the back of the calves and forearms. Her wide eyes were drawn to the tattoo which wound its way down his left arm, beginning at the shoulder and ending at each knuckle. With each movement of his heaving breaths, it seemed to slither like a creeping vine. In each hand he held a short sword, hilts ordained with intricate runes and the pommels adorned with a red beryl and a sapphire. His square jaw speckled with dark brown stubble was set in a ferocious grimace, but this did nothing to sway the natural instinct his mother had to grab at the gaping neck wound that was gushing blood.

She had Seen her son's future, and she was determined to change it at any cost.

Xenia blinked and Brudais stood before her, thin and gangly, the boy she knew, but just below his practice jerkin there was a bleeding gash on the side of his thigh. The blood had saturated part of his trousers.

He seemed to realize that Xenia's magick had left her, because he put up a hand and said, "Mother, I know this looks bad—"

"LEIFIUS!" Xenia shrieked, placing a hand on the wound and grabbing for a cloth next to the cauldron.

"—it doesn't even sting that much—"

"*LEIFIUS!*"

"—anymore."

"How long have you been standing there?" Xenia asked, her voice a few octaves lower now that she had her hands on the wound to staunch the bleeding.

"Not very long," Brudais said, looking anywhere but at his mother.

"Why didn't you rouse me?"

"You were Seeing. It looked important."

It was, she thought bitterly, *but only if my son lives long enough for it to come true*. A pang of fear crept up her spine, and she closed her eyes to send up a prayer that her Sight would not pass into being.

As she wrapped Brudais' leg in the spare cloth, the door to the solar opened and Leifius entered, looking stricken.

"What have you done to my son?" Xenia demanded.

"I was teaching him the importance of scars," said Leifius, placing a hand on his son's shoulder. "A warrior should always have scars. Reminds him why he's fighting, and what mistakes to avoid in future." He looked down at his son with a reproving look. Brudais flinched. "Make sure you leave him one, my love."

Xenia's eyes narrowed in her husband's direction. "I'll leave *you* one if you ever do this again. Now let me heal him."

Leifius held up his hands in silent surrender. Calming herself with a few slow breaths, Xenia mumbled spellverse under her breath. The magick filled her body, warming her to her very core. She touched Brudais' wound, and willed the bleeding to stop, willed the skin to seal itself, and willed—gods be good—a scar to form.

When she removed the cloth, Brudais grasped both sides of the long cut in his trousers, pulled them apart, and gazed at his new scar in awe. With a grin, he turned around to show his father. Xenia rolled her eyes at the pair of them: the legend and his legacy.

As they took their leave of her, Xenia's fear returned. The Sight of her son, the blood gushing from his neck... but even more terrifying was the look in Tarison's eyes—the look of triumph and delight over the gruesome death of her son. Those eyes that never lie.

BOOK I

WARMONGERING

Chapter One

Morvian

The hooves of Commander Morvian's gelding sunk deep into the wet earth. Morvian bent over to slap the horse's flank, as kicking him in the gut no longer elicited an effect on the animal but for an ear-piercing whinny. After a moment of silent contemplation, Morvian turned around to the small company he had brought on this mission with a grim expression.

"We're walking," Morvian said, lifting his leg over the uncooperative gelding and sliding down its side. It snorted in apparent approval. His soldiers would have a much different reaction, he imagined.

Entering the Fayn Forest without horses was idiotic, to be sure. Their chances of becoming lost or trapped were greatly improved without a swift exit strategy, and Morvian hated nothing so much as a plan that crumbled under the weight of mere scrutiny. The king was not known for his military stratagem. As he had clearly consulted no one—least of all the commander of his military forces—of these arrangements, the incompetence of the tactics was... unsurprising.

Only a few days ago, King Eusol had been giving him orders to enter the Fayn Forest with a small detail of men, but he refused to elaborate on the particulars—such as the reason for placing his military leader in harm's way on the brink of war. At first, Morvian had assumed this was an evasive method of disposing of one commander to make way for a new one. The presumption had left a sour taste in his mouth. He knew, however, that if the king had wanted him dead, he wouldn't have gone to the trouble of assigning him a detail and sending him on a pointless mission with the feeblest pretext imaginable. There were far simpler ways to dispose of someone—especially for a king.

Morvian peered up at the ancient trees and their shadowing canopy. The leaves were a deep crimson, and the branches that held them twisted and intertwined. It was as if they were strangling each other.

One of his soldiers approached him with caution. It was obvious that the man was frightened, but the way his too-wide eyes kept darting up to the trees, he could safely assume that the fear was not of getting too close to his commanding officer, but rather of getting too close to the forest's edge. After a brief glance about his detail, he realized the rest of the men had positioned themselves far enough away that even a thrown javelin had a fair chance of missing the mark. Returning his gaze to the soldier before him, he pondered why a twig of a man like him had more guts than the rest to approach. Bravery or stupidity?

"Commander."

"What's your name, Sergeant?"

"Oren, sir. Sergeant Oren of the West Regiment of—"

Morvian frowned heavily and waved a hand, signaling his glaring disposition of not caring in the least what little backwater town the sergeant was from, fearing it might encourage an insipid monologue of his origins and upbringing in the western front and the family he left on the shores of the Recluos River. Oren shut his mouth so quickly at seeing Morvian's jaded gesture, he heard the man's teeth snap together.

"What do you need, Sergeant Oren?"

"Commander," he began, a few beads of sweat glistening on his temples. "I think I would serve you best by staying behind to tend to the horses. I worked in the stables for many years before joining the army, and I have a gentle touch when it comes to the beasts. It seems they'll need something to keep them from bolting; they're a bit skittish in the shadow of the forest."

They're not the only ones. Morvian pondered the increasing desperation in the soldier's voice. He couldn't fault the poor lad for being chosen for a detail most would have abandoned their post to avoid. The fact that he had made it this far was a testament to loyalty, if not healthy common sense. But he recognized resourcefulness in the face of insurmountable odds and, even on a scale as meager as this, found that Oren had some of what Morvian's best captains could not even boast. Some things were beyond a man's control, but making do with aught else is the key to staying alive.

Despite the regard Morvian was fast giving the man, he felt the need to test the theory.

"What exactly are you afraid of, Sergeant?"

The soldier straightened considerably, as if his manhood had just been put to question and the fastest way to demonstrate the opposite was to correct his posture. Morvian barely concealed a smirk.

"Afraid of, sir?" Oren replied, his lips pursing a bit as his face went slightly red. "Not afraid. I just think it might be... ill-advised... to leave the horses here without someone to look after them. There are plenty of thieves happy to take a few healthy steeds off the regiment's hands. And besides, the company will need them to get back to the capital—could take two days on foot."

How very pragmatic.

"And you would be willing to remain here alone with the horses to fend off these thieves?"

"Yes, sir," Oren said, nodding in the assumption that he was winning the debate.

"Even if this meant defending our steeds with your very life?"

"I've defended less with it, Commander."

Morvian raised an eyebrow. Perhaps a story for another time if, indeed, another time presented itself.

"You're no fool, nor are you a coward," Morvian said, brushing the stubble on his chin between his index finger and thumb. "The reasons would be good enough for any sensible general to take you up on your offer, but I'm the Commander of the Hyglenian Army, the most fearsome force in the whole of Kresha. If I were to allow one soldier leniency from this detail, questions would be asked—questions of my aptitude to lead those fearsome forces. So what, Sergeant Oren, do you offer to me on this mission that I cannot afford to risk losing you, besides your experience with shoveling horse shit?"

Oren's eyes quickly flickered to the edges of the forest. The trunks of the first few trees were not farther than a few strides away. They were standing on the roots of some of them as they spoke, roots that looked as twisted and choked as the branches above them. They looked to have an almost black hue with little veins of reddish-brown streaked against the bark. It appeared to be blood-red on first sight, and when Morvian stared at them for too long, he had the sense that they were just waiting to wrap around his calves and pull him down into a bloody grave.

"I have a fair knowledge of what's in those trees, sir," Oren whispered hoarsely. "I lived just north of here my entire childhood, and I've seen the things that walk out of that forest..."

The insipid monologue Morvian had feared was a bit less mundane than expected. After a brief glance around at the rest of the company to ensure they were hitching the horses back to their posts and too occupied to listen to this conversation, he nodded solemnly at Oren as a gentle nudge to continue.

"When I was a child, perhaps three or four, the wolves came the first time. They weren't wolves in the normal sense, though. They were the size of bears, but leaner with more muscle. My mother told me there were only three of them, but for all the devastation they caused, there must have been more.

"My father was savaged, along with five other townsfolk. When we found their bodies, Commander, they were no longer recognizable. The wolves went for the faces first, and then dug into their chests to get at the meat they really desired—their hearts. A normal wolf would drag the bodies off and devour every last scrap among their pack. We didn't see why they had left the corpses until the next time it happened.

"I was fourteen at the time. The town had built meager walls to keep out attacks like the ones from the wolves, but also from the river raiders that frequent the Recluos before it enters the Fayn. The wolves came out of the forest at the northernmost point, just at the shores of the river where a group of us were foraging for berries. They herded us like sheep and picked off six—just six, as before—and savaged them just like they had the last time. We watched in horror as they tore the hearts of loved ones from their chests and—"

Morvian put up a hand, and Oren halted his speech. "This sounds like the kind of superstitious nonsense I would expect from the western front. What is the value of this story, Sergeant?"

Oren grimaced, perhaps imagining an insult where none was intended. Morvian had just referred to the tale of Oren's father's death as inconsequential as a children's story like *The Babbling Nymph of Falla Bay*. He realized the mistake, but his pride wouldn't allow him the fragility of an apology.

"The value, sir," Oren said, his tone a little clipped, "is that I survived the attack, and I saw the beasts up close. I also saw a figure as the wolves ran back into the forest—a figure in fine raiment, with armor of the purest white, and whose skin and long hair was almost as white as the armor. When the wolves passed him, one of them placed the sixth heart into his hand. He stuck his fingers into the meat of it and drew three lines of blood down the side of his face. And then he—" Oren faltered, looking at Morvian with a grim frown. "He took a bite out of the heart and slipped away into the shadows, blood streaming down his chin."

Morvian let the silence hang for a moment, pondering the pragmatism of relaying this information to the king.

"Why was this not reported?"

With a resentful snort, Oren said, "It was. At least the bit about the wolf attacks. No one ever believed me about the white demon in the forest, and any who did were swiftly told to keep their mouths shut. They knew no one would send us help if they thought it was all just... *superstition.* Turns out we were never sent help regardless, so I suppose it doesn't matter now. But that's not the last time I saw the demon."

"And the other times?"

Oren's expression changed from pursed to smug in an instant. "Those are your reasons, sir, for not being able to afford to lose me on this mission."

Morvian tried to conceal his reluctant smile but failed. He gathered himself after a few moments as he watched Oren smiling back, knowing he'd won.

"Stay with the horses," he grunted. "And the weapons."

Oren's eyes widened. Morvian turned away towards the rest of his company, placing two fingers in his mouth and whistling sharply. Soldiers who had been tying up horse bridles or carrying saddles looked up to meet his eye.

"By order of King Eusol, we are to leave all weapons at the borders of the forest. This is to ensure a peaceful welcome." Morvian spat on the ground beside him, giving his men a gesture to appreciate; at least their commander thought less of the order than they did. "I will leave a few guardsmen to look after the horses. The rest of you will stow your weapons and meet me here in ten minutes, ready to march. And bring your balls with you. I'll have no cravens in my outfit."

As Oren walked purposefully past him to tend to the horses, Morvian glanced around at the faces of his soldiers, who seemed unnaturally quiet. Many were simply gazing down at the swords at their sides with longing. Some looked resigned, some forlorn. Morvian would have had a similar reaction had he not been in command. He was the only one among them that had to keep up appearances.

He walked through the small camp they had created to keep the horses from wandering. As he passed by a group of three soldiers untying their belts from their waists, he heard one of them say, "This is suicide."

He couldn't disagree, which is why he'd waited until the last moment to give the order. Tactically, it prevented more than a few deserters—and a few less heads he'd have to take once he returned. If he returned.

The king had made it clear that the Fayn were to be treated with every courtesy. He could not say that they would be provided the same niceties, however. The objective had been to draw out the Fayn and offer them an alliance, one which—were it to succeed—would undoubtedly give Hyglen a superior advantage over their Creetian enemies. But the Fayn were little better than myths, their histories having faded centuries ago. They were known to be skilled warriors, but also vicious killers and their merciless natures were well-known even in the withered texts their ghosts left behind.

An alliance was a precarious thing with the most trusted of allies. Morvian was loath to admit that he was fearful of the bastards, but even he couldn't dismiss the warnings. Eusol had told him he had sent the commander due to his honeyed tongue—that only Morvian could make them believe an alliance would suit both parties. It was doubtful that creatures with the reputation they'd earned would be willing to listen to reason any more than they'd stow their own weapons to put another at ease.

Morvian gripped the hilt of his sword tightly, unwilling to let such a valuable weapon leave his side. *Curse this order to the five hells,* he thought bitterly. His sword was the most dependable thing he had. It felt wrong that he should leave it behind—especially when venturing into the worst mistake of his profession. He unbuckled his belt and let the sword fall from its otherwise permanent position at his hip, catching it before it could touch the ground and sully the fine leather scabbard which held it.

He stowed his weapon on his stubborn gelding's saddle, realizing for the first time that his horse had more sense than him. After assigning another guard to remain with Sergeant Oren, making him the happiest man on this side of Hyglen, he made his way toward the forest's edge where a group of his guardsmen were already gathered. They seemed poised in their travel-worn uniforms, but Morvian could see the hint of panic in their eyes.

"Let's get this over with," Morvian barked, starting into the forest without the slightest hesitation. Hopefully, this demonstration of resilience would give his soldiers something to aspire to on this shit mission. With any luck, they would be insufferably loud, enough to draw the Fayn out of their hiding places, but he doubted that would be the case. Already, his guardsmen were following him so closely that they were quite literally treading on his heels. Other than the brushing of their boots against the forest floor, they were utterly silent. Morvian couldn't even distinguish the sound of a breath from a single one of them.

"Don't just mill about, lads, *talk,*" the commander bellowed encouragingly, startling them. Their backs were as rigid as tree trunks and their eyes danced about the trees, looking for any signs of life. He couldn't necessarily blame them for shitting themselves. With no way to defend against an unknown enemy, it was difficult not to piss oneself over every snapped twig.

"We're rather a quiet lot, Commander," one of his cheekier guardsmen replied.

Morvian's eyes narrowed as he turned to face his company. "That was not a request. The sooner we find what we're looking for, the sooner you can all go back to the comfort of the barracks."

"If you can call it that, sir."

Some scattered laughter rang throughout the group. Once the silence had been shattered, three conversations began at once, undoubtedly begun by those who were most frightened of the forest. Talking not only gave away their position, but it also gave his soldiers something to take their minds off their present predicament.

Morvian's eyes scanned the area with a trained eye, searching for any sign of tracks or movement. The woods surrounding them were comprised of the richest colors he had ever laid eyes upon, and no intertwined root or moss-covered rock seemed out of place. The small smattering of sunlight that filtered through the trees caught on the dew around them, filling the air with vibrancy. Every detail seemed ancient, as though it had only just been discovered. The superstitious babble of his soldiers seemed trivial in the beauty of this place.

When the thrill of his surroundings wore off, Morvian's deft ear picked up one of the conversations amongst the chatter, and he found it rather intriguing.

"...military command is clumsy at best. Creet doesn't even know a good leader when they have him at the head of their army."

"Brudais is still their commander, he's simply sharing the duties with six others. Tarison broke up their command to even out biases."

"To fuck Brudais in the ass, more like. They hate each other more than Jandros loathes the Gods of Life."

"Tarison didn't do it because he hated the man... he's terrified of him. The only thing a king cares about is power, and who has more power than *that* legend?"

"A king's power is one thing. A legend's influence is another."

His soldiers weren't half as thick as they appeared to be.

The situation of Creet's military could be described as nothing short of chaos. There were seven commanders who vied for power and glory in the guise of democracy. Tarison may not have wanted Brudais at the head of his army, but after the regent was executed, perhaps he shouldn't have been so hasty as to restructure the entire military command. Morvian wasn't going to complain, however—this only made Creet that much easier to defeat. He could not imagine having to jostle and debate with six other commanders when he knew his orders were sound. He was sure Brudais knew it, too, which would make him frustrated if not entirely volatile. This would be the first fray since his demotion, and Morvian was sure it was still chafing.

"If I were a king—"

"Yes, you—a king," one of his soldiers spat, laughing until he bent in on himself, holding his stomach.

Morvian shook his head slightly, a small enough movement for no one to notice.

"Go fuck a goat."

"Happily, once we get out of this place. I haven't lain eyes on a woman in far too long."

"For a day and a half, do you mean?"

Morvian heard a twig snap in the distance, distinct from the noise made by the men behind him. It couldn't have been more than twenty paces off. His guardsmen were too busy bickering to hear it. The commander raised a hand, gesturing for the party to halt. Moving into fighting stances, the soldiers searched the trees above and peered into the distance, seeing nothing. Morvian took three careful steps forward and an arrow flew past him, the feathers of its fletching brushing his cheek. It hit the nearest tree trunk with a *thwack!*

Four figures appeared from the shadows of the trees, surrounding the Hyglenian soldiers and cutting them off from their commander. Five more had jumped down from the trees above the party to cut off their retreat.

The Fayn's faces were pale when they stepped into the sunlight shining through the forest canopy—pale but unmarred, uncharacteristically smooth. Morvian had expected them to be rugged, repulsive. At the very least, they should have donned an unsightly number of scars. That was if the legends of their monstrous natures were to be believed. Somehow, though, the smoothness of their skin unnerved him even more than if they had been riddled with marks. Their narrowed eyes held contempt, pinning Morvian where he stood, and he found he could not move even if he wished.

A chill slowly crawled up his spine, but he held off the tremor that threatened to overcome his muscles. Yes, he could believe the stories. They may not have looked like savages, but there was something evil there that not even Jandros himself would deem fit to touch. He didn't need spellcraft to see that.

"Your purpose, trespasser?" said the Fayn, holding his next arrow inches from Morvian's temple. His accent in the New Tongue was thick, as if he hadn't spoken it in a long time. "I gather your search party is meant for us. Our adversaries are not often foolish enough to pass through the woods unarmed."

"I am no fool," Morvian replied sternly. Better not to make mention of being a potential adversary—he was on unstable enough ground where he stood.

The Fayn raised an eyebrow, the edges of his mouth curling upward in a chilling grin. "That is mine to decide."

Two others acted upon some unspoken signal to grab the commander's jerkin by the shoulders and drag him forward. Morvian did not struggle in their firm grasp, but wondered faintly about what they would do to his guardsmen. The leader spoke to the men surrounding Morvian's lads with what were presumably orders, but the unfamiliar tongue sounded so soothing the tone could hardly have been taken as anything but gentle.

The leader took the rear of the group that led the commander deeper into the forest, and the only thing Morvian heard as they walked away were arrows being loosed and the final cries from his guardsmen.

Chapter Two

BRUDAIS

"So, these are the training grounds?" Melius sneered.

Stepping out onto the barren grounds of the castle barracks, Brudais shrugged, holding out the practice sword to the runt before him. A runt Melius certainly was not, by the imaginations of any who had never met the boy and only knew of his wealth and status, but Brudais refused to think of him as anything else until he learned some manners and civility.

"A training ground is much alike to any other, my lord," Brudais said, thrusting the sword into the boy's hand after his prolonged look of disgust at the dirty wooden stick being offered to him. Melius grunted with the impact. "Dirty, raucous, and full of sweaty warriors."

Melius' response was an upturned nose. "I'm sure the training grounds at the Kresha Cup were a bit more glamorous."

Brudais stayed the impulse to roll his eyes at the naivety. The boy was obviously attempting to curry favor with him, but he did not want to rise to the bait too quickly. Instead, he shrugged again, leading him out into some of the lesser squares on the edge of the grounds. The shadow of the castle parapet offered some shade from the morning sun. If they had begun their training in the blistering heat, then the boy may not have sent a dazzling report back to his father, Governor Gailesh. Despite his misgivings of the boy himself, he needed to make a good impression—for Rydril's sake.

"Just a few sessions are all it would take," Rydril had said, squeezing Brudais' shoulder in earnest. "The bill to increase the protective presence at the docks in Kelvs will pass with approval by Governor Gailesh's desk, the Gilded Gems will be forced to disband and sail south, and Melius will get to brag for the rest of his petty little life that he was trained by Brudais son of Leifius. Everyone wins, you see—especially my wife and children, who have already begun the first verses in your heroic epic, 'The Song of Uncle Brudais, the Mighty Vanquisher of Gems and Demons and Such.' It's a working title, mind, but it's not bad—"

"All right, you son of a whore." Brudais shoved off Rydril's hand but could not conceal the smirk. "As long as the song is catchy."

"You won't be able to get it out of your head," his best friend promised.

He'd been right, damn him. The tune had been catchy enough to earn it a place in his memories, even while he escorted the pompous governor's son into the ring for his first session. Everyone wins, Brudais remembered Rydril saying, but no one else had to work very hard for their winnings. He was a swordmaster paying the minstrels.

With a great heavy ax
And his hair all of flax
Did the mighty man fell a big beasty
In the fallen disgrace
Of its pitiful race
The beast fell from the force of the ax

With a fright'ning glare
Set his blade now to bare
On the beast
And it ceased
To be beastly

Brudais smiled with the memory of Dorian and Liska jumping around the table at Rydril and Pallina's villa, belting out the verses at the top of their lungs.

The Gilded Gems were a band of pirates that often sailed up the Recluos River to port towns like Kevilly and Sceryl, but they recently began their infiltration of the capital, Turivaun, particularly the docks of Kelvs District. The pirates usually kept their mischievous antics to the docks—mainly thieving, street brawls, and the odd rape. The city guards had been able to keep the peace until the Gems began moving farther into the city and employing other methods of marauding—extortion, kidnapping, and murder. Kelvs happened to be the district in which three of the commanders of Creet's Royal Military resided—Okriad, Brudais, and Rydril. Those commanders and a few of Kelvs' more prominent noble families drafted a bill for the governor, but as was the way with all politicians, he needed something to sweeten the deal.

"Commander?" Melius' voice brought Brudais from his thoughts, and he whirled around to find the runt. His uniform was loose-fitting. The clasps could have been tighter—especially on the bracers—and his helmet would fly off in the first bout. Were he training any other soldier, he would have reprimanded them for such shoddy showmanship, but the little runt was supposed to be happy with the lesson. The dilemma.

"Are you ready?" he asked, his hand grasping the wooden hilt of the practice sword, a challenge to anyone who was perceptive enough to notice. Melius was not.

"Of course, Commander. Shall we—" Melius' eyes widened in horror as Brudais sprang forward, only just managing to extricate his sword from the awkward position in which he had held it at his side to block the blow. Even with a wooden weapon, it could have shattered his collarbone. "Fuck!" he yelled, the impact from the feeble block sending him backward into the sand. Brudais watched him splutter and spit sand out of his mouth, brushing the uniform with wide strokes of his hands. His helmet rolled on the ground behind him, causing Brudais' lips to twitch in barely constrained amusement.

"As this is meant to be a lesson, I'll thank you not to lie to me again, my lord."

"I didn't—"

"You said you were ready when you most assuredly were not. Your uniform is loose, your helmet unclasped, and you and your sword were not in a fighting stance. I took you unawares."

"Clearly!" he said, spitting out another bit of sandy grit.

"I wouldn't have if you were ready. When I ask if you are ready, I expect you to be ready for anything: any attack, any defense, any type of footwork. I never want to take you unawares again."

The runt stood there for a moment, no doubt weighing the negative ramifications of telling his father that he was quitting the moment he stepped foot on the training grounds. He looked up, his pale freckled face shining in the sun, and he gave Brudais a cocky smile.

"You're right, Commander."

He said it in a way that was insolent enough to assume Brudais required his attestation.

The Great Uncle 'Dais
His swords all of blazes
Rescues damsels and youngsters alike
With his conquering hands
All his foes must disband
Or the wroth they'll get of a good man

"I'll need to collect my uniform before we can continue. You wouldn't mind if I were to do so in the castle barracks."

"I'm afraid we don't have the time, Lord Melius. I have a very busy day, and I don't usually take on students. You'll have to do what you can to amend the errors to your uniform out here."

Melius' eyes were nearly as wide as when Brudais had been coming at him with a sword. "Surely, a champion of your caliber will agree to a little privacy when a man dresses."

"A champion of my caliber was willing to change my entire uniform—armour and tunic—in front of a crowd of three thousand so that I wasn't disqualified from the melee—because I was soaked in blood and my jerkin had been ripped to the chest, and took a strip of me with it."

He unstrapped his leather jerkin and slung it down on the ground. Grasping behind him for his tunic, he pulled it over his head and threw it to the ground, covering his jerkin. He pointed a finger at his chest, across a smooth line of scar tissue that stretched from one bicep to the other.

"Champions aren't particular fans of modesty, Lord Melius," he said, "but we are students of efficiency, expediency, and keeping our armour in pristine condition—on and off our bodies. If we don't, blows like the one that produced this scar—let's just say that losing the Kresha Cup would have been the least of my concerns."

The expression on Melius' face was one of horrified awe. This is what he had come for. He hadn't begged his father to be trained by the legendary Brudais. He had begged to be near him, in any capacity, to hear stories of his exploits—the kinds of things that weren't already whispered in taverns in hushed tones. The famous son of the famous father—a shadow he was beginning to believe he would never outgrow, no matter how numerous his own victories.

"So, tighten your clasps, put on your helmet, and we'll begin with some basic drills. You, my lord, have much to learn."

After his brief success—and undoubtedly hoping for more—Melius grabbed his helmet off the ground and hurriedly began fastening the straps of his uniform.

Brudais grabbed his discarded tunic and jerkin, shaking them free of the sand they had collected, and dressed again. For a moment, Brudais wondered if he'd meant the last part of his lecture for himself.

A few hours into the drills, Brudais could see the sweat on the boy's forehead glistening against the afternoon sun. He was about to dismiss him for the day when a messenger ran up to them. The lad wore a page's uniform of vest and layered leather skirt in the fashion of the military dress, but the crest upon the chest signified a royal summons. Brudais held out his hand for the scroll, but then felt the presence of an armed man behind him and froze, moving his free hand to his waist where he kept a hidden knife.

"I'll take that, lad," said a gruff voice that was pleasant enough but gritty as wet sand. Turning around as the scroll was snatched from his grasp, he looked down to see Commander Gorgid's squat frame. He was a small man in stature, but he made up for it in girth. None of the regiment ever made the mistake of making a mockery of the commander's height—least ways not after his first week in command. He'd proved his worth ten times over and didn't hold with anyone giving him guff for an impediment that he couldn't do anything about. "But what I can do," he'd always say, "is give you half rations and scouting duties for the next three months." Brudais had always admired his fair mindedness and vigor, but he had confiscated his summons from the king, and that could not be tolerated.

The page looked momentarily at a loss, as the Royal Messenger Service no doubt prided itself on prompt and correct delivery, but perhaps the boy was new and assumed that *almost* delivering to the correct person was good enough. As the boy strode away, Gorgid's eyes sparkled with mischief.

"You did that on the chance the lad would get into trouble," Brudais said.

"Of course not," Gorgid replied, huffing in a way that made his intentions obvious. "That was only *half* the reason. We need to talk. Enough of this..." He waved a hand vaguely in the direction of Melius as the runt slashed at a straw figure with a wooden sword. "...nonsense."

"This nonsense may be getting us more protections from raiding pirates."

"Why? You think this little ponce is going to be the savior of Kelvs District?"

"Gods no," Brudais said quickly, letting a laugh escape him. "He's just the key to more oversight. The long game, Gorgid. You've played it before, as I recall."

"Don't like it much. Better to make a straight thrust."

"Not if you lack a sword."

Gorgid's dark eyes met Brudais'. "Aye. True enough. Still... we need to talk. Dismiss your oversight and come to the barracks with me. Aiylus is waiting."

Brudais' own eyes darkened at that bit of news. He liked Commander Aiylus about as much as Gorgid favored the long game, but he knew it was necessary to use the tools one was given. After Regent Cavison's execution, the post of military commander was decommissioned—the reason being obvious to anyone who was paying the slightest bit of attention. Once King Tarison took the scepter of power, he sought to lower Brudais' station as much as he could without fully losing the support of the commonfolk, who were already on the brink of rebellion due to the high taxation and lowered standards of protection offered them against raiders from coasts to midlands.

It was whispered about the realm that Aiylus was favored to take the post, which would have caused quite an upheaval, as Aiylus was thought to be of eastern descent, and the wars with the eastern realms had cultivated bad blood between them and the people of Creet. If an easterner were to be offered command of their military, their quickly ripening suspicions would ensure the impending riots began in earnest.

Instead, the royal decree had been to split the command into a clustered mess, in which commander fought with commander over the scraps of glory and the right to be heard. Ultimately, the king had taken over the position himself with the barest of guises to ensure his goal would be achieved. Brudais was still a commander, but not *the* commander. His authority was a shadow of what it once was, but it wasn't enough to sully Brudais' good name.

There were very few people who knew the true reason behind Tarison's attempt to undermine Brudais, and it hadn't been the favor of Aiylus. Brudais tried to remember this when he saw the man, but his impressive figure did little to discourage the thought.

Before long, the barracks entrance loomed before them with its own impression. The gates were wide open during the day, made of solid iron and designed with slats which left the main hall open to the mercy of the elements. Barracks flooding was a common occurrence, but often kept the newest recruits busy mucking the mud from the passageways. The walls on either side of the gates were dark gray stone with veins of quartz fanning out into the brickwork, which culminated in a design that gave the appearance of tree branches reaching for the tops of the walls of the castle above. It was said that Castle Doriell was once made in its entirety of the dark stones that now only decorated the barracks, but when the castle was destroyed in the Civil Wars, it was rebuilt with sturdier material. The foundation would always remain.

When they had reached the gates, the guard straightened his posture to stand at attention upon recognizing the two commanders, not bothering to challenge their entrance. Aiylus stood inside the gates, the top of his head just shy of the nearest door frame. The muscles on his arms bulged, making him look massive in the dim torchlight of the barracks, while his long dark hair was braided down to the middle of his back. There was no doubt that Aiylus would be a formidable opponent in a fight; Brudais was lucky enough to be on his side, although he had always wondered who would come out on top if the occasion ever presented itself. The son of Grandis had been of a similar build when Brudais had bested him in single combat for the Cup. Brudais flinched, shaking off the memory hastily. He never allowed himself to brood over the outcome of *that* match.

"Aiylus," he said, nodding his head to the giant. "What news?"

"Nothing good, I'm afraid," he replied in his smooth, deep voice. "Best we go inside, away from prying ears."

It must have been serious for Aiylus to suggest something so private, and it was that very suggestion which made Brudais realize what had happened. The moment they had moved into the seclusion of Aiylus' room a few doors down from the entrance, Brudais said, "The trade agreements didn't go well, I take it."

Gorgid grunted a laugh devoid of mirth. "A ghastly understatement. Though I doubt the king ever intended them to succeed."

King Tarison had set up these agreements in a last effort to 'restore the well-kept peace' between Creet and Hyglen. The two had been sworn enemies since before the Crescent Moon Wars, in which Brudais' father had won his fame for the bout of single combat against Grandis the Great. Their peaceful relations were tenuous at the best of times, but Tarison had been restless for far too long. Wartime victories would be just the thing to elevate his status after the atrocities of recent years—the furtive deaths of Parliament, the lack of response to the Ohnville Mountain refugees, not to mention the Xerdin Genocide. His standing with the commonfolk, as ever, was in dire need of repair. Even the ever-present threats of piracy by the Gilded Gems and their ilk was becoming a royal problem instead of a gubernatorial one. There were stirrings of rebellion again, just as there had been before Cavison's death. Brudais recognized that a war might bring people together instead of tearing them apart, but it was a gamble that he would not have dared attempt with a foundation that was already crumbling.

What Brudais bristled at was the callous use of the military to solve a problem that Tarison could easily have resolved without shedding a drop of blood—a military which Brudais commanded, and whose lives would be lost for the selfish bastard who sat the throne.

"When the negotiations didn't meet His Majesty's expectations, he beheaded the Hyglenian ambassador and speared his head onto the castle ramparts."

"Fuck," Brudais whispered fiercely. If his advisors had any compunction about starting a war, it was too late for them to speak their minds on it. "He may as well have called the draft from all the corners of Creet."

"I expect that'll be next on His Majesty's agenda. For now, he calls the commanders to court."

Not that they'd be consulted on the efficacy or morality of the decisions made. "When?"

Gorgid held out the hand that held the scroll. "We didn't want you to be caught unawares."

Brudais looked up at him and smiled ruefully. "I always expect the worst from His Majesty, Gorgid. You should know that."

Gorgid grunted a laugh, but Aiylus' brows drew together. He didn't hold with royal mockery, which was too bad, because Brudais couldn't hold for anything less. It was the only tool he had against the tyrant that wasn't likely enough to have his head speared on the ramparts alongside the Hyglenian ambassador. The only reason his antics were tolerated was because, as much as Tarison hated Brudais, he couldn't seem to be without him. It was Brudais' reputation which made Tarison's rise, and he was certain that dependency drove the king mad. So, he skirted and danced around the royal schemes, making a mockery of the court and the one who ruled it, while enjoying an immunity which would save him from reprimand or execution—until it didn't. Brudais was perfectly comfortable playing on a knife's edge, so long as that edge didn't cut his honor or renown.

Brudais unraveled the scroll, his eyes scanning over the contents. "The 14th day of Spring, in three days."

A sharp intake of breath from Gorgid told Brudais something was wrong, even with the date of his summons. "That'll be the last of them."

Gorgid looked embarrassed. It was normally a great insult to be chosen for the last of the commander audiences, but Brudais was just glad to get some time to prepare some skillfully worded barbs.

"Don't fret, Gorgid," Brudais said, giving him a grim smile. "I'm not easily wounded."

"I heard you're not easily *killed*," Aiylus said, "but wounds are a different thing altogether."

Even the grim smile dropped from Brudais' mouth at Aiylus' words. He supposed he was right about that.

Chapter Three

DANIA

Dania sprinted through the outer halls, holding back the force of her steps just enough so that she could keep her ward within eyesight should she turn her head to look. Behind her, she could hear the boyish giggling of Addie in her wake. He loved to chase her—not that he'd ever catch her. Dania would never merely let him win. He'd need to work for his victories once he was man enough to fight for them, and she wouldn't allow that to be tempered due to his governess' soft heart.

Lord Adrian was a bit young to be tutored, being only seven years, but his parents, Commander Okriad and Lady Jarika, were adamant that he would learn fast enough. It helped, perhaps, that they had secured Dania as a governess after she had grown too attached to the boy to depart as his nurse. She tended to Addie in matters of schooling but went beyond her duties for the pure pleasure it brought her to be with the boy. A woman never knew her last chance at having a child of her own. Granted, Dania was quite young to be thinking of such things, yet in Addie she knew at least that she'd have a foster of sorts. She was content with the fact that she had raised a kind-hearted soul amidst such a wanting environment.

If Okriad and Jarika were not the most attentive or caring of parents, it was nothing compared to the way they treated their servants. Their inability to keep the villa staffed was infamous throughout Kelvs District, but the servants who had stayed on despite the constant belittlement, unfair conduct, and unwarranted docking of pay were like family to one another. Ill-treatment was the bond that drew them together, and that bond was likely the only reason most deigned to stay. The staff's loyalty to one another was something cherished, and it took an unpardonable misstep to sunder it.

"Day!"

Dania heard her pet name, but it had been laced with concern. She looked back and slowed to a halt. Addie was still running, but he had a look of worry on his face.

"What's the matter, Addie?"

Dania watched as Adrian shortened his stride until he was only a few paces away. His dark golden hair was normally long enough to be swept back in waves, but it was now disheveled enough to make his mother faint—strands were stuck to the sides of his face from the sweat, and the rest was a tangled, wind-swept mess. His brown eyes looked up in a pleading sort of way, distorting his customary boyish charm, and showing a side to him she hadn't witnessed in years: vulnerability. It terrified her, and her eyes began to well with unshed tears at the thought that someone or something could have harmed her boy.

She bent down, steadying herself with the effort not to be sick after having run so far, and he jumped into her open arms, grabbing her firmly around the waist.

"Gotcha!"

Dania's eyes flew open, but they were blurry from the tears, and she saw only a glimpse of the proud and unrelenting smile on Adrian's face, which was pressed against her shoulder. He hadn't just tricked her; he had put on such a farce that she had welcomed his victory.

"You..." she began, as if to chide him, grabbing his shoulders and moving him in front of her. Wobbling slightly on her bent ankles, she studied the boy intently. There were no signs of tears in his eyes nor was his expression anything other than pure triumph. "...are doing much better, my lord."

Adrian beamed at her, as if the only thing in the world he desired was her approval. She held onto that feeling of being needed—like a cherished memory that becomes something more. Dania smiled back at him with delight.

"If you can implement that in battle, I wouldn't be surprised at the carnage that follows."

Laughing, Adrian pulled away from her and helped her to her feet. "What's 'carnage'?"

Dania straightened up and began brushing her skirts of dust and dirt. "That reminds me," she said, now with reluctant sternness, "it's time for your lessons."

His eyes went wide, and he began backing away from her. "Wait a minute..."

"You should have kept chasing me a while longer," Dania replied with an unapologetic smile on her face. "I probably would have collapsed from the heat and been too tired to do lessons. See, Addie, there are always consequences to our actions—whether they're good or bad depends on strategy and chance. You must always weigh every option."

"Dayyy!" he cried, reverting back to a seemingly vulnerable state with a trembling lower lip.

"Now *that* is clearly fake. If you'd used that quivering lip on me earlier, I would never have fallen for your trick."

Adrian gazed up at her pleadingly. "Can we play The Hunt, just once?"

The Hunt was a simple game, and a childhood favorite she had played with him since she'd begun her duties at the villa. It was a game of skill and social hierarchy hidden behind the eaves of youthful innocence. Like the playful wrestling of wolf pups in their first years, the offspring of Creetians learned dominance, sportsmanship, and the consequences of risk-taking by partaking in the game. This was not unlike all activities in which Adrian partook—a standard that his father expected, but that Dania more often fulfilled.

The boys of Creet would grow up to be soldiers, whether they remained in the profession or not. When they turned sixteen, every boy was enlisted into the Creetian military for Seasoning. They were trained in wielding spear, sword, and ax, as well as how to defend and attack with a shield. They served for a compulsory three years, so that their training would be fixed in their memory should they ever be recalled for conscription. There was generally no way to avoid the Seasoning… and those who did had no chance of surviving a battle. It was compulsory for two reasons—to save lives and make the army a stronger fighting force.

Being the son of a Commander of the Royal Military, Adrian was expected to be a sufficient strategist, as well as proficient in fighting, by the time he was selected for Seasoning. His motivation for playing The Hunt may have been academic or even out of survival... or it could easily have been a way to escape whatever lessons she had in store for him this afternoon.

"*One* game," Dania finally said, rolling her eyes at the triumphant yell that escaped the boy. "You're the wolf, and we're to stay in the courtyards."

"Only the courtyards?" Adrian cried but stopped abruptly when Dania looked down at him with a raised eyebrow. He was a child, certainly, but there was no reason he needed to make a fuss. She was already succumbing to his whims, and he knew it.

She released an exasperated sigh worthy of the playhouse, which made Adrian giggle behind his hand. "Don't go beyond the walls, Addie."

"Yes, mistress."

Use of formal etiquette. He clearly had something nefarious in mind. Dania closed her eyes, heard his feet scamper against the cobblestone and out of hearing, praying that she hadn't just made a mistake by giving him so much ground.

The strategics of The Hunt were simple enough for children to understand them. A shepherd had the task of looking over his figurative flock while the wolf attempted to surpass him to take the prize of his sheep. If the wolf managed to slip past the shepherd, the game was won. If the shepherd was vigilant enough, the wolf's only option was to fight. Bloodied hands and bruised lips had often accompanied the pastime when eager boys had found time away from their chores to play. It was violent and tactical, but it conditioned young minds to grow into the strong men who protected the realm.

The problem was that the game was more interesting with more than two players, and the tactics could become more complicated having a pack of wolves to contend with rather than a lone wolf, but Adrian had never seemed to mind that it was only himself and Dania playing. He always managed to keep her vigilant with his inventive methods of ambush, which exemplified how intelligent her little ward was.

She walked through the courtyard gardens, her hands behind her back as she kicked at her skirts with each step. Dania usually played the shepherd, but each part had its uses. A general needed tactical skill in both the offensive and defensive. She never made things *too* easy for the boy. She knew he hadn't wanted to be in the courtyards, so she pointed the game there for a time until he'd become too bored wherever he was hiding now and decide to come looking for her, at which time she would move on to the villa halls.

Thinking about Adrian's restless spirit reminded her of her own at a young age, when her father had still been alive. She remembered his brilliant smile, his affectionate praise and pet names like My Gentle Wave and Starlit Night. The years on the oar had chiseled his strapping body and he always returned with his hair and beard brittle to the touch from layers of sea salt. Dania closed her eyes for a moment, recalling the briny smell of him when they hugged, and a sudden tear slid down her cheek.

He was a mysterious man, her father; despite the misfortunes and destitution, his smile had never seemed to waver, his good will always on display for all to admire. He had been what Dania now recognized as an optimist. She had aspired to model him, in her own fashion, but when he sailed off one day, waving and smiling like an excited yearling ready to explore, and he never returned, she knew that making light of your troubles was just a way to ignore their significance. It had been Dania, instead of their distraught and uncompromising mother, who had taken on the responsibility of acquiring income to provide for the family.

She worked for whomever would hire her at the tender age of twelve: fishing on the docks, spooling thread for the ladies in town, copying manuscripts for local clerks, and even a bit of hunting, when she could get her hands on a rabbit or a duck. She considered herself lucky that she was never forced into a more suspect occupation, like the ones *Madam Vaiyor's* solicited—not that they hadn't attempted to recruit her attentively from the age of fifteen. It was tempting to take the shocking sums they offered—if only because her brother had become terribly ill that year. Had she done so, she could have afforded to pay the mender's fee, and Browyn might have recovered.

Her brother had contracted a disease by the name of Gray Throat that Summer, for which only magick was a known cure, and magickal remedies were expensive to procure. Dania loved her brother fiercely and often wondered, if her moral scruples hadn't interceded, if she could have saved him from the fragile existence he now suffered. She had to watch him wither away from a growing boy full of laughter and joy into a wasted husk who could barely hold his own soup spoon at times. Their mother had appointed herself as his caretaker and held him under her control—recognizing that the only one of her two children she had authority over in any capacity was the one whose existence depended upon others.

When Dania was offered a job in the capital, she took it under the assumption that her wages would be able to fund Browyn's recovery. She settled into the Okriad Villa household as a nurse to Adrian, and all her spare income went straight back to Kevilly to support her mother and brother. Once Adrian had rather outgrown the need for a nurse but certainly required instruction with his newly expected studies, Dania realized the full extent of what Adrian offered her in return for her services—a little piece of the childhood she had never had.

Dania heard a twig snap and wheeled around, her skirts circling her ankles and twisting there, rooting her to the spot. *Damn fabric,* she thought, giving it a little kick with the heel of her foot while she searched the courtyard around her. She didn't see anything amiss; her gaze wandered up to the trees in search of the boy. She was between the fountain and the courtyard wall. The only place she hadn't bothered to look was behind the fountain and—

Her heart skipped a beat, then seemed to stop altogether. *Don't go beyond the walls*, she had said. Slowly, almost begrudgingly, her eyes traced the length of the stone wall to her right until it reached the top, where Adrian crouched, wavering on the edge with all the grace of a balancing pewter plate.

"ADDIE, NO!" she screamed, but he had already begun his descent, leaping off the top of a wall that was more than three times his height.

Dania jumped forward, as the boy had leapt too far to the right to jump directly onto her, intending to break his fall and not caring for the consequences. She had misjudged his trajectory, and the bronze basin of the fountain turned an odd red color in her mind's eye, like a desperate warning, but one that was given too late. Dania's feet could not propel her any further given the skirts that were twisted at her ankles, and she could only reach out her hands enough to break the contact of his jaw with the stone rim, but she watched in shock as Adrian's wrist smashed against the basin, watched as the bone shot out of the bottom of his hand like his skin was as supple as the flesh of a peach. An arching trail of blood shot out of the wound mimicking the fountain above it.

Dania's hands and arms were battered and scraped with gravel, but she didn't care. Her hand went to Adrian's face, who was biting his lip so hard that it was beginning to bleed.

"Adrian," she said gently, a slight tremble to her voice. His eyes were wide when he looked back at her. "You don't have to be brave all the time, Addie."

A few tears began to fall from his face, as if he had been waiting for permission to cry. Her hand went up to his cheek and she shuffled her hips forward to embrace him. He sobbed into her apron as she ran her fingers through his hair, making soothing sounds.

"We've got to get you to a mender, Addie," she said after giving him a few moments to collect himself.

He sat up, cradling his wrist to his chest, hissing and crying at the pain it caused.

"Let's go. Quickly now," she said, gathering her skirts in one hand and her ward's uninjured hand in the other.

They found the commander's manservant, Lindon, once they entered the main hall.

She must have looked quite the spectacle, her hair disheveled, dirt all over her arms and hem, and a blood stain across her apron, but Lindon was quick to act. He called for the page and bid him collect the mender with due haste. Then calling the maids, he gave them instructions to prepare the lord's chambers for the mender.

While this transpired, Dania led Adrian slowly to his chambers. She laid him down in his bed once the maids had stripped it and laid a few white linen sheets on top. Pulling one of the sitting room chairs into the room, she placed it next to the bed and sat down.

"Addie," she said sternly as the maids bustled about them making preparations. "You know how dangerous that leap was. Why did you make it?"

His face contorted in pain and a tear leaked from his left eye. After a moment, he managed a rueful smile. "You said not to go *beyond* the walls, so I thought…"

"You thought you were being clever," she said, unable to control the smile that formed on her lips. "Do you think you're clever now, little lord?"

Adrian bit his lip, but the laugh escaped regardless. He looked directly in her eyes. "Day?"

"Yes, Addie?"

"You're my favorite person," he said gently, coyly, as if he wasn't supposed to mention something like this. Dania's cheeks flushed, and a warm smile lit her face.

"And you're mine, love."

Adrian nodded back, but he didn't return the smile. He grew very solemn, tightening the hold on his wrist. "I won't let them send you away."

Dania's head jerked up to see the maids staring in their direction—some with tears in their eyes, but others with stern looks on their faces. She looked back down at her boy and gave him a reassuring nod.

"I'll do everything I can, Addie. You just worry about your wrist, hm?"

She sat with him until the mender came and told her she must leave. She kissed the top of his head and squeezed his good hand.

"I'll be right outside," she said. He nodded in response.

She wondered how a boy—even one as young as he—could have no concept of cruelty even when he was surrounded by it. He knew they might discharge her for this situation, but he still had the idea that she would be there tomorrow to teach and play with him. He was an optimist, like her father. Even if all the servants were on her side, she doubted she'd get anything resembling fair treatment when the Okriad's only son had been injured on her watch.

Dania walked into the kitchen, where Lindon and the head housekeeper, Mira, were whispering fiercely to the head cook, Shaylon. She had always liked the three of them—their own collective triad of power in a house where there seemed to be none beyond the screeching of Lady Jarika and the monotonous disapproval of Commander Okriad. There was nothing else so pressing to discuss as the predicament of the little lord upstairs and his negligent governess. Dania's jaw clenched at the thought of the staff turning against her, even after all the ways she had stood up to the commander and his lady on behalf of their staff in the past.

She recalled the day when Mira herself had been accused of stealing a necklace from the lady's chambers, but Dania had found it in Adrian's things before Mira could be dismissed. Or the time when the page, Victys, had been noisily chastised for returning late with a message marked urgent and Dania had reminded the commander of the four other messages he had tasked the boy with that day (and the fact that the message was not, in fact, marked urgent on the outside). The commander's voice had lowered but his eyes had narrowed considerably when he told her to "mind your own bloody affairs, nurse," but the page was not punished with more than the scolding.

Dania stopped just before the bottom of the stairs, hugging the wall and listening to the conversation as best she could with the kitchens abuzz preparing luncheon.

"She's a sweet girl, and it's a shame, really…" said Shaylon.

"She's a sweet girl?" Mira said, her voice sounding harsh. "She's been a godsend to us! Her grit is the only thing keeping the tyrants from treating us all like the diseased vermin they think we are."

"Hush, now, Mira." Lindon's voice now. "There is no cause to panic. The boy may not heal, but we shall dig in our boots for Dania. We all know that the lady will wish to seize the opportunity to be rid of her for her persistent… what was it you called it, Mira? Grit? Yes… we all know she's been wanting another governess for some time, but that no one will take wages so insulting."

"Dania doesn't do this for the wages," Shaylon said. It sounded like she'd grown a bit of backbone since last she spoke. "She does it for the boy. They're inseparable! I wonder if she were discharged if she'd come back to steal him away—and a good thing it'd be, too, for the both of them."

"Hear, hear," said Mira, a little louder than the rest of the whisperings.

Lindon and Shaylon both shushed her.

"And yet," Lindon said, dropping his voice even lower. "The boy may have been injured beyond repair… on her watch."

"Blast it, Lindon! Are you a parent? It's hard enough to nurse a child from infancy to boyhood without incident; you'll begrudge her one misstep? The boy admitted to me that he thought to disobey her—as a jest, he said—but he realizes it was a mistake now. We all make silly mistakes in our youths. Some come at a greater cost than do others."

"Yes, yes," Lindon said. "So, we are agreed—to resist dismissal at all costs."

"Aye," Mira and Shaylon whispered fiercely.

When she heard the last whisper and a few footsteps in opposite directions, she carefully made her way up the stairs again, catching the eye of one of the kitchen maids, who smiled at her shyly before returning to the pot she was tending.

She reached the top of the stairs and began pacing from one end of the corridor to the other. She lost track of how long she'd maintained her vigil, but when she looked up on her last turn, the sun was low in the blood red sky. She spun about, her skirts twisting in a way that reminded her of her inability to leap forward to prevent Adrian's fall this morning.

She was headed towards the stairs to Adrian's chambers, for surely the mender had finished his work and Adrian had gotten some much-needed rest. Her heart thumped in her chest at the thought of seeing that little face again, with his swept-back hair and pleading eyes. Would he seek forgiveness from her? Recompense? Her thoughts began circling with all the ways he could pay her back, most of them playing games that *she* liked to play. Her footsteps on the flagstone floor echoed as she raced towards the staircase.

"*DANIA!*"

It wasn't a call or even a shout. It was a scream. She had never heard her name said that way in all her thirty-three years—not even by her own mother. There was malice in that voice, and it sent a chill down Dania's spine with the cold knowledge that if she didn't ignore it and run up those stairs to Adrian's chambers, she may never see him again. The part of her that recognized it urged her to lift her skirts and take the steps, but her frozen spine kept her rooted.

"My lady?" she said, doing her best to keep her voice even and strong. "Have you seen Lord Adrian yet?"

"I don't *have* to," Jarika spat, walking towards her with purpose. "I received a note from Lindon."

"Please allow me to escort you to his rooms," she said, curtseying low when Jarika walked up to her. "I'm certain he desires to see you." *Not more than he desires to see me*, she thought.

"The boy can wait. I have pressing business I need to tend to."

Normally during a reprimand, a curtseying servant was expected to remain in place until the lord or lady allowed them to stand. Jarika gave no indication that she intended to release Dania from her humiliation. Dania heard the servants begin to gather in the corridors, where tentative footsteps and hushed whispers gave faint echoes off the stone passages.

"I cannot allow," Jarika began, her tone full of haughty disdain, "the governess who looks after my only son to be so careless. Lord Adrian was injured on your watch, governess. What do you have to say for yourself?"

Dania's muscles were clenched with the effort of remaining steady in such a low curtsey. She opened her mouth to respond when Lindon stepped out from the crowd of onlookers.

"My lady, Dania was playing a game with the lord, on which he insisted. He seems to have taken it upon himself to disobey his governess's rules and jumped from a height which might have caused far more damage if Dania had not been there to break the fall. Lord Adrian has repented his folly—"

"Enough!" Jarika shrieked. "I will hear it from her own mouth."

Dania closed her eyes. Maybe not seeing the mess she had made would help her to focus. "I told Lord Adrian not to go beyond the walls, my lady. Trying to be cunning, he climbed onto the courtyard wall to jump down on me from above. As soon as I realized his intention, I made to catch him, but my skirts had twisted and prevented me from shielding him more from the fall."

Continuing her low curtsey, Dania kept her eyes closed so as not to see Jarika's expression. She didn't want to know that this was the end, that she could have run up those stairs and seen Addie one last time.

"I think everyone in this hall will agree that you know Lord Adrian best," Jarika sneered, grabbing Dania's chin with her hand and lifting her head. Dania's eyes fluttered open, a single tear running down her cheek. "So, how did you not perceive his… cunning… to evade your instruction?"

Dania couldn't answer because she *had* known—or at least, she had suspected—and yet she hadn't done anything about it. Jarika may have been a terror, but she was right. This was all Dania's fault.

The hall suddenly broke into a ruckus of protestation. Dania's eyes darted from kitchen maids to pages to stable hands who were all coming to her defense. Jarika's hand slipped from Dania's chin, and she spun about, sweeping her hands in a quieting gesture. The room slowly calmed to an eerie silence, the staff stepping back against the walls again.

Jarika turned back to her, giving her the signal to stand. With effort, Dania untangled herself from her curtsey and stood, legs shaking.

"You will never see Lord Adrian again," Jarika said viciously.

Dania's legs gave out. For a moment, she didn't know what had happened, but Mira and one of the housemaids had come to support her on either side. Where was Addie? She needed to see him.

"And you will never," Jarika said, leaning in close to Dania's ear, but loud enough for the maids to hear, "touch my husband again."

Dania balked, her face contorting in confusion. There were gasps above her, and suddenly her support was gone. She toppled to the ground; her hands were just quick enough to find the ground to prevent her nose from cracking against the flagstone.

She had never laid a hand on Okriad in all the years she'd resided here. There may have been moments where he made his own fancy known—a hand placed on her shoulder, fingers trailing along her dress skirts—but she would *never* stoop so low as to bed him, even in her most desperate destitution. But Jarika knew this. She had simply been waiting for the right opportunity to catch the staff unawares with the accusation. Dania shook her head madly, angry at herself for not having anticipated this. Was it worse than having perceived it, as with Adrian's boyish trick, and done nothing?

"Collect your things and remove yourself," Jarika said with a bite, but she was smiling most insidiously. "Immediately."

As Dania got to her feet, she looked around at the faces that surrounded her and lined the walls. Many of them were filled with pity, some with confusion, but there were a few that held contempt. The staff who have relations with the lord they serve is a disgrace to all the staff, and that might have brought a measure of disgust, but when the lord is a tyrant… she could understand the loathing in their eyes, if not the utter lack of trust that she would never do such a thing.

She passed by Lindon on her way to the servants' quarters. She curtsied to him and gave him a wavering smile. He didn't smile back, and when she saw this, she shook her head in a small gesture. "The lady is mad, the lord is soft, and I care not for either."

Lindon's expression changed, his eyes widening almost comically, then changed to reflect some of the staff that surrounded him, in forlorn pity.

She managed to make it to the servants' quarters to collect her few possessions—her knife, her favorite book, *Fe'lyn Nevermore*, her pair of trousers. She kept looking up at the ceiling, wishing she could go upstairs and wake up Addie, give him one last cuddle, tell him everything would be fine.

But nothing would be fine. She didn't want her last words to be a lie. She briefly considered stealing him away in the middle of the night, like Shaylon had suggested, but that wouldn't be fair for the boy. He needed a more attentive governess—one who would know the gleam in his eye and stop the fall before it had the chance to happen. Dania had made a mistake, and it was going to cost Adrian his sword hand.

She couldn't stop them now. The tears fell like rain—hard and unrelenting.

Everything would be fine, she lied to herself.

Chapter Four
Brudais

Brudais had decided to walk up to the training grounds today, and with the sun beating down after a rigorous training session, he now realized that it had been a foolish endeavor. 'Decided' was a bit of an exaggeration, however, as his stallion, Ælon, was courting a rather feisty dappled mare in the adjoining pasture, and saddling him in the midst of his frustration could have been disastrous. He wondered who the true master was in their relationship; Brudais felt like he made more allowances for his horse than for his entire battalion.

The only grace he was permitted this afternoon was that going home was entirely downhill. Castle Doriell had been built on a cliff face overlooking the Recluos River, with the city having sprouted up along the breadth of the cliffside below. Its strategic advantage was undeniable, as scaling the cliff to Doriell was impossible for an army of thousands. They didn't boast of impregnability in an attempt to stave off the ambitious from calling their bluff, but a foreign army had not attacked Turivaun for over three hundred years. If there was any fighting at all, it was off the coast or in southern port towns like Kevilly and Sceryl. During the Crescent

Moon Wars, Krashkin had often raided these port towns to force a surrender, but Creet held strong in their resolve. If they hadn't, the kingdom would have dissolved into a vassal state under the will of the Eastern Triad. He wondered for the briefest of moments whether that would have been preferable to the conditions in which Creetians now lived under the rule of Tarison II.

His gorge rose as an image of Regent Cavison's bloody corpse came to his mind. His hands had been red for days after he had found the man who was like a second father to him, a knife wound in his neck. A series of memories followed the unceremonious execution, just as events had played out in the past—mysterious disappearances, the ban on magick, moving the non-Human races to the slums, and the horrors that ensued from those decrees. Brudais shook his head as if to remove the thoughts with mere force. He hadn't thought it had worked until he stopped at the entrance to a familiar villa.

The open door frame was wreathed in vines and dark purple flowers on the cusp of budding, while the front courtyard was likewise bursting with vibrant foliage. High shrubs lined the walkways to make a labyrinth of the living space. It was easy to get lost, and Brudais had done so many times, but for reasons beyond his fathoming, he never seemed to mind, no matter how much of a hurry he was in.

Stepping through the archway, he took a sharp left at the white lilies. He knew the way to the main house, but he was hoping to speak to Rydril before his lovely wife and children distracted him from the news of the day. Another left, a right, and he was nearly to the inner garden when he heard a quiet noise coming from the other side of the shrubbery. Humming. The voice was deep and honeyed, with a softness that wasn't expected from one with such a tenor. Brudais halted, turning quietly in the direction he had come and starting off for the main house. He would never intentionally disrupt his friend from his prayers, but he wondered for whom the man was praying and to what purpose. *For me*, he often wondered, bemused at the thought that the only reason the gods ever saw fit to favor him was the humming and mumbling pleas of his best friend. Rydril only kneeled for two things: the gods and the king. He shuddered to think what bad news had him kneeling twice in the span of one day.

When he emerged from the labyrinth, he heard Pallina singing in the kitchen and smiled at the thought of the married couple making a peculiar kind of music together, if only in Brudais' mind. Pallina kept a staff, of course, but she still liked to bake and could often be found in the kitchen wearing a flour-speckled apron and rolling dough. Brudais stepped into the doorframe and heard a chorus of childish screams greet him.

"Uncle 'Dais!" Liska yelled breathlessly as she and her brother, Dorian, flung the small balls of dough they had been working onto the surface of the oak table, pushed out of their chairs so clumsily that one of them fell over, and ran towards him. Brudais' eyes widened considerably after witnessing these hysterics, but he was quick enough to squat for both to clamber onto his shoulders—instead of into his more delicate parts. The act had seemed the most prudent at the time until Brudais' ankles gave way to the force of the impact, and he toppled over the doorstep onto his back with a *thud*, the children cradled safely in his arms.

The collision and fall had surprised them, but all three of them soon began laughing wildly.

Pallina walked over to the pile of them and swatted them with the cloth she normally kept on her shoulder while baking. "Hellions!" she said, but there was no real chastisement in it. Her smile was too bright to relay any notion of punishment to come.

Laying on the ground, Brudais saw her from a different perspective than usual. Pallina had light brown hair which she always kept up in a twisted bun. Her eyes were a piercing sapphire, yet somehow one always managed to find warmth in them. Many years ago, before the children, she had been slender, but her now-plump figure complimented her in the best of ways. He thought she was more beautiful than ever, even with the streak of flour crossing her forehead.

"Get up now, my loves, and let your uncle walk *through* the door before you ambush him."

"It's no bother, Palli," he said, helping the little ones to their feet before standing up himself. He brushed at his tunic with his hands, but it was filthy enough from training this morning. A little dirt wouldn't make much of a difference. "What are you making?"

Pallina had turned to make her way back to the stone counter, but she turned her head to look at him, one eyebrow raised. "I knew the moment you entered the villa that you were going to be stealing my treats."

A surprised chuckle escaped Brudais. "I had no such intentions, Palli. I swear."

"You may not have *had* them, but you have them now, don't you?"

He couldn't hide the smile. "I must admit that the lady of the house did put the idea in my head."

Brudais guided the children back to their seats, and Liska looked up at him pleadingly when she sat down. She was the tender age of five, and her wavy, black hair cascading down the sides of her face made his heart ache at the adorable creature before him. "Uncle 'Dais, can you help us with the dough?"

"Liska!" There was shock in Pallina's voice. "You do not ask guests to help you with your chores."

"Ahh," Brudais said, pushing her chair closer to the table and leaning down next to her. "But I'm not a guest, am I?"

"You're family," said Dorian. The dark-haired nine-year-old said it so naturally that he didn't even lift his head from the dough he was kneading.

Looking up from Liska's smiling face, Brudais found a mirror in her mother's. He sat down in the extra chair facing the rest of the kitchen. "I don't work for free, you know."

"I'm making *pasteli*," Pallina called as she made her way to the fireplace.

"With dates?"

"Pears and hazelnuts."

"Then you have me for as long as you want."

Liska cheered loudly. Dorian pounded the table three times in such an impressive imitation of his father that Brudais had to choke back a laugh, causing a brief coughing fit. After the choking had settled, he began kneading a ball of dough which Liska had gingerly pushed to his side of the table.

"How long has Rydril been on his knees?" he said, the question directed at Pallina who was bustling about collecting ingredients.

She looked up from her work to scold him. She had never liked how he mocked their religion, and this particular phrase was usually accompanied by a hissed, "Your vulgarity knows no bounds." But this time there was no comment from her. The scathing look would have to suffice.

"Since before midday."

A long time. The gods would be bored stiff of Rydril's humming by now, surely. "And when was he kneeling before?"

Pallina didn't hesitate in her response. "His audience with the king was this morning, as you well know. It was not... productive."

Brudais watched the children from the corner of his eye to see if they were listening. Liska was concentrating too hard on her dough formation to be comprehending the conversation, but Dorian's pace had slowed, and his head was tilted to one side with one eye closed, as if trying to concentrate on two things at once was a strenuous physical effort.

"So much so that an audience with me will be... chaos?"

Pallina chuckled. "Isn't it always, Brudais?"

He smirked when he caught Dorian looking at him, which startled the boy and had him back to kneading quickly. He stuck out his hand to tousle the boy's hair when a deep voice from behind said, "If you get flour in Dorian's hair, you'll be giving him the bath yourself, *Uncle 'Dais.*"

Turning in his seat, Brudais watched as Rydril stepped into the kitchen, a small smile on his lips. He was not much more than Brudais in age—a lively forty-six—but he wore his cares on his face. The man was incapable of bluffing, which made him a good friend to have. However, it also made him vulnerable and often in need of support because of it, which Brudais was happy enough to provide whenever the occasion arose.

Rydril was of average height, only a bit taller than his best friend, but his build was more toned than muscular. His chestnut eyes gave him a natural countenance against his dark skin, but the lightness in them made him seem harmless to those who did not know him. That was his only bluff—his physical appearance allowing him the element of surprise, so long as he kept his facial features impartial.

Brudais turned back to his dough. "How are the gods? Balanced as always?"

Rydril rounded the table, his long cloak trailing the ground as he walked to his wife and gave her a gentle kiss. "The gods are good. You'd know that if you bothered to speak to them."

"The gods offer only promises and platitudes," Brudais said casually, as if he were discussing the coming harvest. "They've never listened to me before."

"Your position is one of offering," Rydril said, putting his arm around Pallina's back, his hand cupping her neck. She smiled but swatted him away with her cloth and went back to her baking. "If you go to them in search of answers or desires, they'll give you nothing."

"And what do you offer, brother? Your beautiful singing voice?" Brudais' temper was rising, and he was kneading so forcefully that the dough was beginning to break apart.

Liska looked up after hearing Brudais' tone change, and she put a small hand over his fist. He froze, unable to move while those little fingers held him. "Uncle 'Dais, the dough is crumbly. You have to be gentle."

All anger dissipated. Glancing sheepishly into Liska's expectant eyes, Brudais said, "Of course, darling. I'll be gentle."

From the corner of Brudais' eye, he saw Rydril and Pallina facing away from them, their backs and chests rising and falling, and their hands pressing against their mouths with the effort to keep their laughter at bay. *Damn them.*

It was a while longer before all the dough was kneaded to Pallina's satisfaction and she sent the children off to wash, giving the adults some time to discuss more serious matters. Pallina set a plate of fresh *pasteli* in front of Brudais, grinning from ear to ear as he broke off the first bite with his teeth and moaned with pleasure.

Rydril slid the plate back to Pallina when Brudais grabbed for another.

"I've earned these!" Brudais objected loudly.

"I need you to concentrate, and you can't do that while you're drooling and dribbling onto the table."

"I can listen and eat at the same time."

"I'm not even sure you can *listen* at one time."

Brudais brushed the flour and bits of dough off his hands, then crossed his arms over his chest and leaned back in his chair.

"How bad is it?"

Rydril's expression was grim. "We may have the numbers on Hyglen, but we also have the march, which will weaken the troops before we ever get to our destination."

"How do we have the numbers? The last council estimated them roughly equal. Where are we pulling from? This year's Seasoning was minimal—"

"We're adjusting for the last six Seasonings."

Brudais stared at Rydril, his eyebrows drawn together. "We're recalling *six* battalions?"

Rydril looked over at Pallina, whose expression was as grim as her husband's.

"Six years? Which means at least three regiments of unfocused, ill-trained, unwilling soldiers. And Tarison expects that this will make the difference?"

"He's given a quarter each to Aiylus and Okriad."

"So, he expects them to be *better* trained?" Sarcasm filled the room with an eerie weight.

"And the other to me," Rydril said softly, his eyes never leaving Brudais'.

His jaw clenched. "Which half?"

"That would be the unfocused, ill-trained, and unwilling half."

Pallina stood up and placed her hands on the table, drawing both men's gazes. "Rydril has been dealt a bad hand—"

"If you knew the dealer," Brudais mumbled under his breath, "you'd know it was deliberate."

"—but this is an opportunity for him to prove his worth," she continued as if she hadn't heard the mutterings of the man across the table. "You'll just have more work to do, my love."

"Think of it as a challenge," said Rydril, watching Brudais carefully, as if expecting him to burst into furious curses at any moment. "A very tedious challenge."

Brudais' expression began to soften at the looks of hope and determination on their faces. Retraining what amounted to insolent draftees for a few months before marching them off to war, commanding their own battalions, and coordinating with the rest of The Seventh Order on tactics and strategy was meant as a type of royal punishment. Okriad may have deserved such a fate by his attitude alone, but Rydril? Even association with legends had its fallbacks at times, he supposed. But if the king desired to be petty and pick a fight, he would refuse to rise to the bait. He was determined never to allow the king to be seen as victorious in his endeavors—especially when those endeavors were to stain his reputation, or the reputation of those he loved.

"A tedious challenge, eh?" A smirk began to form on Brudais' lips. "Retraining Seasoned troops who can barely remember how to pick up a sword."

Pallina and Rydril both cringed, expecting that his retort was going to be pessimistic and unwelcome.

"Sounds like I'll need to develop some patience if I'm going to be challenged *this* much."

The couple looked at each other, their confusion quite an adorable sight.

"I'm not going to let you do this alone, brother," he clarified, reaching forward and grabbing another *pasteli* off the plate, "but sweet Masiya, this is going to be a long war."

Brudais shut the door to his townhouse with exaggerated slowness, trying not to let the sound of the door creaking closed announce his presence. When he turned his back to the door to look into the inner rooms, he found Nelera standing in the foyer. Her hand was on the hip of the sheer dress she wore which parted so high on her left thigh it drew his eye immediately. After a moment of admiration, he swiftly raised his glance to her eyes, which held the embers of lust or rage—he wasn't quite sure which he had earned… if any.

"Brudais," she said. Her face was puzzlingly stern, but the tone of her voice and the suggestive motion of her tongue as it glided along her upper lip held no mistake as to her intentions.

"Nelera," he replied, his fist now clutching the king's summons hard in his palm, unwilling to share the news if something more agreeable might be in store. "I should tell you, my lady, a gown such as that is not suitable to appear in when we are at court. We should get you out of it quickly, lest we get a tongue thrashing from all the nobles in the realm."

The woman's expression softened slightly at the lewd jest. She was always beautiful—the pale skin and light freckles that graced her cheeks, the delicate eyebrows which never failed to mirror her emotional state with comical accuracy, her fiery red hair which framed her face in luxurious curls—but when she smiled in earnest, he remembered why he had chosen her amongst the other women who desired a place in his bed and on his arm.

His arrangements with women were contracts brokered due to mutual necessity. Brudais was often required, to his intense dislike, to make appearances at court. The first few times that he had attended alone, however, he had come to realize that the female nobles had invented a game, and the winner was either to wed or bed the Commander. It was made apparent to the subject of this game that the latter would be preferable. Despite the wound to his pride, he wasn't all that surprised. He may have had the right bloodline, a decent title, and an enviable physique, but apparently his personality was lacking. This may have been his downfall for the prospects of marriage within the noble class, but it also happened to be the only one of those aspects that he could easily control. He had no intention of wedding a noble, so perhaps his abominable manners and conversation skills were slightly manipulated to ease that concern and keep the noblewomen at bay. His plan had succeeded for a time, but the moment that Lady Oria of Nesliarc had glided her hand up his trousers causing Brudais to spill his wine on the Ambassador of Zethland, he decided it was time for a change of tactics.

His strategy was to enlist the aid of a woman to ward off the clutches of the handsy chits at court. She didn't have to be high born to attend court because Brudais' station allowed him to escort young ladies of just about any class. He tempted them with the knowledge that they would be introduced at court and begin to accelerate their own position in society through association. The first woman he had made the offer to had slapped him in the face. The second, the amenable Kaeveri, had asked how often they would be fucking—a question which caused Brudais to choke on his ale. She had also been the first woman at court to *hiss* at a flock of hens who were determined to roost in Brudais' vicinity. The looks of utter shock and dismay on those hens' faces were what made him realize that this new strategy would be a success.

From then on, the women came and went, but the arrangement was always the same. It suited him well over the years. He may have been the Creetian court's most conspicuous rake, but his reputation in the arena wasn't tarnished by his bedroom habits. He had not deceived the young women who were willing to keep away the hens. Many of them had advanced to higher status or had secured themselves a high-ranking official as a lover. One of them even bore a son to a Geldivinian prince, he'd heard tell. He liked to remind himself of the ladies' achievements on the eve of an arrangement's conclusion. It was easier to swallow any remaining guilt at leaving them knowing that their time together had been fruitful.

It was time to say goodbye to Nelera. The proof of that was the crinkled scroll in his hand. He would need to spend the next few months training draftees and honing the Creetian army's strategy against Hyglen. He would have no time for court, nor would he have time for Nelera, regardless of the enticing incentives she offered. Their contract was up, and the summons in his hand grew ever smaller as he stood watching her walk slowly towards him in that barely-there dress, pinned together at the shoulders with the only things holding the garment in place.

"You'd better take it off, Commander," she said in a sweet voice with a wicked grin.

It was over.

"And maybe you can give me a tongue thrashing instead."

Best to make a clean break.

"Or I could give you one."

Crunch. The wooden rod of the scroll broke in half in his hand and fell to the floor.

One more night wouldn't hurt.

As the evening grew dark, they realized none of the candles had been lit before Brudais had been accosted in the foyer. He was just getting up to light a couple in the bedroom when Nelera pulled him back onto the sheets. She kissed him hungrily, but his kiss lacked enthusiasm in return.

"What is it?" she said, nudging him playfully.

He sat up and moved to the edge of the bed. After a long moment, he said, "It's time."

He waited for the onslaught—the curses, threats, complaints—but he only heard a very prolonged sigh, that of a woman who is disappointed but resigned that the choices she made were hers. He breathed a little easier.

"I'll admit," she said, "I had hoped I'd have you for a little while longer, but I suppose… we had a deal. Is it another woman? Or war?"

"It's… not another woman."

"Oh dear. It must be very bad."

"Yes," Brudais replied, grabbing behind him. When he found her hand, he squeezed. "Do you have lodgings?"

"I can stay with my sister in Drens."

"When?"

Looking back, he saw the faint outline of Nelera's shoulders shrugging. "Tomorrow, if need be. Unless…"

She wrenched Brudais' hand so hard that he fell over into the sheets, and she planted a few kisses on his neck, from his Adam's apple to his earlobe. He shivered involuntarily.

"Tomorrow," he said sternly, "would be best."

Nelera sighed that long, disappointed sigh. "I'm sure you're right. I just don't know why."

"I am," Brudais replied with a smile that seeped into his words.

As he lay there in the dark with a beautiful, naked woman next to him, he realized the absurdity of his position and his insistence on breaking their engagement. But it *was* for the best. The one thing he could count on was that women could not be a distraction during wartime—especially on the battlefront.

Brudais had never formed any lasting attachments to his lovers throughout the years. In fact, he had not even been jealous when a few of them had told him they were leaving him for another man. They had been sweet, fierce, willful, beautiful, feisty… but none had been his match in strength, intelligence, or cunning. He didn't want a lover who would do what was necessary to gain a good position. He wanted a rival who would love him—someone whose character and cleverness could make him question his own. He didn't want a lover. He wanted his match.

He brought Nelera's hand up to his lips and kissed it gently.

No one had stood up to the challenge yet, and he had doubts that he would ever find her. Despite his misgivings, he still clung to a shred of that hope, a dormant dream. It was better than surrendering to solitude.

Chapter Five

ELDEVA

The Shadow turned toward Eldeva, lifting its hand to its face to brush away a stray black hair from its stunning brown eyes. Its caramel skin glistened in the moonlight pouring in from the high windows of the solar. Eldeva studied her Shadow closely, assessing. It twirled in a pirouette, the skirts of its dress billowing in the air like the makings of a maelstrom. Before it had completed its third spin, Eldeva sent a thought command, causing the Shadow to gracefully come to a halt and begin teasingly taking off her gown.

It looked like a woman in her prime, a ripe fifty years old and at the height of her sexuality and her child-bearing years. It was beautiful: the perfect blend of sensuality and poise. How deceiving appearances could be!

This Shadow was of Eldeva herself, a sixteen-year-old witch of the Old Order, a princess of Sycil. Although a Shadow could be manipulated by the sorceress who conjured it, this one had not been. Eldeva had begun in the Order at the age of thirteen. A typical apprenticeship lasted eight years, but the daughter of the king had completed it in a mere three. She strove hard to complete the tasks assigned to her, but it came at a cost. She, like so many others, had succumbed to the craving when magick was used without thought of the consequences, which were dire. In the last three years, she had used magick so often and with such ever-increasing complexity that the toll on her body had accelerated its aging. The physical aging of thirty-four years had not been an easy thing for her mind to grasp. That same sixteen-year-old mind had not endured the demands that were expected of a fully-grown adult woman. In this body, her outward appearance dictated a heavy toll on the psyche, for she was treated as a woman grown when her mind was still attempting to catch up. She didn't have the years of experience required to determine a good choice from a bad one, and yet everyone expected her to know the difference.

Due to this self-made gap, she had made some very poor choices thus far in life. The last had been a few moons ago, when a brainless oaf had made a lewd suggestion in her ear at dinner, and she had replied by touching his face with a sensuous caress which had become a writhing torment as flames lit the side of his jaw, ear and hair. If he had been any other brainless oaf, she may have gotten away with it, but it had been the Ambassador of Krashkin, so her father the king had given her a punishment just as unkind if not as marring. The princess had been given to the Order where she had endured being burned alive—a spell where she felt the sensations and experience of the act within the confines of her mind. Eldeva was loath to admit that the punishment had been effective. She had not used fire magick since.

Eldeva gazed at the Shadow again, now standing naked before her with her gown pooled about her feet like a jade island against the dark tiles of the solar floor. She still had a good seventy years, if she was careful. She hadn't been thus far.

A thought command had the Shadow dressing slowly, carefully, as if someone were watching it and it was waiting to be told to stop. The princess was simply practicing for tonight when she sent the Shadow to her lover. He had been on the road for two days, making his way to the Jaguar Hills.

It was a spit of land nestled between the Fayn Forest and the Recluos River. It had been quarreled over for centuries between Sycil and Creet, but it was currently under Creet's control—if 'control' was the appropriate word. The people of the Hills were a wild folk. Because of their rule under Sycil, they practiced magick to grow the barren hills into a habitable and profitable agricultural land. The Creetian ban on magick had not sat well with them, and they refused to put aside their practices for the king's law. Luckily for them, there was more profit in allowing them to practice, so the king looked the other way.

Eldeva had never understood the benefit of banning magick. Tarison was a greedy, power-grabbing ruler, but he wasn't a fool. The only advantage of putting oneself at a disadvantage was if there were a greater prize to be gained than the potential of losing one's kingdom. She supposed that banning magick kept the people of Creet compliant—especially when the higher classes seemed to use it without penalty. *A tyrant knows his own business*, she thought. *It's none of mine.*

What *was* her business was that his brother had traveled across the river tonight and was camped on the shores of the Recluos. A potent magick settled there between the Fayn Forest and the Jaguar Hills. It would only make her Shadow that much stronger.

"*Melo guant vod req*," she said, and the Shadow vanished into the air like a wisp of smoke.

Eldeva sat down upon her bed, which was lavishly adorned with feather pillows and silk sheets. She shifted into a cross-legged position, her eyes glazing over, and a warm sensation crept up her spine. She waited patiently, focusing on her breathing and the warmth in her back, focusing on her lover and what she would entice him to do tonight. She imagined his hands gliding along her skin, his lips brushing her neck. The magick pooled at the base of her spine, spreading throughout her body, catching like wildfire. She shut her eyes tight, grabbing hold of the sheets beneath her for support. Her mind was twisting and turning on the precipice of madness.

Then, just as if the fire had been doused with a bucket of icy water, the embers cooled and Eldeva opened her eyes. She looked into the well-crafted tent with a golden hammer and silver saber crest adorning the flaps. A thought command had the Shadow moving forward, and through its eyes she watched as it moved the flaps back and ducked into the tent.

The inside was sparsely furnished with but a cot, a small table, and a weapons rack with a short sword propped up against it and a knife with a bejeweled hilt hanging between the posts. In the cot lay a man, brunette, with almond-shaped eyes and a meticulously trimmed and short beard only a little darker than his hair. He was taller than some, lean but strong. He was beautiful—and he was Eldeva's.

The Shadow sat on the side of the cot and touched his face, a little sigh of contentment coming from Eldeva. When the phantom hand began to caress the man's cheek, he started and grabbed at it, but his hand passed through the air and landed on the opposite side of the sheets. He looked up, his fierce expression turning to something more like concern.

"Princess—" he began, the tone drowsy but laced with anxiety. She cut him off with a harsh look.

"Don't play titles with me, *Prince*," she hissed through her Shadow.

Sitting up on his elbows, Ithiador studied the Shadow's face. He reached his hand out to touch its face, and despite the hand going right through, Eldeva sighed, dipping her head back as if almost feeling his fingers on her neck.

"Are you in trouble?" he said, pulling his hand away and moving to the edge of the cot. "Your father—"

"My father is a blind old bat. I could run circles around him with my hands tied behind my back."

"You don't need your hands to run circles," Ithiador said, his lips twitching.

"True, but I do need them to do spellcraft."

"Aye," he replied warily. "And this is the spellcraft you've chosen for tonight, is it? A ghost."

"A Shadow, my love."

"And what does this Shadow do, other than drive me wild with longing?"

"You haven't been to the palace in an age. So tonight, I come to you." The Shadow leaned into him, its breasts rubbing up against his chest, and she imagined his pulse quickening. "Would you like to keep longing, or would you rather I show you just how good a Shadow can *feel*?"

Ithiador watched her, his eyes burning with need. Then he closed his eyes tight, grimacing. He looked quickly toward the tent entrance. “My guards are in the tent next to mine,” he cautioned. “If they hear anything…”

“You don’t want to use it?” The Shadow stuck out its bottom lip, then rubbed up against him again. “Such a waste. I conjured it to see you tonight, and you’re too afraid that your guard dogs will hear? I can be very quiet, Prince, but I won’t make promises for *you*.”

His eyes burned brighter, watching her carefully. It didn’t take him long to decide.

“Make it corporeal.”

Warmth worked its way down Eldeva’s spine and into her legs. She became the Shadow and the Shadow became her. She didn’t waste a moment on the peculiar sensations of being in two places at once. She straddled Ithiador and their lips locked in a fierce kiss. And neither of them cared what noises they made.

Eldeva’s Shadow shifted so as to wiggle its arm from underneath Ithiador’s body. Once it was free, it brought its hand up to his face, gently gliding its fingers along his cheek.

“Prince,” she purred, her nails trailing down his face, making their way down his neck.

“Yes, my love,” he replied huskily.

“Why are you here?” Eldeva’s voice was crisp, with no illusions of further play at hand. “What is it that your brother wants with the people of the Jaguar Hills?”

“Is this mere curiosity, Princess? Or is it your father asking?”

The Shadow moved to prop itself up on one elbow, displaying her bare chest. Ithiador seemed to struggle to keep his eyes on hers. "You think my father has made a spy of me?"

"Of course not, though you've never shown the least bit of interest in the goings on of Creetian politics before."

"Unless they involve an ambassador being sent to the palace, of course."

"I do find myself particularly lucky to have been the only ambassador to leave Sycil unscathed. I wonder if your father has made note of that and works to play it to his advantage."

"He's a fool. If he knew, the entire palace would be humming with the news."

"Those you did not pay to keep their silence, you mean."

Pay. Her lover could be so terribly naïve. When he came to Sycil the first time, two years ago, he had told her she was the most beautiful woman he had ever met. What woman could be unmoved by such a compliment? He did not know how old she was, and if he had been aware that she was a scant fourteen years, he would never have agreed to follow her into her bedchambers. The king would have been furious for her fraternization with a potential enemy, so when they had been found out by two servants, she took no chances.

There was always a risk to paying someone off. That risk was eliminated when the person had no memory of the event in question. Eldeva had used a spell on the two servants, but her training in the Order had not been complete at the time. The servants had soon after been dismissed when they had been found drooling on the floor, unable to remember their own names. She had felt a touch of remorse for her mistake, which only made her wish she had killed them outright.

When Ithiador had asked about the incident, she had told him a simple lie to hide the truth. She would not admit to how much she loved him. He would see it as weakness and leave her, surely. It was a tenuous first year, and the two servants whose minds had been liquified had not been the only casualties in her bedroom games with the Prince of Creet, but she was much more thorough and subtle in her disposal methods now. It was almost sweet that Ithiador still pretended to believe that the worst thing to come of their indiscreet liaisons was a lost bag of gold.

"I am curious," Eldeva said, the Shadow rubbing its naked breasts up against his bare chest. "They are our people, after all."

"I thought you didn't want to get political."

"Let's call it historical."

"Hysterical, maybe. Creet has laid claim to the Hills more often than Sycil has. They are Creetian lands."

"Damn the land. I said they're our *people*. I am concerned for their welfare."

Ithiador gave her a wicked grin, then moved with feline grace so quickly that Eldeva didn't even realize the Shadow had been moved and was now splayed on its back, its arms held at the wrists with gentle force.

He kissed her hard, his tongue forcing her mouth open. She began to struggle, but when his right hand released her wrist and gingerly glided down the side of her body, goosebumps rose along her skin at his touch, and she surrendered to him, parting her legs expectantly.

Ithiador withdrew his tongue, moving away from her to sit up on the side of the cot. "The Jaguar Hills could be used to strategic advantage… if we can coerce *your* people to help us win the war."

Eldeva moaned in a way that showcased her displeasure and frustration.

"My brother sent me to find out if they would be amenable to such an arrangement, and how much gold would be required to procure their services—their loyalty, that is."

Eldeva shifted her pelvis, nudging him in the back, moaning frustratedly again, louder. Ithiador placed his hand over her mouth to silence her.

"I'm only telling you what you want to hear, Princess."

What she wanted to hear right now was that delectable noise he made every time he thrust into her. She relaxed her muscles, which made him drop his hands from her mouth and wrist.

Foolish male.

She pounced on him, twisting around his torso and straddling him as quickly as he had pinned her with just as much grace. She encircled his neck with her arms and grabbed his mouth with hers in a forceful kiss. When she finally released him, they were both out of breath.

"The man who is free," she said between ragged breaths, "is always more amenable than the one who is chained."

"Except perhaps one who is chained by your thighs," Ithiador muttered, burying his face into her neck.

"I mean," Eldeva continued, tightening her thighs' hold on his waist almost as an afterthought, "your ban on magick has the Hillpeople chained to life outside the king's law. Make it easier for them, and perhaps they'll strive to be a little more helpful."

"How?" came his muffled reply.

"Draft an exception to the law," she said simply, as if the answer were obvious.

Ithiador lifted his head, his hair disheveled in a way that made Eldeva's inner self scream, *Mine!*

"That is not as easy as you suppose."

"If you want any help from the Hillpeople, you should find a way to make it easier."

She leaned forward to kiss him, and he caught her lower lip between his teeth, running his tongue along its length. She was trapped, but she didn't care. Not with him. She moaned a little until he let go, then she moaned again in protest.

"Tarison doesn't make exceptions, not in any good ways."

Eldeva scoffed. "You are second in line to the throne. Tarison might not make exceptions, but he should listen to reason. Make your own exception, then make him see reason."

Ithiador paused, considering. Eldeva ran her fingers through his already disheveled hair. He groaned, grabbing her hand and holding it behind her back.

"You have a very clever mind, Princess."

"And you have a very accommodating tongue, Prince."

Ithiador smirked. "Is that an invitation?"

"That," Eldeva purred softly, "is a command."

Chapter Six

BRUDAIS

Ælon whinnied again, pounding his hooves into the dust and kicking it up into the air around him. Brudais grit his teeth, holding one hand to the horse's flank and the other to his powerful chest in an attempt to calm him.

"Ælon, you frightful beast," he said, brushing his hands along his mane in slow, deliberate motions. "Are you still on about that bloody mare?"

The horse snorted with all the grace of a mule.

Brudais grabbed for the brush that had fallen from his grasp, but the stallion made to kick his back leg, and his owner was forced to retreat.

"That's *enough,*" Brudais said through clenched teeth. He dodged a well-aimed kick. Perhaps Ælon thought that if he could not use his balls, Brudais should not be able to use his either. Moving around to the stallion's front, he grabbed the bit at both ends and pulled the horse's muzzle towards him. Ælon's eyes rolled furiously, but Brudais gripped the bit tighter, jerking it down once. Twice. Ælon's eyes met Brudais'—fury meeting fury.

"You are acting like a *foal*," he said, spitting the last word to release some of the impatience and anger boiling just under the surface. This day was already destined to be joyless and frustrating. He had hoped that going for a quick ride this morning would help offset some of that frustration, but the damn horse had been a terror in and out of the paddock. He knew that Ælon had been courting the dappled mare in the lower field, but he had not guessed at how serious his affections were and how unwilling he was to accept a graciously phrased "no" for an answer to those attentions.

"So the lass spurned you," he continued, his eyes never leaving the stallion's. "She may not have wanted you, but there are plenty of mares in that field. Fix your gaze elsewhere, old son."

Brudais watched Ælon's eyes slowly waver from fury to calm. He knew this behavior wasn't common among other horses, but he would swear on his father's gravestone that Ælon understood him. Even knowing this, it still amazed him each time his horse reacted to something he said. Because of his apparent intelligence, Brudais always spoke to him as though he were capable of comprehending every word.

Ælon snorted, shaking his head and rattling the reins. Brudais took that to mean his tantrum was concluded and he had finally seen sense. What his master willfully excluded from his advice was that Ælon would not be using his balls anytime soon, because Brudais had no plans to breed him. Perhaps one day, when the demands of his military career were not so all-encompassing.

The day when Brudais had seen Ælon step off the ship from Madidus, he had designs to breed him—a magnificent-looking buckskin stallion with a fine pedigree. His tawny coat glistened in the sun, his dark brown mane flowing in the sea breeze. In that moment, Brudais fell in love—if not with the animal himself, with the idea of what offspring he might sire. He had never imagined the kind of feral intelligence that might be spawned from Ælon's brood, but he had assured himself he must try before the beast was too old to breed. His plan could no longer wait until he was an old man himself now that he had the perfect stallion with which to carry it out.

Moving his thoughts to the back of his mind, he put his forehead against Ælon's and sighed heavily.

"I still have a great deal to do to ready you, not to mention myself, for a visit to the castle. Will you let me make you pretty?"

A trumpeting snort was Ælon's reply.

"Yes, I know. You're very particular about your appearance."

He got to work brushing the horse's coat and mane of the tangles from their morning jaunt.

His Seventh Order audience with the king was in a few short hours, and the unpleasantness he so often felt when going to court had pervaded his entire morning, but with each stroke of the brush, his temper waned. By the time Ælon was saddled, Brudais smelled strongly of horse and manure, but he didn't have time to return to the townhouse to bathe and dress. Having foreseen this predicament, he had brought his uniform—or his court costume, as he often called it—to the stables.

When he came out in his courtly attire, the three stable hands stared at him. They had never seen him in anything more glamorous than his "good" riding clothes, which consisted of a woolen vest to cover his linen tunic and trousers.

The ghastly excuse for attire he now wore was a hard leather doublet over a linen shirt, paired with creased pants, all dyed or stained shades of forest green. The doublet had solid, pointed shoulders, with the royal crest worked into the leather at each point, and down and across the right breast was a ladder of sewn stars against a deep purple silk sash. This sash was where all the commanders displayed their various achievements. Brudais' sash included his five-years of triumph at the Kresha Cup, his advancement through the ranks of lieutenant, captain, and major, his victories at Altroch and The Fennan against Firdeshian invaders, the Seventh Order crest, and the command stars he had received upon his promotion to Commander of the Royal Military. Admittedly, he was not permitted to wear those stars, as he had been stripped of his singular post by Tarison, but he kept them pinned to his sash for the satisfying look of fury on the king's face whenever he happened to take notice of them.

Brudais self-consciously straightened his doublet, a faint jingle coming from his sash. "Well?" he asked, eyeing the stable hands warily.

Gable, the least timid of the three, walked up to him, removed a piece of hay carefully from Brudais' hair and brushed a bit of dust from his sleeve.

"You look splendid, Commander," he said, standing back with a genuine smile.

"I look like a fool," he replied, grabbing his bag from the ground and lacing it into the saddlebag. "All the pomp of nobility with none of the status. But I thank you for your help, and your flattery. The beast and I look suitably outfitted thanks to your diligence and care."

"It's an honor to assist you, Commander. The beast… not quite as much."

Ælon kicked his back leg out towards the other stable hands, who swiftly scattered. It could only have been a purposefully aimed kick, because there were very few flies in this part of the stable.

"It would appear you've hurt his feelings."

Gable shrugged. "He's hurt worse than my feelings before."

"Fair enough," Brudais said, a smile tugging at his lips. He mounted Ælon, drew up the reins and started for the gate. "You have my permission to pay him back in kind."

Gable walked alongside them until they reached the gate. He held it open for them, and as they passed, he said, "He's not one you want as an enemy, much like his owner."

Brudais chuckled, waving back at Gable as they rode up the causeway towards the main street. "A formidable pair we make, eh, my friend?" Clapping his hand on the stallion's balmy neck, Ælon shook the reins in what his owner supposed was agreement.

Three Sons Stables was nestled at the very bottom of the city, as it had the lushest pastures for grazing. There were a few stable yards in the city center, which would have been a much closer walk for Brudais, but Three Sons was a more reputable establishment and treated their boarders well. However, the distance meant trekking through the entire length of Turivaun to reach the castle walls. He had not considered the disruption he would cause by his formal dress and the direction of his travels until he was faced with the eerie silence and open-mouthed faces turned his way as he trudged through the lower markets of Drens district.

The silence unnerved him, so he searched the crowd for a friendly face and called out.

"Aurelius! What have you got for me today?"

The blacksmith's head perked up when he heard his name, and his serious expression swiftly passed to one of wry amusement.

"Nothin' for the likes of you, Commander," he said. "Only repairs and refittings today."

"I may have need of some repairs soon," said Brudais, the smile dropping from his face. He hoped not only Aurelius would heed the warning in his words.

"Aye," said the big man, lifting his hammer to rest over his shoulder. The grimness saturated his expression and tone. "My forge will be ready when the time comes."

Brudais nodded sternly, then urged Ælon forward into a steady trot. In his wake, he heard a smattering of conversations erupt at once. The little he could make out was talk of the beheaded ambassador, fear of raiding parties, and the rumor of a coming war. Now Commander Brudais rode through the streets in military dress towards Castle Doriell. A dark omen of the days ahead. An omen of death. But whose death was not certain amongst the commonfolk. Some said Brudais was meant to bring about the death of Creet's enemies. Others proclaimed the needless wars would bring much death to both sides. One was even so bold as to suggest the death of the king and was quickly hushed by his fellows.

He should have known better than to parade himself in front of the crofters and laborers of the city, whose perceptions were keen if not entirely accurate. However, the king had not explicitly forbade the commanders from making appearances or cautioning, and someone needed to warn them of the blood on the horizon;

if not their king in a formal proclamation, then a whispered threat would have to suffice.

Ælon trotted up the streets past *The Moon & Myth*, a frequent refuge of Brudais' which straddled the districts of Kelvs and Quies. He made similar overtures to the proprietor there, with similar reactions from the patrons and surrounding townsfolk. His hope was that by sundown the city would be humming with news of war with Hyglen, and their involvement might demand a forthright response from their king.

It hadn't been his intention to cause such havoc on his ride to the castle, but once the opportunity had presented itself, it was hard not to steer the ship with a straighter heading. The cost of that choice might not be felt for some time—and certainly not on this visit to court. Word may have traveled swiftly, but gossip needed time to steep before it was properly brewed.

"Careful, lad," he said, tossing his reins to the stable hand and dismounting. "He's been a bit testy lately, so have a care. Take him straight to Nav. He'll know what to do with him."

The stallion snorted harshly when the boy tugged lightly on his reins. The boy jumped and backed away quickly.

Brudais watched the exchange and then rolled his eyes. Ælon looked back at him and whinnied, but Brudais waved his hand toward the royal stables dismissively. Ælon may have hated coming to the castle as much as his owner, but he knew he had the better deal of the two of them. He would be rubbed down with refreshing spring water, and lathered with lavender and honey-scented soap and fed the freshest grasses imported from the midlands. If Brudais could have stayed out in the stables, he would have. Alas, his business was within the dark walls of Doriell.

He climbed the gray quartz steps to the outer doors, his face stoic as he made his way past the two guards standing on either side of the great oak doors.

Once he was within the confines of the castle, he had an innate sense of not knowing where the hell he was. Throughout his childhood and again during his tenure as commander, he had been obliged to come to court quite often. The fact that he didn't have even the main level memorized was a credit to his constant hope that he would never set foot in the place again.

As he made his way north, he came upon a guard standing just outside one of the castle courtyards.

"Afternoon, soldier," he said, moving his hand to rest on the ceremonial sword hilt at his left hip, an instinctive movement occurring any time he was in the presence of an armed unfamiliar.

The guard straightened his posture, keeping his hand well away from the sword at his side so as not to invite a challenge. "Commander," he grunted brusquely.

Brudais looked him up and down. "Am I taking up your time, soldier?"

After a moment, a look of puzzlement crossed the otherwise indifferent face. "Sir?"

"Usually when I hear grunting, I look for pigs." Brudais tilted his head. "You don't look like a pig."

"Apologies, sir." The guard bent his head in a makeshift bow. "I meant no disrespect."

"Mm." Brudais didn't care to discipline a guardsman, as they were typically never reassigned to a battalion after retaining a position in the castle. It was a dreary life, so he could understand the lack of decorum, but his disrespect would have earned a much harsher punishment if he were a soldier in Brudais' battalion. "Can you tell me where the receiving room is?"

He watched the uncertainty in the guard's face as he attempted to piece together this next puzzle. It took a terribly uncomfortable few moments before he said, "Is this a joke, sir?"

Brudais sighed, relaxing his stance. "Indeed, lad. A cruel one."

The guard gave him a set of detailed instructions which would lead him to his destination, but Brudais had no intention of meeting with the king on time if it could be helped. He took an unnecessary turn about an abandoned corridor, taking an interest in a bust statue of an old man. The description below it identified him as Meddin son of Uked, a deeply renowned mender who had saved countless lives of citizens who had been injured during the Krashkin Raids. Apparently not renowned highly enough, thought Brudais as he glanced about him, since his only tribute was a stone mount of a face no one recognized in a corridor no one frequented.

The end of the hall led into another courtyard, and the bright sunlight dancing on the dark stones drew him forward. He still had at least a few minutes to spare, which was plenty of time to pass through one of the castle's less prominent gardens.

Stepping out into the pleasant breeze, he inhaled deeply. Next to the confines of the stale bowels of the castle, the fresh air was practically a godsend.

There wasn't much to admire save the bright flowers decorating the edges of each wall. A miniature, unadorned fountain spouted water from the spigot at its center, a pathetic stream running into the basin, which could have been considered laughable. In contrast, one of the most beautiful women Brudais had ever seen was sitting demurely on the stone bricks that made up the fountain's base. The breeze shifted suddenly, and he picked up on the scent of the perfume she wore, which mingled with the flowers' scents in a strange, alluring way.

Nothing about her had seemed familiar to him when his eyes first met her figure, but as she turned her head to acknowledge his presence, he recognized her immediately.

"Livy," he muttered aloud, the tone of his voice mirroring his panic. He prepared himself for the worst.

The woman stood up quickly, all the grace and delicacy she had previously displayed disappearing in a single instant. She ran to him and encased him in an embrace so fierce Brudais momentarily failed to breathe. When she relaxed her grip from around his ribcage, he took both her shoulders in his hands and held her at arm's length.

"I don't believe that was one of the three acceptable formal greetings permitted of ladies of the court," he scolded lightly.

"I haven't seen you in ages, Brudais," she replied huskily. "Allow me a moment to adjust."

Her voice bit him like ice, prickling across his skin, causing a barely concealed shiver down the base of his spine. It wasn't cold or cruel, but in some strange, perverted sense, the very sound of her voice aroused him. It was an uncomfortable feeling, given the innocent background on which their relationship was based.

Staliva was daughter to Cavison II, the regent-uncle who had helped to command the throne while Tarison grew to manhood. Due to Brudais' position, he frequently joined the court for important occasions, which the regent's children were also forced to attend. The young Brudais had been good friends with Cavison's sons, Ryvius and Kritun. Their charge, their sixteen-year-old sister, would often join them during the festivities. Over the years, Staliva had come to know Brudais as another elder brother, an adopted relation. Following her father's execution, she had stayed in the Zethland court with Brudais' mother, exiled but safe from Tarison.

So when Brudais felt an all-too-familiar tug at the crease of his trousers, he was disgusted. Either he had briefly put aside the idea that she was like a younger sister to him, or she was playing with magick far too liberally in a realm which did not hold with the practice.

"After years of grueling instruction on the matter," he added teasingly, "I'd expect more of your ability to adjust."

Staliva eyed him carefully. "You're right, of course. Would you prefer a curtsey or a slap on the cheek?"

"I haven't been to Zethland in some time, I'll admit, but I don't ever recall a formal greeting involving bodily harm."

"Oh, yes, Commander. It's the formal greeting for rogues and rakes."

Brudais' lips twitched. "A rogue, am I?"

Staliva placed a hand on her pale gray dress, pretending to smooth out the wrinkles. "If the gossips are to be believed."

"The gossips of court should never be taken to heart. They only see half the picture—and not the flattering side."

"So, you deny your involvement with eleven women whose bloodlines can be traced to the gutter?"

Her alluring voice suddenly turned savage, biting him now not with a playful lust but as shards of ice. The light teasing that he usually peppered their conversations with seemed to have struck a harsh chord with her, and he pondered at the reason before realizing his mistake. She was a woman now, full-grown, and women did not often tolerate being made fools of. Still, he would not allow her to spout scurrilous rumors, even if many of them were true.

"Did the ladies of the Zethland court teach you this?" he said mildly.

"Teach what?" she spat.

"Dereliction. Arrogance. Malice. Take your pick."

Staliva's eyes grew a touch wider before her cheeks grew a delicate shade of pink.

"Or is it now customary in Zethland," he said, bending his head to whisper in her ear, "to bewitch one's relations with carnal spellcraft? That lesson you might have kept leashed within the castle whose rule calls for its banishment, if you had any sense left."

"I didn't—"

Brudais leaned back, watching Staliva's expression pass from remorseful to wary. Perhaps she really hadn't realized the danger she was in, and the Zethland vultures had picked her clean before sending her back to Creet, as disgraced carrion who had remained a rat in their presence for far too long. He had the beginnings of a strongly worded lecture to his mother on this subject, as it had been her idea to send Staliva to Zethland for safety. That 'safety' was likely to get her executed in Creet—or worse. The kind of spellcraft she had used on him was just as likely to entrap a real rogue, whose only desire would be to take her for his own pleasure. Whether that led to a marriage or not, neither outcome would be beneficial to her.

"You are a woman now," he said, straightening up to his full height, "and you may have been taught the means with which to defend yourself, but you have a lot to learn yet about people, Livy."

Staliva stepped back, her eyes taking in his figure, showing a gleam of defiance. "And what do I need to fear from *people*?" She said the last word in a mocking tone.

Brudais stepped toward her, bringing his hand up to her face and brushing a strand of her blonde hair away from her unsettling dark eyes. He looked at them closer and recognized the magick in them, the deep purple irises which shown with glints of lightning through the pupils. Where were the brilliant green eyes he knew so well?

The lust grew in him, his body feeling suddenly hot, a restless sensation boiling like a rising geyser. She pinned him with her gaze, rebelliously refusing to release the magick despite his gentle warnings. He growled low in his throat, an animalistic sound, suddenly gripping her beneath her shoulders tight in an attempt to resist. Every instinct told him to pounce on her, kiss her madly and take her on the ground. Every instinct save one.

"*People*," he snarled, increasing the pressure on her arms until he watched in triumph as she winced and withdrew. He let her go. "People can be monsters, and not all monsters can be slain with magick."

They stood together, apart. There was a cold silence which stretched between them as the desire melted from Brudais' body. His physical faculties had returned to him, and he no longer felt the longing—the need to touch her, take her—but the prickling frustration remained, digging into the edges of his resolve.

She stood holding her upper arms where he had surely left bruises, her face an odd mixture of uncertainty and confidence. When she looked up at him, her eyes were the beautiful green he remembered, but he could not recall ever having seen in them the determined mischief he now witnessed.

Staliva straightened, lowering her arms to her sides and balling her fists. “I’ll take my chances with the ones that can.”

Brudais let out a slow breath, his eyes cast down in defeat. He said, “And how will you tell them apart?” and began to walk past her, then moved into a flourishing formal bow. “My lady.”

As he made it to the outer walls of the corridor, he heard a small sob concealed behind a hand. He did her the courtesy of not turning back. She was a woman now; if her choices were her own, so too were her sorrows.

King Tarison II sat on the throne on the raised dais, not attempting to hide his distaste. The king’s short, light brown hair was styled back and away from his face. A curious blend of whale’s oil and maple sap—a mystery that Prince Ithiador had uncovered years ago—ensured it stayed in place in an unkempt-looking way that was his fashion-setting flair. He had a medium build, a square jaw which always made him look severe and unyielding, and a dark brush of stubble framed his jawline. His eyes may have been kindly in the presence of others, but when Brudais was near enough to notice, the king’s eyes always held contempt.

“You have kept us waiting, Commander.”

Brudais glanced around the receiving room without turning his head overmuch. There were a collection of chairs on the right side of the room, which accommodated a large assemblage of the king's advisors. Some were dozing, some looking straight on, past Brudais to the other side of the room to admire the tapestries or the high windows. Only a few dared to meet Brudais' gaze.

What did advisors know of the intricacies of warfare? During wartime, the commanders *were* the advisors. Good counsel should not have been checked by the ignorant ramblings of a few aged noblemen.

He bowed his head slightly to the king and clasped his hands behind his back in a military stance.

"Nothing brings me greater shame than to waste your time, Your Majesty."

One of the guards at the inner doors to the throne's left stifled a cough with his sword hand. There wasn't another sound in the room. It did make the commander feel rather elevated to inflict a blow so carefully worded that it was known to be an insult but could not be marked as one to merit penalty.

Brudais broke the silence. "If we might begin this meeting, I've prepared a few select strategic queries, but I am sure a more detailed account of the coming war is forthcoming, and my questions can wait until I've heard the full proposal."

Caldwell, a lean and simpering advisor, stood from his seat and began a rapturous account of Creet's plans to invade Hyglen. Many of the details were already known to Brudais, such as the recall of the six Seasonings and the march along the northern borders of the Fayn Forest, but he had not known of the intention to encamp the army on the eastern edges of the forest, so far from Hyglen's capital, Bentixt. They may have thought it would be safer to have a forest at the back of the camp, and he might have agreed that any other forest would provide decent shelter from a rear attack, but not the Fayn Forest. There was so much they didn't know about that wood, and it was best for all concerned to steer well clear of it.

After Caldwell had returned to his seat, Brudais turned back to the king. He'd start with the more obvious of the disastrous implications of this plan and work his way to the most critical.

"Why is it that we're marching to Hyglen?" he asked, sweeping his gaze swiftly over the murmuring advisors. "We lose the advantage if we instigate and fail to wait for retaliation. Our position is stronger than Hyglen's. We have the upper hand and could use Hyglen's anger to fuel their desire to lay siege to Turivaun, which would be only to our advantage. With the river to our east and the height of the city itself, it would be almost impossible for them to sustain a siege for long."

"We go to Hyglen to protect the people of Creet, Commander."

Brudais bristled at the boredom in the king's voice. It rubbed against his already raw temper.

"We could easily evacuate the city to the midlands or the mountains and house the people in temporary settlements before the Hyglen army could make its way here."

Murmurs and whispers. He could not make out whether the tone was one of agreement or dissent.

"Our people are safer where they are. The army will move to Hyglen and keep the people safe from the atrocities of war."

There had never been a time when Tarison would willingly put his people above his own agenda—unless it would yield some profit for him. It didn't take more than a moment for Brudais to see the king's benefit. To quell the stirrings of rebellion while the army was fighting the king's battles, he needed to secure their protection from enemy forces. A tactful move that a good king would never have needed to make.

Brudais nodded, signaling his assent if not his disapproval.

"And the location of the encampment. The forest may give us a small advantage on our west flank, but the danger it poses may be a greater threat to—"

"Hold your tongue on the subject of ghost stories, Commander. Any counsel on mythical beasts will quickly be brushed aside."

"Stories and myths originated somewhere, Your Majesty."

They stared at one another, unblinking, with determination and unwillingness to yield.

"Do you know, Commander, why I *honored* you with the last of the Seventh Order audiences?"

Brudais stiffened. "I assumed it was to insult me. A wound I will not easily heal from."

Tarison sneered, his face a mask of scorn. "In addition to the insult, it was to ensure that no matter what you have to say, it has already been presented by one of the other six commanders, so we have little need to listen to your *prudent* advice longer than is necessary."

"Perhaps," Brudais replied, keeping his tone even, "you should have begun with the wisest, or else dispensed with the niceties and gathered a war counsel, as is custom."

The golden and bejeweled crown on Tarison's head glimmered in the sunlight as he drew forward in his throne, looking down on Brudais. "Had I done that, I could not have insulted you."

A vindictive answer to an insignificant problem, just like when they were children. During Brudais' adolescence, he had been called to court on many occasions by the regent to befriend the boy-king. It was hoped that friendship with Leifius' son would help smooth out the rough edges that Tarison had honed over his boyhood, if not only for appearance's sake. But the boy-king was loath to associate with the legend's son, and he often spurned Brudais' company whenever it was conveniently made available. After one of their tussles over the younger boys' 'lack of respect,' Brudais had found Prince Ithiador getting into mischief in the castle kitchens. Instead of turning him in—which might have been the honorable thing to do, according to the regent—Brudais joined in, and together they repurposed two blackberry pies and all the soup ladles they could find. Laughing raucously, they ate the entirety of the pies while listening to Cook yell at his subordinates for misplacing the ladles while making rabbit stew. They had been inseparable ever since.

Brudais often thought the reason that Tarison hated him was the animosity between the brothers, and how he had widened that gulf with his alliance with the prince, but that had never explained Tarison's disdain and why he had so consistently snubbed Brudais' advances toward friendship in the first place. The king had always seen him as an enemy—even when he tried to be a friend—and at some point, he had stopped trying to be the latter.

"Majesty, tell me truly," said Brudais, leaning in conspiratorially, "is this war only about insults? Because those hurled by the Hyglenian king may not have held credence, but the state of your manhood is nary a reason to go to battle. If that's all my men are fighting for, I respectfully request redress."

Tarison's entire face was bright red, a pot ready to boil over. Brudais straightened up, pulling at the edges of his doublet, and waited.

One moment. Another. A few coughs from the guards in the back.

"OUT!!!" Tarison's voice boomed through the receiving room with surprising force, the echoes climbing up into the rafters.

Perhaps he had gone too far, he thought as two guards dragged him bodily from the room, but he had never quite been able to back down from a challenge.

Chapter Seven

Loya

Damn it all!

Governor Loya of Drens watched with a carefully displayed mask of indifference as two guards dragged Commander Brudais from the receiving room. It was a testament to her self-control that she didn't stamp her foot at the unfairness of the situation. Not for whatever—probably wholly inconsequential—reason that the commander had been forced to vacate his audience with the king, but because Loya had secured an audience with His Majesty afterwards. Now that the king was likely stewing over whatever frivolous comment Brudais had made, he wouldn't be of a mind to seriously consider her proposal.

She had known this was a possibility. It always was when dealing with males—especially those with even a modicum of power—but if she had waited any longer for her audience, she may have been forced to admit defeat until next season. The king's schedule, his aid had told her, was simply fraught with urgent matters. So her audience had been postponed multiple times, thus giving the governor the impression that her presence itself was unwelcome—not just the subject matter of her intended discussion. It had taken bribing a lower-level aid to secure this spot, but when she had realized it would be following the king's audience with Brudais, she had nearly demanded her coin back.

"Get off me," Brudais growled at the guards who were holding the shoulders of his uniform tightly. He shoved against one of them, causing him to stumble, leaving the other open to attack. The commander lurched forward to unbalance his opponent and, instead of a shoulder to the guard's ribs as Loya had expected, Brudais moved swiftly out of either of their reach and walked briskly forward, straightening his doublet and smiling in a self-satisfied sort of way.

"Commander," Loya said from the shadows on the other end of the hall, managing to form the word into an exasperated sigh. "Please tell me you were not just thrown from your audience, and your escort was simply a sign of respect from a grateful monarch."

The commander looked toward her as she skulked in the corner, clearly not thrilled to have had his disgraceful antics on display but enthusiastic enough at seeing her to bring a warm smile to his lips. The latter, she shamefully admitted, caused smugness, accompanied by a faint flutter of nerves. He was a handsome devil, as the ladies of the court frequently stressed in both word and impropriety.

"Governor Loya," he said, walking towards her. When he reached a polite distance, he made a formal court bow, the stars on his command sash jangling in a none-too-subtle reminder of his station.

She curtsied in reply, extending her hand expectantly. He trailed his fingers along the side of her forearm in a coquettish flourish before he took her hand, bending forward to kiss it. He lifted his head enough for them to lock eyes, blue to green, before he gently dropped her hand from his.

Such a dangerous male, she reminded herself. How could the man who built the good reputation of the realm afford to be such a scandalous flirt?

"*Really*, Commander," she replied scoldingly. "I must needs an answer."

"Unfortunately, my lady, you already have the answer. Armed escorts are uncommonly rare forms of respect from a king, unless the journey ends at the gallows."

She hadn't really expected a better answer, but hope lingered ever so gently on the edge of the chasm of despair.

"A black pall is cast over my own audience then, I suppose?"

With his hands behind his back in an unobtrusive fashion, he turned slightly to the left to admire the closed doors of the receiving room. He turned back, his expression one of the keenest remorse.

"Black pall is somewhat hyperbolic, don't you think?" he replied. "A gray cloud, perhaps. A dismal hailstorm, at worst."

"Neither sound inviting or agreeable to my purposes."

The commander suddenly found the edge of his shoe fascinating.

Loya snorted in a very unladylike manner.

"Truly, lady," Brudais said, looking up at her, "had I known your audience was to follow mine, I would have stifled the need to balance the king's inflated head—"

"With your own?" Loya interjected, a wry smile forming.

Despite the move he made as if to stab himself in the gut with an imaginary knife, she caught the impressed smile he quickly tried to hide. "You wound me, lady."

"You'll heal, and quickly enough to rebound with another witty remark, no doubt."

"What is life but a joke of increasingly intricate scope?"

Loya rolled her eyes. "That, my dear sir, is called irony."

"No." Brudais' tone turned serious. "It's called 'injustice.'"

He turned to walk away with a curt nod of his head.

"Brudais," Loya called after him, stepping out from the shadow of the tapestries, wariness warring with concern. "I will need your support on this proposal."

Without turning back to her, he called, "I make a point never to support a doomed cause… but if you prove it has merit, I'll sign the damn thing—not that my name means much in this place," he added bitterly.

Loya's smile brightened. His name meant a great deal to a great many. Perhaps not the king, but many of his advisors—not to mention the other commanders—counted Brudais' counsel and support to be dearer than gold. The weight of Brudais' signature on her proposal could propel it in the appropriate direction. She need only prove its merit.

Turning about so that her skirts followed her, she swept down the hall until she stood before the doors to the receiving room. She shifted her gaze to the guard at the right, giving him a pointed stare before he got the message and opened the door for her.

Stepping through the archway, Loya straightened her back, causing her chest to display to full effect in her plum-colored dress, the corset of which she had requested to be rib-crackingly tight. Her breasts had not gotten her the governor's seat—though many rumors had spread due to her distinction as the only female governor in the history of the city—but she did not forgo the advantage they served as a distraction for her male colleagues. Distraction was a most useful tool when dealing with imbeciles.

The receiving room was impressive in its structure, sparsely decorated so as not to welcome the petitioners who came to make requests of their liege lord. A few dull tapestries hung from the high, imposing ceilings whose rafters made a cross, obscuring the high windows which offered the majority of the room's light. The stone pillars on either side were carved in a fluted design, accentuating the castle's remarkable age, as the style had gone out of fashion before the Pelyrian Wars. A dais was positioned at the back, lifting the elaborate throne centered between two tall beams, their peaks carved with snarling wolf heads—the symbol for the royal House of Dagmere. Before the Civil Wars, the Dagmerian line was strong and flourished in their love of the land and the people. Once Soville the Heartless ascended the throne, it was a rarity that the king aided his people without ulterior motive, and the land had suffered, decaying into ruin and wilderness without tender hands to care for it.

Soville was the king's thrice great-grandfather, and Tarison's heart seemed similarly absent even prior to his coronation. But Loya did not require a king with a heart, only a large treasury and an open mind. Whatever else he was, Tarison was a maverick, his unconventional methods often causing panic and dissension.

His dismantling of Parliament, for instance, brought about the "disappearances" of all its members. She could appreciate the subtle craft required to accomplish such a feat—especially given that all fifty disappearances had occurred on the same night, and not a single body was ever found. No one had seen a royal or city guard go into a member's home. Loya was sure of this; she had issued enough bribes to secure her certainty. It had been a calculated risk, as well as an insurance policy. With Parliament being eradicated with such efficiency and swiftness, the governors could easily have been next on the king's discreet chopping block. It was to all their relief when the king made it clear that he wanted nothing to do with Turivaun's politics and would gladly leave the city's governance to them. The only good thing about having little power was that it was not often squabbled over.

Loya reached the back of the room, sparing a cursory glance at the rows of advisors seated on the right wing. As to why the entirety of the king's advisors had been called to this meeting—and presumably Brudais' audience, as well—she could only guess it was the king's hope to intimidate them. It hadn't been effective with Brudais—given whatever flippant remark had him thrown from the room—and she was determined not to allow it to intimidate her… despite the trembling in her legs.

Halting before the dais, Loya moved fluidly into a formal curtsey and remained unmoving, her eyes downcast, as was customary before a monarch.

"Lady-Governor Loya," the king said, his tone a little hot. "Please rise and do us the honor of presenting your proposition. We have been told it regards the military and is of great import." His tone did not indicate that it was of great import in the least.

"My liege," she said, rising from her curtsey, her eyes falling on the king's face which was rather red and moist from the sweat across his brow—the sweat of exertion. She would murder Brudais. "I have been in communication with Lady Selene, the ambassador of Phesius, who has made several inquiries into our military's numbers and standing. I had, at first, believed those inquiries to be nothing more than an ally sizing up potential support should the need arise, and so felt no need to make further inquiries on her behalf. That was until the true reason for her curiosity was divulged.

"Ambassador Selene, in response to a remark made by King Wenyar of Phesius, would like to offer... advice... on how we could increase the number of our ranks."

King Tarison placed his elbow on the throne's armrest and raised his hand to his face, stroking his thin beard. "Lady-Governor, our ranks are sufficient for our purposes. We have the ease with which to supplement our forces with Seasoned citizens should we wish, which is *our* method of increasing our ranks... but pray tell us, what is the good ambassador's method that she so desperately wishes to share through her Creetian puppetry?"

There was hushed murmuring from the advisors as Loya made a face which clearly showed her distaste for the king's description of her part in these activities. King Tarison saw it before she could rein it into a more neutral expression.

"You disagree with my assessment of the circumstances?"

"Your Majesty," Loya said, bowing slightly to hide her face, the mutinous turncoat. "I would never presume to oppose your judgment; however, might it be put off until the full tale has been told?"

She looked up in time to see the king's gesture for her to continue.

"King Wenyar's remark, Your Majesty, referred to my position in Creetian politics. He confided in the ambassador that now, since political circles could tolerate a woman, the army might, as well."

Outraged murmurs began to spread through the assembled advisors. King Tarison did not move, but his eyes shifted towards the commotion. He allowed it to continue for a few moments before raising a hand for silence. He then nodded to Loya to continue.

"As I'm sure you are aware, my liege, Phesius has, for nearly eight years, allowed women to be trained for combat. Their fighting force has nearly doubled, and their army is stronger than it has ever been."

"In peacetime!" yelled a heckling advisor from his seat in the back. A chorus of approvals followed before once again being silenced.

"Indeed, my lords, in peacetime. Phesius has prospered from their various treaties, but they are always ready for confrontation—or that of their allies."

Loya almost smiled when the king's expression and posture stiffened at her words.

"I was asked by the ambassador to bring these words to you, and I graciously accepted to be a puppet should my lips soften the delicate words required to bring forth such a proposal. But I have gone beyond that duty to assuage the doubt I'm sure still lingers.

"My study of this matter has reasoned that our Seasoned forces could be substantially increased by the inclusion of women. At first, it may be only as volunteers to assess the reasonableness of this undertaking, but in time, we could have full regiments of women, which would only necessitate a few accommodations. With the increase in our numbers, we could implement them with ease.

"I have had everything drawn up for Your Majesty's perusal. I think you will find the accommodations and increased expenses satisfactorily determined, based on the last ten years of the realm's military intervention, and, as was mentioned by my puppeteer, King Wenyar, the need for increased numbers may be to your mutual advantage."

King Tarison grinned at her. *Grinned*. She didn't like the bastard. He may have been brilliantly conniving in his politicking, but he was vile in his character—she knew this based on the numerous wayward advances she had spurned over the years—especially those directed to her while his wife lay on her deathbed. But she had only a small amount of power, and her ambitions were large. The king had the power to grant her first real political desire, something that could change the very fabric of the realm. She almost wished she had simply given in to his advances to secure his favor.

"King Wenyar's proposition has us intrigued," said the king. *The thought of invading another realm is not just stiffening his posture*, Loya thought mildly. "However, I cannot possibly risk the lives of so many citizens on assumptions alone. I will not consider this proposal until I have seen for myself that a woman is capable of surviving combat with the training we would typically provide.

"Unfortunately, this *intriguing* venture will have to wait. As you know, Lady-Governor, we are in the midst of preparations for a war. Leave your documents with our aid. We will peruse them at our leisure."

Dismissed. Loya ground her teeth as she curtsied to the king and turned to leave.

"Oh, and Loya," he said, making her turn again to make a full circle, her skirts swishing the marble floor with increasing idiocy—a twirling marionette in the hands of her puppeteers. She curtsied again, and when she rose, King Tarison's eyes were raking her body with a lewdness that made her teeth ache. "Your hopes for this endeavor may require additional incentives. You may need to see to those prior to any… remuneration."

Loya smiled demurely while her insides burst into flame.

"My king, I have faith that the contents of these documents will speak for their own merit, but should additional incentives be required, I'm certain enough funds can be raised."

King Tarison's leer transformed into a hard frown that reached his eyes. *You are not the only one, my king, who can turn a phrase.*

"Good day, Lady-Governor."

"Your Majesty."

Chapter Eight

Morvian

Morvian opened his eyes to little effect, as his surroundings were just as dark as the back of his eyelids. It had been this way for days, perhaps even weeks.

His lodging with the Fayn was a hole carved out of the side of a rocky hill, the width and breadth of which was just large enough to accommodate a moss-covered cot, a crude latrine, and himself. The heavy stone placed in front of the opening sealed out all the light, and he was lucky to see it more than twice a day.

He had tried to move the stone, but even when he hadn't been half-starved by his meager rations, he had been no match for its weight. How the Fayn were able to move it with such ease told him just how strong they were. He had not attempted to escape if he was brought out of his cell for any reason. It would not have been worth the possibility of reprisal.

The Fayn had brought him before a priest of some kind upon his capture. The priest wore pure white robes which flowed to the forest floor, only revealing his feet when he walked. His skin was pale and drawn, but he held himself as one of nobility. The other Fayn seemed to revere him, parting and bowing as he passed. They had not told Morvian that he was a priest, but it was not difficult to assess.

They seemed to be a warrior race, and he had seen very few of them, even the females, in garments other than brushed metal armour of the most intricate designs, ranging from copper to steel, and even some of the darkest ebony, the metal of which he was unable to identify. Their class structure seemed to be acknowledged by the type of metal of their armour, with the darker metals being the highest class, which was why Morvian was so confused by the priest in his bright white raiment, adorned with no metals to determine his class. Perhaps he was 'beyond' such earthly stigmas—he'd heard the priests in Hyglen's capital proclaim as much, even as they grappled for their parishioners' coin.

Still, a warrior race revering a priest seemed incongruous, he had believed... until he had seen a ceremony that the priest officiated on one of his excursions from his cell. The screams of the sacrifice, a young Hyglenian girl, continued to haunt his dreams.

Images of Oren's family in the small river town north of the forest crept into his mind, and he wondered if she had been a sister or a daughter. It made him ill more than once, disposing of the contents of his revulsion into his latrine. Having witnessed the violence and skill of the priest, he now understood why the warrior Fayn backed away from him in respect and fear. If Oren had been right in his fairy tales, the white-armored demon who had tamed the vicious wolves of the forest was most certainly this priest, or another like him.

A pang of fear passed through Morvian, causing him to clutch his chest. He prayed there were not more like him.

Turning his thoughts away from the priest, he continued to worry about why he had not been granted an audience with the king—even though Morvian was, strictly speaking, an emissary to their 'realm.' His accommodations made it clear that he was a far step down from emissary in this land. The king's name had been mentioned several times in the last few days in his presence, as if they were taunting him. They could starve him, harm him, use spellcraft to make him comply, but they would never take his dignity. He refused to beg.

The stone slab was pulled aside, and light flooded the hole, blinding him. Hastily, he threw up a hand in front of his eyes, shielding them from the light he craved with his entire being. The irony was not lost on him.

A fluid stream of the Old Tongue came from the opening, followed by a curt, "Up, Human."

Morvian made to stand, but the guards were too impatient. They hauled him to his feet and swiftly tied his hands behind his back. Everything he did seemed to fill them with irritation, which made him begin to believe that nothing he could say to these people would sway them from their own purposes. It was as if they were tolerating his presence just long enough to shatter his confidence in his own influence. It appeared they knew when that final thread had snapped before even he had, for his guards were moving in the direction of the citadel at the center of the city, towards the living quarters of the king.

Morvian's heart began to pound in his chest, but he stiffened his resolve. This is what he had wanted, was it not? A chance to speak to the King of the Fayn and convince him to fight with Hyglen. Now that he had been amongst them and had seen what they were capable of, he knew that the only way to win a war that involved the Fayn was for them to be on your side. But the trust he had in his own voice had faltered, and the doubt that his words would sway them prevailed even before he had begun the attempt. After weeks of being treated like vermin, the ability to stand up straight was greatly diminished, let alone any faith that his squeaking would be heard.

The guards brought him through the citadel, a beautifully decorated garden sweeping the outside circle with all manner of alien foliage—flowers of unnatural colors whose vibrancy made him stare, transfixed, and bright green plant life that seemed to glow in the shadowed square.

At the center of the stone ring lay a knoll covered in dark mosses which spread out into the cracks of the surrounding bricks. An intricate basin on a silver stand spread out at the edge of the bricks filled with a liquid which seemed to illuminate against the bowl's edges like the shining light of a full moon. When he saw it, he felt a desperate need to move towards it, to look into the basin, but in his weakened state, he was no match for the guards' strength.

Glancing up, he followed the height of two enormous trees as they wound up high into the forest canopy. One was of the deepest black, but it was not dead. It was alive with leaves of shimmering gray splayed out in five-pointed stars, and as they rustled in the slight breeze, Morvian heard a discordant song, like a chorus of unlearned pupils singing off-key to a beautiful melody.

The other tree was of the purest white from roots to branches, and its leaves were of a dark gray, three-points with bright veins of glowing light. As the guards moved Morvian past, the song he heard in the whispering leaves of the white tree was the melody the black tree had failed to attain—a harmony so beautiful and soothing that it caused Morvian to drift into sleep on his waking feet. He stumbled and his guards dragged him up, lifting him as though he were as light as a feather.

He felt like a feather as he gazed up at the white tree, but then he noticed that the two trees were linked, their branches knotted and tangled in a way that supposed a deep connection. Morvian looked down at the roots splayed out in the knoll and realized they too were entwined. Unlike the trees in the rest of the forest, which seemed to be choking each other with relentless violence, these two trees seemed to be coexisting in a magnificent dance. It seemed that one could not survive without the other. *Lovers*, he had thought at first, but then the word came to him, and he could not imagine it was anything else: *Twins*.

The guards led him through a dark metal archway, which opened out into a dim, circular chamber lit only by a few torches at the entrance and the back. On each side of the room, a lower dais jutted out in ragged metal points. The torchlight lit the faces of many Fayn, all in dark armour and standing stiffly in rows. At the back of the room, there was a high dais, the spikes from its edges looking big enough to impale a man. Upon the dais were two thrones, ornate in their fashion, with imposing spikes protruding from the sides with two spear points at the back on each end.

In the center throne sat King Auphier. All the faces of the Fayn were unnaturally smooth and unmarked by age or illness, but the king's face was almost glowing, a paleness in the dark which shone with deadly severity. His long, dark gray hair was streaked with white strands, but his face was a hard mask of cruel, calculated indifference. Morvian could only glance at his eyes for a moment, for they were deeply unnerving—a light gray which glowed in the darkness, which flashed and flared with a malevolence reminiscent of lightning against a night sky. Morvian had seen that eerie look in the eyes of those who used magick, but this was somehow deeper, more frightening. He noticed that the customary shade of purple, showing the magick inhabiting the user, was not present in the king's eyes. Somehow, this unnerved him still more.

When Morvian glanced to the right throne, he almost did a double take. It was Auphier—only not quite so. The facial features were only slightly different, the face still severe and pale, but the lips and eyebrows more delicate, like a female's. The eyes, though, were the same as the king's. Identical. Morvian didn't know what position this female Fayn held in the king's court, but her throne suggested one of great import—even that of a queen. *But surely*, Morvian thought, his eyes dancing between the two of them in confusion and growing disgust, *they are twins*.

The thought regarding the trees outside began to make sense. Lovers *and* twins. A reflection of their makers. He wondered, his teeth clenched with the effort to remain stoic, which of the two would reflect the discordant song. That was who he would need to be wary of.

A voice lanced through the dark stillness. "Kneel before the Great Auphier, King of the Fayn and the Forest, the Ruler of Order and Protector of the Old Faith."

Morvian hesitated, as his wits had been scrambled by his realizations in this room. The guard dug the back end of his spear behind Morvian's knee, and he collapsed face-first onto the stone floor. A chorus of harsh laughter echoed inside the chamber. He tried to maneuver himself to get up with his hands tied behind his back, but the butt of his guard's spear had dug into his back and remained there.

"Kneel before the Noble Omaiya, Queen of the Fayn and the Forest, the Ruler of Chaos and the Protectress of the Old Faith."

Morvian did not move, thinking it best to remain prostrate regardless of the spear butt in his back.

"Rise."

He could not even if he wanted to. The spear was removed, but he still had no use of his hands. The guards did not help him up. He grit his teeth, aware that all his efforts would be watched, writhing so that he could move his chest and finally get onto his knees. Panting as their mocking laughter moved about him, he maneuvered his feet so that he could stand, one by one. He was shaking by the time he was standing, but even he wasn't sure whether it was from exhaustion or rage.

"You are Morvian," Auphier said in a thick accent, looking down at him with little interest. "Commander of Hyglen's armies." It wasn't a question, so Morvian simply nodded. "We sent a message to your king that we desired to meet you. I take it from your… entrance… into our forest that you did not come willingly, and your king did not abide by our message's… request."

Morvian's head spun. Eusol had never mentioned a word of this, the bastard.

"My king, Your Majesty," Morvian said, attempting to keep his tone even, "did not make me aware of your requests."

It would be best to keep it vague and hope that they could supply more information.

"Obviously," the king replied drolly. A light laughter filled the room. "Our instructions were implicit. You were to come alone, unarmed, and we would treat you well, returning you on the next full moon." After waiting for a response from Morvian and not receiving one, he continued. "My queen is a Seer, Commander. She has seen you intend to fight a great war over an Agent of Change. Is that not so?"

Morvian was still, contemplating the riddle.

Auphier looked over at Omaiya expectantly.

The queen tipped her head to one side. "'Change does not mind the seeker's path,'" she said in a sinister voice, full of midnight and shadows, making Morvian's skin crawl. "'The depth of its desire finds purchase in the legend's mirror. Three lures there are to quell the tyrant, just enough for blood to sing.' Three lures, Commander."

An even stranger riddle, and much more complex. Morvian stared at the queen, his eyes never leaving hers. She sat back, her armour clanking against the metal of the throne, her eyes boring into Morvian's soul.

"Well?" Auphier said, his voice sounding like a cool flowing spring against the harshness of the queen's. "We have allowed you to glimpse into the Secrets of the Wood. You are bound to reply in kind."

Morvian broke his gaze from Omaiya's with effort, and looked back at the king. "Your Majesty, I will need time to ponder these… secrets before I can provide a response."

Auphier glared at him, considering. "Perhaps the Human mind is too… frail to receive what is offered?"

"No, Your Majesty," he said quickly, taking a step forward before he realized his mistake. His guards grabbed his elbows, drawing him backwards and onto his knees again. He grunted as one of them jabbed the butt of their spear into his back. "I apologize, Your Majesty. Our minds are perhaps slower than the Fayns'. We need time to understand the riddle you offer."

"Riddle." Auphier said the word, but it sounded like a curse. "I do not punish you for such insolence only because you are ignorant of our ways. The Secrets of the Wood are sacred. We share them with you, Commander, because you are the only one who can draw them out, making them *vywn*... true.

"But from your ignorance, we see the last part of the Secret must be realized as well."

Auphier lifted his hand, and from the shadows walked the priest, in white armour, his face cold and hard.

Morvian's mouth went dry, his stomach dropped, and his face and chest were suddenly slick with sweat.

Omaiya's face contorted into a hideous smile. "'Only silence will keep the seeker on his path.'"

Morvian barely heard her words as the priest approached him, his eyes dark skies full of lightning. He grabbed Morvian by the neck and squeezed, and a burning fire coursed relentlessly through his throat.

He wanted to scream. He wanted to die.

His vision swerved, catching the blurred but indifferent faces of the king and queen before he succumbed to the pain, and darkness took him.

Chapter Nine

Dania

Legs to her chest, Dania sat against the alley wall with her pack nudged against her lower back—the best way to prevent thievery while she slept. It was as good a place as any to sleep while waiting for the next ship to Kevilly—that is, if you have no more coin to spare for more appropriate accommodations. She'd spent the last few nights in *The Moon & Myth*, a sizable inn a few blocks from the Okriad Villa, but if she were to buy passage to her home village, she realized her last night in Turivaun must be spent in an alley along the ship lanes.

Her time at the inn hadn't been entirely wasted on a few comforts. The patrons were positively buzzing with the cryptic hints they'd received from one of the commanders that war was brewing—and quickly. Dania hadn't been certain what her plans were after her dismissal from the Okriads' service, but now she knew exactly what she needed to do. Despite the ache in her heart from leaving the city with Addie still within it—and her desire to see him one last time serving as little more than hopeless longing—her path now took her south. If a war was starting, and a recall of the Seasoned would be deployed, her brother was in the greatest peril.

Browyn's infection with Gray Throat had begun only a few months before he turned sixteen, and through the good graces of well-placed bribes, Dania had managed to have his name overlooked on the rosters when the officers came to collect the boys. Her brother had never been Seasoned, but when they drafted the men of Kevilly for war, Browyn would be expected to be trained well enough to fight. If he could not convince them, he could be executed for absconding on the Seasoning. Even if he were lucky enough to pass by and complete the retraining, his illness wouldn't allow him to fight. He would never survive an actual battle.

Dania's duty was simple, regardless of her desires. She needed passage on the fastest ship to Kevilly and would steal away with her ailing brother. Perhaps she could find a carriage to the midlands where they could find shelter for work. If they were careful and clever, they might even make their way north to the Ohnville Mountains and across the borders into Geldivin. There were many variables to consider in her venture, but one thing was quite clear: she would not abandon her brother to death.

The first obstacle had become apparent almost immediately. She had missed the last ship to Kevilly by several days before she had ever known she'd need to take it. The next ship was scheduled today, and with news of war in the east, the cost of the fare would be difficult to attain. What she could not afford in coin she hoped she could make up for in labour. Most ships' captains didn't shy away from an extra hand even if it lost them a bit of profit. Dania had changed plenty of slop buckets on board a ship to get from one place to another. No matter what she had to do to get to Kevilly, it would be worth it to see her brother safe.

A horn blew in the distance, sounding the warning for the early morning departures. Dania rose to her feet, grabbing the pack from behind her and tossing it over one shoulder. Walking down the alley, she tried not to focus her eyes on any one of the grungy, suspicious-looking men she had just spent the night with. Had she not had her knife—and had displayed it openly—she could easily have been robbed, if not much worse. One of the men, covered in filth and missing an eye, leered at her as she passed by. Her best efforts to ignore him fell short when he reached out to touch the folds of her dress.

"Don't touch me," she hissed, pivoting backwards and out of his reach. In doing so, she ran into a young man who'd been leaning against the alleyway wall and who caught her shoulders from behind. She shivered violently at his touch and tried to shift out of his grip by twisting her shoulders, but his hold was too tight.

"She says, 'Don't touch me,' and then falls into the arms of another man." The man's voice was mocking, but in a most sinister way. She knew that *this* man would be far more dangerous than the old man pawing at her skirts. He leaned in, his lips touching the shell of her ear, causing her to squirm in his grasp. "You wanna tussle, maid? I've got enough coin to make a good girl like you beg to be bad."

The way his voice scratched at her, scraping her nerves and her fears, she knew that no matter how she responded, she'd end up against the wall, wishing at the very least that she'd taken his coin. Her teeth grit at the prospect.

She moved quickly, ducking down and twisting to escape his grip, sliding her knife from its hiding place in the folds of her skirts. It was in her hand and pointed at the man's chest in an instant.

Her arms were outstretched and her feet in a fighting stance, eyes assessing.

"I may not be as good a girl as you think," she said, her eyes narrowed. The young man slowly raised his arms in a placating gesture, watching the edge of the knife carefully. "But I'd sooner die than beg."

"That can be arranged," he said harshly, his mouth twisting in a nasty grin. "After."

He didn't believe she would kill a man. He may have recognized her knife was a danger, but he still didn't take her seriously as a threat. That rankled, not only because it mattered greatly in her current predicament, but also because she wasn't sure herself if she could kill a man. Perhaps today was the day she'd finally find out.

A smile formed on her face as she shifted, moving the knife under his jaw, the blade sliding across his neck and drawing blood. The young man snarled viciously, but she was no longer afraid. If he'd had a knife, he'd have drawn it by now.

"Why don't you be a *good boy* and sit down."

He growled a little at her jest, but it was the growl of a dog who knows they've been beaten. Slowly he sat down, her knife following his movements, drawing a little more blood as it slightly changed position.

Dania stepped back a few paces, holding the knife outstretched tight in her grip. As she stood, she kept her eyes fixed on the young man, whose face was nearly feral with rage.

"Now you can stay there and sulk that things didn't go your way, or you can get up—and my knifepoint can finish what the edge started. Your neck, your choice."

As she gazed down at him, measuring the probability of whether he would do anything further, the young man muttered a sulky, "Bitch."

That, more than anything else, decided her. Perhaps if he'd had a weapon, he could have presented a real threat to her, but right now, he was all talk. She turned around and quickly walked out of the alley, keeping her knife visible. The rest of the alley's occupants seemed to press themselves against the walls as she passed, seeing the weapon at her side smeared with blood.

When she reached the upper docks, she quickly wiped the blood off her knife in a fold of her skirts and placed it safely back into its hiding place. The bright sun shone down on her, and she let her neck relax so that her face could feel the full force of the sunbeams. Her hands had been steady while she'd needed them to be, but they suddenly began to shake. She closed them into fists, but the shaking would not stop. Heaving a heavy, ragged sigh, she grabbed the railing that would take her down to the lower docks. At least her grip on the rail aided the trembling in her hands.

The city of Turivaun rested on the back of a great hill, a jutting rock which sprung out high beside the great Recluos River. Due to this, the docks were a strategic marvel which most cities could not contrive. There were upper docks to house the cargo, which would be shipped elsewhere, both within the kingdom and without, but they were situated well above the river. A series of staircases and pully systems allowed the crew, passengers, and cargo to find their way from the city streets to the lower docks, where the ships were anchored. It was an arduous journey, but it was a defensive design which allowed Turivaun to be easily secured by barring a few gates and hoisting the ladders at the docks.

"Dania!"

She had made her way down three flights of stairs before she heard the voice and wasn't quite sure it was meant for her.

The horn blew again. The second warning. She had better step up her pace if she was going to make it to the ship. She couldn't afford to wait until the next one came. Browyn needed her.

"Mistress Dania!"

She lifted her head to see a small boy leaning over the rails of the first staircase.

"Catch me up, lad!" she said, not bothering to lessen her pace. He was young. Surely he could reach her before she boarded the ship. Dania couldn't keep looking above her to see if the boy was making headway, so she continued to bound down the steps in haste.

"Mistress Dania!"

His voice was pleading, and she could hear the strain in it. She grit her teeth and turned around. He was two staircases above her.

"You haven't made much progress," she yelled, the wind whipping her hair to and fro.

"Could you find it in your heart to stop?"

She paused, her need of haste pulling at her to move forward. She didn't know what the boy wanted, but it couldn't be more urgent than her brother's life. Still, her curiosity was piqued.

"Get down here! Quick!"

He ran down the wooden stairs as quickly as he could manage. Dania's trembling fingers tapped the railing impatiently as she watched him. When he finally made it to her, he bent over, panting in exhaustion, holding out a letter to her. Grasping it and quickly breaking the seal, she read over the contents. Then she read them again.

Mistress Dania,

I have recently been made aware of your unfortunate predicament in relation to your service at the Okriad Villa. I will be praying to Masiya daily for the boy's health.

I know that your plans must be to return to your family in Kevilly, but I hope you will do me the honor of visiting me at my villa in Drens. I have a few personal matters that must be discussed with you, your brother's position among them.

I believe I can help.

My page will bring you to my villa, should you like to hear my offer.

Sincerely and respectfully yours,

Governor Loya of Drens

Dania's plan to 'rescue' her brother was minimal at best. There were a great many flaws, and at any point, it could easily go wrong. She was aware of that—especially with the lack of funding. But to have the help of a governor of Turivaun… She would need to hear the governor's proposal before she could be sure that it was feasible, but it seemed like a better plan than the run-and-hide designs she had in mind.

The boy looked up at her with expectant eyes.

How did the governor know about Browyn situation? Did she know he had absconded the Seasoning? If so, she could easily have turned him in or had him executed. Was she planning to blackmail them? What would she want in return when her family had nothing?

Regardless of the answers to any of those questions, Dania felt that she must see what the governor desired of her. She was a politician; secrets were never safe when a politician took an interest in you. But maybe her secrets were the reason why Loya was interested in her in the first place.

Her hands were no longer shaking as they rested on the railing.

The horn blew for the last time, the signal of departure. She watched as her ship weighed anchor and glided away from the docks.

Dania sighed, turning and holding the letter out towards the upper docks.

"I guess we're going to see the governor," she said, looking down at the page, who gave her a pleased look until he started up the stairs again.

It was nearly an hour to the governor's villa by foot, but it was an easy journey going almost entirely downhill. Dania watched the sun as it rose in the sky, the feelings of regret washing over her for missing the ship and slowly overshadowing the hope that the governor might have a better plan.

The page, whose name was Arrik, seemed more used to delivering messages on horseback; the distance from Drens to Kelvs and back seemed to be weighing heavily on him. When she had asked if the governor had horses that could be lent to page service, meaning to find out a little more about Loya's character in the process, Arrik had replied that there was always a horse ready for him for the delivering of messages. Then he had halted suddenly in mid-speech, turned to her sheepishly and said, "But the, uh, horses have been lent to another task today."

Dania hid a smirk. He was naught but a lad, so she could forgive the none-too-subtle subterfuge, but she knew the real reason the governor did not want to lend a horse to Dania: it would be easy for her to steal away on it. Arrik may have been a sharp lad and good with horses, but it wasn't easy to control two horses at once—especially with another rider atop one. Loya was taking the measure of her, trying to discover whether she could follow orders, and put trust in another person she didn't know… to learn how curious—and perhaps how desperate—she truly was.

She could have stolen a horse easily. It wouldn't have gotten her to Kevilly as fast as a ship, but maybe with enough time to get Browyn on a carriage to the midlands. It was not honorable, and it would have driven her to great grief to have robbed someone's goodwill and hospitality so, but her brother's life was worth the guilt. She had made a promise to her father, and she would not break it even if ill came of it—even if Dania herself were considered criminal because of it.

Loya didn't know Dania, but it seemed that she needed her for some of her purposes. What could she possibly want with a dismissed governess?

"Mistress Dania," Arrik said, his hand brushing against her arm to draw her attention to where he looked. She turned, giving him a quick glance before gazing up. "This is Governor Loya's villa. She's expecting you for breakfast."

The villa was a lavish retreat from the cottages and houses that lined the streets of Drens District. She supposed all the governors must have similar accommodations, though she'd never cared to take notice of them before, if she ever saw them. Loya's villa was tucked into a blind alley, hidden away from the rest of the populace and surrounded by thick foliage so as to keep others away and the building beyond notice. The exterior gave the impression of well-kept secrets. She was curious what else was hidden in the extravagant villa.

When they had stepped over the threshold, no servants greeted them. Odd. Usually, a villa such as this would have servants at every corner. The Okriad villa certainly had. Arrik took off his coat and offered his hand to take her own. Reluctantly, she relinquished her woolen coat to the lad. After arranging the coats on a contraption by the door, he held out his hand again, looking down at her bag. She stiffened, straightening her stance and gripping the bag tightly.

"I'm sorry, mistress," Arrik said, watching the pained look on her face. "I must take your bag, lest you have any… weapons. It's my job to protect her."

Dania assessed him, then surrendered her bag to him. Before he could turn to set it aside, she pulled out the knife from the hidden pocket of her skirts and handed it to him, hilt first. His eyes widened, and he took it, giving her a look that was filled with gratitude.

"I have no wish to harm the governor," she said. "Do you believe me?"

Arrik didn't even turn his back to look at her while he set the blade carefully by her bag. "Aye, mistress. I'm not worried, but the governor is a careful lady. 'No use in being reckless when you can use your head,' she often tells me. Come along this way. I'll bring you to the dining room."

They walked along a wide hall, which branched out here and there. As she followed the page, she was lost in the first few minutes, but she noticed that there were so many grand windows lining the walls, looking onto a beautiful courtyard, or the foliage outside, or a glimpse of the city beyond. Windows that caught the light of the sun as it shone in, casting rainbows against the walls lined with pictures and portraits of landscapes and individuals—places and people she had never seen, had never hoped to see in her wildest imaginings.

She followed the light of the sun's rays to a portrait on the opposite wall, and she halted in front of it, gazing at the face before her. He looked… familiar… somehow. He was a dashing man in his prime, with sandy-blonde hair swept neatly back with a part to the side, above his left eyebrow. He wore a military uniform, adorned with a royal purple sash over his left breast. The sash held a great many emblems, but she didn't know what any of them meant—save one. There was an emblem of a crescent moon with a four-pointed star.

"Commander Leifius," said a soothing female voice behind her. "So many had thought that he would lead us into glory and hoped his influence would give us our freedom."

Dania turned her head to see the speaker. Her red hair was striking, almost as red as the color of blood as it's washed away by rain. Her tresses were full and sank nearly to her elbows. Her eyes were a vibrant green, piercing in their gaze, and her frame was slender in the way most men found pleasing. Her dress was a dark green which moved with her easily, silently.

"He gave us glory, most assuredly, but the freedom that his greatness promised could not be attained before his untimely end."

"Freedom, my lady?" Dania asked hesitantly. She knew the answer before she had asked the question, but she was curious to see how far Loya was willing to go to proclaim her beliefs.

Loya turned to her, her smile hiding the truth of her convictions. "Dania, I presume? It's a pleasure to welcome you to my home. Please follow me. Breakfast is prepared."

"My lady," she began to protest, but Loya turned back and gave her a look. Those piercing eyes held her for a moment until her feeble protest abated. "I would be honored."

"You don't like porridge?"

Dania looked up from the bowl that was placed in front of her. She wasn't sure what that bowl contained, but it wasn't porridge. She must have shown her confusion on her face, because Loya let an amused smile escape her otherwise stony control.

"Perhaps this is a more… select… way to prepare oats, but I assure you it's quite good."

Poking at her bowl's contents with her spoon, she moved around an assortment of berries—raspberry and boysenberry—and the dark brown swirls at the edges. There was a dollop of yellow cream in the middle which made the dish even more confusing—especially given the dark brown shavings sprinkled on top.

She didn't want to look up to see Loya's bemused expression, so she focused on the food before her and raised the spoon to her lips. Her eyes popped open, the single taste of the brown swirls causing her to slaver like a hound in heat. She brought her hand to her mouth, embarrassed.

Once she had control of her faculties, she put her spoon down and looked up at Loya, whose eyes were filled with mirth. Her expression, however, was carefully neutral.

"What is it?" Dania asked.

"They call it *gova*. It's a Firdeshian spice with a sweet, poignant taste. It pairs well in many dishes, but I've always found porridge to be a bit… bland. I think it enlivens it, gives it a new palette."

If you can afford such a luxury, Dania thought. Importing spices from Firdesh must have cost her a fortune, but with the look of the small palace she lived in, perhaps it was but a trifle expense.

"Fascinating," Dania said, giving her praise not only to the foreign spice but also to the way this wealthy woman lived.

Loya's face was stony once more, but Dania sensed that she took her full meaning well enough.

"Have you finished?"

Within Loya's eyes, she saw the divergence in the question. Was she finished with her dish, or was she finished taking Loya's measure?

"If you'll permit me, Governor, I'd like to take my time. A new spice may be jarring, but it can be equally enjoyable. After all, I am not accustomed to seasoned fare. It may take more time for my tastes to adjust."

Dania braced herself, grasping the arms of the dining room chair. Her boldness could have left her back scalped if she weren't more careful. She was a peasant chastising a politician for their abrupt behavior.

"You're clever," Loya said, smiling. Dania sighed softly, her tight grip relaxing on the armrest as Loya continued. "Cleverness can be quite useful to me in these circumstances."

"My lady?"

Loya put down her spoon and sat back against her chair. "You're afraid for your brother, one of the only men in Kevilly who escaped his Seasoning."

Heart racing, Dania stiffened in her seat, drawing forward. She knew this had been a possibility, but the letter had said Loya could help. She held onto that possibility with her last ounce of hope.

"It's not difficult for a woman like me to obtain this kind of information. I normally would have no use for it, but I have a proposition for those who might wish to evade the consequences of such action. Browyn is the only man in Kevilly who escaped his Seasoning and also has a sister."

Dania watched Loya, her attention so focused on her words that the surrounding room and everything in it became a dark blur. *She wants me?*

"I have a proposal set to the king to introduce women into our military. I have full confidence I can see it done—not to mention the resources to see it well-funded—but the king and his advisors require… evidence of its efficacy.

"I would like you to be my evidence, Dania. As recompense for joining the military, I will see that you take your brother's place in his assigned unit. He will remain in Kevilly under gubernatorial protection, should anyone try to collect him—not that anyone will, seeing as he will technically already be enlisted under your guise."

After a moment of staring into the bowl of porridge, Dania pushed back from the table, the scraping on the floorboards by the legs of her chair so loud it made her wince. Her gaze met the governor's, their eyes locking in contest—the last measurement each had to take of the other.

Their gazes were steady. Loya's eyes held a ravenous hunger and impatient expectation. Her desire for this scheme to be brought to fruition was clearly a passion none would willingly avert, but Dania's eyes did not reflect any unwillingness or fear. If any emotion could be seen in her eyes, it was undoubtedly relief.

The burden of protecting her brother with an inferior plan was lifted from her shoulders. Here was a strategy that addressed Browyn's protection, while also giving Dania a chance to prove her worth, to be released from the chains of duty and prosper in her own right. She was being given the chance to see what she was made of, and the limits of what she could endure, without worrying what would happen to those who relied on her should she fail.

Dania leaned back in her chair, her hands pressing against the armrests. "What if I die in battle and prove your cause false?"

Loya nodded. "I had considered that possibility. But having met you, it no longer worries me."

"Why is that?"

Grinning, Loya placed her elbows on the edges of the table, leaning in. She whispered, "Because you're made of sterner stuff than you imagine, and your willful wits are bound to lead you true."

Normally, Dania would have flushed at such a shrewd compliment, but something had changed, like a subtle shift in the wind.

"I accept your offer," Dania said, grinning back at the governor, "but I take no responsibility if my death and that of your schemes are connected."

Pushing her chair back delicately so that it barely made a sound, Loya stood and nodded. "We are agreed on that point—although, again, I do not think it will be a necessary amendment to our contract."

Dania stood quickly, the napkin she had placed on her skirts falling to the floor. "Contract? You said nothing of a contract."

"My dear girl," Loya said, a bit of laughter in her voice, "I am a politician. Everything must be in writing."

Dania's narrowed stare was meant to be intimidating, but it caused Loya to laugh outright, bringing a light flush to Dania's cheeks. Loya spun around to grab a piece of parchment from the desk in the corner of the room.

"You will thank me for this in the future, I promise you."

Chapter Ten

ELDEVA

Prince Ahnvil's pointed gaze was beginning to unnerve her. Eldeva sat in the very back of the proceedings where the other females gathered over matters of state, but she was the only one of those females who was listening to her father's counselors. The skirts around her were more focused on gossiping behind their hands and delicately waving their fans in the direction of whatever diplomat they thought to cuckold their husband with tonight. Eldeva's eyes had been following the direction of the conversation, trying to glean as much from the meeting as she could for her own purposes: blackmail, extortion, political advantage. It would have been a fruitful yield—if only the eyes of the Krashkin prince had not been boring into her all morning.

It had become a point of pride for her not to look in his direction, but after missing what she assumed was an important bit of information on the raiding parties near Hoefke, she shot her gaze towards him, her eyes glowing with a faint purple hue as she barely constrained her anger. He watched her like a hunter, and his gaze did not shy away when confronted. In fact, he *smirked*. Such a show of disrespect! Her nostrils flared in annoyance, and he smirked all the more. A more insufferable man she had never met—the taunting and teasing and jests since he first began his visit were enough to make her long to give him a hot, fiery touch down his neck. Alas, she was bound to diplomacy. He was the heir to the throne of Krashkin, and their relations with that realm had been strained enough as of late.

"...so that we can accomplish our holy mission of reclaiming the Jaguar Hills."

Eldeva tore her gaze away from Ahnvil to rest on Counselor Freq.

"It appears that Creet's prince has made a bargain with his brother to extend goodwill to their northern neighbors, and there has been an... exception to their magickal ruling. The Hillpeople have been allowed leniency and are now able to practice magick openly again."

"This is an outrage!"

"What will we do?"

Eldeva was not quick enough to conceal her triumphant smile. So Ithiador had taken her advice after all and stood up to his brother. She felt the delight wash through her, then flood her sex. Gods, how she missed him. Her flushed face turned to find Ahnvil staring at her again, this time with an expression of curiosity. She looked away quickly and held her hands firmly in her lap.

"There is not much that can be done, my lords," King Ulden said firmly. "Now that they are established and secure in Creet's arms, our hopes for a rebellion are thwarted. The only way we will win them back is through Creet's defeat in battle."

The room quieted considerably, the entire assembly seeming to wait with bated breath. Would there be war? Only the king could command it, and he had been known to make such proclamations in counsel.

"For now," he said, his tone more supple, "we shall continue to provide what aid we can commit to the Hyglenian advantage. We are allies, but we are a small country with insufficient troops. Our strength in this endeavor will be in our magicks. What preparations has the Old Order made for the requested succor?"

Eldeva's attention began to wander as they spoke of spells and hexes that could be used against Creet in their war with Hyglen. Such petty inclinations—things that could cripple an opponent when it would have been so much simpler to summon a firestorm or a few demon warriors to lay waste to their armies. It would have required sacrifices, certainly, but if the Hyglenians wanted it so badly, they could provide their own Human fodder. Not that she would ever suggest such a notion—not when Ithiador may be amongst the troops. So, she pondered again the prince's willingness to cede to her counsel, and the inherent trust that it implied.

"Princess," said a gravelly voice, old and wizened. "What are your thoughts on the matter?"

Looking up, her eyes found her mentor from the Old Order staring at her from across the room. The rest of the counselors had turned to face her, and the sycophantic lot around her quieted their gossips, the room going eerily still.

Without having the time to contemplate a more skillful approach to the subject, she used her discontent to her advantage.

"Ealdor Gunmai, I find that these tactics are rather... trifling... for the Order's extensive knowledge and skill. Must we debase ourselves to common tricksters?"

Muttering erupted throughout the hall, a stream of indignation running throughout the chairs of the representatives of the Old Order.

"Please, respected ealdormen, hear me: We will not hatch our designs from being cautious, but only by sleeping with dragons."

A foreboding silence filled the room, as if she had just spoken prophecy. Ealdor Gunmai looked at the king, who nodded his head once. Gunmai returned his gaze to Eldeva.

"You may be right to ward off caution, Princess, though our hearts do not burn as yours does. Your task as Priestess will be to show us that you can birth a dragon—but do not expect you will not get burned in the undertaking."

Eldeva offered a demure smile, a royal expression which showed neither contentment nor rage. "Fire and I are old friends, Ealdor. Give me a fortnight to make my preparations."

"You have it," he said.

Everyone returned their gazes back to the center of the room, a few of the counselors glancing back at her with fear in their eyes. She drew her own gaze away from the ealdorman and her father and back to Prince Ahnvil. His eyes had been those of a hunter before she spoke; now, the curiosity mixed with hunger in those eyes made *her* smirk. She sat back, crossing her legs so that her slip would fall apart, displaying the length of her leg. She watched him carefully as his gaze fell to her exposed, golden skin, his expression like a dog after a meaty bone. *Males,* she thought, looking away and purposefully ignoring the prince's stare. *No matter how clever they think they are, they are so very pliant.*

"A thrilling performance, Princess."

Eldeva halted outside the council chamber doors when she heard the prince's voice. She moved gracefully to the side as the counselors and ealdormen walked past, and rolled her eyes at Ahnvil as she spun to greet him, palms outstretched in formal greeting.

"I'm delighted you think so, Prince. The dreariness of my father's court required a delicate spark of interest to enliven it."

Ahnvil held his hands above her wrists to acknowledge the greeting, then let his left hand fall as the fingers on his right traced the full length of her arm, a sly smile openly displayed. "I'm certain a council chamber is not the only place you… enliven… with your presence, Princess."

Eldeva twisted out of his reach while nodding politely as two of her ealdors of the Order made their way past them. Her skin crawled with the effort to suppress her shudder.

"Prince Ahnvil," she said, her posture erect and deliberately formal, "you presume too much."

"I presume nothing, Your Highness."

He took a step forward, hooked the slip of her dress in his fingers, and gave it a gentle tug. Eldeva hissed, lifting her foot and landing her heel squarely on the toe of his boot. His grunt silenced the rest of the council members who were loitering by the chamber doors and caused them to glance in their direction. When they saw Eldeva's fiery gaze, they looked away again quickly, resuming their previous conversations.

When Ahnvil righted himself after the injury, he laughed. *Laughed*. The bastard.

"Feisty, aren't we?"

"Don't you have a serving girl to ravish against her will?" she spat.

"When I have the opportunity to taunt you?" Ahnvil threw his hand into the air as if to wave away the suggestion. "Besides, I hailed you because I'm fascinated to know about your Order's task. What devilry are you concocting inside that wicked mind of yours, Princess?"

Eldeva considered spitting a biting retort but stayed herself. There was no point in getting him even more riled—especially since he seemed to enjoy it so much. She had spoken up because she had wanted the assignment—only then could she control the outcome to better benefit her lover. She had taken immense pride in her contribution to how Creet fared with the Jaguar Hills—despite the blow it had been to her father's court.

In twisting the task this time, she would have to keep her father happy with the results, as well, since she had not played this out in secret. Ulden's rage was not something one wanted to witness firsthand. The gods knew she had been the victim of it enough times to merit her fear—especially since he had learned to silence her first so she could not use magick against his attacks. His fists on her were the reason she had become so proficient in healing craft, even though it had not been a requisite of her Old Order apprenticeship. After her first few instances of appearing at court with a black eye or a bruised lip and seeing the king's look of triumph, she was determined never to give him the satisfaction.

None of this could be voiced to the insufferable man standing before her. He was likely too dim-witted to comprehend or appreciate the entirety of her schemes, even if she were to trust him enough to reveal them. There was only one person she trusted with her plans. Not even her lover had gained such trust.

"Wicked though my mind may be, it is closed to you, as is any devilry I may be concocting."

Eldeva shifted her gaze beyond Ahnvil's intolerable smirk to her father, who was approaching them with Counselor Freq. She moved fluidly into a curtsey as Ahnvil turned and bowed low.

"Ah, my cunning Prince," Ulden said, his tone a colorful chastisement that held no real malice. Eldeva knew when his voice held malice—every time he spoke to her. "I take it that you could not wait until dinner to relay the happy news?"

Eldeva and Ahnvil rose from their formal positions, her eyes raised to her fathers' in silent question. Ahnvil smiled, a seemingly innocent gesture, but one that was returned by the king and could therefore only have meant something sinister.

"I had not had the pleasure yet, Your Majesty."

King Ulden grinned, looking at his daughter. "Well, it seems I'll have to commandeer that pleasure, Prince Ahnvil."

Eldeva grit her teeth. It was unbearable when her father toyed with her like this, like taunting a caged and starved tiger—a foolish and dangerous endeavor.

"My king," she said, her tone edging on meekness, "what news is there to relay?"

Ulden leaned toward his counselor, Freq whispering something in his ear. When Ulden whispered back, she swore she heard the word 'witnesses.'

"Daughter," said the king in a mirth-filled voice, "you will be wed to Prince Ahnvil to further our alliance with the realm of

Krashkin. It is a most advantageous match, for both our great nations."

He inclined his head toward Ahnvil, who spoke some platitudes which Eldeva did not hear, as her entire body felt as though it was burning under roaring flames. They licked up the sides of her dress, burning, burning away the fabric until she was naked under the gazes of these animals, these swine. The flames engulfed her hands, her face, the fire in her cheeks so hot it could be seen.

"Princess?"

Eldeva blinked. She had contained the rage, but just barely. An indifferent smile was plastered onto her lips.

"I am honored beyond words."

She heard the mumblings of approval at her response, then watched dumbly as the king moved off toward the throne room. She felt Ahnvil's presence on her right, then the nausea as he brushed his hand against her cheek, down her exposed neck. Her eyes followed him as his gaze dropped to her breasts, taking in the fullness of his prize. She had thought he was a hunter eyeing prey in the council chambers, but he was just a wealthy patron admiring a recent purchase.

"I cannot wait until you're mine," he said, his eyes locking onto hers. He didn't seem to see the lightning that was surely swirling in her pupils. The fool. "Princess."

Eldeva growled, "Prince."

Ahnvil smirked, moving backwards, and bowed.

The princess of Sycil stood in the same position for a long time, not daring to move. She had called the magick to her, but she hadn't given it an outlet or allowed herself to cast spellverse. She hadn't even known she had done it until she felt the flames, the burning heat, engulf her body. Trapped in her own skin, she had stood there, waiting for the anger to dissipate, the rage to cool, and the magick to leave her, but it didn't. Until it did, it was best for her to remain still and silent. Calling magick without a purpose was perilous, and the chaos could easily turn rogue. Eldeva slowed her breathing until it became calculated and intentional. One false move and the magick inside her might escape, razing this wing of the castle to smoldering ash in a matter of moments.

A servant stepped past her, moving toward the royal suites. Eldeva risked the movement of her hand enough to grasp the servant's arm.

"Bring me my sister. *Now.*"

Chapter Eleven

BRUDAIS

His mother's Shadow was sitting in the armchair of his study, its demeanor that of a graceful princess calmly studying a potential ally—only, the man she was studying was her son, and the information he had just received could have broken that alliance.

Brudais paced furiously from one end of his study to the other. His gaze did not leave Xenia as he paced. He took in her features as a way to distract himself from the news, but the Shadow presented itself just as Xenia would if she were sitting there before him. Her body had aged, withered in the years since Leifius' death. The part of her dress showed a long stretch of her leg, once smooth and delicate, now wrinkled and thin. There was a time when men would have fought each other to place themselves between those thighs.

She was too lax with her magick use; he had told her a million times to ease up on her practice, but she would not listen to him. He growled a little at her stubborn resistance. The magicks she called to her consumed her youth, and she was now sixty-two, in the prime of her life, and looked like an old crone. Her face was still beautiful in a matronly way, but those years she lost… years she could have found another husband, had another life. When he had berated her about it, her response was always the same: her husband, her son, this life was enough for her. He sometimes wondered if she used the magick deliberately.

"Tell me again." Brudais' voice was rough in his throat, as if he hadn't spoken in a while.

Xenia crossed her arms over her chest. "The eyes never lie."

"No," he said, frustration lacing his tone. "The battlefield."

Cringing, Xenia said, "You are kneeling on a battlefield, surrounded by dead soldiers. You hold your sword in one hand, your neck wound with the other. Tarison stands before you, grabs your hair—"

Brudais held up a hand, causing Xenia to stop. "Which sword?"

His mother blanched, as if struck. Brudais stopped pacing and went to kneel by the armchair. He reached out a hand to brush away the tear that rolled down Xenia's cheek, but it went through the Shadow. A quivering smile was her response to the gesture.

"Which sword was I holding, Mother?"

Her eyes had a far-off look, as if reaching into the memory to grasp the answer. When she locked eyes on her son again, she shivered. "Ire."

A triumphant smile formed on Brudais' lips. "All right."

"All right?!" Xenia howled so suddenly that Brudais leaned back on his heels, his eyes widening.

"Yes," he said, his smile wavering.

After a moment, Xenia said, "Do you care to explain your vanity? I have been carrying the burden of this prophecy since you were a boy, and you deign to dismiss it?"

"I don't dismiss it. I just won't let it affect my decision."

Xenia choked, a hand going to her throat. “You will *die* if you go to war.”

Brudais put a hand on the arm of the chair, a comforting gesture. He sighed, his head falling forward onto his chest, then rising to look at his mother in exasperation.

“Mothers have been telling their sons that since the dawn of time. They don’t need prophecy to See the inevitability of war.”

Xenia’s face set into a hard mask. “Don’t chide me, boy. I was Seeing before the thought of you existed.”

A smile tugged at Brudais’ lips again. “Forgive me, Mother, but I’ve been fighting since I was old enough to walk. I know how to take care of myself on a battlefield.”

“And if you’re wrong? If you’re fighting both sides?”

The possibility of being stabbed in the back in battle was a good one—especially since Tarison planned to accompany the army to Hyglen, but he had few qualms about enduring the fight, so long as he was surrounded by his Blood Guard. Those insolent bastards wouldn’t let anyone infiltrate their ranks—even the king’s own guard. If Tarison was considering Brudais’ assassination on a battlefield, it would take more than a turncoat and a quiet blade to get the job done.

“Do you trust me?”

His mother’s eyebrows rose in surprise. “The last time you asked me that, you stole your cousin’s horse and rode it to the edge of Leida Lake. It threw you from the saddle and you came home covered in mud and limping.”

“Exactly,” Brudais said, getting up off the floor and standing over her Shadow, smirking. “I came home, and in one piece.”

Xenia glanced up, a pleading look in her eyes. “Home?”

Brudais sighed heavily in response. "Zethland is *your* home, Mother."

"It could be yours, too. I spoke to the king, and he once again offered—"

The look Brudais gave her cut her off in the middle of her explanation. He knew what offer his uncle, King Heqvelt, hoped to entice his nephew with, and Brudais would not trade one military command for another. His duty was to Creet, to his father's people. Brudais may have been half Zethlandian, but his father's legacy meant too much to abandon. He was bound to it, bound to fight and die in the name of Leifius, connected to his father in an inseparable tie. Zethland was a place full of happy memories and doting relatives, but it could never be home.

"You may not realize," Xenia said, running her fingers along the knee of her gown, "how sought after you are for your military stratagem. A number of courts have expressed their wish for your aid and counsel among our allies. I doubt Tarison has brought this to your attention, but my brother wants you to be aware."

One of Brudais' eyebrows rose. "Why?"

His mother smiled. "Because he wants his nephew to know what a prize he is, given your… demotion. Will you not consider the offer?"

"*Mother*," Brudais said bitingly. "I am my father's son."

Instead of the cold indifference he expected from her, Xenia laughed, a velvety thing that played with the air. Her laugh lines were more pronounced than ever. "I'll tell you something about your father that you seem to have forgotten, boy. He never imagined you to follow in his footsteps so carefully. He wanted you to live your life by your own creed. You are your own person, not his legacy. You don't have to live in his shadow. Make your own. The world already knows your name. Now make certain they don't forget it."

Brudais' hand rubbed the back of his neck, considering her words.

"You will go to war."

It wasn't a question any longer. He looked down at her.

"You once told me that fate is a message sealed in wax, not welded in steel, and that any break in the wax can tear it asunder. If fate is as you said, Mother, there are a thousand paths I can choose to keep myself alive."

Xenia's Shadow stood up, her hand resting gently on Brudais' cheek. "You were a far better student than I gave you credit for." A small smile played on her lips and then quickly vanished. "You will need a great change to tear this wax seal, my son."

Brudais nodded. "So long as passion rules me and not fury."

It seemed that Ælon had given up on the dappled mare in the lower fields; he almost pointedly ignored her as they moved from the stables, even after she gave a little whinny of disapproval. *Bitch.* But Ælon held strong and moved on at a bit of a trot, though Brudais had not urged him faster than a walk.

He allowed the horse to have the reins while his mind wandered. The conversation with his mother brought memories flooding back to him of Zethland. He recalled the monstrous pine trees climbing snow-capped mountain sides, its beautiful icy lakes so clear that the fish could be seen from the bank. The blankets made of bear hides his older cousins had hunted for, and huddling in them at night to keep warm. The first hunt his cousin Berrik had taken him on, and the archery practice he had endured to ensure that he caught the elk in the eye. The feast in celebration of the young man's accomplishments. The pride in his father's eyes. It was a cold country, but his memories felt warm enough to thaw his frozen heart.

That had been the last visit to Zethland before his father's death, the sickness burning through Leifius like wildfire. Even his mother's spells could not stop the spread, though she tried with every drop of knowledge and power she could muster. The next time he had returned to his mother's homeland, he had been a ghost in silent mourning. Berrik, Verra and Herralt did their best to distract him from his cares, but the sound of his mother's keening as she held Leifius in her arms, his lifeless body slack against her, the wrinkles beginning to form on her face from the magickal strain… it would haunt him for the rest of his life.

That was the moment he realized how weak love could make you, how desperate. Watching Xenia's hollowed-out shell as she walked the castle grounds, his vibrant mother laid waste by the loss, made Brudais determined to stay strong when the death god came for those he loved. If Jandros were intent on their departure from this life, he would avenge it and move on. Grief was a weakness he could not afford.

His horse came to a sudden halt, jolting him in his saddle. Brudais looked up to see the lower castle gates towering above him. They were slightly ajar, the soldiers guarding them on the other side undoubtedly too involved in a game of dice to hear him approach.

Ælon saved him the trouble of shouting by whinnying loudly enough to produce a slight echo through the training grounds. Two soldiers rushed around the corner, spears in their hands but helmets askew atop their heads.

"Commander," one of them called, as if hailing him was apology enough for being caught off-guard.

"Who is in command here?" Brudais said, leaning over his horse's head to peer down at the soldier.

"I am, sir," he replied, straightening his helmet.

Brudais grunted. "Put away the dice," he said, giving the soldier's command straps a glance, "Lieutenant. Your job is to prevent infiltration of this camp by spies. How can you hope to prevent that eventuality if the gate is open, and you and your men are occupying your time with… children's games?"

It was meant to sound like the reprimand it was, and the lieutenant's cheeks flushed red. He gave a few orders to his men, who swiftly opened the gate fully for the commander and stepped aside.

"Lock the gate behind me, lads," he said, placing his hand on Ælon's rump to turn to face them. "A spy may trick you, but they can't trick a closed gate open."

One of the soldiers muttered, "Unless they use magick."

Brudais grabbed the reins and steered Ælon back around to face the soldier who spoke. "If you were expecting magick, Sergeant, why in the name of the gods were you playing dice with an open, unguarded gate? Did you expect that if magick were involved, you were powerless to stop it and might as well let it through? Is this how much your guard duty means to you?"

The soldier's eyes bulged, and he visibly gulped. The lieutenant moved over to his man, placing a hand on his chest and making him step back a pace, placing himself between Brudais and the soldier. That was a gesture Brudais could appreciate in a lieutenant.

"We apologize, Commander. It will not happen again."

Brudais nodded and moved the reins back around. "It had better not."

He wondered if these were some of the Seasoned who had just made it to the city. Undisciplined, untrained, frightened pups. It was a wonder they were allowing some of them to stay within the city. Even if they had an entire legion of Seasoned to defend Turivaun, it wouldn't do much good. He prayed it would not come to a siege, not with rascals like these guarding the gates.

Once they approached the stables, he dismounted and Ælon began walking off towards the entrance without a lead. Brudais laughed aloud at the thought of Nav's face when he found the commander's stallion poking his head into the royal stalls and stealing hay. It was enough to pull him out of his foul mood from the incident at the gate.

Walking off towards the barracks, Brudais spotted Aiylus leaning against the entrance, his stance stiff.

"Commander," Brudais said.

Aiylus's frown deepened. "Brudais, your troops are getting… restless."

"They always are."

"I wanted to warn you before you entered. Violence has been threatened."

Brudais smirked. "They're *veritas*. Violence is in their bones."

"Usually only towards their enemies."

Patting Aiylus on the shoulder, he said, "*Veritas* know their enemy by their leader's command. Don't fret, Aiylus. I won't point you out directly." Brudais winked at the grave look on the commander's face and moved into the barracks.

"*Brudais! Brudais! Brudais!*"

The roaring chant echoed off the walls, pounding in Brudais' ears until his own name seemed a curse. The crowd of soldiers parted for him as he walked through them, his stance erect, but a waning smirk could be seen on his face. When the noise subsided, he turned to his soldiers and called, "The honor of being your commander cannot compete with the deafness in my left ear." A chorus of laughter rumbled through the crowd. "Form up in ten minutes on the training grounds."

The clattering of armour and unsheathed swords were the only sounds that could be heard as the crowd dispersed at his command.

The men in his battalion were named *veritas*, a title they gave themselves after being proven worthy. Brudais had led them into battle at The Fennan, the bloodiest battlefield Kresha had known in centuries. All those who had survived crowned themselves as Brudais' warriors, as *veritas*, a fighting force so deadly that the name was feared by enemies and allies alike. When they reached the field at Altroch, they were outnumbered by Firdeshians two-to-one, but Brudais had used his *veritas* to greatest effect in one-on-one combat. He blocked the Firdeshian cavalry charge and forced them on foot, where his battalion wiped them off Creetian shores and had the survivors running for their ships.

His soldiers had proven their worth twice over, and yet they still continued to honor him as their leader. They would follow his command without hesitation, which was one of the reasons why Tarison could not afford to imprison or exile Brudais, or even to insult him too deeply. Brudais had unwittingly created his own army—and a bloodthirsty one at that—within the Creetian hosts. They were his friends, his troops, his collateral. They knew it as well as he did, but they never held it against him. They acted like a shield wall, protecting him with the threat of their existence. The king could batter against that wall with blunt weapons, but the moment he aimed to shed blood, *veritas* were there with a perilous promise.

Once Brudais entered his empty barracks chambers, he walked to the chest at the end of his rickety bed and dropped to his knees before it. He opened the chest, pulling out a little beauty from a Phesian trading vessel bound for Utica, a stunning steel dagger in an intricate sheath. He rummaged around in the chest a little farther for his hunting knife when his fingers brushed past the breastplate of his father's armour. They traced the stag and crescent moon crest at the center, the symbol of his household. Brudais eyed it for a moment, his hand placed gently on the crest as if he could glean a bit of the power that it had once held, the power his father had once known.

Mother thinks it will take a miracle for me to survive, he thought, sending up the prayer. *Do you doubt me, too, Father?*

He withdrew his hand from the breastplate, opening his eyes to stare at the symbol of the hero of the Crescent Moon War, the many-pointed antler rack crowning the stag's head like a bouquet of thorns.

You are your own person, not his legacy. His mother's words seeped into him, coating the doubts, easing the fears.

He shook his head, plunging his hand deep into the chest to retrieve his unadorned hunting knife, and then closed the chest. It was not time. Not yet. Perhaps not ever.

"I thought you'd given up praying to the gods. Are you so desperate for their appeal?"

A wry smile was on Brudais' face as he turned to greet Rydril.

"I look to you for that, brother. You have the better singing voice."

Rydril stood against the doorframe, leaning casually in his gray cloak, his military uniform looking pristine. Brudais got up off his knees and went to stand at Rydril's side.

"I have prayed to Esriella every day to wash away your terrible arrogance, but the gods must have a use for it."

"Perhaps you should try praying to Kronos instead."

"For balance? Measured against what, exactly?"

"Humility?" Brudais said, unsure.

Rydril guffawed. "Even if you had any, Kronos wouldn't be able to steady it against all that pride. Especially as he is dead."

"I never understood why the god of balance is the only dead god."

"Because," Rydril said, placing a hand on Brudais' shoulder, "life would be too dull if it were so predictable."

They walked into the hall where the troops were pouring out into the training grounds, leaving them a wide wake.

"Are you meeting my Seasoned today?" Rydril asked.

Brudais chuckled. "I think they'll have enough to piss themselves over when they meet your Blood Guard."

"Fine," Rydril said, "but remember that you promised to *help*."

"I have every intention of training your miserable draftees, brother. Despite the wound to my immense pride."

Rydril's boisterous laugh hit the stone ceiling and echoed along the damp corridors. "Your pride can survive it; I have no doubt."

CHAPTER TWELVE

DANIA

"Not over here," said a growling voice from behind her. "This is where they keep the Seasoned meat."

Two massive forms brushed past Dania, making for the outer corridors of the barracks. One of them shoved her as they passed.

"Watch it, boy," he said in a gravelly voice.

Dania rubbed her shoulder and muttered, her voice coming out in a lower mockery of her own, but enough to have fooled the guards and courtiers at the gate into believing it was male. "Yes, as you are the injured party."

The two soldiers turned around, their expressions reflecting the depth of the insult. Dania took in their bulk with increasing panic. The muscles on their arms and chests were solid and defined. She could trace slash marks in the dark leather jerkins of their uniforms to the skin on their arms, the scar tissue healed over from years ago. It gave her a small taste of their experience; these battle-hardened bodies were as dangerous as they came. The murderous look on their faces had Dania backing up, but she realized there was nowhere for her to go as bodies filled the corridor.

"You want to talk down to us again, you little shit?"

Dania pressed herself into the bodies behind her, wondering if she could wedge her thin frame between them and escape into the mass filling the corridor.

"Do we have a problem here?"

The voice came from one of the chambers on the right, a deep voice belonging to a man who had to duck underneath the door frame when he emerged. His uniform was tight-fitting, and the muscles beneath showed through, despite the layers. Dania glanced at the command straps on his bicep—four broad straps signified a commander.

One of the soldiers' nostrils flared, as if he were about to challenge the commander, but his fellow threw a hand up to block his advance.

"Aiylus, when will Commander Brudais be here? The *veritas* need to get the fuck out of these quarters. We're not used to shoveling through so much filth, and we might develop a *problem* if it's much longer."

Dania blanched at the informal way the soldier spoke to the commander. She wondered whether it was how all soldiers spoke, or if only the *veritas* were allowed such leniency. The stories she had heard of them made her certain of the latter.

Veritas were elite soldiers of Creet. Their unit had gained fame throughout the country after their victories over Firdesh in a failed invasion four years ago. When they returned to Turivaun, their renown spread throughout the realm. When Commander Brudais had been demoted, they had made certain threats to rebel against the crown. To appease them, Tarison had united the *veritas* and placed them under Brudais' sole command. Dania didn't want to consider the possibilities if they hadn't been satisfied with that arrangement.

"Soon," Commander Aiylus said, crossing his arms over his powerful chest, "but if Brudais' unit starts to make trouble for the rest of us, he'll be the one to end it. He'll also be the one to answer for it."

The two *veritas* warriors grunted, but they seemed to be cowed by the response enough to move along without further complaint. Brudais clearly commanded a great deal of loyalty from his battalion for that threat to be effective.

Commander Aiylus didn't even look in Dania's direction before he moved off to the barracks entrance.

Her heart slowed to its normal rhythm—something she hadn't even had a chance to notice was amiss once the soldiers had locked their gazes onto her. She had thought that the hardest part of this endeavor would be acting like a male, but she now realized it might be curbing her sharp tongue. There were things that a male would allow from a female because he enjoyed her quick wit or feisty remarks—no doubt bringing to mind what bedroom games he imagined playing with her. However, he would never take the same treatment from another male—especially one who was significantly smaller than himself.

Dania's body was now as close to Browyn's as she could remember, though older and less sickly. Loya had warned her that she'd need to pick a form that wouldn't bring her undue attention. The less attention she received, the less likely her ruse would be uncovered. Browyn had brown eyes and tousled, wavy hair. His frame was slight, but she had added a few muscles to the spell so as not to stand out as weak.

The spellcraft that she used was called a Glamour. It made something appear as whatever the Keeper wished. The spell Dania was using would last for one week before the effects began to fade, so she would need to carefully mind the days of the week to ensure that it wasn't fading prematurely. Loya had informed her that replenishing the spell would be necessary every seventh day.

"Magick is not how it was described in the stories you heard as a child. It is a real entity. When you call it, it will come, but it may not be pleased to do so. Your spellverse is the only thing keeping it from tearing your body apart, but it may do that anyway."

Dania's eyes widened as she surveyed the governor. "I could die?" A flicker of fear and doubt came over her as Loya's words sank in, but it was quickly washed away by her resolve, as Browyn's face flashed into her mind.

"Magick comes at a cost," said Loya. "With each spellverse you recite, the magick that you invoke will consume the energy of your body to bring about the spell. If you are young and the spell is simple, the magick will only take a few days or weeks of your lifecycle."

"And if I were old and the spell intricate?"

"Years, perhaps decades. If one were not careful… it would not be a quick death."

Dania kept these words close to heart as she used the spellverse. It was an odd sensation when the magick was called. Heat flooded her body, invading her as it consumed her, sometimes painful in its pursuit. Then, as if the fire were quelled by a mere command, it waited patiently to do her bidding. Once the magick was cast, it would slither out again and back into the darkness of the world. Dania did not trust it, so she would only use it when it was necessary, every seventh day. She did not want it inside her any longer than necessary.

It was going to take time for Dania to get used to her perceived male body—not to mention the use of magick. Loya had only taught her some basic spellcraft she would need to carry out her mission, including the Glamour, a sight shield for her intimate needs, and a memory modification—in case she mistakenly revealed something she shouldn't have. Spellverse was known only to a chosen few: scholars and Keepers. If spoken, the magick would be called to the speaker. There were some Keepers who were powerful enough to merely think the spellverse to bring it about, but it took years of study and practice. However, saying the spellverse was not enough. Calling magick was a matter of intention. It had taken Dania several attempts to cast her first spell before she felt the insufferable warmth filling her limbs. Loya had been absolutely thrilled with her progress—particularly because not everyone had the ability to be a Keeper. If Dania hadn't been capable, their little farce would have been doomed to fail.

She had remembered her father using spellcraft on his weapons long ago, years before the ban, and how easily the Old Tongue seemed to flow from his lips. Dania had marveled at him, as well as the pale glow that framed the edges of the blades, an eerie warning to those who thought to take up arms against him. She had never imagined that she would use magick herself—especially once the ban had been enacted. Never in her wildest imaginings…

"*Brudais! Brudais! Brudais!*"

The barracks were filled with the chant of the commander's name, the echo reaching all the way into the farthest corridors. Relief washed over Dania as she heard the name. Now that Commander Brudais had arrived, the vicious *veritas* would have no more cause to incite violence.

She had not had the chance to revel at the realization that she would be in close proximity to the legend. Brudais son of Leifius was in the barracks now, about to address his battalion. She had heard stories of him and his father since she was a small child. Dania recalled her father's recounting of the renowned duel between Leifius and Grandis the Great. The slashing of the swords, the clash of shields, and every last scratch the two legends had suffered... her father's words rang in her mind, coloring a picture that was bright enough to make her believe she had been there.

"Twenty minutes," came the sharp voice of a lieutenant just down the corridor. "Get your asses out on the training grounds. Form up into straight, even lines, twenty columns, fifty men to a column. Keep to the very back. The Blood Guard will form up in front. Oh, and the *veritas* will be leaving as you get out there. Don't give them a reason to pound you into the dirt."

Dania had a feeling from the nervous shifting around her that she wasn't the only one who thought being late to form up would be worth it if those bastards could be avoided.

Commander Rydril stood at the front of the battalion on a makeshift dais so that he could be seen and heard by all. It was a clever way to marshal the troops to a focal point, while also displaying who they would answer to.

Her commander was tall, muscled but not large in the imposing ways of Commander Aiylus. Rydril wore a tight-fitting military uniform, his greaves fastened around muscled calves. She could not see the insignia on his breast, but his gray cloak swayed behind him in the breeze, making him look almost regal.

"Welcome back, friends." His voice was deep, soothing, approachable. Dania liked him instantly. "The opportunity to defend your country has come. It seems Hyglen doesn't have the balls to come to us, so we are marching to them. We have drafted from the Seasoned, as many of you know, and we have two moons to retrain them.

"We will set up camp on the borders of the Fayn Forest and form a plan of attack soon after. Commanders Brudais, Nezaun, Aiylus, Gorgid, and I are marching, while Okriad and Sliven are staying behind to protect Turivaun and the cities surrounding the capital. Pray to the gods that no one attacks Creet while we are away."

A chorus of laughter came from the men up front, but no one in Dania's unit so much as cracked a grin.

"We will have an impressive force of eight thousand soldiers and two thousand Seasoned—"

"More impressive without the Seasoned!" yelled a soldier from the midsection of the formation. Chortling, many of the men looked behind them with disgust. Rydril raised a hand, causing the men to quiet.

"Those two thousand Seasoned could mean the difference between us losing a battle and winning it. You may dislike them because they didn't volunteer for the death they may receive, but just think of them as cleverer, untried versions of yourselves."

Dania blinked, supposing that his words would surely have his entire battalion ready to throw up their arms in protest, but to her surprise, many of them laughed. If they did not laugh, they at least grunted in agreement.

"We believe Hyglen's forces to be about seven thousand strong, giving us a distinct advantage. Now, I know that my men could conquer this force with their hands tied behind their backs." There were roars of approval from the battalion. "And I know that we can put aside our petty differences with Brudais' brutal *veritas*, Nezaun's aging warriors, Aiylus' querulous rout, and Gorgid's limp runts, and we will give Hyglen the timely demise it rightly deserves." Another deafening roar rang throughout the training grounds. "Report to the campground north of the city in four turns. Men, fall out. Blood Guard and Seasoned, stay where you are."

As the majority of the battalion moved towards the gate, Rydril motioned to a few of the lieutenants who immediately began shouting orders at the Seasoned to march forward, closing up the gap between them and the Blood Guard.

"Blood Guard, about face," Rydril said. His tone was clipped, having dropped the companionable manner he'd held with the rest of the battalion.

As one, two hundred men pivoted on their heels and turned to face the Seasoned. Dania breathed a silent sigh of relief that she was in the midsection of the unit and not in the front. From her place in the fourth row, she could see the Blood Guard as they lined up to face the front row of Seasoned. They reminded Dania of the *veritas*, but she saw more scars on their faces and shoulders, their expressions so fierce they looked like they were about to leap onto the battlefield. She heard a few whimpers from the Seasoned at the front and cringed at their cowardice. *They are on your side, you fools.*

"Seasoned," Rydril called. "There are a thousand of you in my battalion, which means I have more men than the other commanders. I have the task of retraining you—so your whimpering will do little to serve you in the coming weeks. I will turn you into men—whether you're ready for that challenge or not. You will have three mentors through these next two moons. My Blood Guard will be doing the brunt of this training, while Commander Brudais and I will instruct as needed. You will meet Commander Brudais in a few days in the encampment."

A hum of talk began among the Seasoned, but Dania stood still and silent, imitating the Blood Guard as they quietly surveyed the mass of uncooperative draftees before them.

"Silence!" Rydril barked, his first show of real anger. His expression was stern as his eyes swept over his Seasoned unit. The silence that followed was biting. "Excited about training with Commander Brudais, are you? Why don't you ask my Blood Guard how *exciting* that experience can be? How many of those scars are from drilling with him?"

Dania watched as the Blood Guard took in the looks of surprise from the Seasoned and grunted. The look on their faces read, *We can't wait for you to find out.*

"These men are my personal bodyguards during battle. They have been tested and proven again and again. Every one of them is a swordmaster and, if I'm not mistaken, would lay down their lives to defend my sorry hide."

A sudden chant was sent up, so loud that Dania was sure there were more than two hundred men participating in it. When it was over, Rydril wore a wide grin.

"Two hundred of Kresha's finest warriors, and you have the honor of being trained by them. Appreciate this gift. It may save your own hides."

Dania wasn't sure whether she should be grateful or startled out of her skin, but there was no turning back now. By signing the contract with Governor Loya, she had exposed her brother's abscondment. Browyn's life hung in the balance if she were to break it. They would both be implicated and executed if she were to run now.

Despite the consequences, she knew this was the only way she could save Browyn from this war and the illness that had consumed him for the last six years. She was his Blood Guard, and she would do anything—lie, conceal, cast dangerous magicks, even lay down her life—to protect him. Anything.

CHAPTER THIRTEEN

MORVIAN

Morvian moved quickly down the stairs of the library, his hand tracing the railing in the dim light so as not to trip over his feet on the way to the inner archives. The silence had, at first, unnerved him. The only sound in the library's stacks was the rustling of paper as scholars carefully examined old tomes.

The muscles in his left leg suddenly seized, and he was forced to stop, gripping the railing tight, until it passed. He ground his teeth together in frustration. Those bloody Fayn were the cause of this pain, having housed him in an earthen cell for nearly three weeks. His sore and weakened body, however, was the least of his problems.

When the Fayn had released him—voiceless and weakened, on the brink of starvation—he had found Oren and the other guard he'd left waiting with the horses. He hadn't expected to see them again, but it seemed that their proximity to the forest had kept away any thieves who might have thought to take advantage of their cache of weapons and steeds. After a humiliating display of miming his orders, the pitiful remainder of his unit rode for the capital with great speed. Eusol had been livid with the news that his commander was… 'crippled,' was the word he'd used. Better to be crippled in voice than in mind, he'd thought in response; if his king had been at all clever, none of this business with the Fayn would have occurred.

The cramp in his leg subsided and he moved on from his place on the stairs and from his thoughts.

The Library of Bentixt was a beautiful secret. Ornate tapestries adorned the walls while stained glass encircled the tower in a spiral of color and light. The walls of the tower were lined with bookshelves while turrets jutted out to reveal alcoves with wooden tables and cushioned chairs for pompous asses to sit and study. It was a house of worship to knowledge, and despite Morvian's disdain for the usual class of citizen who frequented its hallowed halls, he appreciated the necessity for such a secret wonder. He had often been known to peruse the shelves—particularly in the lower levels where tomes on military history were kept. Those in positions of power could be sustained by knowledge, and Morvian's ambition kept him coming back to the library whenever a question entered his mind that he did not have an answer for. It was an ever-flowing stream of response and authority, as long as one knew where to look.

Morvian's current dilemma was that he didn't have the familiarity required to read the books on spellcraft, which was the only way he was certain he could regain his voice. Since the Fayn had taken it away using spellcraft, he was sure there must be a method of reprisal, but his search for answers had been thwarted by a simple educational failing: he had never mastered the ancient runes of the Old Tongue, which the majority of the books on spellcraft were written in.

He despised relying on others for aid, but he had little choice in the matter. He had written a letter to the chief librarian explaining his quandary, who had since employed three of his most trusted scholars to piece together the puzzle. A brief note had informed him that they had discovered a way for him to write without ink or quill—simple spellcraft that he had since put to good use—but it had been three weeks, and there had been no word from the chief librarian of further progress. Tonight's visit to the library was to remind him and his scholars who had made the request and put the fear of the gods into them.

The inner archives loomed nearer as he trudged down the final few steps of the spiral staircase. There was a light in the chief librarian's chambers; the dim flickering of candlelight could be seen from under the door. Morvian walked across the tiled floor, his heavy footsteps echoing against the shelves. He knocked on the door three times, a clipped noise that echoed into the library's spiraling heights.

The door slid open quickly, the chief librarian's girth filling the door frame. He wore a simple linen nightshirt that reached his ankles where a pair of fur slippers poked out from the fabric. His expression was one of utter incredulity. *A rare occurrence for such a learned man*, Morvian mused.

"Commander," he said, flustered. "I did not expect you at such an hour."

Morvian stood silently, giving the man a withering stare.

"Won't you come in?"

The silent response weighed heavily in the air between them, the librarian's jowls quivering slightly.

"Commander, I know you were expecting regular reports, but my scholars are rather occupied by a few of the nobles' requests; I haven't had an opportunity to inquire further."

Morvian's stare bore into the man. Beads of sweat began to form on the librarian's forehead and temples.

"I apologize for my lack of expediency, Commander! I will call for the scholars at dawn and we will—"

Morvian's eyes widened slightly, then narrowed.

"Immediately! I will call for them at once."

It took an uncomfortable half hour for the scholars to be wrangled from their beds and gathered in the inner archives. The circular hall towered around them, making Morvian's presence that much more menacing.

"Present your findings to Commander Morvian on the quandary he presented us with. Have we uncovered any solutions to his... silence?"

Noting the use of the word, Morvian gazed at the three scholars, who stood barefoot in their nightclothes on the cold tile floor of the archives, shivering slightly at the cool drafts—and perhaps the look in the commander's eyes.

"We have not found any cure to the Fayn's spellwork, Commander. The spell tomes are often cryptic when it comes to voicelessness. There was one solution that may be of some use to you, but we were attempting to search for the actual cure, so we had temporarily dismissed it."

Morvian's eyes flared and he took a step forward. All three scholars stepped back, and even the chief librarian's hands went up to his chest as if to ward off a blow.

"Our sincerest apologies, Commander, for our singular focus. We can teach you the spellverse for this solution. It will allow you to speak through another, using a mind link. However, it should be used with someone who you trust, as the link does not only pick up on what you will want them to say aloud, but also your thoughts and emotions. You have to be explicit about what you want them to say and what thoughts you want kept to yourself."

Someone he trusted? Morvian scoffed. He trusted no one so much that he would allow them into his mind for any length of time—unless, of course, they were expendable. It would require more thought, but it wasn't the solution he was expecting.

He stepped up to the scholar who had spoken, ignoring how the rest of them skittered out of the way like beetles. Wearing his most menacing expression, Morvian stared at the man.

Quivering, he said, "We will continue our research and find a more permanent solution, Commander."

Walking up the stairs of the library a few moments later, leaving behind a terrified pack of pompous asses in his wake, he smirked. Whether the Fayn had made him mute for amusement or as a punishment, he still seemed capable of voicing his opinions loud enough to be heard.

Morvian gazed blankly down at the desk between him and his king. Eusol's berating had done very little to ease his dour mood, and this latest remark was more than he could stomach—that *Morvian* had not made the proper precautions before undertaking his mission.

He ground his teeth in annoyance, because even had he been able to yell, he wouldn't have. If his king had any notion of strategics, he would have informed his commander of the real reason the 'mission' had been staged, and Morvian might have been able to prevent the deaths of seven good soldiers and his own voice, but Eusol had been too afraid of the Fayn, concocting some bullshit about an alliance and leading his greatest asset into a realm of hostiles so that he could avoid an unpleasant response to his refusal.

Eusol cleared his throat, snapping Morvian out of his thoughts. He looked up to see the king leaning back in his seat, resting his elbows on the arms of the chair across from him.

"I hear you've coerced the scholars into a magickal remedy to this… affliction?"

The parchment placed before Eusol began filling once more with carefully inked words, although there were no quills in sight. The librarians had taught him this skill the moment he'd returned from the forest. Though he could convey many messages with his eyes and facial expressions, he'd realized it was far easier with this little magick trick. It was not a long-term solution—especially since more than half his soldiers couldn't read—but until he found an appropriate puppet, it was necessary.

Eusol looked up, his eyes speculative. "Another person? One whom you *trust*?"

Morvian shrugged, nodding his head toward the parchment as he wrote out, *Or someone of no consequence.*

The king read over the line and looked pointedly at the commander. "Do you have someone of no consequence in mind?"

Ink dribbled across the parchment. *One of the soldiers I took with me on your… mission.*

"No." The king's answer was so emphatic, it took Morvian aback. "I will not have you attempting to raise the dead again, Commander. I am aware of its uses, but it was far too dangerous the first time, and they cannot be controlled."

Morvian waved a hand, signaling a request for the king to look down. When Eusol raised his head from the parchment, he looked relieved.

"A far better solution, Commander, so long as you can trust his allegiance."

Morvian wrote nothing but nodded once. He could trust Oren's allegiance in opposition to the Fayn, that was certain… and what mattered.

"Can you have him collected and put to use quickly?"

Again, Morvian nodded.

"Excellent. Then we can dispose of this." The king waved a hand at the parchment in disdain. "And we can proceed to matters of urgency."

Yes, because his commander's ability to speak was a mere trifle. An inconvenience. Not that the fate of his entire army rested on this one man's ability to speak.

"Now, on to my nephew. How is he fairing amongst the Creetians? Has he made any reports in the last few moons?"

Nothing we didn't already know from speculation and rumor. The thoughts flowed from Morvian's mind onto the parchment in fluid strokes. *He has confirmed the size of the Creetian troops: eight thousand strong—although, strong may be a slight overstatement, as they have called in six battalions of their Seasoned fighters to supplement their numbers. Their real strength will undoubtedly be in Commander Brudais' battalions. His* veritas *are more riled than usual. Perhaps they suspect…*

"No, no. He would not be so foolish."

As you say. It would not be the first time his pride got the better of him.

"Are you referring to the Cup?" Eusol made a dismissive noise. "Still bitter about that, my dear commander?"

It was not a fair fight.

Eusol grinned when he read the last scribbled text. "For Brudais or you?"

Morvian's eyebrows drew together. *Both of us.*

Laughing, Eusol drummed the armrest of his chair. "Men of honor you believe yourselves to be, but you are both the most conniving snakes ever to walk the earth."

Grinning, the commander sent a thought to the parchment. *Why can't we be both?*

"As long as you are *my* conniving snake, Morvian, I don't care what you call yourself."

Morvian bowed his head, then gestured to the parchment. *This would be a perfect opportunity for your nephew to make himself useful. While they are retraining the Seasoned troops, he can gain a good deal of intelligence from the war councils. We'll be able to glean their exact position and get the most recent strategy—at least, so long as he is able to report in.*

"You know those reports are few, Commander. What if they change tactics after a report?"

I'll improvise. You know how good I am at pivoting, my king. Now the task I have in mind is in supply disruption on the march. It's easier to fight half-starved men. Additionally, if there are enough disruptions, they may begin to suspect an interloper.

"We don't want him found out."

And he won't be, but it will sew dissent amongst their ranks. If we can get Tarison to turn back and desert his troops, their morale would be so weak... imagine the rallying it would take to get them back in line.

"Brudais would set it right, would he not?"

He is no longer the sole commander in their army. He could be dismissed by a majority rule—and he will be if your nephew does his duty. Then our armies can sweep through the Creetians like the Reapers of Jandros.

Eusol lifted his fist to brush his jawline, scratching his beard contemplatively. "A well-reasoned plan, Commander. See that my nephew is assigned his new duties. Now, what of this alliance between Sycil and Krashkin? Have you heard of the marriage pact they've made?"

Morvian nodded, his lips pursed. *Ulden thinks he can buy Krashkin loyalty to bolster his army, which Sycil has little to speak of. Their magicks have protected them, but the Old Order is dwindling. It's not as strong as it once was. They need men, and they know that we cannot assist while we fight our own battles.*

"Pray tell, *why* do they need men? They are currently at peace."

From the rumors circulating the Sycillian court, they are looking to take back the Jaguar Hills from Creet. They aim to do it while the majority of their armies are in Hyglen.

"Sneaky bastards, aren't they? Though I suppose we're allies... but will we be for much longer once the sorceress marries the Krashkin prince?"

Morvian grunted. Sycil could have chosen a better ally than Krashkin if they wanted to retain their alliance with Hyglen. Since the end of the Crescent Moon Wars, Krashkin had detested Hyglen—with sound reasoning. When the war was over and the peace treaties were being drawn up, Eusol's father had demanded that Krashkin banish Grandis the Great from their realm. It was a petty move, and one that the previous king had made only to weaken the Krashkin resistance in case he made designs to invade their lands. Krashkin banished their hero—if only to keep the peace—but they broke their alliance with Hyglen in the process. It was a foolish move on both sides—particularly because Hyglen's king died soon after and left his kingdom to a skittish lout with no intentions of invasion. It seemed that the legend, Grandis, was lost to the winds after stepping off Krashkin soil, but the feud between the two nations had held strong since. Hyglen was not even allowed trading rights along the Krashkin coast as the other eastern realms had been.

Now that Sycil was advocating for an alliance with them, it meant a strained accord going forth.

They are still willing to aid us in the coming war... with their magicks. In fact, they have reported that Princess Eldeva has been brewing a few surprises for the battles to come.

Eusol's expression slid into a leer. "I'm sure she is, the little siren. If I could choose the princess over the whole of Sycil... for military support, I mean."

The girl was a mere sixteen, and yet every Hyglenian nobleman wanted to fuck her, even with her chaotic tendency to crisp any man who spoke an unseemly word to her. Without allowing his disgust to show on his face, he sent a thought to the parchment. *Of course, my king.*

"As long as we have your mind and the aid of the sorceress, we can expect a swift victory. Inform me of anything else pressing in the next fortnight. I expect you'll have your puppet speaking for you by then."

He'll do as he's told scratched across the parchment as Eusol rose to his feet. The king walked out of Morvian's office, the sound of his footsteps trailing behind him. *Or else.*

CHAPTER FOURTEEN

LOYA

Loya watched the end of the corridor carefully, pressed back into the furthest reaches where the shadows were darkest. No one frequented this part of the castle for anything other than transit to other areas. She had chosen it for that very purpose. The darkness was a calming pleasure to her; the mixture of silence and near-blindness gave her the feeling of desperation that was necessary for these types of meetings. Desperation, but not recklessness.

One could be desperate for information but not reckless with the ways in which it was used. Loya had made it her mission to handle the information she had with the utmost care, but she would never have sought the need to employ her spies if she hadn't felt that glorious desperation—something that was subtle enough to propel her aspirations without males caring to take notice.

If she weren't so careful with her success, people would begin to suspect her of having ambition, and a woman's only ambition should be to find a distinguished marriage. Loya had no plans to find a husband who would simply steal her accomplishments for himself the moment she made them. The only male she would consider an appropriate match would be someone as blind and mute as the shadows that now surrounded her. They would keep her nestled comfortably and keep him ignorant and mediocre enough to ensure that her triumphs would remain hers alone. Unluckily, her need for power had led her into politics, and these males were too scrupulous and conniving to be trusted with a blind imbecile tied to her. They would surely buy his loyalty and turn on her, like all the rest, which is why she had remained unmarried and nearly celibate for the last fifteen years.

It was not easy to abstain from the sex, a challenge which had almost cost her her good name when the king had made overtures. He was a very handsome man—despite his utter depravity—but she didn't think she'd ever lament the lonely life she had led. There was no need to attach herself to another. Loya was happy to exist in the silence, so long as she felt fulfilled. The only thing that had ever come close to giving her blessed release was the thought of rising to the top. If she had to refrain from a man's touch to ensure that feeling, she'd do it gladly.

Loya's eyes shot up to the opening of the passageway, where a dark silhouette had just stepped. It looked from left to right, then proceeded down the corridor to where Loya stood. When he got within ten steps, she smelled him. The reek of onions and garlic wafted from his uniform.

"Jamis," she said, crossing her arms across her chest in an expectant gesture. "So glad you could get away."

"Apologies, lady," he said in his thick western accent. "Cook wouldn't allow us a break 'til we—"

Loya waved her hand between them. "Report."

"The troops are going to be heading out in the next few days. The king's been restless and wants the Seasoned trained on the march. The Commanders don't seem too pleased w' that. It don't make no difference, though. What the king says goes, eh? They're starting to dismantle the camp and load supplies. A lot of supplies—mostly grain and rice, potatoes and ale. They'll be eating well w' the amount of bags we have stored."

"And what of the castle itself?"

"Provisions have been made for a siege, too. We've been getting wagons from the midlands for the last fortnight w' the surplus. They'll still be coming for another moon, supplying Kevilly and Sceryl, as well."

"Good. Any word on command of the city?"

Jamis scratched the back of his neck. "As the king plans to join the troops, and Prince Ithiador is doing his tour of the Hills, he's leaving Steward Venhil in charge. The Commanders Okriad and Sliven will be residing at the castle, too, while the war is on."

Steward Venhil was a lecherous middle-aged male with as little political savvy as a sea urchin in the desert. Loya tolerated being underneath Tarison (politically) because he was cunning and adept. She couldn't imagine being forced under Venhil. His most notorious talent was underpaying the fourteen-year-old whores because they didn't have a bosom worthy of more crowns, and then using it as an anecdote at state affairs. Tarison tolerated his unsuitable antics because he found him amusing, but the only value that Venhil had was as a figurehead. This move could prove to be more advantageous than vexing.

"Anything else of note?"

"There was one thing, m'lady. The Countess Staliva has returned."

Loya blinked a few times. "From Zethland?"

"Aye. She's been staying in the lower family wing and frequents the courtyard just a few passages down on the right here. She spends most of her time alone, but she eats with the king at dinner. There's been some talk about marriage, but nothing's settled. The king mostly gives her sultry looks, and she ignores them. It's been whispered about that she's been trying to snag a husband on the sly, like, before the king can bed her, which of course would never do. He'd likely have them killed before talk spread. But I did hear from a maid that she and Commander Brudais were in a tiff a few weeks ago. She said it looked like a lovers' quarrel."

"The Commander wouldn't be such a fool." She hoped. "But what is the king's interest in Staliva? She's disgraced—blood of a traitor and all that."

"Don't seem to care too much about that when the king saw how pretty she is now that she's grown."

"The political advantage, Jamis," Loya said in a monotone voice.

"Keepin' it in the family, I suppose. He doesn't seem to want to marry any of the matches that have come from Phesius or Geldivin. Since the queen died, Staliva's the first woman he made designs on, excusin' yourself. And he's not being too quiet w' them, neither. Not 'round the staff, anyway."

Staliva could be a powerful ally, and someone new to the game who she may be able to mold. It wasn't often someone like that came about.

"The courtyard down the hall on the right, you said?"

"Aye, lady. Likely there now. Want me to show you?"

"I'll manage. Thank you, Jamis."

Loya turned the corner a few moments after Jamis had made his quick exit. The governor had an abundance of reasons for being in this part of the castle—or at least, she could easily invent some. The cook's assistant didn't have the luxury of authority to pacify curious guardsmen, so his departure required more stealth.

She moved along the corridor briskly, lifting her skirts slightly to prevent a fall. She had become adept at walking swiftly in a dress since her realizations of politicking had solidified the need for expediency. There were only so many opportunities, and the ones that were placed in her hand needed to be snatched up before someone else could claim them.

Moving gracefully around the corner of the courtyard entrance, she slowed to a halt and took a few steps backward, moving into the shadow of the archway. Loya's eyes sparkled as she beheld the sight before her.

The woman sat on the edge of the fountain, donning a beautiful crimson dress. The bodice and skirts were adorned with small gems and a delicate lace that could only have been crafted by one of Kresha's more esteemed dressmakers. Tarison had spared no expense for his intended bride. The lace that trailed down her shoulders glittered in the sunshine. The beauty of the dress complemented its wearer well, but there was no brightness in the young woman's face. Her vacant stare was affixed to the western wall while the tips of her fingers just trailed the water's surface, causing a slow maelstrom in the fountain's basin.

Loya's observation of Countess Staliva was calculated; there was more than just the melancholy brooding of a female who had been roped into an unsuitable match. After Regent Cavison had been executed for treason, his children had been exiled. Princess Xenia had taken Staliva under her wing and nestled her in the Zethlandian capital of Lolaith, where she had been trained in genteel social circles, giving her the grace and political esteem that would be advantageous to her future. Her brothers, Ryvius and Kritun, had taken flight to Gwendalir and Nesliarc, where they had both secured high-ranking positions in the lower courts. In doing so, they failed to oversee their sister's education and ensure her welfare—something that Loya had every intention of exploiting. Zethland was a wonderful place for a young lady to flourish, but not a place where she *could* flourish without the use of magick. It was ingrained in Zethland society, and it was to be expected that such lessons had been favorites of the young girl who had lost everything in the span of one evening. The power she would have felt through the use of magick would have been insatiable.

Loya could see in Staliva's sullen manner that she either missed that power or that the use of it in Creet had elicited some unfortunate consequences. Normally, Tarison would have turned the other way if he saw a noble using magick for their own ends, but Jamis had told her that Staliva may have been attempting to entice a husband before the king officially asked for her hand. *That* he would not tolerate, whether magick was involved or not.

Her spy had also mentioned a 'tiff' between Staliva and Brudais. Had she weaved a spell around him, causing him to do something he regretted? Loya bit her lip hard enough to break skin. If Brudais had bedded Staliva before the king had his chance, there would be bloodshed. This told Loya that the young woman before her, idly trailing her fingers along the water's surface, was playing with fire—the question was whether it was deliberate.

"Countess," Loya said, stepping out of the archway and moving into a low curtsey. Rising, she found Staliva's gaze on her, and all the vacancy was now hidden behind a mask of pleasant indifference. "I am Governor Loya of Drens District. It's a pleasure to make your acquaintance."

"The pleasure is mine, I'm sure," she replied. Her voice was as soft and supple as warm butter, her accent a strange mixture of southern and northern. On any other tongue, it may have sounded coarse, but her tenor gave it a lilting quality that made her sound like the royalty she had once been. "What brings you to the castle today?"

"I had a meeting with an advisor." Not exactly a lie. "I thought to explore some of the courtyards during my stay. The castle has so many of them, I like to seek out a new one each time I visit."

"What a lovely idea," Staliva said, a small smile lighting her lips. "Perhaps I should explore them more myself."

It was idle talk. From the look of it, Staliva had no intention of leaving this courtyard for another. Perhaps it was because Tarison had never found her here. Perhaps he didn't even know it existed.

"Countess, are you well?"

Staliva stiffened, her eyes shifting from Loya to the wall. "Do I not look well?"

"You look as beautiful as the stars are bright," said the governor, stepping towards the countess with a look of deep concern on her face, "but I have learned that one's appearance rarely reflects the turmoil within."

Staliva's eyes turned back to meet Loya's gaze. There was panic in them. "I should not discuss such things."

Loya sat down on the fountain's edge next to Staliva, thinking that perhaps towering over her was causing the concern. She took one of Staliva's hands and gave her a friendly smile.

"There is no need to, if you feel uncomfortable," she said, "but I have found that taking on a confidant can ease the pain at times. Nothing is so heavy that the burden cannot be shared."

Lies, all. At least, that had never been Loya's experience. There was no one she trusted so much, but Loya read in the look on Staliva's face that she needed someone to talk to—someone female—and if that burden weren't shared soon, it would cause a great deal of pain for herself or others.

Staliva inhaled slowly and clasped Loya's hand. "The king wants to marry me, and I cannot abide it."

Loya schooled her face into a serious expression, but all she could think was, *The foolish girl took the bait.*

"What can be done, Countess? He is the king." *And better you than me.*

"He is not all-powerful. I will spurn his advances. I will find a husband of my own."

Loya frowned. "Any man you bed or marry would be executed immediately."

Eyes widening, Staliva said, "You're joking, surely."

"My dear, if the king has laid claim to you, he will not tolerate another male with you. It would cause humiliation to his royal person."

Staliva slid her hand out from under Loya's, placing both hands in her lap in a picturesque scene of innocence.

"Is that how you have evaded his advances? You refuse the company of other men."

Loya wanted badly to grin at the countess' astuteness, but she managed to look shocked, recovering quickly. "I refuse the company of men for different reasons, not because the king has laid claim to me. He has only made overtures in the past."

"The not-too-distant past, I've heard. As recently as a few weeks."

Moving her hands into her own lap, she shrugged. "The king does as he pleases."

"But I may not?"

"No, Countess. We are all bound to serve King Tarison."

Staliva's gaze fell from Loya to her lap. "Even if I am more powerful?"

Loya straightened her posture, trying not to look too interested. "And what do you mean by that?"

Staliva's head snapped up, and her eyes were a light purple, the depths of which were a storm of lightning. She blinked and it was gone. The pupils returned to their natural green. Loya's lips formed a gentle smile. Oh, the ways she could use this girl, this all-too-trusting girl. Her knowledge of magick was something that Loya could glean—especially now that Dania was secured in her mission. It would be good to check in on her once the troops moved out, and Ambassador Selene only knew a few choice spellverse for her to supply Dania with on her travels. If Zethland's Order had trained Staliva, her knowledge of spellverse had to be far more expansive.

But the countess would never help her simply because she was asked. She would need incentive, and her greatest cause of woe was that Tarison wanted to marry her. With what she had just learned from Jamis about Steward Venhil taking over command of the realm while the king marched with the troops to Hyglen, the time seemed ripe for a change in power. No coup, however, was complete without a replacement to sit the throne. She could think of two men she'd be willing to stay underneath, to serve loyally. One of them had no designs to rule and never would; the other was conveniently the heir to the throne. Both had great claims, and neither could currently object. Staliva would make a great match for either.

Loya could barely contain the excitement and pleasure she felt from the beginnings of her schemes as she said, "Countess, are you entirely opposed to marrying kin?"

BOOK II
THE BLOOD OF TWO HEARTS

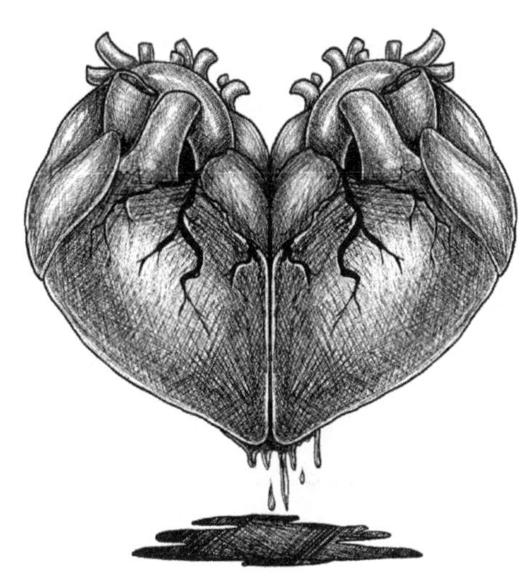

Chapter Fifteen

BRUDAIS

Ælon whinnied loudly enough to spook all the mares in the column. Tarison's cavalcade had just passed Brudais' position on the hill, overlooking the troops. The stallion had his eye on one of the royal steeds, a chestnut mare with a golden mane and tail, and he had been determined to get her attention the entire march.

"You set your sights too high again, my friend," Brudais said, leaning forward to pat Ælon's balmy neck. "Why don't you mount a nice country mare whose owners wouldn't give a damn?"

Ælon snorted and shook his head. It was likely to discourage the flies from landing on his ears, but Brudais imagined the more intelligent response.

"Do what you wish," he said, straightening his back as he watched a familiar horse and rider gallop up the hill to meet them, "but know that those mares are forbidden. You risk being gelded, and there won't be a thing I can do to stop it."

Stomping his foot on the ground, Ælon backed up a few paces as Rydril's horse drew near. Rydril spun the lively colt about and settled next to the stallion.

"And why is the Great Brudais on scout duty?" asked Rydril. He was wearing his weathered cloak that made him look older than he was. There was a gleam in his eye from the mild jest.

"Someone has to make sure the king gets through this pass unharmed. Why not he with the keenest sight?"

Rydril snorted. "How you manage to inflate your arrogance with a common foot soldier's duties is beyond me. And besides, if Tarison had chosen the scouting party for this pass, you would have been chosen last."

Brudais shifted in his saddle, holding the reins a little tighter than was necessary. "He can imagine all manner of hubris in me, but all I really want is to be left alone—chiefly, by him."

A rough laugh escaped Rydril. "I'm afraid you'll never get it, brother. If only our grumbling monarch would obtain a wife. Perhaps then he would divert his attentions to her."

"That is a crude jest. Why would you wish that on some unsuspecting female? Can you imagine the torment?"

Rydril frowned in a pronounced way as if he were considering. "I don't pretend to know His Majesty's bedroom habits. He could be a very tender lover."

"Queen Ceryl would have said aught else if asked, but her eyes read differently. *Much* differently. I don't doubt her untimely death was due to lack of affection and the stresses of attempting to please an unpleasant man."

"You knew her better than I," Rydril replied, moving his gaze away towards the column.

Tarison's lot was winding through the entrance of the pass. High hills surrounded the marching columns, making it the perfect place for an ambush. They couldn't manage the slopes with all the supply carts, so the pass was their only option. Brudais had stationed himself on one of the highest cliffs, while his scouts were positioned all along the foothills that formed the pass. Gorgid's battalion had gone through first without issue, after which Tarison's retinue meandered along. It was Brudais' battalion that followed and was expected to scout the pass as the entire army marched through. In a show of solidarity with his overworked scouts, Brudais had taken a post himself. It lifted his soldiers' spirits, which were in dire need of lifting.

After only a fortnight of training the Seasoned in the encampment on the outskirts of Turivaun, the king had gotten restless. He had overruled all seven commanders' unanimous advice to remain in the capital until the Seasoned were trained and ordered that they march for Hyglen at once. The commanders still grumbled about the use of their positions if they were to be overruled at every turn and began to feel as no more than military advisors to a very flighty monarch. At the last war council, after Tarison's unpopular decision to march, Brudais had simply smiled. When Rydril and Gorgid had turned to ask him why, he said simply, "I have known all along what the rest of you are only beginning to understand." Their grim expressions hardened further at this realization, but they didn't seem to begrudge him his joke. He had been the commander for five years before his demotion, and they for only two—without seeing combat. Now that all seven commanders were seeing Tarison on the eve of battle, the illusion of their power would soon be extinguished.

The problem with moving out early was, of course, that the Seasoned were barely trained. Rydril and his Blood Guard had done what they could with the rascals and Brudais had lent his hand to their training, but very little could be done in a fortnight. Tarison had been adamant that they could be trained on the march, but it was far more difficult to train if the pace the king required was to be maintained. Brudais hoped that once they were camped on the forest borders there wouldn't be an immediate attack, because they could use the time the rest of the army was setting up to train the Seasoned.

"I did have something to report," Rydril said hesitantly. Brudais raised his eyebrows, signaling for the commander to continue. "Okriad sent out a scouting party for the prince." Brudais' back stiffened, his entire focus on Rydril's words. "As I'm sure you know, Ithiador was sent to the Jaguar Hills to parlay. He sent back a proposal to the king, allowing for the Hillpeople to use magick—regardless of the ban. Wisely, the king accepted, thinking that this would provide us some magickal assistance in the war that would be... above board. Ithiador was meant to spend a moon in the Hills before sending word that he was returning with his guards. That word was never received."

Shaking his head slightly, Brudais said, "He would never miss a report. The dolt lives for his letters."

Rydril nodded grimly. "Aye. It didn't take long for them to send out a search. He was last seen by a few of the villagers on the northern Hills. He had been discussing agricultural techniques with the village elders when he stepped out for some fresh air. He and his guards seemingly vanished after that encounter."

The hairs on Brudais' arms rose in response to this information. The Hillpeople had nothing but respect for Prince Ithiador. In fact, he was the only dignitary in Creet who cared for them as a people and not as a political tool—although he had proven to his brother that he could shoulder the political minutiae well enough to be useful there. He did not suspect their hand in this—although those who were in charge in the capital might have. Steward Venhil and Commander Okriad were not known for their geographical knowledge or political scheming. It was likely that their first command would have been to harass the Hillpeople until they admitted wrongdoing. Brudais grimaced at the thought of their soldiers haranguing the primitive people, destroying dwellings and livestock pens, battering the elders until someone spoke the words they wanted to hear—the whereabouts of their prince. Brudais knew the Hillpeople would not have been involved, but there may have been a people on the northern borders of their land who could have been.

"They haven't heard word since," Rydril continued, "but they did espy a small hunting party to the east of the Hills a few days past. They couldn't make them out in their pursuit, but the banner they carried was strange. One of the scouts reported it as a blood-red banner with two trees intertwined."

"I've never heard of such a crest," Brudais said, his brows drawing together in thought. "Not even from the boroughs in the mountains."

Rydril nodded, clearly disappointed. "If any knew of the more minor and arcane crests, it would have been you. Your expertise of lineage is unprecedented amongst the troops. But I wonder if this crest is new…"

A moment of silence stretched between them before Brudais said, "Or very old," looking up at his friend with a pensive, bleak expression.

Rydril looked at Brudais intently and straightened in his saddle, clearly uncomfortable. “You think the Fayn might have taken him?”

“I think,” Brudais said, lowering his voice, “that if the Fayn have awoken and are meddling in Human affairs, Ithiador would have been an easy prize. But what they mean to do with him… we know how Morvian the Mute’s encounter with them ended. What might they do to a prince?”

“Do we tell the king?”

“And risk him sending the entire army into the forest? He has little love for his brother, granted, but his pride he adores above all else. He would not stand for the abduction of his brother by an enemy. He would invade without thought.”

“You’re right, of course, but what can we do?”

Brudais’ mind was racing with the possibilities. The thought that Ithiador was a prisoner of the Fayn was maddening. He was having a hard time not steering Ælon south and riding for the forest himself, but it would do little good and more harm to abandon his troops on the brink of war. His instincts had his heart racing; the drive to find and protect was a persistent need. But his duty kept him seated and still, kept him centered and mindful. Only in this state would he be able to form a plan.

“We can’t leave Ithiador to whatever devilry the Fayn have in mind, and we can’t tell the king. We send some of our troops into the forest disguised as scouting parties for Hyglenian forces. Tarison will believe this readily enough. It’s a smart strategy regardless of the reason. We tell the scouts that we believe there may be imprisoned Creetians within the forest and if they find any sign of this, they’re to report back to us immediately.”

"Are we keeping our suspicions to ourselves entirely?"

Brudais pursed his lips. "Do you need more of us clamoring their opinions on the matter, or do you want to find the prince in one piece without decimating the entire Creetian army?"

Rydril sat back, his spine straight as an arrow. "You know my answer."

"Good," said Brudais. "Talk to your scouts tonight and have them round the forest on the eastern edges so as not to arouse suspicion, but have them circle back to the south where the hunting party was last seen. The trail may be cold by the time they get there, but it's the only start we have. I'll send my scouts straight through."

"No." Rydril's voice was firm enough to cut Brudais' concentration, and he looked over at his friend. "You will not sacrifice your men so easily and leave mine a safer path. Ithiador may be your friend, but he's my prince, too. Give us equal footing."

Brudais ground his teeth. "Fine. I'll send them around to the west and get more information from the Hillpeople, if they can stomach it. Then I'll send them in north of where Ithiador was last seen."

Nodding, Rydril pulled on his reins. "The king's column is through." His colt began moving off toward the southwest. "I'll send you word once my scouts have departed."

Ælon stomped his hoof in a show of impatience, but Brudais did not move from his position. He could not stop thinking about that absurd Ambassador's Ball. The prince had thought it a splendid idea to invite all the Kreshan ambassadors to Creet for three days of discussion. This was followed by the most lavish ball thrown in Creetian history. It had been held three years ago, when Creet and Hyglen had been on far better terms, so every ambassador had attended. Much to Brudais' chagrin, he had been forced to attend as well—not by the king, but by the incessant pleadings of Ithiador. He was to be a sort of spectacle, as many of the ambassadors from the east had expressed great interest in meeting him—to take his measure, Brudais had thought. When he was introduced, however, he realized it was his reputation as a Kresha Cup champion that held their immediate interest. Still, festivities of any size and design held little appeal for the commander, and he had found himself hiding on the outskirts of the party with drink in hand, hoping to go unnoticed.

"You're supposed to be mingling," said Ithiador in a withering tone, as though he knew he'd have to have this conversation tonight.

"I am," Brudais said pleasantly, turning to face him. "I'm mingling with this cup of wine. And the one before it."

Ithiador's handsome face barely concealed his grin. His brown hair was short enough to sweep back into a slightly disheveled state, which both did and did not resemble his brother's style. His was a more natural flourish, whereas Tarison used a greasy mixture to keep it back. Ithiador's build was slighter than a common soldier's, but still enviable enough when paired with his impressive height. He had begun growing out a little stubble, which had an auburn tinge to it that the ladies of the court seemed to love. It was interesting that ever since Ithiador had begun his duties as an ambassador, he had shown very little interest in companionship. When Brudais had finally insisted on an answer to this riddle, he had admitted there was someone, but she was far away and none of his business. However, this didn't mean that the ladies of court did not fawn over him like lost lambs.

"You were invited here tonight—" Ithiador began.

"—forced to be here tonight—"

"—to impress upon our allies and enemies alike that we are both accommodating and foreboding."

"Ass-lickers and hardasses, you mean."

"Your delicate speech would make the ambassadors' wives cheeks more enflamed than the wine."

Brudais raised his cup in a salute, then took another gulp of wine. His glass was almost empty. Again. "I am on display, and this uniform is chafing."

"I'm sure some of the ambassadors' wives would be happy to help you out of it."

"And you yours."

"Nothing would bring me greater shame than to seduce a colleague's wife."

"And yet you suggest it of me."

Ithiador grinned openly now. "You have no shame, so I cannot advance it."

A sharp laugh escaped Brudais. Then he looked around warily, hoping no one noticed.

"I need you, brother." The look on Ithiador's face was serious now, pleading in a way that reminded Brudais of the times he had gotten into trouble with this rascal when they were boys. Ithiador always had a knack for imagining mischievous antics, and Brudais always had a way of getting them out of trouble.

Brudais sighed, chugging the last of his wine and moving into the party, grabbing another glass off the nearest table. "You owe me."

Ithiador hid a smile. "I always do." Then he moved over to one of the pillars where a severe-looking man stood, his eyes deep and watchful. "Brudais, may I have the pleasure of introducing Commander Morvian of Hyglen?"

"We've met," said Brudais, bowing low. "A pleasure to see you again, Commander."

"And you," Morvian replied, his voice gravelly, just as Brudais remembered. "I was wondering why I was invited, but now I see the reason."

Ithiador blanched, an act which was very convincing. "I'm sure I don't know what you mean, Commander."

"Indeed," he said, crossing his arms over his chest.

Looking over to Brudais, Ithiador's pleading eyes lit up. Brudais blinked slowly in the only show of annoyance he was allowed.

"Commander Morvian, I was invited for the sole purpose of being shown off to curious diplomats like an old trophy. I'm envious of the fact that you have been invited due to your veritable knowledge and legislative propensity."

Morvian looked from Brudais to Ithiador, grinned, and turned back to Brudais. "I see your tongue is as quick as your sword, Commander. I'm pleased to have found that neither has dulled with time. That business at the Cup should be forgotten."

"Agreed. There is nothing so abhorrent to champions such as us as foul play. If only we'd had a chance for a rematch."

Grunting, Morvian lowered his arms to his side, a more open gesture. "I was too old to be matched against you the first time; now it would just be an embarrassment."

"Surely not," Brudais said, grabbing Morvian's shoulder hard. "I would be honored."

As Ithiador and Brudais walked away towards a couple that Brudais knew as the ambassador of Zethland and his comely wife, Ithiador whispered, "I knew you could crack the old villain. He's been seething all night. Now I believe he'll have a drink and slip quietly into some courtyard, thinking the whole affair as dull as you do. But at least he won't continue scaring people away."

Brudais shook his head. "You are shameless, too, you know."

Ithiador's charming smile shone bright when he turned to Brudais. "That I am, and readily admit to."

The amusing memory washed over him like a gentle Summer rain. Growing up with Ithiador had been like having a little brother, someone he loved and mentored. The prince had grown into a fine man: intelligent, scrupulous, and just. Brudais was proud to have had a hand in his upbringing and in keeping him away from the influences of Tarison.

A horse hoof pounded into the ground, shaking Brudais in his seat and causing him to glance up. There was a small skirmish going on in one of Nezaun's columns. Likely nothing to worry about—just some disgruntled soldiers with high tempers—but someone needed to see to it. Nezaun was too far ahead to fall back and Aiylus was too far behind. Putting his fingers to his mouth, Brudais whistled loudly to the scouts on his left and right flank. When they looked his way, he signaled for them to stay put. When he saw their nods of consent, he spurred Ælon to an easy trot down the hillside.

It took the Creetian army twelve days more to reach the Hyglen border, and another three to find appropriate ground for the encampment. They had decided to settle between two thickets of blood-red hawthorns which jutted out from the forest borders like menacing horns. In this way, the camp was protected partially from the north- and southwest, but against Brudais' recommendation, as it enclosed the entire army, enveloping them in the eerie embrace of the Fayn Forest. A few of the other commanders had agreed with him at their last war council, but Tarison, Aiylus, and Nezaun had ganged together to overrule him—despite the good arguments made for camping in the hills west of Hyglen's capital.

Rain had begun pouring down the day they set up camp. A bad omen, many of the men said. Brudais tried to dispel this notion as often as he could, not wanting morale to plummet further. He urged the commanders and captains to say that the rain was a blessing from the goddess Esriella. "It's her way of showing she is with us!" Having a god's blessing amounted to good fortune and vitality, while a gift of water or air was life-affirming. Gifts of earth and fire, however…

"Those grain stores were kept quite secure, I can assure you, Your Majesty."

"It would seem they were not quite as secure as you assure us, Commander Gorgid."

Last night, one of the supply wagons unexpectedly caught fire and half the wagon load was burned to cinders. As the guard had fallen to Gorgid and the wagon was on his section of the camp, he had to answer for it.

"The campfires were nowhere near the wagons, so it could not have been by accident."

This caught Brudais' attention. He looked around the king's tent, moving his eyes from commander to commander to see their reaction to the words, but only Rydril looked back at him with a hard expression.

Brudais cleared his throat. Tarison and Gorgid turned to look at him. "Forgive the interruption, but did we not lose an entire wagon of rice on the road back in Phesius? And the four bags of grain by the Recluos? It seems there has been an epidemic of lost supplies since we began our march. Perhaps we ought to be looking inward for the cause."

Tarison rolled his shoulders back, giving Brudais a withering stare. "Do you mean to tell us that you suspect an insurgent?"

Brudais looked pointedly at Gorgid, who piped up, "Aye, my king. We might, at that."

Aiylus stirred. "It's too often to be called a coincidence."

That surprised Brudais. He didn't often get the support of Aiylus, which the king seemed to take note of, as well.

"We will consider this," he said, nodding slowly. "In the meantime, put a double guard on the supply wagons and post a few dogs by the main stores. We can't afford to lose more food if we're going to withstand Hyglen's forces."

Rydril put his hand on the table, drawing everyone's attention to the great map that was displayed there. The map was made of pressed leather, and the lines drawn divided the realms of Kresha in an approximate record of their borders. Small figurines were scattered strategically throughout the map, including the eight white pillars of the Creetian camp, two at Turivaun, and a few smaller ones along the river, coast, and mountains. Seven black pillars stood at the foot of Bentixt, Hyglen's capital. Sycil had a small host of brown figurines—mostly at their capital, Vorsai—and Zethland and Phesius had a smattering of blue and green figurines. In fact, the only realm which did not have any figurines placed on their portion of the map was Krashkin. Their isolation after the Crescent Moon Wars left a didactic gap for ambassadors; the information gleaned about their military numbers was minimal at best. No one seemed to know what the realm's military status was, which made their involvement in any war both a mystery and a gamble.

"We should spread the supplies throughout the encampment," Rydril said, pointing his finger to a few different places on the map. "That way, it will be more difficult for anyone—enemy or spy—to compromise our stores."

Tarison nodded. "Agreed."

"I would," Nezaun said, his thin voice quavering, "respectfully, request not to have any of the supplies stored in my division."

The king turned to the commander, eyeing him warily. "And why would we grant you this concession?"

Nezaun's hand trembled as he held it out to the southern edge of the camp on the map, more likely from his advancing age than from any real fear of the king. "My division lays on the southern border of the encampment. I fear a southern advance may be imminent. If we were attacked, I'd like to have the stores as far away as possible."

"Are we preparing for a southern attack? We are partially shielded from the thicket extending from the forest. Would it be wise for Hyglen to attack there knowing they are already crippled by the trees?"

Brudais tried to hide his smile by turning away from Tarison, but this only drew the king's attention.

"Commander Brudais. Have you something to say?"

After suppressing the urge to roll his eyes, Brudais turned toward Tarison, their eyes locking for a moment with a fiery intensity that seemed to cause the other commanders in the tent some discomfort, as they began to shift their stances and rub the backs of their necks. Brudais broke off eye contact first, looking toward the map.

"The thicket provides minimal cover for the southern divisions of the camp. It only extends about halfway through the borders of Aiylus' division, and none of Nezaun's. In another circumstance, I would say it's barely enough cover to deter Hyglen from attacking in full force. However, there are a few reasons why we need not worry about a southern advance."

Rydril caught his gaze with an intense look, as if warning him off his next words, but he couldn't help himself. Rydril would not ruin his merrymaking.

"There are three possible situations in which Hyglen would attack from the south. The first is if Hyglen were to divide their troops into two to three units, attacking from multiple angles. This might leave them with a good starting advantage, but Morvian knows that strategy will fall apart quickly enough, given our advantage over their numbers. If Hyglen attacks our camp, it'll be a straight eastern attack, with their full numbers behind it.

"Another possibility is that Sycil joins the war and comes straight from Vorsai to attack us. Unlikely, seeing as their military force is minuscule in comparison, and their strength lies in their magicks. If they do join Hyglen, it'll be with magick, which we can't hope to overcome, as we lack the Seers and Keepers to withstand them.

"And the last possible southern advance would be if Hyglen had enticed Krashkin to join the war in an attempt to rekindle their old alliance. Krashkin might overpower us, or they might not. As we have no intelligence on their military numbers, Krashkin is the biggest unknown, which would be very concerning—*if* we did not know our history, that is. And with their abhorrence of Hyglen since the exile of Grandis the Great, I can say with surety that Krashkin would not ally with Hyglen for any reason, for any coin. So despite the riddle they pose, they are of no consequence here."

Brudais stepped back from the table, straightening his uniform and placing his hands behind his back. He looked first at Rydril, whose expression was comically exasperated. Then he moved his gaze between each of the commanders in turn. Gorgid was nodding in acquiescence, and Aiylus and Nezaun's eyes were wide and unblinking. Then Brudais turned to Tarison, who was glowering. Brudais smiled pleasantly back at him.

"Why must you goad him?"

"I didn't goad him," said Brudais, clasping a hand on Rydril's shoulder as they walked out of the tent. "He asked me a question. I deliberately tried not to get involved."

Rydril snorted loudly in response, clearly unconvinced.

Before he could retaliate, he heard his name from behind. Brudais turned and saw the hulking form of Aiylus stepping out of the tent.

"Commander, can I have a word?" he asked.

"Is it private?" Brudais asked, starting to smile. "Because Commander Rydril can't be away from me for very long. He feels jilted."

Rydril shoved his shoulder, a reluctant smile forming on his face. "Bastard."

"It isn't private," Aiylus said with a half-smile, as though he wanted to be in on the joke but wasn't. "I just wanted to tell you that I was very impressed by your strategies today. I think we all were."

"Now, don't tell him that, Aiylus!" Rydril said. "He already has a big enough head as it is."

Brudais laughed, but Aiylus' face was serious.

"Maybe he needs a big head, to fill it with all this great knowledge and plotting."

When Aiylus walked away, Rydril turned to stare at Brudais incredulously.

"You are insufferable, you know that?"

"I don't know what you mean," said Brudais off-handedly. "You had the great idea of spreading out the supplies to all divisions. Fantastic work, Commander Rydril. Really, top-notch stuff."

Rydril kept walking down to his division, then grabbed Brudais by the arm and hauled him forward.

"Why don't you use that big head and big mouth to inspect my Seasoned?"

Brudais groaned. "Can you just keep berating me instead? I promise I'll lay down and take the beating quietly."

"No," Rydril said. "The last time you told me you'd inspect them, you were nowhere to be found. Vanished! Like a ghost. It's your turn to make sure my draftees are… how did you say it? 'Top-notch.'"

Brudais ran a hand through his hair and sighed. "All right, but only because you asked so nicely."

Chapter Sixteen

ELDEVA

Eldeva sat with her legs folded, her hands gently placed on her knees. She had sat in this position countless times before when she had used the Sight, but this was a different endeavor than simply peering into the future. She was attempting to see through the eyes of an enemy, without knowing who that enemy was. The princess could easily have fallen into a magickal trap, becoming ensnared in her enemy's mind if they were to realize her intrusion. It was a risk she was willing to take if she could reach out to Ithiador.

She had not heard from him in over two moons. Normally, this lack of communication would indicate a need for discretion, but she had heard word from the Sycil moots that the ambassador had gone missing. Eldeva had done her best to act nonchalant in the face of this news—especially when the next questions in council were directed at the spells she had promised—but her heart ached for her lover. Determined to discover his whereabouts, she had delved into deeper Sight magicks in the Old Order's library. No matter how she attempted to uncover Ithiador's movements, the magicks seemed to be blocked. She had been close when using the Sensate Touch spell. She remembered holding out her hand in a desperate reach, nearly touching the prince between the fabrics of time and space, but the only thing she could tell for certain before the link snapped was the smell of him wafting over her, like a teasing caress. Throwing her spellbook to the ground had not alleviated her frustration at having been thwarted yet again.

This time, she had found a possible solution to the blockages. Instead of attempting to see through the eyes of a Human, she had decided to expand the spell's depths to animal communication. She supposed the reason that her magick was being thwarted was due to an interloper whose magicks were more powerful than her own, so she would sink to the level of primal beings. At the thought of Ithiador's capture by powerful Keepers, her desperation was ripening, and she would use any means to unveil the truth.

To ensure that the spell was effective, she needed to pinpoint an animal mind that was adjacent to the enemy who had kidnapped her lover, and that was a dangerous pursuit. She had never entered an animal's mind before, but she assumed it would be easier than entering a Human's.

She was wrong.

Her body was thrown back and thrashed against the mattress beneath her as the magick swelled inside her, battling with the primal mind she was attempting to enter. The temperature of her body rose and sweat began to drip down her skin in rivulets. The barriers of the animal's mind were thick and inlaid with a magick of its own, woven in simple but effective stitches across the breadth of the surface. It was like trying to enter a steel chest by whacking it with an ax. Eldeva stretched to the limits of her power, fighting for a way in, before she realized her mistake. She would never find a foothold by fighting against the magick. She would need cunning to invade it.

Calming her body to still against the silk sheets on her bed, she stopped her onslaught and backed away from the animal's mind. It calmed in response, backing away with a quiet yelp. Then Eldeva caressed the outside of the barrier lightly with gentle touches, like petting a cat until it purred against her leg. The animal was stupid enough to mistake her gentleness for affection, and allowed her to tap the barrier until she found what she was looking for. Her fingers felt a crack in the barrier, like a bone that had not quite healed from a break, and she wedged her fingers into the crack mercilessly. The animal thrashed again, but it was too late. Eldeva was inside its mind, pawing through its simple brain and coiling around it, snake-like, squeezing its will until it submitted. It didn't take long. The animal was under her control now.

She sat up on the bed and breathed heavily for a few moments, hoping to regain some of the energy it took to breach the barriers before she began her task in earnest. But the animal's drive was relentless—even under her command—the need to hunt, the need to kill. She decided it was best not to fight that instinct and allowed the animal enough control so that she was guided towards its destination.

Seeing through its eyes, she watched the red leaves fall against the forest backdrop. The woods were dark and misty, and there was a heavy quality to the air. The animal's sight was keen, and she could see sunlight far ahead. It was daytime—although the forest canopy was so thick, it was impossible to be certain if not for the bright glow between the trees ahead. Suddenly, it stopped, lifted its head to the skies above, and howled, the sound reverberating against the trees but almost swallowed by the red leaves above. The wind shifted, and a chorus of other howls shook the forest to its roots. A hunt. They were about to attack. The animal bounded forward, its hulking form bursting through the trees and entering the sunlit grounds of the Creetian war camp. Horns began blowing throughout the encampment, but the animal stalked cautiously around a tent before it lunged at an unwary soldier, claws tearing against leather and ripping into flesh like knives. The animal's teeth were ripping at the neck of the soldier, tearing the skin open to reveal the wet, sticky blood beneath.

Eldeva's stomach roiled. She grasped her hands against the animal's mind and tore it away from the feast underneath. It struggled for a moment, then decided Eldeva's command wasn't worth fighting. *More meat further in*, it thought carelessly. Eldeva shuddered at the way it thought of Humans as 'meat.'

The animal went farther into the camp, snarling as it passed by fleeing soldiers, but Eldeva kept it from pouncing on any of them. She needed to know where Ithiador was, not lose her breakfast watching Creetian soldiers torn apart like empty sacks.

Was Ithiador here in the camp? she wondered. Why would the spell have brought her to this animal mind if he weren't nearby? She growled in frustration. She would never find Ithiador in a camp this large by inhabiting one animal mind. It would take days—perhaps weeks—to make a conclusive search.

Suddenly, she watched as a soldier turned to face her, holding up his sword and running straight at her. The animal didn't move—despite Eldeva urging it to do so. It stood there, rooted to the spot, watching the man run closer until their eyes met. He froze in mid-attack; his grasp on his sword loosened, and the blade fell from his hand and thudded to the ground. The animal snarled, moving forward lazily, watching the panic in the frozen man's eyes as teeth snapped around his neck.

Curious, Eldeva thought. She expected that the animal had some kind of magick, what with the difficulty of entering its mind and the magickal barriers protecting it, but she was fascinated to see the power behind it. Then she realized the danger if one of these animals were to come into contact with Ithiador.

With a powerful push, she surfaced from the animal's mind and rocketed towards her own, the impact like a collision between two boulders. She shook violently as her mind returned to its own body and time, but she forced herself up to grasp her spellbook. Her fingers trembled as she paged through the book, seeking out the spell she needed.

Reading the page carefully, she breathed deeply for several moments before whispering the words of the Old Tongue.

"*Greya voral phil kay*."

The heat flooded her lower back until it lifted her mind once again to the Creetian camp on the edges of the Fayn Forest. Her intention was to send a warning to Ithiador, but frustration and fear leaked through the link as she once again failed to find any sign of him. She urged the magick to search out his closest kin in the encampment, and it sped through the maze of tents, her mind burning with the effort to keep conscious long enough to deliver the message.

She entered a tent with a flurry of wind in her wake, stopping before a tall man with sand-colored hair and a defined jawline. He looked both like and unlike Ithiador, but his uniform showed that he was of high rank. If Ithiador could not receive her message, at least someone with authority would be able to spread the word to the rest of the troops. With any luck, it would reach Ithiador in time.

"Do not look them in the eyes. Their magick is strong. Tell Ithiador," she said, gasping his name with effort as she began losing consciousness. "Tell him—"

Her vision darkened and the last thing she saw were blue eyes staring at her in concern and alarm.

"Eldeva!"

A gentle nudge suddenly became much more forceful, and she startled awake. Her eyes opened to the bright sunshine streaming across her bedchamber and onto the bed where her prone body lay slack against silken sheets wet with her sweat.

"Eldeva, what happened?"

Her sister crouched over her, her hands against Eldeva's cheeks, and her brown eyes wide.

It took all her effort to sit up, moving to the edge of the bed and clasping her palms against her temples. When she looked up at Mayora, her sister gasped.

"Why are your eyes white?"

Eldeva's head shot up, and she glanced at the mirror on her armoire on the opposite side of the room. Her face was drawn in pain, sweat speckling her forehead, cheeks and neck, but her eyes were a brilliant white, glowing against her sun-kissed skin, with no pupils or irises. She shut her eyes tight, thinking herself dreaming, and when she opened them again, she watched the glow fade, and her brown eyes stared back at her from her reflection.

Mayora stood back, trembling slightly. "You go too far, sister."

Eldeva tore her eyes away from her reflection to look into her sister's. "I am fine, Mayora."

"One day," Mayora said gently, sinking onto the bed beside Eldeva and grabbing her hand, "you are not going to come out of one of your trances. You take too many risks."

Eldeva took in her sister's full frame, seeing herself at sixteen in her sister's features. She was so young, and yet they were the same age. It just showed how experience was the true test of life—not the number of years one spent living it.

"And what do you know of magick, little sister?" she asked sweetly, giving Mayora a pointed look. Mayora hated being called 'little' by her own twin.

"Only what the Solemn Priests tell me," she admitted. "Father Junil says that magick ensnares the unwary."

"Father Junil," Eldeva said, heaving a great sigh and willing her hands to stop shaking, "is a prick of the highest order." Mayora shot her a surprised look, then giggled. The sound washed over Eldeva like a balm. "This is the only power I am allowed over my life, sister. I am going to use it to my advantage, and as frequently as it pleases me."

Mayora frowned. "Can you promise me something?"

Eldeva retracted her hand from under Mayora's and sat upright. "And what would that be?"

Mayora's expression turned hard, and her frown deepened. "He's important to you, I know, but don't let him take everything from you."

Rolling her eyes, Eldeva said, "He isn't."

"Important? Or taking everything?"

Eldeva sighed dramatically. "Either. Both. Must you make such a spectacle about it?"

"If you truly love him," Mayora said slowly, as if weighing her words, "perhaps you should tell Father—"

A wail of laughter escaped Eldeva before she could contain it. She wiped her forehead with the sleeve of her dress, and it came away soaked in sweat. "You truly don't understand the place of a princess, my dear sister—even though you are one. We are not bred to love. We are bred to breed, making alliances with foreign powers. That is why I am engaged to a swine, who has condoned raiding our lands his entire life—and probably participated in many himself. Father does not care whether I love a Creetian prince. He will see I am married only to whomever suits him. And your fate will be no different.

"Besides, I cannot find my Creetian prince. I fear that perhaps..." Eldeva stopped suddenly, looking up at Mayora with a pleading gaze. Her sister's eyes softened at the vulnerable look. "Don't ask me to call off the search, sister. I couldn't bear it."

Eldeva's insides warmed at the look of pity on Mayora's face. She was so easy to deceive, it was almost embarrassing.

"Fine," she said, "but please... be careful. When I found you in the hall two moons ago and had to coax you back from the edge... I have been worried sick since."

Eldeva fell backwards onto the bed sheets, closing her eyes. Mayora was more a mother to her than their own had ever been. Desperate for this conversation to end, and her body enticing her to sleep for a week, she smiled up at her sister.

"I will be, beloved. I promise."

She felt Mayora stand and walk to the other end of the room. When she heard the door shut, Eldeva fell into a deep sleep, healing the parts of herself that she had damaged with her own foolishness.

Chapter Seventeen

BRUDAIS

Brudais stood at the head of the column, looking out at Rydril's Seasoned unit. Amongst the columns, there was an intense silence, but the noise of the remaining encampment as soldiers made their way between the tents to deliver messages, train, and move supplies filled his ears. The noise was muted as the commander peered out at the Seasoned he was to inspect. His gaze fell on one soldier who appeared to have an itch on his face and kept wrinkling his nose because he wasn't allowed to scratch it. Brudais groaned internally. Why had he agreed to this? Rydril and Pallina's expectant faces came to mind immediately. Oh yes. He had promised to be helpful. The only reason Rydril was in this predicament in the first place was because of Tarison's hatred of him. He lamented that this particular promise didn't merit an additional ballad from Dorian and Liska. He should have specified his terms.

He stood in the front-center of the column, drawing in a deep breath. He would need to shout for the full unit to hear him.

"Seasoned," he said, his voice carrying so that even the bustle in the immediate vicinity of the training grounds halted for an instant before they continued about their business. "I have been asked by Commander Rydril to inspect this unit for battle readiness—particularly, your weapons. As Seasoned, your weapons are inspected because they are your own property, and not the army's. If your weapon's edges aren't honed regularly, or your guard or hilt is in disrepair, your weapon might become unusable on the field of battle, thus rendering you a liability to your comrades. Soldiers who fail inspection are sent to the front to undergo punishment. I've decided that punishment will be addressed by Commander Rydril's Blood Guard. Sergeant Wren has volunteered to assist with this. If your weapon fails you when you are up against him, in addition to the cuts and bruises you can expect, you'll face an even greater disciplinary action—cleaning out the latrines.

"Hopefully, the thought of shoveling shit for four turns will teach you that weapon maintenance is of the utmost importance. Always take care that your weapon is in pristine condition. It is the only thing keeping you and your brothers from becoming mincemeat to your enemies. Remember that you are no longer only responsible for yourself. You are a part of this army. What you do—and fail to do—affects us all.

"You will comport yourselves at attention until I say otherwise."

Brudais looked over at the soldier whose nose was itching, who met his eye, blinked stupidly, and stopped wrinkling his nose. It took a great deal of effort not to roll his eyes.

Moving down the first four rows, he sent two soldiers to the front for dull blades and one for a compromised hilt. He also sent up the soldier who couldn't control his baser urges and had the audacity to actually try to scratch his nose without being noticed. On the fifth row, he was inspecting a fine piece of craftsmanship when he noticed Aurelius' mark on the pommel. He turned it over in his hands, feeling the perfect balance. How, by all the gods, had this little blond pipsqueak afforded such a fine blade? He looked closer at the soldier, who stared straight ahead with his hands clasped firmly behind his back. He was thin and gangly with a mop of blond hair and blue eyes that sparkled in the sunlight. Brudais blanched suddenly, drawing back as he looked closer into the boy's eyes. There was a hint of silver lightning in their depths.

Brudais was no Seer, but he could recognize magick when he saw it, just as he had with Staliva. His mind raced with all the reasons why a common foot soldier would have to use magick amongst Creetian troops. His first thought was of subterfuge—perhaps the lad was an assassin disguising his true appearance so that he could murder a high-ranking officer. He looked closer at the boy, whose forehead beaded with sweat. Perhaps something of a less nefarious nature, then—concealing a disability. If that were the case, it would be better to have it out now, instead of in the midst of battle when he could cause a real disadvantage for his fellow soldiers. Pity swelled in his chest, and he decided he would not alert the entire battalion but only reveal the disability for himself.

After a moment to recall the proper incantation, he whispered, "*Quel vyn foreth.*"

Before his eyes, the boyish façade melted away to reveal a wave of long blond hair and the soft facial features of a female. Her hazel eyes widened in panic at his use of the Old Tongue, but she remained steadfast in her position. Brudais' eyes roamed over her: the delicate eyebrows, the soft, pale lips that parted just barely as she breathed slightly more quickly than before, the contours of her jawline and chin, and the skin that looked as smooth as silk when compared with the ugly, pock-marked faces of the men he had just inspected. When he glanced below her neck, he admired the way her uniform was just slightly too tight about her chest. He didn't even allow himself to look below her waist, where he was certain the sight of her bare legs would cause him to forget himself. His uniform was becoming increasingly hot with each passing second.

Clearing his throat, he realized just how long he had been staring at her. "To the front, lad," he said, and the words came out far huskier than he had intended.

Her head turned, eyes cautious, as she took the proffered sword and began walking up to the front of the line. Brudais couldn't help himself from watching as the leather skirt of her uniform shifted as she walked, grazing the middle of her bare thighs with each movement.

Fuck. At the risk of him becoming noticeably aroused, he turned on his heels and went to the next soldier in line.

She had left him with no choice but to call her out. If he hadn't sent her up, the soldiers surrounding them would have thought it suspicious. Without giving her away, he did the only thing that he could have done in that moment. With sudden amusement, he realized that he was defending her. He didn't even know the girl. He didn't discount the idea that she was a Hyglenian sleeper, and his life very well could be in danger—although he suspected something more banal. Perhaps she had taken the place of a relative with failing health. It had been known to happen—though not with so little care for Creetian law. They were generally found out within a fortnight and sent back home, but this girl had been using magick to disguise herself. Who was to say just how long she had spent amongst them at this point?

When the time came to decide what to do with her, he admitted grudgingly to himself that he had sent her to the front to watch her fight. His curiosity was piqued, and he was determined to make quick work of the remainder of the inspection so that he could see how she fared against Rydril's Blood Guard.

Does that make me cruel? he wondered as he inspected the hilt of a sword that wobbled as he held it. *Perhaps.* But whether she was an assassin or had been training with the Seasoned for these past few moons, she should stand a chance against Wren. Brudais allowed himself a small smile. He had never been more eager for the end of an inspection.

CHAPTER EIGHTEEN

DANIA

Dania made her way up to the front of the Seasoned lines, conscious of just how many eyes were on her. Sweat gathered at her temples and began to run down her lower back over her growing apprehension that they could see her female form. Suspecting that there would have been a great deal more commotion from the men if they could, she contented herself with believing she had only been revealed to the commander.

She was not the only one of the Seasoned to have been excited at the prospect of being inspected by Commander Brudais. The battalion had been abuzz with the possibility since the evening before. During her training, she had not had the opportunity to learn from him back in Turivaun. The commander's presence in Rydril's unit had been sparse, but every time he joined them, she was not in the lucky unit that held his attention.

When she had seen him walking down her line during inspection, butterflies fluttered in her stomach. She was about to come face to face with a legend that she had only ever heard stories about, whose lineage aligned with Leifius. Her father's voice echoed in her head.

"He used his shield to great effect, mind—as its own weapon, as well as a defense. He drew it up over his head and hooked Grandis' blade, drawing it down and away. Their steel clashed, and the armies surrounding them roared with approval, with anticipation, as Grandis gained footing over Leifius. Their faces taut with concentration, steel slid across steel and they both retreated but stood their ground again. And again."

She had listened to the story so many times, she had memorized it—even the inflection in Riven's voice as he told it.

When Brudais stepped up next to her, she wanted so badly to turn her head to look at him, but he had been adamant about the soldiers remaining at attention. She couldn't let him down.

He held her sword in his hand for a long time after examining the pommel. Her mind wandered off to Aurelius back in Kelvs District, wondering if Brudais knew of him. Then she panicked, expecting that perhaps he knew something about this sword, and that Aurelius had accidentally mentioned for whom he had made it. Then she heard the words of the Old Tongue on his lips, whispered like a secret, and her eyes widened in horror as she stared straight into his and saw the recognition in them.

Dania positioned herself between a few of the men who had been sent up, giving her sword a glance before she placed it back in its sheath. She was certain nothing had been wrong with it. It was only a few moons old, and she was meticulous about honing it with the whetting stone she'd won in that game of dice back in the Turivaun camp. She wondered if the commander's decision to punish her was due to her use of magick to conceal her identity, rather than any fault of her weapon's keeping. Nothing else could have accounted for it.

She supposed he would be right to do so, but she wondered why her punishment had not been greater. It was against Creetian law to use magick, but Commander Brudais had just done so to reveal her own use. He wasn't a common foot soldier. Status made quite a difference in terms of what was considered to be 'legal.' No Inquisitor would find a noble guilty of charming the dice to roll in their favor. Perhaps he felt pity for her, or a greater punishment was forthcoming. Whether she owed him for mercy's sake or she owed him further abuse for her forbidden practices, she liked neither alternative better. Whichever it might be, it meant he held power over her. That feeling was not comforting.

When the inspection was over, and Commander Brudais returned to the front, she watched as he put his hands behind his back and shouted, "At ease!" The entire unit relaxed in unison—except for those who had accumulated at the front lines. They remained at attention, and Dania followed suit. Brudais nodded to Sergeant Wren, who stepped forward, towering over them.

Wren pointed the end of his sword at the first Seasoned in line and, without a word, led him to the main practice ring. The moment he turned to face him, Wren pounced with the grace of a wildcat. The soldier staggered back, holding out his dull sword and parrying as much as possible. Wren had him on the ground in a matter of four blows.

The next soldier didn't fare much better. It took six blows and a slice on the forearm, but he was down in the sand, bleeding, before Wren had broken a sweat. His sword guard had dislodged from the blade and was lying on the ground next to him, like a fallen comrade. Dania glanced over at Brudais as he shook his head and said, "You will bring that sword to the smithy immediately for repair, and then report to the latrines. And I don't want to hear any shit about it, either." The faintest of smirks had formed on his lips, and a few laughs came from the Blood Guard. Dania was surprised that she found this display of lightheartedness endearing. It seemed to humanize him.

Wren stepped up to the line, pointing his sword in Dania's direction. She followed him to the practice ring, drawing her sword as she walked. By now, she could anticipate that he would round on her and immediately attack, so when he did, she held up her sword to parry, sweeping his blade away from her. She continued to parry Wren's advances, sidestepping a heavy blow as she had learned on the road to Hyglen, causing the sergeant to stumble slightly. He regained his footing quickly, but it gave Dania time to move to his left, which she had determined was his weaker side.

Wren was on her with a renewed fury, and the blow she blocked reverberated the blades of their swords, the metal kissing as it slid down the length of her blade, causing a slicing metallic *twang!* to ring through the practice field. Opening some distance between them allowed her a breath, but only for a moment. Wren came at her again in a high guard attack. There was little she could do to block or parry, so she took the only escape allotted to her and dove, sword-first, straight between the man's legs. His open stance gave her plenty of room, and when she emerged at his back, she somersaulted away again, jumping back into a fighting stance as Wren spun around after once again regaining his footing from his failed attack. The Blood Guard's face was livid.

"The longer you evade me, boy, the harder it'll be when I pummel you into the ground."

Dania's back and hands were slick with sweat, but she was determined not to make a fool of herself. Not while Commander Brudais was watching. "If you can catch me, that is," she said, with more confidence than she felt.

Wren roared with rage and started her way again, then stopped suddenly. A howl had sounded in the distance, off towards the forest. Every soldier stood frozen, looking in the direction of the trees. A chorus of howls erupted from the forest, and a palpable panic began to sweep across the entire battalion.

"Seasoned, to your barracks. Now!" Brudais shouted at the troops. "Wait for your superior's command!"

With the push and shove of a thousand frightened men making their way west towards the Seasoned barracks, Dania turned to join them, still shaking from the fight. Wren pushed past her in the opposite direction, his face still red from exertion. As she breathed a sigh of relief that he didn't grab her in the confusion and make good on his promise, she felt a hand grasp her upper arm. She started, thinking Wren had changed his mind, and turned to find Commander Brudais.

"You're coming with me," he said firmly.

Dania blanched. "I'm Seasoned, sir. I have my orders."

"And my order for you is to come with me."

The heat from his hand on her arm was almost burning to the touch. When she looked into his eyes, they were as black as embers. She could have sworn they had been blue before.

"Come with me?" It wasn't an order this time, but a plea. She licked her lips, tasting the salt of her sweat, nodding slowly. The chorus of wolves sounded again, and she wasn't sure if it was her imagination, but they seemed to be getting closer.

Chapter Nineteen

BRUDAIS

Brudais made his way through the throng of bodies that were making for the barracks, but he looked behind him frequently to ensure that the girl was following. It would have been so easy to lose her in this swarm, but luckily, she seemed to trust him. He wasn't certain he deserved that trust, but he would take it all the same. This wasn't a time to waver.

The howls were getting closer, which meant the wolves were not far away. The reason for the superiors' concern and the men's panic was not that a few wolves might visit the camp and make for their rations, but rather that they were on the borders of the Fayn Forest. They didn't know what obstacles would be posed when they made camp here, but Brudais had expected retaliation of some kind.

So much was unknown about that wood, and the tales that were whispered about it were filled with blood and horror. The Fayn were characters in well-known Creetian bedtime stories. He had once seen an artist's rendering of a Fayn in a book of fairy tales. The otherworldly, pale and drawn face had hideous scars, blood dripping down the corners of its mouth, and a wicked grin with pointed teeth. There was another fairy tale that he recalled once the picture of those creatures came to mind—black wolves as big as bears, snarling and baring their bloodied fangs. The Fayn were said to ride them and could control them with their minds.

Brudais was jostled by the crowd. He took the opportunity to look back to see the girl. She didn't seem as concerned as the others. Perhaps she had never heard the stories.

When they made it to mid-camp, Brudais took a sharp turn and headed towards his tent. There were far fewer men in this section of the camp, and he was glad he didn't have to explain why he was housing a single soldier in his quarters. Parting the flaps, he motioned for the girl to enter. She looked wary, and he saw her eyes dart left and right before she realized that they were very much alone. A scream sounded from the west, causing the girl to startle and make for the shelter he was offering. Once she was inside, he followed her and pulled the tent flaps closed.

His tent was roomier and more private than any comfort the barracks provided, so he wasn't surprised by the shocked look on the girl's face when she took in her surroundings. He was a commander of the Royal Military; of course his lodgings were more favorable than the infantry's. When he glanced at her again, he read the longing on her face and realized that his quaint wartime lodgings could have been more elegant and spacious than any place she had ever been accommodated in. Something shifted in Brudais' mind at this realization. He needed to remind himself to appreciate his station more often.

A sudden strong gust of wind blew through the tent entrance and knocked Brudais over. The girl tried to grab him to steady him from the fall, but her hands clasped around his bicep and tore his command straps from his arm. He fell to his knees before her and a frantic voice whispered in the shell of his ear.

"Do not look them in the eyes. Their magick is strong. Tell Ithiador—"

And then the wind subsided. The only sound he could hear was the tent flaps rustling.

"Commander?" The girl's voice. He looked up to see her crouched over him, her hand still on his arm. Their faces were so close together, he could see a hint of blue in the hazel of her eyes. She blinked, and he looked away. She offered her arm, and he took it, standing.

"What was that?" she asked.

He didn't have time to explain, nor did he think he could without sounding raving mad.

Clearing his throat, he said, "Stay here," and stepped out of the tent and into the daylight.

Before he had made it halfway across the path, Captain Yurik of his Blood Guard came into view.

"Captain!" he yelled. Hearing him, Yurik turned around and ran to Brudais' side.

"Commander," he said, a little out of breath. "Four wolves have been spotted slinking their way into camp. At least one casualty so far."

"I heard," he said.

"What are your orders?"

Brudais took the horn that was slung underneath Yurik's arm, faced away from the captain, and blew a long, piercing note. Yurik winced at the noise. "Gather the men here. Make a sweep of the camp in groups of twenty, spread from this point in each direction until you make it to the borders of the encampment. And Yurik—" The captain had turned to leave, but Brudais reached out a hand and took Yurik's forearm. "Don't look them in the eyes. They have some kind of magick."

Yurik's eyebrows drew together, and he nodded solemnly, then looked down at Brudais' arm. "Your command straps, sir..."

Brudais glanced down and saw his skin indented where his command straps had been ripped off. "Not really the issue at hand, is it?"

He gave the captain a shove, and Yurik moved in the opposite direction, towards the *veritas* barracks, where Brudais' Blood Guard would be gathering once they heard the horn.

The commander turned around to find the girl outside the tent, watching him from across the path. She didn't seem intimidated by the commotion, or the screams that occasionally came from the western section of camp. Instead, her eyes were focused, taking everything in. He wondered if the horn had drawn her from the tent. He also wondered about the shaking of her right hand by her scabbard, as if she had just realized she was weaponless. She must have dropped her sword in the dirt of the practice field in all the commotion. *That's a shame*, Brudais thought. *It's a beautiful sword.*

"Follow me," he said, turning to head north. He heard her tentative footsteps behind him, and he drew his knife from his belt and held it tightly in his right hand.

"How do you know Aurelius?" Brudais glanced behind him to study her face, which was carefully neutral.

It took a moment for her to respond. He wondered whether she was concocting a lie. "He was the first friend I made in the city."

Interesting. So she wasn't from Turivaun, but she had lived there. If he had to guess at her lineage by the look of her, he would have said she was from the west. Nesliarc or Geldevin, perhaps. Creet had an influx of western immigrants in recent years, so it wouldn't have been difficult for her to make passage over the mountains or by ship. That still didn't explain the rest of the myriad questions that were circling his mind.

After a long silence, she said, "How do you know him?"

Brudais smiled fondly. "He forged my swords, and my father's before me. He's a talented blacksmith."

He could hear the surprise in her voice as she whispered, "Oh." A moment passed before she added, "And a kindhearted soul."

"Aye," he replied, his tone soft. He wondered if her sword had been a gift from Aurelius. He was known to be charitable with his craft and tell the recipient he had needed the practice. The man had been making swords since before Brudais was born. He certainly didn't need 'practice,' but the idea that she might have accepted his gift without that knowledge was… intriguing.

They walked through the camp at an even pace, passing by soldiers who were running in the other direction to help in the fight. They came across the bloody remains of a soldier, his guts splayed across the path, as if an animal had ravaged his torso but had found nothing worth eating—or perhaps it had been interrupted from its meal. A heaving sound came from behind him, and he turned around to find the girl leaning over the side of a tent, vomiting. *Not an assassin, then*, he thought, bemused. He hid his smile well.

"Is that the first time you've seen a corpse?"

"No," she said defensively, wiping her mouth with the back of her wrist. "Just... not so..."

"Messy? You stick around long enough to fight in a battle, and you'll find that this poor sod was a clean kill, compared to some."

Brudais watched as the emotions rippled across her face: disgust, rage, uncertainty. He crouched down to unsheathe the knife on the side of his greaves. When he stood back up, he offered it to her. Her wary expression was beginning to annoy him.

"Will it help you feel safer?" he asked.

She seemed reluctant but nodded. He held it out to her and her hand grasped the hilt, their fingers touching for a moment before she pulled it towards her.

They started moving again, but the silence did not last.

"Why are we heading north?" she asked, gaining some confidence.

"My horse is stabled this way."

"Your horse?" she replied, in shock. "Don't you think we should be helping to fight off the wolves?"

"The *veritas* are sweeping the camp for them and will protect the rest of the army. My horse, however, has no protection, and he can be as clueless as a milkmaid in a hen house when he's in mortal danger. Besides, we'll need a cavalry to beat back Hyglen, and if all our steeds are slaughtered tonight, we can forget about half the strategies I've devised."

She scoffed lightly. "An inconvenience to you, then."

"If you call losing thousands of lives an 'inconvenience,' then yes, I suppose."

"I'm sorry," she mumbled. "I didn't mean..."

"To pass judgment as if you knew me?" he said with a mirthless chuckle. "It's fine. Everyone seems to feel entitled to the act. For me, lady, the cavalry is desperately important, and I can guarantee that no one else has given a thought to the stables in this mess." As an afterthought, he added, "And if Ælon has been harmed, I'm going hunting for pelts."

"Dania." Brudais turned to face her, as she was no longer walking behind him but on his right side. "My name is Dania."

A smile tugged at the corner of Brudais' mouth. "A pleasure to meet you, Dania."

"And you, Commander."

Brudais' eyebrow arched as she said his title instead of his name, thus solidifying his theory that she was indeed part of Rydril's battalion. They might as well get it out now.

"You've been with us since Turivaun?"

"Yes," she said, then quieted. She had spotted the stables after they rounded a corner. They spotted something else, as well. The hulking form of a giant black wolf was moving stealthily towards the stable tent from the west. Horse hooves beat against the ground as it made its approach. A few whinnies broke out, alerting all the horses to their peril. Brudais held out a hand to stop Dania from moving forward.

"I can handle this," he whispered, pulling Ardent slowly from the sheath on his back. "Why don't you keep a lookout for any other members of the pack?"

Dania looked like she was about to protest, but then nodded her consent. She crouched low to the ground, grasping his knife firmly in her palm, one hand on the wet earth to steady herself.

Brudais slunk forward, keeping his knees bent and his eyes fixed on the wolf's paws. A twig snapped beneath his boot. His heart raced as the beast turned toward the noise and spotted him. A low, monstrous growl came from behind its bared teeth. Brudais stared at its paws, watching in his peripheral vision. Suddenly, the wolf spun around and charged toward Brudais. When it was only a few feet away, it lunged, claws extended, intending to rip the flesh from his bones. Brudais closed his eyes and sank to his knees just before the wolf collided with him, plunging Ardent straight up and into the wolf's belly. He felt the hot, sticky blood pour over him as the wolf yelped and came crashing to the ground behind him.

Brudais leapt up, circling the creature with his sword outstretched. The black form thrashed on the ground, yelping desperately, before it was silenced by Brudais' blade. A pool of black blood darkened the grass and dirt as it spilled from the slice down the wolf's underside. Carefully, Brudais looked away but felt for the beast's eyes, ensuring that they were closed with his fingertips. One could never be too careful. The magick could have still inhabited the wolf—even after death.

Brudais rose, holding Ardent at his side.

"Well, you look a mess," said Dania, rising from her position.

He smiled, wiping his hand over his face. "I've looked worse."

Dania walked carefully around the wolf's carcass, heading for the stables, and Brudais followed her. It didn't take long for him to find Ælon, who had wandered off-lead, his post having been kicked over by a frightened neighbor. He was munching on the grass near the water trough.

Brudais gathered his reins in his hands. “You could have been killed, you great lout.” Ælon gave a prolonged snort. “And your only thought is for food.”

He yanked on Ælon’s lead, but the horse reached down again for another mouthful.

“You’re hopeless.”

Ælon nudged him in the shoulder, and he smiled despite himself. He led the stubborn horse back to the stables. It took some time to right the post and secure him again, but it was obviously necessary.

Brudais had turned around to lay Ardent against one of the other posts, and when he turned back he saw Dania stroking Ælon’s muzzle. The horse nuzzled his nose against her cheek. The commander stood mesmerized by this sweet encounter, juxtaposed with the intense fighter he had witnessed on the practice field just a short while ago.

“Where did you come from?” He didn’t mean to say it aloud, but the words had certainly left his mouth. He stared at her so she’d know the question was meant for her.

Dania’s eyes shifted to the ground, contemplating her next words carefully. When she looked back at him, there was a determination in her eyes that made Brudais tense his muscles in anticipation. He almost reached for Ardent behind him, but instead placed a hand on the dagger sheathed at his hip.

“Lady-Governor Loya of Drens sent me to fill my brother’s position in Commander’s Rydril’s Seasoned unit.” Her lips tightened, face resolute. “Her intention is to prove to the king that Creetian women can enter military service.”

A memory swam before him of Loya outside the throne room, entreating him to sign her proposal. *If you prove it has merit, I’ll sign the damn thing.* This entire situation was his fault. His hand fell from his dagger, and he burst out laughing.

Chapter Twenty

DANIA

Dania watched in horror as Commander Brudais continued to laugh, and her face began to grow red with anger.

How dare he pass judgment over her and her mission? Over the past four moons, Dania had dedicated herself to this cause. Her training had been rigorous and harsh, but she had endured it to the best of her ability. She had been able to withstand a Blood Guard for more than a few minutes of combat, had she not? How dare this male think that what she was doing was laughable? Heat flooded her lower back and chest as the anger consumed her. Before she could stop herself, she stepped forward, drawing back her arm, and punched the commander square in the jaw.

The laughter ceased. He took a step back, putting a hand to his jaw to massage the area.

Instantly, sweat began to pool on her brow. *What have I just done?*

Until Brudais smirked. "You're strong."

"Yes, I am," she said, his composure giving her license to be as unbridled as she liked. "Women can be, if given the chance."

Brudais' eyebrows drew together, then relaxed as he seemed to realize something. "I'm sorry that I led you to believe I found

Loya's proposal comical. That was not my intention. I was aware of Loya's plans before we left for Hyglen; I just never believed they would come to fruition with such expediency. Though, I've underestimated her before."

The tenderness with which he said Loya's name made Dania want to blush. Perhaps his laughter was nothing more than a jest between lovers.

"I apologize for my… spirited response," she said.

Brudais' smile warmed her bones. "Dania, please," he said, and she was fond of the way her name sounded on his lips. "Think nothing of it. Although, I'll have to explain to my men why I have a welt the size of a fist on my face. If you come up with a worthy excuse, let me know."

Dania smiled and put her hand up to Brudais' jawline. "*Med veq raw*," she whispered, and the bruise that was beginning to form disappeared, his skin tone evening out. He watched her intently as she did this, his eyes never leaving hers, and as she moved her hand away, he caught it in his own.

"You didn't have to do that," he said. "I see you have little faith in my ability to justify a wound to my men."

"I was merely righting my wrong," she said, pulling her hand gently free of his grasp. "And don't you have appearances to keep?"

"Appearances?"

"Legend of Kresha, Champion of the Cup," she said haughtily, teasingly. "What would your men say if they knew you were wounded by a woman?"

Straight-faced, Brudais said, "They'd probably say, 'That's quite a woman.'"

Dania's mouth twisted into a reluctant smile.

They stayed at the stables to protect the horses, but no other wolves came for the beasts. They walked among the horses, calming them and ensuring that they were tied down properly. They didn't speak much, save to communicate the horses' welfare. Every so often, Dania would glance over at the commander and watch his comportment with the animals. He was gentle, speaking to them in hushed voices. Even if a horse was frightened, snorting and whinnying in fear, they quickly calmed at the commander's touch and soft words. She was surprised by the gentleness in his voice, and his patience while he waited for them to accept his touch. Dania smiled ruefully as the horse she was currently stroking snorted and nuzzled at her, knocking her chin and causing her to bite her tongue.

They heard a mustering horn in the distance, and Brudais came to her side.

"We should go back to mid-camp," he said, grabbing his sword from where it was propped against Ælon's post. "I'd like to hear Captain Yurik's report."

They made their way back to Brudais' tent, passing by soldiers as they ran hither and thither along the paths that connected the tents. The encampment had been constructed so that it resembled a maze. If an enemy were to break past the fortifications, it would have been impossible for more than three soldiers at a time to fit between the tents, thus making things a little more even in a fight with close quarters. It also made it difficult for the Seasoned to navigate anywhere other than between their barracks and the practice field. She supposed it was meant to be that way. The Seasoned were the lowest rank in the army; they didn't need to know anything except what their superior officers told them, and it wasn't often that they were tasked with navigating the encampment on their own. Brudais, however, moved through the tents with a surety that told her he had been instrumental in the camp's construction. He rounded corners with confidence and never once made a turn that led him where he didn't expect to go. Dania followed close at his heels so that she wouldn't lose sight of him. If she did, she would certainly never find him again, and probably wouldn't be able to find her way back to her barracks. She did, however, make note of the mess tent as they passed it, where she saw soldiers already lining up for their meager rations after the fight.

By the time they reached the commander's tent, the captain was standing outside, ready to make his report. Brudais motioned for Dania to enter the tent, but when she passed by Captain Yurik, he asked, "Who's the runt?"

"None of your concern, Captain," Brudais said tightly. "What are our losses?"

Dania ducked under the flap and entered the tent as she was bid. She didn't want to argue with the commander in front of others—especially since they only saw her as a Seasoned 'runt.'

The tent was more spacious than it looked from the outside. It boasted a full-sized bed with a pillowed mattress and warm blankets lining the foot. A heavy-looking chest stood at the foot of the bed, and a table and chairs lined the tent wall on the southern side beside a wash basin. Another table stood in the corner with a large leather map spread across its length, while a weapons rack was positioned by the door, filled with intricate knives, daggers, and several swords. One was a longsword with a jeweled hilt. The other was a short sword, which was unadorned—save for the runes carved down the fuller. They shone dark against the sword's bright steel. Dania took a step forward to examine the blade before taking two steps back.

She knew this blade. Its name was Ire. One of the two famed blades of Brudais, son of Leifius. Her hand shook with excitement as she held it out to touch the hilt. This was the blade that won Brudais the Kresha Cup against Halvian son of Grandis. This was the sword that ended his life. Looking up to the tent entrance, she realized that the blade that had sliced clean through the wolf near the stables had been his other sword, Ardent. Dania shook her head, disbelieving. She was walking in the world of her father's stories. She knew they had happened, and that these legends had lived amongst them, but she had never expected her path to cross with them.

The tent flap was pushed aside, and Commander Brudais entered the tent, his expression grim.

"We lost one of our *veritas*, and at least twenty-five from the other units. We managed to kill six wolves, but their numbers were at least thrice that. We'll make a pyre tonight for the valiant dead."

Dania put her hands behind her back, waiting for him to continue, but he seemed lost in his own thoughts.

"And what of me?"

He glanced up from the floor of the tent, his eyes locking with hers for a moment. They were the deepest blue. As she gazed into them, she almost forgot that she had asked a question, so when he began to answer her, she was confused at first.

"If you're to continue with Loya's mission, I think it's best that—"

A flash of brilliant, white light spread across every corner of the tent, but only for an instant. Brudais' expression grew concerned and his eyes scoured the tent for any abnormalities, but before he had made a full circuit of the room, Dania watched as a dark form appeared between them, materializing from thin air. She stepped back, unable to take her eyes off the shape, as it formed into a perfect copy of Governor Loya. From the red hair cascading down her back to the pale skin and dark green dress, which hung gracefully on her frame, Loya stood in their midst now, where nothing had been before.

"Loya?" Brudais said, his voice sharp with shock. "What in the five hells are you doing conjuring a Shadow?"

The tenderness that had been on his lips when he'd spoken her name earlier had evaporated, giving Dania the distinct impression that whatever relationship lay between them was a complicated affair. She wondered what he meant by 'Shadow,' but could see clearly that Loya's form was almost translucent and had an otherworldly quality about it. If she were to reach out her hand and place it on Loya's shoulder, would it pass right through her?

"Dania, why are you with Brudais? Have you been discovered?"

Loya's voice was clear but seemed far away, as if it were disconnected with the form in front of them. The concern that showed on the governor's face was evident, and Dania's face reddened from embarrassment. She had promised the governor that she would stay hidden. This was the first time that she had checked on her, and Dania had already been found out—and by one of the most senior commanders in the army, no less.

"Only by me," Brudais said as he watched Loya glower at him. "I saw her eyes during an inspection. I had no intention of exposing her until I knew what her schemes were. When I found out they were of your making, I realized my mistake."

"Mistake?" both Loya and Dania said at the same time, caution and surprise mirrored in their mingled voices.

"Yes," he said, standing up straighter. "I mean to bring her before the king as soon as possible."

Dania's heart sank. She had thought he was on her side. It had seemed that way when he spoke about his knowledge of Loya's plans. She had hoped that she had obtained an ally in her mission, not the catalyst of its ruin.

"You can't be serious, Brudais! A great deal of effort and coin has been put towards this venture. I can't allow you to ruin it with some haughty sense of—"

Brudais put a hand up, interrupting Loya. "I won't ruin anything. We'll tell the king that Dania was hiding in the supply wagons and was eager to join the battalion for your schemes. This way he need know nothing of your use of magick. If he were to learn of your methods, my dear Lady-Governor, he would have you both arrested. Besides, he'll want to know if the girl can fight on her own. If she kept up her guise, no one would ever believe she accomplished anything. The men will need to see it for themselves."

He waited patiently as Dania and Loya looked at each other, caution warring with the commander's unwelcome common sense.

"Who taught you how to conjure a Shadow, Loya?"

Loya's cheeks turned a delicate shade of pink, but she crossed her arms over her chest. "The Countess Staliva," she said quietly.

Brudais swore viciously, causing Dania to look at him in surprise and take a step back. "Why must all women insist on defiance when a man, in good faith, urges you to quit the use of outlawed practices? You're all determined to advance yourselves so much that you're willing to ruin yourselves in the process, is that it?"

Dania shot him a hurt look, but Loya scoffed. "If there are no decent alternatives to what magick can provide, I'll do as I please, thank you, Commander."

"It's your pretty wrists that'll be clapped in irons should you fail, Governor. I thought you valued your position more than this."

Loya pursed her lips. She turned to Dania and ushered her away from Brudais with an outstretched hand. Dania stepped to the edge of the tent, Loya gliding along behind her.

"I'm loath to admit it, but I agree with Brudais on these matters."

Dania looked up at the Shadow in shock, but Loya cut her off before she could make a comment.

"The men—especially men like the king—will never believe something just because you tell it to them. We need proof. Brudais is right, damn him. I should have realized this sooner. You'll need to reveal yourself in a way that will not incriminate you. A white lie should suffice. I should not visit you like this again, but I do want regular reports of your progress. Once you are established in your new situation, you should be free to write to me."

Dania's head was spinning. They had been looking at things from a female perspective, imagining that her presence there would not be welcome and hiding it was the only way to encourage the kind of behavior and inclusiveness that a male interloper would be afforded. They had not taken a male viewpoint into consideration. Dania's hidden presence would never be discovered—unless the magick that she used were revealed to the men. They could not do this without admitting to their outlawed conduct. Brudais' way forward seemed the only way.

"I'll do as you say, Lady-Governor."

Dania looked back at the commander, who was eyeing them at the other end of the tent, his expression calculated. Loya's eyes shifted from Brudais back to Dania, and her lips pursed again.

"Oh—and Dania," she said, her voice soft against the shell of Dania's ear. It was odd, but even with the Shadow being so close to her physically, she did not feel her breath against her skin, as she would have if the governor were really there. It was unnerving. "Don't get too attached to Brudais. He's a good enough man, but he's a notorious rake when it comes to women. Ignore his wiles while you can."

Before Dania could turn around, Loya's Shadow had disappeared. She considered Loya's last advice carefully. There had been a few moments of what Dania perceived as tenderness between her and the commander since he had discovered her, moments that she had thought might have meant something. Given Loya's last words, perhaps those moments had just been his normal way with women and had held nothing more than a sexual undertone in his eyes. *Although*, she wondered, finally turning around, *why would Brudais support our cause enough to risk his own station by helping us if he thinks so little of women?*

"What did she say?" the commander asked, his voice a little gruffer than it had been a moment ago. She wondered if perhaps he had heard Loya's last words and taken offense.

"That I was to trust your strategy." *But not your character.*

Brudais held her gaze for a moment, and Dania wondered whether he had read her mind, as his face was grave.

"Good," he replied, and then a smile lit his lips. "Let's go meet the king."

Chapter Twenty-One

Loya

A heaviness seeped into Loya's bones as her mind settled back into her body. She had never traveled by Shadow before, and it was a most jarring experience. The magickal heat that had flooded her extremities was now beginning to dissipate, but when she opened her eyes, she was not ready for the wave of sickness that crashed over her. She leaned over the side of the armchair and dry heaved, finding it difficult to breathe.

Staliva was there to steady her, holding her shoulders to keep her from falling over. Rubbing Loya's arms vigorously, Staliva helped her stand.

"It will help you come back to your body," she said softly. "How did it go? Did you find her?"

For the last few moons, Loya had wondered how best to contact Dania. Staliva had come up with a way for her to project an image of herself to the girl, but they had needed to find her first. The solution was a combination of three spells: one to find Dania amongst the troops, one to check to see if she were alone and could be contacted safely, and one to use a Shadow to communicate.

Developing the plan and researching the correct spellwork had taken quite a while, as Staliva had never managed the first of the three spells before. Once she had obtained the correct spellverse to find a Keeper amongst a hoard of other Humans, Staliva then had to teach Loya what she had discovered. Learning spellverse was simple enough, as it usually involved passing knowledge from one mind to another, but the intention behind the spellverse was sometimes more important than the words themselves. It had taken Staliva years of practice to perfect her meditation practices and pinpoint her magickal focus. Loya was still learning how to calm her own thoughts enough to make her intention known, and it could be felt as the magick roiled within her, waiting for instruction. When it didn't have the proper incentive and direction, the magick took more energy than it otherwise would. After each spell Loya cast, she was spent, whereas Staliva was able to recover within a few moments.

"She was with Brudais," Loya said, wobbling with the effort to stand.

Staliva's eyes lit up, concern washing over her face.

"It's fine," Loya said reassuringly. "He's amenable to our cause. He's devised a more honest plan, which I believe—gods help me—will be more effective in this instance."

Staliva led Loya through the solar doors and into the governor's bedchamber, lowering her onto the bed. "Since when has Brudais cared about women joining military ranks?"

"Since I asked him to support it," she replied, grunting as she hit the mattress.

Staliva gave her a wary look, nibbling her lip heedlessly.

Loya grinned. "Are you jealous, Countess?"

"Of course not," she replied immediately, rolling her eyes in an almost believable way. "Although, I should know if you have other ties that could compromise our schemes."

"Other ties?" Loya's grin deepened, then she sat up on the bed, leaning in and placing her lips gently on Staliva's. The Countess' eyes fluttered shut and her breath caught. She leaned into the curve of Loya's body, deepening the kiss.

Staliva's mistreatment at the hands of the males in the Creetian court had caused her to despise them. Loya had produced a more enticing plan for the Countess to side with her in marrying her cousin, Ithiador, over forsaking men altogether, but it had required Loya to offer herself up instead. Staliva was a restless youth. Since Loya had forsaken men for so many years to sustain her power and waylay the king's advances, she had decided that experimentation was the only way either of them would get any release, and she had been right. This hadn't been Staliva's first relationship with a female—and it was abundantly clear in her expertise—but Loya was eager to become equally enticing for her prized pupil. She needed Staliva to remain satiated—otherwise she might have strayed from Loya's plans entirely.

They separated, breathless, Loya smirking and tracing the shell of Staliva's ear with her fingertips.

"Brudais is a good friend, but nothing more. Is he more for you?"

"Yes," Staliva said, licking her lips. "He's like a brother."

"A brother you'd like to fuck?"

Staliva snorted, but she turned away and could not meet Loya's gaze.

"He shunned your advances, didn't he?"

"He reminded me of our relationship."

"And that reminder stung, didn't it?"

Staliva backed away, getting up from her sitting position and stepping towards Loya's bedroom armoire, which boasted of a large mirror that stood at its back. Loya watched as Staliva gazed at her own reflection, a look of confidence and arrogance lighting the countess' features.

"A legend has his creed. It was not through any fault of yours. Besides, had you succeeded, and the king found out, you may have started a war."

Staliva waved her hand dismissively. "Tarison would have just reprimanded him, as always."

"You underestimate the king's hatred and pride. Civil war would have erupted over that precious body you're admiring."

Staliva cocked her head, looking somewhat pleased with the idea. She was ever so dangerous.

"The person you see staring back at you will be queen before this war with Hyglen is over. Queen of Creet."

Smiling, Staliva turned back to Loya. "What needs must be done before that can happen?"

Her eagerness was both an encouragement and a warning. Staliva's ambition to be queen had risen quickly with the realization that it did not mean she must wed Tarison for the privilege. Her ambition was insatiable, and she was willing to do anything to see Loya's plans succeed—including using and teaching Loya magick. She had been an extremely useful tool—especially in collecting information on Loya's colleagues. Her network of spies had not been able to collect half the amount of intelligence that Staliva had in the past fortnight. Using the Sight for such methods would have been considered ill-gotten and ill-used by her Zethlandian mentors, but Staliva was eager to please her new mentor.

"First, we'll need to discredit Tarison, which shouldn't be too difficult. He's given the people enough fodder for dislike in the past. So, all we need do is remind them of his past indiscretions."

"High taxation, increased poverty, his unpredictable nature with foreign and domestic politics—not to mention the Xerdin Genocide during the Gray Throat outbreak."

Loya's eyebrows rose.

"What? I had good teachers in Zethland, and good reason not to want to marry that abominable oaf."

Loya smirked. "The easiest way to spread the rumors is through my spies. They're nestled in all walks of life, so the messages will get through to the right people. Next, we will need to introduce the idea of Ithiador taking over and show them that he would make a suitable alternative. His work with the people of the Jaguar Hills, the peace treaties he's brokered with our allies and enemies since becoming an ambassador, and the goodwill missions he's implemented for the poor will make a good start. It will let the people know that he is for the reinstitution of magick, which will aid all peoples, and shine a beautiful light on his determination for peace instead of war and his hopes for a more prosperous future for all. He will sound like a saint compared to the slander circulating about the king."

Staliva smiled wickedly. "And then?"

"Then all that is left is to make it happen. Steward Venhil will need to be deposed, of course. His… demotion… will assure us a swift victory when Ithiador returns."

Staliva's eyebrows drew together. "And what if he does not return?"

Loya placed her hands on each side of her thighs against the bedsheets, smoothing them out. "He will return."

"But what is the plan if he doesn't?"

Loya looked up at Staliva, drawing her gaze. "Then there may be a lot more blood to shed."

Chapter Twenty-Two

Morvian

Pexix had assured Morvian that he would be able to report by mid-day, but he had surpassed their scheduled time and Morvian found himself waiting on the king's nephew for more than two hours, gazing into a bowl of water which would be used for their magickal communication. He knew it wasn't a simple task for the man to get away from the throng of Creetians, but it should not have taken hours for him to appear.

In the meantime, he mused about the man standing next to him. Sergeant Oren had agreed to be his… assistant… while the scholars continued to search for a cure to Morvian's voicelessness. The men called him "Morvian's Mouth," and other things more vulgar, because they were inseparable. The more biting retorts were silenced quickly when his men realized Morvian was just around the corner. Oren had, overall, been very accommodating. Once their mind link had been formed, he never pried about Morvian's inner thoughts, and never relayed information that was meant to be kept private. If he had, Morvian would have known. It was nearly impossible to keep something from someone who had access to your every thought. Oren also didn't rue the unfounded torments his fellow soldiers committed due to his new station. They were all simply jealous that their commander favored someone so rustic and untried. Oren's main concern, as Morvian had expected, was to outwit the Fayn for the terrors they had committed upon his village. As long as Morvian continued to be against the Fayn, he could count on Oren's loyalty.

Oren glanced up at him, a resolute expression on his face. He'd been listening to that internal monologue, but at least he was smart enough not to respond to it.

The bell by the side of the water basin rang as if it had been hit from the outside. That was the warning that the king's nephew was about to connect with them. The water in the basin rippled, and Morvian hung over it, hands on either side, looking directly downward.

Pexix appeared in the water. His image was faint but unmistakable. His chiseled jaw, black hair and narrow eyes swam in the water within the bowl. He would have been the spitting image of the king if Eusol were more handsome and well-toned.

"Commander," he growled, his voice as deep as ever. "The Creetians were just under attack."

Morvian blanched. Oren said, "By whom?"

Pexix winced, as if in pain. "Wolves. They came out of the Fayn Forest. They had some kind of enchantment; it froze men in their tracks. Lost an entire unit's worth of men." He grimaced. "Once the men were mobilized to fight them, they managed to kill about six of the beasts."

"How did they evade their enchantment?"

A grunt sounded from the basin. "Commander Brudais spread the word not to look in their eyes. We would have lost a lot more men had he kept quiet."

"How did he know?"

A lazy shrug from Pexix. "No one knows. Tarison has called a war council to assemble after the commanders have had a chance to recover and see to their battalions. Perhaps he'll tell us there."

Morvian watched as Pexix's expression turned pained again. "Are you injured?"

"It's just a scratch," he replied. "I'll have it tended to as soon as I'm done here."

"Given their weakened state, it would seem a good time to mobilize our forces for an attack."

"It would," Pexix agreed. "We'll be reeling from this for a while still. The Creetians will want to take further precautions against the forest and fortify the western encampment against another wolf attack. If you're quick about it, you can be here in two day's march. Tarison will have a watch over Pelosia Field, but it's the best time to move regardless of the Creetians knowing. They won't be able to do anything to prevent it or attack while our forces are on the road. Although, I would highly recommend coming from the north. Only one battalion is stationed there, along with the stables. If you get close to the forest edge, you can penetrate the Creetian defenses there."

"That is too close to the forest," Oren said, reading Morvian's thoughts. The commander shook his head. "Their numbers are vast, and they don't look fondly on those who trespass, as you well know."

Pexix looked confused. "Do you mean to say you think the wolves were acting on Fayn orders?"

Morvian scowled. "I know it," Oren said behind him. "I've met the beasts before. They do the Fayn's bidding. It's why their magicks are so strong."

Pexix mirrored Morvian's scowl. "When will you attack, and from which direction?"

"East. Give me three days' time. We'll need a short rest after the march. I'll ensure the army is camped in the hills to the west of Pelosia. It'll provide enough cover."

"Three days," Pexix agreed, nodding. "I'll leave the door open for you."

Morvian nodded back, and the image of Pexix disappeared from the basin. He looked behind him, and Oren appeared confused.

"What did he mean, he'd leave the door open?"

The commander smiled. *He'll ensure the Seasoned forces are on the front lines.*

Morvian sat at his desk, scribbling a note to the captain of his guard. He had informed the king of Pexix's report and his intentions to mobilize Hyglen's forces with Oren's help. He had then told Oren to return to his quarters and rest. He would need his assistance far more in the coming days now that Creet was encamped on their borders. The king had made it clear that it would be too risky to for Morvian to travel with the army, but that he was to remain in Bentixt to command from the sidelines. He saw sense in the strategy, but that didn't mean he would enjoy it. It was difficult enough to control the troops when one was there to reprimand them in person. He would now have to rely on messages from the Hyglen encampment, which would take time to receive—time which could mean the difference between victory and defeat.

He trusted his captains to command in his absence, and admitted to himself that to lead, the men would need to hear the conviction in their superiors' voices when they went into battle. That was something that Morvian could not give them. Despite Oren's willingness to help voice Morvian's concerns aloud, he was not the most confident speaker. The men would hear the fear in his voice and waver in their resolve. This was for the best.

A hesitant knock came from his closed office door.

Morvian grew impatient. He couldn't even voice his consent for someone to enter his office. He got up from his chair, rounded the desk and made his way to the door. He yanked it open and glowered down at the messenger boy standing in front of him.

"Commander," he said, his voice cracking a bit with the effort not to squeak. "A message for you."

Morvian grabbed the piece of parchment from the boy's hand and shooed him away. He closed the door and went back to settle in his chair. He unfolded the parchment, expecting a note from the king or one of his officers, but the script on the parchment was not written in ink. It looked to be written in blood.

His spine tingled. He read the contents carefully, scanning the page for hidden messages.

The Agent of Change that you seek commands without office.
Our pets are felled, but eyes see clearer in death.

Kill him, Morvian the Mute. He seeks to ruin the world.

Morvian snarled, his muscles tensed with hatred. How dare they command him after what they had done? His mood soured when he realized that their intent and his were already aligned. He desired nothing more than to throw the message in the fireplace and change his entire strategy to avoid their involvement, but his plans were already in motion, and Eusol had agreed to this course of action.

He thought about the look of panic and suspicion in Oren's eyes when he next read Morvian's thoughts. Was he colluding with the Fayn? *No*, he imagined himself saying, trying to dissuade his Mouth. *Not until now.*

He didn't take commands from the Fayn, and he didn't require their cryptic aid. He knew what he had to do, and he had already devised his approach long before the Fayn had interfered.

Murder took a great deal of planning, after all.

Chapter Twenty-Three

BRUDAIS

Brudais led Dania through the encampment again, heading northeast to Rydril's battalion. The look on Dania's face was fairly amusing as they wound their way through the maze of tents. She had no idea where they were, but once they made it to the practice field, she blanched.

"I thought we were going to the king," she said, her voice a little unsure.

"We will be," he replied, turning from the field and walking up to Rydril's tent. "We need to make a stop first and get a few things… settled."

She gave him a tentative look, as if, despite Loya's assurances, she shouldn't rely on him. He smiled reassuringly.

"Trust me; this will make things much more convincing."

He held the tent flap open and motioned for her to enter. Her eyebrows drew together, but she did as she was bid. He followed her in and took in the sight before him.

Rydril stood hunched over the map laid on a table in the middle of the room. Captain Peric of Rydril's Blood Guard was moving a few pieces across the map in a sweeping fashion, as if indicating an attack. They both looked up from their studies, giving Brudais quizzical looks.

"You're alive," Rydril said cheerily, gazing back down at the map before him. Captain Peric saluted Brudais in the common military fashion, standing at attention.

"At ease, Captain," he said, and Peric's posture slackened. "I need your commander for a moment."

"Yes, sir," he said and quickly strode out of the tent. The look he gave Dania as he passed was one of little consequence. It was odd to see Dania's presence go unchallenged, but Brudais reminded himself that her female form was only visible to his own eyes. Peric just saw a Seasoned runt, likely thinking him a messenger.

Rydril didn't look up again, still studying the map. Brudais held a hand out to Dania to indicate that she should stay where she was, and then he crossed the tent to stand on Rydril's left. He bent down, whispered spellverse in his friend's ear, and watched the look on his face morph from confused to shocked and then livid as he looked up at Dania.

"What the—" he began, and he pushed away from the table, stumbling backwards a few steps.

Brudais chuckled softly. "Commander Rydril, meet one of *your* Seasoned soldiers. Her name is Dania."

Rydril stared at her. Before long, Dania looked away, blushing slightly. Brudais watched her cheeks redden with embarrassment. When had she become *shy*? Looking back towards Rydril, he saw that his friend was still staring at her in disbelief. A feeling of jealousy was roused in him, and he shoved Rydril in the shoulder.

"You can't be here," Rydril said tersely. "We'll send for a horse and a guard to escort you back to the city."

Brudais rolled his eyes. "She's here for a reason, brother."

"I don't care," he replied, his eyes narrowing at Brudais.

"I do."

Brudais' and Rydril's eyes met, and they stared at each other, neither giving way. Finally, Rydril grabbed Brudais' shoulder and hauled him to the other side of the tent, out of Dania's earshot.

"Are you mad?"

"Debatable."

"What possible reason—"

"Loya."

A small pause, considering. "Fuck Loya."

"I will not," Brudais said, smirking. Perhaps if he could bring a smile to Rydril's lips, he could win this argument. "She's a dear friend and nothing more."

"Brudais," Rydril said in an almost pleading voice. "I know you have stuck your neck out for her before, but this is too great an ask. You could be arrested for helping her."

"Only if they're aware of the magick she's used, which I intend to keep a secret. You can keep a secret, can you not, brother?"

Rydril cursed viciously, then peered at Brudais for a moment too long. "Is this for Loya, or the girl?"

Brudais' eyes widened. "I barely know her."

A tight-lipped smile came to Rydril's lips, but Brudais doubted he was winning. "Lust, then. Just as dangerous for you."

Brudais scoffed, then glanced over to the other side of the tent where Dania stood, playing with the fabric of her tunic as she stood awkwardly, looking at the ground. He turned back to Rydril, who was now smirking outright.

"I don't tell you how to fuck your wife, so don't tell me when I can use my cock."

A burst of laughter came from Rydril, then he grabbed his friend's shoulder, hard. "As long as you know what you're doing, and why."

"I made Loya a promise," he said coolly. "Besides, I'm curious."

Rydril made a face. "That's never good."

Brudais chuckled, then turned back to Dania.

In a voice loud enough for her to hear, he said, "Dania, Commander Rydril has consented to help you. I think it best that he advises the king that you were found amongst his Seasoned. If the news were to come from me… well, let's just say it will be much better received coming from someone else."

Dania's eyebrows drew together, but she nodded consent. "Thank you, Commander."

Rydril said, "I'll consider this a favor, for which I will require payment in kind."

"Whatever you need, Commander."

Most accommodating. He doubted she knew just what she was getting herself into with that agreement.

A rustling came from outside, and they all turned to face the tent's entrance. A young soldier entered, his breath ragged.

"Commander, the Hyglen army is on the move! Scouts spotted them marching on Pelosia Field and heading for the hills. They estimate two days before they arrive. The king has ordered the war council to be moved up. He wants the commanders there as soon as may be."

Rydril waved him off, and he exited the tent.

"Fuck," he said absently. Brudais could see the wheels turning in Rydril's mind, just as they were in his own.

"They'll consider us weakened from the wolf attack."

"We are," Rydril reminded him.

"Yes, but we have time to fortify the camp while they march. What are our weakest points?"

"North, west."

"Morvian wouldn't come through the forest. Not after what the Fayn did to him."

"Both will need to be fortified regardless. We don't want another attack from the forest."

Brudais looked up suddenly, seeing Dania hanging on their every word. Rydril sighed.

"What do we do with her in the meantime?"

Dania was resolute as she said, "I'll be fine on my own."

Suddenly, doubt seized Brudais. "You're going to run, rework your spell, and we'll never find you again. Loya told you to trust my strategy."

"And I intend to!" she said hotly. "It's *you* who doesn't trust *me*."

Brudais rounded on her. "And why should I?"

Her mouth was set, and she crossed her arms over her chest. "Because you gave me a knife and I never used it."

"Fine," he said, incensed. "You'll need to stay hidden until after the battle so that we can bring you before the king when it isn't utter chaos. The conditions need to be ripe for your reveal."

After a moment, Dania's arms fell to her sides and she looked at him, confusion coloring her face. "Shouldn't I be fighting in the battle?"

Brudais looked at Rydril in surprise, seeing a similar reaction on Rydril's face.

"Wouldn't you rather have more time to train before putting yourself in that position?" asked Rydril.

"None of the other Seasoned get that choice," she replied evenly.

Rydril turned to Brudais. His expression read, *She's got a point.*

Brudais shook his head, holding out a hand in a cutting gesture, as if the move would help them both see reason. "The other Seasoned don't have anything to prove. You do. You're here to demonstrate to the king that females can fight and survive, be assets in battle. This war has been a travesty of an example for how women would be trained if they were meant to enter a battlefield, and you were never Seasoned to begin with. You don't even have the proper foundation."

"I held my own against Sergeant Wren."

Her expression was confident, stubborn even.

"You are insufferable," he said hotly. He tried and failed to ignore the smirk forming on Rydril's lips in his peripheral vision.

"So, you don't deny it," she said triumphantly, smiling. "My footwork is at least decent enough."

"Footwork is one part of fighting," Rydril admitted, "but what about your attack?"

They watched as Dania pursed her lips and her eyes sank to the floor.

"You need more training, and *you* have a choice. Are you going to take it?"

After a moment of silence, Dania sighed and nodded.

"Wait outside for a moment," Rydril commanded. They both watched her make her way outside of the tent before Rydril turned to him slowly. "The girl is different," he admitted with a curious expression. "I see what you see in her."

"Defiance and naivety?"

Chuckling darkly, Rydril followed Dania out of the tent, leaving Brudais alone with his thoughts.

Chapter Twenty-Four

DANIA

Her mind was reeling from the conversation she had just witnessed. The way the commanders' minds worked was fascinating, as was how they could read each other's thoughts before speaking, their minds in tandem. They hardly needed to converse at all. In contrast, all she had done was gape at them, and insist she was ready for something that she knew she wasn't. She had made some valid points—that was evident from the look on her commander's face—but it wasn't enough to convince them. Secretly, she was relieved. The more training she received, the better use she could be in a battle, and the easier it would be to prove herself.

Rydril emerged from his tent, looking bemused.

"Walk with me," he said. He turned to the east and she matched his stride. "I don't have much time to instruct you before the war council begins, so you'll need to return to your Seasoned unit. The next few days, we will be fortifying the encampment for Hyglen's attack. Now, more than ever, the Seasoned will be training... *hard.* Brudais may be supportive of Loya's proposal, but even I will take some persuasion—and I am one of the more open-minded of the commanders. Train hard and prove me wrong."

Dania looked up at him, his dark, handsome face stone cold in the bright sunlight. "I intend to, Commander."

Commander Rydril nodded, the corner of his mouth twitching. She knew she had won some points with him for that remark.

"Go to the barracks and find your commanding officer. He'll inform you of your duties."

The lieutenant she reported to had asked her to join her Seasoned unit on the practice field with one of Rydril's Blood Guard as her instructor. She was determined to prove Rydril wrong, of course, but she found that she was more determined to prove Brudais right. Despite his intractable behavior, she felt as though he were on her side. She wondered why Brudais had such faith in women to fight in combat when, according to Loya, he treated women with all the deference of a soiled rag. He was vexing, but she had to admit that he was also very enticing. Regardless of Loya's dissuasions, the more time she spent with the man, the more she realized her attraction. It wasn't just the look of him—and, gods, the smell of him—though his chiseled biceps and handsome features didn't hinder her desire. The way that he looked at her and spoke to her were as if he saw into her soul, knew her every desire, and wanted to be the reason they were all realized. She imagined those eyes on her, those gorgeous blue eyes… turning black, like fiery embers. Heat flooded her sex, and her nipples hardened against the linen cloth of her tunic, pressing hard against her leather jerkin.

"Browyn!" someone yelled from the middle of the field. Dania straightened and ran across the training ground to meet her lieutenant. He glowered down at her. "This was found on the practice field this morning after the wolf attack. Commander Brudais said it belongs to you. Don't let me catch you losing sight of your weapon again, runt. Embarrassing enough that you lost it, but that Commander Brudais of all people retrieved it for you… give me a lap around the northern encampment for your negligence."

Dania turned to run, then quickly turned back around to take her sword from his outstretched hands. The lieutenant rolled his eyes. Her entire run around the barracks, supply tents, and mess was consumed with the thought that Brudais had intentionally retrieved her sword before it could be lost or stolen. She wondered if maybe the maker of the sword had something to do with it, but if that alone were the case, he might have kept it for his own. Perhaps by giving it back to her, he meant to teach her the same lesson as the lieutenant. How could she have dropped her sword in the midst of an attack, when danger was all around her? She had to rely on the goodwill of others to obtain another weapon, so as not to be utterly defenseless in the fight. She could not rely on that goodwill during battle. She deserved whatever punishment the lieutenant doled out.

When she returned to the training grounds after her punishment, she was immediately thrown into a paired fight with a menacing-looking Blood Guard, who pounded her into the dirt for five minutes before lifting her to her feet and instructing her on better form.

"You tarried between the second and third thrust. You need swift action. Don't be afraid to slash an arm or a leg if it'll help interrupt the flow of your enemy's movement. Even a few moments will give you the advantage. You don't use the opportunities you're given to attack; you'd rather prance about with fancy footwork. While you're prancing about, know that there are enemies on your left, your right, behind you, with swords in hand, ready to use every chance they have to catch you unawares, cut you down, and leave you for the crows. Your sword and your wits will be the only things supporting you in a fight. Ensure you don't lose either."

So, he had heard about the incident, as well, had he?

He tensed his shoulders and held his sword up. "Let's see if you've learned anything."

Dania smiled and moved into a fighting stance.

Chapter Twenty-Five

BRUDAIS

Two days later, Brudais stood outside Rydril's tent, leaning against one of the posts that held it up. His arms were crossed over his chest, and with the heat of the day, his skin stuck to the leather jerkin he wore whenever he shifted his stance.

The wolf attack had come swiftly after the encampment had been established on the borders of the Fayn Forest. It had been a clear sign that they were not welcome. Their war council on the matter had been shunted aside for more pressing concerns—namely, Hyglen's advance. The council's solution had been to fortify the western borders of the camp with stakes and nets, while increasing fortifications elsewhere—especially in areas with little manpower. Rydril had been correct; their main concentration had been on the northern borders. The men who would not continue training the Seasoned were aiding in the fortification efforts. When Hyglen attacked, their camp would be safe, but Tarison had every intention of meeting them head-on in battle, from whichever direction they deemed fit to attack. Brudais and a few others had strongly recommended reserve units to the north on the outskirts, particularly a cavalry, but Tarison had refused.

"Our numbers are more than enough to beat Hyglen back with our infantry," he had said.

Why had they brought the horses if not to use them in battle? Brudais had thought. It would have been a boon to their struggling forces to have a cavalry at the ready to aid them. Tarison, however, had been adamant that a cavalry was only to be mobilized in time of need.

"Our need is now, when the whole of Hyglen's army is upon us," Brudais had responded hotly, but he had been overruled.

The strength of the army's infantry would need to be enough to break Hyglen's lines. Tarison had clearly never heard the term 'reserve forces' before, and Rydril had to calm Brudais down after the council with an amusing anecdote about Dorian chasing Liska through the flowerbeds in their courtyard gardens.

"Why does he shun my advice when he knows it is sound?" Brudais said grumpily, after the laughter from the story had died.

"Because he is a stubborn fool," Rydril said quietly. "Every suggestion you make is an opportunity for him to diminish you. You have given him good enough reason in the past to want to discredit your expertise. Perhaps if you stopped challenging him, he would be more amenable to your strategies."

"A good king would heed good advice."

Rydril laughed softly. "Even a good king would be fed up with your antics by now."

"Ah, but a good *king would not encounter them in the first place."*

After two days of preparing the encampment for invasion, they would march out to meet Hyglen's forces of their own volition. They only had to wait for them to make the first move, which was folly of a different kind—especially given their intelligence on Hyglen's position.

Brudais shook his head, trying to clear the thoughts of impending battle. Instead, he raised his eyes and brought his gaze back to Dania in the practice fields. Her blond hair shone bright against the sun, so she was easy to pick out from a crowd—at least, for one who had unveiled her magick. He watched her as she moved fluidly through a set of drills. She had an instinctual grace which lent itself to the dance of a fight. He respected her tenacity, passion, and stubborn pride, which led her to strike a commander without a thought as to the consequences. He brought his hand up to his jaw, rubbing the spot where she had punched him. He smiled at the memory of her eyes widening in panic once she'd realized her folly. She was determined to prove herself—and not just for the sake of Loya's scheming.

There was something else in her demeanor which gave off a confidence she hadn't quite earned. If he had to guess, she wanted to prove her worth at the edge of a sword. He'd seen it many times throughout his career, but never with a woman. Some men may have laughed at the concept, but Brudais applauded it. He had known many women who thought their worth lay only in a good marriage or political ambition. Dania wanted to prove herself through hard work, dedication, and learned skill. It may have been marked as unnatural by some, but that made it still a greater feat. She may yet pave the way for other women to have the same opportunity. She was, in fact, a marvel.

Brudais felt the tent flaps shift, and Rydril emerged, squinting into the sunlight. When he spotted his friend, he walked over to him, shoving him in the shoulder. Rydril's gaze followed Brudais' across the practice field.

"Admiring the view?" he asked.

Brudais smirked. "Something like that."

"I've had some good news from home. Pallina has received the bill from Governor Gailesh. His son had nothing but praise for your training sessions. There will be a host of city guard stationed at the docks, and there's been a reward posted for members of the Gilded Gems, who are to be arrested on sight."

Thank the gods, Brudais thought. His services to Kelvs District had been fruitful.

"I'm glad I could lend my assistance—though, by the third session, I may have wanted to choke the little bastard into the dust."

"Surprised you were able to show the restraint."

"I'm a marvel."

Brudais smiled at his use of the word, looking back out onto the training grounds and searching for Dania's blond hair. She was now waiting on the sidelines as she watched one of her unit spar with Wren.

"My scouts have reported back," Rydril said, drawing Brudais' attention back to the conversation. "There has been no sign of the prince. They even rounded back to Turivaun to gather a report. The steward's scouting parties have come back without answers, so he's enlisting the help of the Turivaun governors for their aid. Hopefully, someone in the Ten Kingdoms knows something of his whereabouts."

"I have not heard from my scouts at all," Brudais said ominously, "and if yours were able to circle the forest in the same amount of time, I wonder if—"

"Who took the lead in your scouting party?"

"Captain Jaalin," Brudais replied. "He's a good man, but I chose him for his… eccentricities. I told him to do whatever it took to find Ithiador. It's likely they went straight into the forest when they reached the Hills."

Rydril stared at him. "You promised me you wouldn't do anything rash."

"I didn't," Brudais said, turning to face his friend, their eyes level. "If anything rash was done, it will be Jaalin who will answer for it."

Scowling, Rydril looked away. "You play on a knife's edge, my friend."

"Ithiador is the heir to the throne of Creet. If his life is not worth the risk, whose is?"

Rydril must have decided to ignore this sentiment, for he said, "Hyglen will be attacking soon."

"We're ready for them."

"If they do as expected."

"Morvian knows he doesn't really have a choice. What I'm worried about is Sycil."

"You think they'll intervene?"

"I'm almost certain of it, but there's no way to know *how* they will intervene."

"We'll have to leave it up to the gods, brother."

"Hope is not a strategy."

"No, but it's a good practice. Keeps the worry at bay."

As Rydril walked away, Brudais muttered, "Worry can be useful." He looked back out at the practice field, and spotted Dania in the line of waiting soldiers, holding a wooden sword in both hands in front of her. "It can be a warning."

Chapter Twenty-Six

ELDEVA

Eldeva stood in the center of the temple where a half circle of deity statues was displayed. She stared into the eyes of Jandros' statue, which had been positioned on a small dais, elevated above the rest. His statue had the look of a dragon about it, with dark wings framing his scaly body, and extended claws clutching the edges of the dais in warning. His face was the only Human feature, which was handsome, boasting a chiseled jaw, high cheek bones, and deep, fathomless eyes.

The other gods paled in comparison to Jandros' greatness. When the temple had commissioned his new statue, Eldeva had only just begun her duties in the Old Order, but she was still a princess. Her word held sway over the Solemn Priests, and she had demanded that his statue be the largest of all the gods. She argued that if they were to once again be conquerors, like their ancestors had been, they would need Jandros' help to accomplish the feat. King Ulden had approved, and Eldeva's request had been granted.

Masiya's statue stood to Jandros' right, as an ever-present reminder that the goddess of life's power juxtaposed the death god's in a potent and immediate way. The statue made her appear like a pregnant Human, but with cat-like ears, a serpentine tail, neck gills, thick legs and flowing white hair to incorporate as many of the races of the Seven Bloods as she oversaw. Humans, Crendors, Agros, Xerdins, Lowens, and Traps all owed her homage, given Masiya's bargain with Jandros for their various lifespans. The only race that shunned Masiya's loving arms was rumored to be the Fayn. They were said to have made their own deal with Jandros for their immortal lives. Just what that deal entailed, none knew.

The rest of the gods lined the half circle, which represented a crescent moon—waxing or waning, according to the spellwork being used. Havelior, the god of air, stood like a proud eagle, his wings tucked tight against his back. Esriella, goddess of the waters, curled in on herself, a sea serpent whose scaly, pointed face sprouted fins on either side. Ghavole, god of earth, was portrayed as a strong farmer, muscles rippling as he spread his seed over the barren plains. The last deity was Kronos, the god of the Balance. His frame was that of the Crendor he had created, a tawny cat in the garb of a man, but his figure was prone, lying against the cold ground, holding out a feeble paw, as if to ward off a blow. Kronos had been murdered by Jandros in the great myths, a trick that the death god had concocted to rid the world of Balance and restore Chaos—a plot that certainly seemed to have worked.

Eldeva turned her attention back to Jandros' statue, breathing in deeply as she readied herself for the ritual.

"Everything is going according to plan, Princess." Counselor Freq's weedy voice permeated her concentration, her meditations. She opened her eyes, turning to stare at him with a withering look. He had been walking towards her, then stopped in his tracks when he saw her malign expression. "Pardon me, Your Highness."

Eldeva sighed dramatically. "So long as you've procured what I asked for."

"Yes, of course, Princess. Here they are."

Freq waved his hand, signaling to a guard at the temple door to usher in a line of six slaves. They were dressed modestly in white linens. Their expressions as they walked slowly, chained together, through the temple doors made Eldeva's heart race with delight. They were terrified. As they should be.

"Ah, good. They're not covered in filth like the last time. You know Jandros likes his sacrifices kempt and comely."

Freq sent a nervous glance to the death god's statue. "Are they for the god alone? I thought the sacrifices were for more potent magick."

"That is why you are a politician, Counselor," Eldeva said smoothly, getting up from her knees and making her way towards the white altar at the back of the temple. "The gods *are* magick."

The gods had a will over magick that could cause it to intensify, should they will it. When the proper sacrifices were made, they were used up by the magicks that the spells called to increase their potency without harming the Keeper. This was an Old Order practice, which had led to the uncouth name of Reapers. However, a sacrifice could also entice a god to lend his goodwill to the spell for greater success. Human sacrifice only worked with Jandros. The other gods preferred animal sacrifices, such as goats, sheep, bulls, and the occasional horse if it had some poetry to it. The female gods were of a different breed. They delighted in riddles that were often too obscure for Human understanding and preferred games, rather than blood. Eldeva rarely had time for such nonsense. It was vastly easier to slaughter than to puzzle out what a female god wanted in that moment.

She had worked with Jandros several times and knew exactly what he most desired.

"Bring the sacrifices behind the altar and chain them to the post. Leave me the key."

Freq bowed sycophantically and relayed her instructions to the guards.

Eldeva clasped her hands together. Her pulse raced with excitement. This would be one of her most interesting and daring spells yet. She would need all of Jandros' help to summon an ether into a specific location, without allowing it to consume both armies. She prayed everything would go according to plan. If anything went wrong, her father may suspect her duplicity—or beat her regardless of it. She didn't take pleasure in envisioning either scenario. She still hadn't heard that Prince Ithiador was with the Creetian army. All she knew was that every attempt to contact him thus far had gone awry.

"It's nearly dawn. Let us begin."

She wheeled about, her dress cascading down the temple steps as she began singing. The Solemn Priests who had been waiting silently at all the temple's pillars began their ritual humming in tune with her song. When she stopped, they continued the rhythm. It pulsated against the marble as if it had a heartbeat of its own.

"I am thine instrument, O Great One! Suffuse my being with the power to vanquish my enemies. Fill me with strength and magick, and I will give thee what thou most desires: death."

Eldeva went to the slaves huddled in the corner, grasped one of their wrists and unlocked it from the chains. The girl whimpered and shook violently, but Eldeva traced her fingers along the slave's face, shushing her.

"You know, Jandros loves a fearful sacrifice."

Then she dragged the girl to the altar, flung her over the edge and grabbed the ritual knife that lay on the altar's surface.

"Fear sweetens the blood."

A scream echoed eerily along the marble walls of the temple. Eldeva pulled the blade across the girl's neck, and a spout of crimson blood erupted from the wound, dribbling over the edge of the glistening altar and pooling onto the temple floor. Eldeva's neck snapped back as Jandros' magick poured into her, her eyes a deep purple. The girl's body collapsed to the floor. A chorus of screams filled the temple, as the remaining slaves witnessed their fate.

"Bring me another."

Chapter Twenty-Seven

BRUDAIS

"I won't be made a coward!"

Dania's voice was tight, her posture stiff. Her cheeks were flushed and her eyes blazed with open defiance.

"Dania," Brudais said softly. "No one can make another person a coward. Even the king, when he learns of this, will agree that you have less training than the average Seasoned soldier, and it was wise of you to recuse yourself from battle before you were ready."

He spoke to her as if the matter had already been settled, and he saw the fire in her eyes when she realized this. As far as Brudais was concerned, the matter was settled. She was not going to battle with the rest of the men.

Dania had only been training for three more days while the camp's fortifications were made. The entire army was on edge, waiting for Hyglen's next move. The commanders had tried to calm the men's fears by reminding them that they were ready for the fight, but his whole battalion seemed ready to strike out at the simplest provocation. If Creet's next move had been up to Brudais, they would have sent out several units to attack the Hyglenian camp, causing disruption to their plans if nothing else. Waiting and watching was driving the men crazy—especially the *veritas*. Their anticipation and enthusiasm for the fight had been difficult to keep leashed. He already had to put down two rebellious units, who were keen to put Brudais' plan into action against the king's wishes. Now Dania was fighting direct orders to stand down. He wasn't sure he could take much more of this. He was about to send Morvian a strongly worded message to get on with it already.

"You are intolerable," she said, her eyes blazing.

"Because I'm right?"

"Yes!"

Brudais was smug as the heat drained out of Dania's face. He looked over at Rydril, who was sitting on the side of his bed, smirking.

"Good, now that we are agreed..." Dania let loose a frustrated snort in response. "I'll see you to my tent in mid-camp. It'll be safer than Rydril's on the outskirts."

Brudais stood, walking toward Dania and grabbing her elbow to steer her out the door, but she stood firm, moving her arm out of his reach.

"Do I need to carry you over my shoulder, or will you come willingly?" Dania narrowed her eyes. Brudais bent down to her ear. "Determination is one thing, Dania. Pigheadedness is another."

She turned to glower at him, then moved with expediency towards the tent entrance. Brudais looked back at Rydril with a smile and a shrug and followed her out of the tent.

They were silent as they made their way to Brudais' lodgings. He wondered what was going through her mind. Embarrassment? Defeat? Relief? He had a feeling that as much as she was determined not to admit it, relief was high on the list of emotions winding their way through her psyche. As much as she wanted to prove herself, she wasn't a fool. At this stage, battle was not the way to accomplish this feat. It was simply ill timing that Hyglen had decided to march when they had. Perhaps a fortnight more of constant training and she might be ready to spar with real weapons. Another few moons and perhaps she could be included in a skirmish, but battle was out of the question. They had not even gone over the basics of the shield wall. How could she hope to support her fellow soldiers if she didn't understand how to use a shield?

"Make yourself comfortable," he said, motioning to the bed once they'd entered his tent. She grunted, and he tried desperately to hide a smirk from her. "There are latrines down by the barracks, but try not to stray too far, as the Black Guard will be patrolling the encampment during the battle. If you find yourself restless, practice with the wooden training swords and sticks. Just, please refrain from using this one." He laid his hand on the hilt of Prophet, his longsword. "It is really for… sentiment rather than use."

Dania nodded, watching as his hand retracted from the blade as if it had bit him.

"How long?" she asked, her eyes catching his and holding them. She looked woeful.

Brudais shook his head, breaking eye contact. "Hard to say. Every battle is different."

A long silence followed his words, until Dania quietly asked, "Are you afraid?"

He smiled sadly. "Fear can paralyze you on the battlefield. I find that a clear mind is best. No anger, no fear; just an objective."

"And what is your objective?"

Brudais held her gaze. "To stay alive."

He watched Dania as the simplicity of this message sunk in, but she did not look away from him. A hardness set in her hazel eyes, an understanding.

"I have to go prepare my troops," he said. "If anyone finds you in here, tell them I sent you to get my lucky dagger."

"Which one is your lucky dagger?"

Brudais smiled playfully. "Any of them."

He moved closer toward her, bridging the gap between them, and he heard her breath catch in surprise, but he knelt by the chest next to her, opened it, and grabbed his Phesian dagger from within. When he stood—slowly—he was quite close to Dania, their faces mere inches from each other. Her inquisitive eyes searched his, and he took in the details of her features, the beauty of her. Once he stood at his full height, his hand moved to her upper arm, so close to touching her, but hesitant. She could have stepped away from him, making it clear she had no interest in this closeness, but she hadn't. She seemed rooted to the spot. He felt her quavering breath against his neck. She blinked, and he stepped back, his arm dropping to his side as he cleared his throat.

Staying alive. He had to remind himself of the objective that would rule him until they beat Hyglen back. He could not be distracted from that goal.

He glanced down at her, unable to help himself. Was it his imagination or did she look… disappointed?

He turned, making his way to the tent entrance.

"I'll see you in a little while," came Dania's voice from behind him. When he reached for the tent flap, his head turned to show her his uneasy smile.

"You may."

Chapter Twenty-Eight

DANIA

Dania watched as Brudais exited the tent, her lip quivering slightly. She would see him soon, she assured herself. He was a legend of Kresha. This battle with Hyglen would be nothing to him.

She stepped back, her foot knocking into the chest behind her, and she sat clumsily on top of it.

Her heart was still racing from what had just happened. She gripped the edges of the chest so hard that pain lanced up her fingertips.

What *had* just happened? She replayed the scene in her mind. They had been so close, and he had almost touched her. He had, of course, touched her before, but not in this way. Not when their faces were inches from each other, and they could feel their breath mingling. He had been about to kiss her; she was sure of it… but he had decided better of it.

Her racing heart skipped a beat, and she loosened her grip on the chest. Despite Loya's warnings about Brudais' rakish nature, he had never attempted to get close to her in that way before. He had never so much as made a disrespectful move towards her. Now that he had closed that gap, created the opportunity for so much more to happen, she could not help but feel rejected when he had not followed through.

He has a lot on his mind, she thought, trying to justify his inaction. *Battle is on the horizon. Had he not just mentioned that he needed to empty his mind during such times, focus solely on survival?* She contented herself with this explanation, hoping that it was the right one. Perhaps things would be different when he returned. Perhaps he would try again. Her stomach gave a pleasant lurch at the thought.

She tried to shake her head free of the thoughts of him, but the more she tried not to picture them on the bed behind her, him naked underneath her, her straddling his hips, her bare breasts pressed tight against his chest...

Fuck.

She stood up, beginning to pace around the tent. She was restless. Hadn't Brudais mentioned something she could do in such an instance? Her gaze spun around the room and landed on the weapons rack. She grabbed one of the wooden swords off the rack and held the hilt loosely in her right hand, examining the weapon's weight. The last few moons of training came back to her, and she chose a sequence of movements to practice. Thankfully, the tent was large enough for her to make all the required defensive movements: a series of blocks, sweeps, guards, and retreats. The motions of the light wooden sword moving through the air calmed her, and her slow, deliberate footwork allowed her heart to slow to an even rhythm.

When she had spent a full hour recounting the defensive and offensive sequences taught to her by Rydril's Blood Guard, she placed the wooden sword back in the weapon's rack, beads of sweat dripping from her forehead. When she retracted her hand, it grazed against the hilt of the sword Brudais had requested she not use. The movement caused the sword to swing back and forth lightly against the rack, drawing her attention to the runes that colored the fullness of the hilt.

She bent down, peering at the runes. She couldn't see them well upside down, and she wondered if Brudais would mind her examining it more closely. He had asked her not to *use* it, not to ignore it entirely.

Feeling slightly rebellious, she grabbed the hilt of the sword firmly, pulling it from its place on the rack, then brought it to the bed, laying it gently on one of the blankets.

The runes were in a Zethlandian dialect—something she was unfamiliar with, but she could pick out some of the words that were close to the Creetian. She had been a governess, after all. She had needed to teach Addy a number of dialects—especially those who were allied with Creet. His father had demanded it.

A sudden pain filled her chest as Adrian's face flooded her memory, his mischievous smile encouraging the best sort of impishness. She pushed the memory away, forcing her attention on the task before her.

She could make out the first runes which circled the pommel. *For my son,* they read, and her eyes widened at the realization. She backed away, still on her knees. Brudais had said the blade was sentimental. This was a sword made for the commander by Leifius. Despite the nagging feeling in her chest to put the sword back in its place and leave it alone, she knew she could not rest until the remaining runes were translated. Her curiosity heavily outweighed her sense of propriety for Brudais' privacy.

It took her another hour to decipher the runes that spread along the crossguard. She had determined that there were two juxtaposing kennings along each side. One was either "world-breaker" or "-builder"; the other was "peace-" or "anarchy-granter." By the end of the hour, she had realized that it was not one kenning or the other that was meant by the runes, but that both kennings were deliberately cryptic. It was foretelling and purposefully ambiguous in its meaning. She had heard of such things during her studies, but had never seen one written out before.

It didn't surprise her that a prophecy had been delivered about Brudais. He was a legend in his own right, not to mention the son of Leifius. But—and gooseflesh rose across the length of her body as she came to this awareness—she was now part of this legend's story.

She put the blade back in the weapons rack and lay down on the bed, her arms behind her head, her mind spinning. *What part of the story do I play?* she wondered faintly as her eyes slid closed. *Will it be as ambiguous as the runes?* Before she could reassure herself, she had fallen fast asleep.

Chapter Twenty-Nine

BRUDAIS

Ardent plunged into the nearest Hyglenian, sliding through his armpit and into his chest cavity in one fluid motion. Blood spurted from the wound in a stream as Brudais pulled the blade out, and the Hyglenian collapsed onto the ground. Without a backward glance, Brudais pushed forward, assuming that if the soldier weren't dead, his Blood Guard would deal the killing blow. As soon as he turned around, a sword was rushing past him. He held out his blade to block, shoving it back with as much force as he could muster, and the offending sword was forced backward in time for Ire to slice cleanly through the Hyglenian's neck.

"Forward and out!" he yelled, motioning towards Hyglen's forces with Ire.

The whole of the Blood Guard that surrounded him moved with fervor, screaming in rage and ecstasy. The *veritas* were in their element here, amongst the vanguard. It was their task to push through Hyglen's lines like an arrowhead through solid wood, dividing their forces in two. They were doing a damn good job of it—until they ran into a unit of Hyglenians led by their prince.

Muxvor was of giant-make. He was a legitimized bastard of King Eusol, the result of an indiscretion with a Lowen female forty years earlier. He was a head taller than any other on the battlefield, and Brudais had been keeping a close eye on his movements since the *veritas* had entered the fray. The morale of the men surrounding Muxvor was potent, but two could play at such a game. Brudais just needed to get close enough to the bastard for a real fight.

Suddenly, the sky darkened around them where bright sun and few clouds had been. Brudais looked up to the skies to see a black abyss high above them, moving slowly downward. He didn't know what it was, but he bet his life Sycillian magicks were involved. He shouted at the men to ready their shields. It wasn't likely they could beat it back with a defense, but if the magicks only affected the Creetian troops, then they would be prepared for the swift attack from Hyglen once the abyss reached them.

A howling sound filled their ears as the abyss crawled closer, and the winds picked up, the flag-bearers struggling to keep hold of their charges. A tendril of black mist flung out from the abyss, grabbing one of Brudais' soldiers around the torso and yanking him into the air, hurtling him through the blackness. He did not emerge on the other side, and his scream of terror was cut short as he disappeared behind the veil. Two more soldiers were lifted in similar fashions, but both of these were Hyglenians. Their screams were prolonged as the tendrils swung them around above the heads of the fighting vanguard, but were again cut short once their bodies disappeared behind the blackness.

The Hyglenians who were not engaged in combat cowered below the abyss, holding out their shields in desperation.

Seeing the opportunity, Brudais yelled, "Shield wall!" and his *veritas* moved in a fluid motion, linking shield with shield. "Push!" They herded the Hyglenians, pushing them back against their reserve forces. "Spearhead!" The soldiers on both ends of the shield wall retreated, still linked with their fellows, but moved into the shape of a point, driving through the Hyglenian forces, pressuring them to retreat to either side of the Creetian wall. Once they had made it to the middle of the column of Hyglen's vanguard, Brudais yelled, "Break!" The shield wall broke apart, and his *veritas* made their way through the scattered Hyglenian forces with a ferocity that would frighten most men. Their tongues lolled from their mouths, eyes bulging in challenge, daring the Hyglenians to move against them. To their credit, some did. Other, smarter ones ran for their lives in the face of such animosity.

The abyss that had so frightened them began to dissipate as the Creetian forces charged. The blackness retreated slowly, and the sun peered out from behind it until it was no more than a passing dark cloud.

"Muxvor! Muxvor!"

Hyglen's chant brought Brudais' gaze back down to the battle and issued a challenge to Brudais son of Leifius. He moved through the throng of soldiers, cutting down Hyglenians in his path, a few of his Blood Guard at his back, as he made his way towards the large figure of Muxvor at the other end of the battlefield.

Brudais pointed Ire towards the Hyglenian prince. "Do you want me to kill the bastard?!" Brudais shouted over the din, and the *veritas* who heard him cheered in response. Captain Yurik, who was on Brudais' left side, shouted, "Brudais! Brudais!" The whole of the *veritas* caught on quickly, drowning out the Hyglenian chants for their prince.

Brudais smiled coldly, swinging Ardent in an arc before him, cutting down a brave but stupid Hyglenian. The respective vanguards seemed to part when Brudais made it within a few strides of the half-giant, deliberately vacating the space. Muxvor had seen Brudais' ascent, and the moment that the crowd cleared, he swung his longsword in his enemy's direction, the broad sweep missing Brudais by a hair. Brudais smirked, dodging another powerful blow, clambering over a few dead soldiers to get closer to the prince.

Brudais held out both his short swords to each side in challenge. Muxvor gave a howl of rage, veins popping out of his neck, and moved to attack. Brudais lunged forward and down, sliding under the giant's longsword and appearing at his back, turning nimbly and slashing Ardent across Muxvor's spine. The blow didn't hit as it should have, but it made a thin slice along Muxvor's lower back. The giant's hand reached behind him, and he turned, sweeping his longsword in the other hand. It might have had the power to carve Brudais clean in half at the waist if he had not anticipated the clumsy response and moved back several feet to avoid it. When the longsword moved back again, Ardent and Ire trapped it between them, and in one swift movement, Brudais plunged the offending sword into a nearby corpse. Releasing it, he moved to Muxvor's unguarded left side and plunged Ardent into the giant's boot. His howl was pained this time, and the Hyglenian response was immediate—the once-clear circle filled with Hyglenian soldiers, and the *veritas* who had been holding back at the other end charged to meet them. The throng divided Brudais from his enemy and he was carried off while Muxvor retreated.

Damn it!

Yurik's voice pounded in his ear. "Commander, we've been called away to the east! Ailyus' Seasoned are being torn apart!"

Brudais watched Muxvor's head disappear from view, and he cursed viciously. "Fine! Disengage a quarter force to assist Aiylus. We have to hold this area or Hyglen will attack the camp from the north."

Nodding, Yurik ran to deliver the message to the *veritas* closest to Rydril's forces.

Brudais spun around, holding Ire in a high guard and Ardent in a low guard, but his enemy turned out to be Rydril.

"Fuck, brother, I could have killed you," he said, breathing hard.

"No, you wouldn't have," said Rydril, his face grim. Brudais looked down to see the knife pointed at his ribs. "I've sent half my Seasoned to assist Aiylus."

"And I a quarter of my *veritas*."

"You knew this would happen," Rydril said darkly. "We should have called in a cavalry."

"Aye," he responded, taking no comfort from the fact that he had been right. "I had a hunch."

Rydril clasped his shoulder with his left hand, moving back through the throng of *veritas* to his battalion.

Brudais' eyes darkened with bloodlust as he moved back through the vanguard, barking orders at his Blood Guard. He thought it would be impossible for his mind to drift in the thick of battle, but he found himself thinking about Dania more than once. *Stay alive,* he reminded himself irritably, but another emotion kept surfacing that seemed more important, more urgent—Dania's pleading hazel eyes and her words, *I'll see you in a little while.* It was lucky for him that those two objectives coincided.

Brudais carefully removed his cuirass, grunting in pain as the wound in his armpit re-opened.

"I'm surprised that you of all people are acting shy about taking your clothes off in front of a woman."

Rydril's commentary was not helping with the pain. He was sitting on the side of Rydril's bed instead of his own for a very particular reason, and Rydril didn't need to know that he and Dania had nearly kissed before the battle—mostly, because he didn't need Rydril's commentary on *that,* and he didn't want to see the look of intrigue on his best friend's face when he asked why he didn't follow through.

"I'm not shy. I'm simply addressing her modesty," he lied.

"How do you know she's modest?"

Brudais' eyes narrowed. "You are a meddling old man, you know that?"

Rydril's laughter bounced off the walls of the tent. "Meddling, not concerned?"

"There's nothing for you to be concerned about."

Almost as if in direct defiance, the memory of Dania's lips came into focus in Brudais' mind. He thought of what he would have done, had he not been so preoccupied; he would have grabbed the back of her neck and kissed her, their lips locking passionately and their bodies moving closer together, filling the gap between them. Heat flushed across his torso and face. Was it passion or shame? Now that Brudais had removed his tunic, Rydril was privy to at least the idea of his intimate thoughts.

"Clearly," his friend said, a smirk forming on his lips. "So, you expect me to believe that you weren't thinking about her during the battle?"

"No," Brudais lied again, placing a hand over his wound. "I thought about her before."

"And you're thinking about her now. She must have some skill to have ensnared you so quickly."

Brudais scowled at Rydril from across the tent, offended. "You go too far."

Rydril raised his hands, then peered at Brudais questioningly. "So, you haven't bedded her?"

"Meddling. Old. Man," Brudais said through clenched teeth, in time with loosening his greave strings.

The smile was evident in Rydril's voice. "So, you thought about her before and after the battle. Were you thinking about her at all while you and Muxvor were pummeling each other?"

Brudais took off his greaves one at a time and started on his sandals. "I was thinking about survival. That's all."

He slipped off his sandals and tossed them aside. It wasn't a complete lie.

"Good," said Rydril, nodding slightly. "At least she hasn't bewitched you entirely."

"Bewitched?" Brudais rounded on him. "What the fuck does that mean?"

"It means that we need our legend at his strongest if we're to win this war. If they're distracted, even the best legends can fall. I'm still not certain females in war lend to the efficacy of it. I have yet to be proved wrong."

"Did I fight well today?"

Rydril looked at Brudais, puzzled. He had never asked his friend that before.

"Yes, of course."

"Better than usual?"

"Well, you took on Muxvor and lived, so I count that as an improvement on most men."

Brudais nodded with a satisfied expression. "The entire battle, I was thinking about survival. I was thinking about what it would mean to die never having kissed her."

He looked up in time to see Rydril's eyes widen in shock.

"She's not a distraction, brother," Brudais said, grabbing a clean tunic from the bedside and lifting it carefully over his head. He grabbed his armour from the floor and as he passed Rydril, he leaned down, so they were eye to eye. "She's a reason."

He walked out of Rydril's tent, leaving his friend behind, mouth still agape.

Chapter Thirty

ELDEVA

Mayora's hands shook slightly. She clasped them together in an attempt to stop their violent tremors, but it only made them shake in unison.

"Don't fear for me, sister," Eldeva said, brushing her long black hair behind her shoulder.

"I'm concerned," she replied, her voice relaying none of the tremors that her hands failed to hide.

"Father will do as Father always does. His wrath doesn't concern me."

"What does?"

Eldeva couldn't suppress the shiver that spread down the length of her spine. Her spell had failed. The ether had opened for mere moments before it closed again, dissolving into a menacing cloud. The earthquake she had summoned had been no more than a weak tremor under the soldiers' feet. She didn't lie; she was not afraid of what her father's reaction to the failure would be. She was more afraid of why the spell had failed in the first place. Her fear was for the gods' wrath.

"Perhaps Jandros was not pleased with my sacrifices."

"The sacrifices were flawless," said Mayora quietly. "I saw to their preparation myself." No wonder they had looked so pristine. "Maybe Jandros is not pleased with something else... something more... intimate."

Eldeva shot a look at Mayora, who blanched. "You mean to say that my affair with a foreigner has impeded my magickal connection to the gods?"

Mayora looked down at her trembling hands. "I just wonder... Jandros is not favored in Creet. He is seen as a demon rather than a rightful god, whereas Krashkin sacrifices to Jandros regularly, as is his due."

"Jandros couldn't care less about my choice of suitors." But even Eldeva didn't believe her own words. She considered whether her feelings for Ithiador were worth the alleged consequences of such a union. She could live without love, but without magick? She would not dream of it.

Mayora glanced up, studying her sister's face.

"Perhaps you need be more concerned with the present, sister. Our father will not be pleased with the outcome of this battle. You've endangered our relationship with Hyglen."

"He's doing that already by selling me off to Krashkin."

"Yes, but that was intentional; this was accidental. It's a matter of pride for him. He cannot abide being embarrassed. You know what happened to our mother."

An image of Queen Hysinia at the bottom of a snake pit entered Eldeva's mind. Her screams echoed, increasing in volume, as guards held the princesses in place. They had watched their mother being bitten repeatedly, cobras and rattlers pumping her with venom, her look of terror as she gazed up at them one last time, holding out her hand… The princesses' tears wet the hot sand. Her father's voice rang resolutely against the chirping of the cicadas: "I will only tolerate a wife who produces an heir. You will do well to remember this. Your future husbands may not be as merciful as I in this regard."

Mercy, she had thought, watching her mother's corpse twitch as the snakes continued to lash out, piercing the dead flesh with their fangs.

A single tear slid down Eldeva's cheek.

Suddenly, there was a loud knock at the solar doors. Mayora jumped, her hands grasping the sides of the chaise.

"Come," Eldeva said, turning her face away from the door and wiping at her cheek furiously.

The doors burst open, and King Ulden strode through them. Mayora scrambled to her feet, but Eldeva took her time, slowly rising from her chaise with deliberate poise, like a king cobra preparing to strike.

"Leave us," the king said harshly, as he spared a cursory glance at Mayora.

She looked back at Eldeva, who nodded once, holding out her hand. Mayora's shaking hand grasped hers for a moment before the princess fled from the room, her skirts trailing noisily across the marble floor.

Ulden sat on the chaise that Mayora had vacated, making himself comfortable. Eldeva remained standing, waiting for her opponent to lash out.

"So, my daughter claims she can summon the darkest magicks to aid our allies in war, proclaiming her powers to the council and in front of foreign dignitaries, and what does she do? My beautiful, foolish daughter summons the darkness for mere minutes before it is no more than a passing rain cloud." He leaned back, his face turning savage. "Tell me how I am to explain this to Hyglen. They were assured victory. It was a certainty."

"Victory is never certain, Father. The gods did not favor us in our endeavors."

"You made the damn sacrifices. Your magicks should have been appeased. What more is required?"

Eldeva rolled her eyes at the naivety of the question. It took research, skill, energy, meticulous preparation, ritual, and a blessed blade, but she wasn't about to contradict him when he was in such a mood. The darkness in his eyes told her all she needed to know about how this conversation would end.

"Jandros may waver in his favor. I cannot claim to know what the gods intend. Perhaps it is with Creet that Jandros has thrown his lot, and I selected the wrong god to curry favor. Not even with the best preparations could I have anticipated such a thing."

"Or perhaps... you're just not as great of a sorceress as you claim."

Eldeva smiled, returning to her seat and crossing her legs. Rage blistered at the corners of her resolve, but she would not let him know that he had wounded her. "Your words cut deep, Father—or they would, if I had not proved just how powerful a sorceress I am. Perhaps the reason Jandros did not favor us was that you refuse to pay him his due homage, and instead make sacrifices to Hevalior. The god of air may help us conjure up a mighty wind, but I don't see how that will help crush our enemies without killing our allies in the process."

"I don't condone the sacrifices you made—even slaves have their uses—but I allowed you to perform the ritual for the sake of victory. A good sorceress learns to work with the tools she's given."

Eldeva could not conceal her surprise. Had the king of Sycil just referred to the gods as 'tools'? She knew he didn't have much respect for religion, but her father's blasphemy was going to rain down consequences, and she couldn't be in the line of fire when they appeared.

"You had best leave me to my devices, Father. I need to prepare for my next spell."

Ulden's knuckles reddened as he gripped the arm of the couch. "What am I to tell Hyglen?"

Eldeva sneered, "Perhaps that they should choose their allies more carefully, because some don't even recognize their folly when they anger the gods."

Ulden's eyes were dark as the abyss. Without warning, he sprang from the chaise and covered Eldeva's mouth with one hand before she could utter a curse.

She could have done without the slight. She would pay for that insolence.

Chapter Thirty-One

Loya

High Hall was an imposing structure nestled in the quiet streets of Quies District. The main chamber was where the governors of Turivaun met to discuss the affairs of the city. Its high ceiling and the windows that circled the dome at the top poured down bright sunlight from above, while the cool stone walls produced a voluminous effect on any who rose their voice to be heard.

Currently, Steward Venhil was speaking, his rasping voice carrying throughout the chamber. There was a half-circle of governors' seats, and the steward sat in the middle with Commander Okriad while they recounted their tidings from the Jaguar Hills. Prince Ithiador was the topic of discussion, as he so often was since his disappearance. Losing an heir to the throne was... problematic, at best—disastrous, at worst.

Venhil's voice rose throughout the chamber. "We have sent scouting parties through the woods near the borders, but no trace of him has been found. We will need to keep this information quiet until we know more to tell the king."

Loya sat up in her seat. "Pardon, Steward Venhil," she said, her voice carrying melodiously across the chamber. "Do I take it that your intention is to hide this from the king and the Creetian people? Why are you sharing your findings—or rather your *lack* of findings—with us?"

Venhil shifted uncomfortably in his chair. "We need more resources," he rasped, his expression a little hostile. "We understand that the Turivaun governors have a lot of… pull… in foreign circles."

"I see," she replied, "and we're more discreet than your military operations, I suppose."

Venhil glowered. "Yes, Lady-Governor."

It may not have been a secret in the city that Ithiador had gone missing, but there were still certain aspects of the search for the prince that could have been kept from the people's ears. Venhil had authorized the use of extreme force against the Hillpeople to ascertain the prince's whereabouts, but he did not foresee the backlash this would create. Before his disappearance, Ithiador had sent Tarison a drafted bill which gave the Hillpeople immunity to practice spellcraft without persecution or additional taxation. Tarison had signed the bill before departing for Hyglen in the hopes that this rare concession would provide the crown with a legal method for implementing magickal support for the war efforts.

In Venhil's enthusiasm to find the lost prince, he had essentially stripped all hopes that Creet would benefit from the bill. The Hillpeople had suffered injustices at the hands of the royal guard—injustices that Loya preferred to be kept in the dark about. Regardless of the specifics, the Hillpeople were no longer willing to support Creet in any way, and were becoming once again increasingly hostile towards the rest of the country. Ithiador had been their sole protector and advocate against the impending consequences from the crown. His disappearance left them vulnerable to the steward's unorthodox methods and any future support against their unwelcome Creetian rule.

The Jaguar Hills had been contested land for centuries, and Sycil was chomping at the bit to seize it from Creetian control. The Hillpeople's animosity towards Creet's crown would make it that much easier for them to lay down arms were Sycil to invade, which was becoming more of a possibility now that the Creetian army was on the other side of the Fayn Forest.

Loya glanced at her colleagues one by one. Ithiador was not just an important figurehead, but the key to Loya's plans to oust Tarison upon his return to the capital. If Ithiador were not here when that eventuality occurred, it would be much more difficult to instigate a coup.

Her eyes fell on Governor Gailesh who noticed her keen stare and sat up, surprised.

Loya drew her glance back to Venhil and said, "I will employ all my resources in Phesius along the borders of the Fayn to notify us if they espy the prince, but Lord-Governor Gailesh, don't you have a troupe of hunters in your employ? You're always regaling us with tales of their exploits. Would they not entertain the idea of searching within the forest if the purse were enticing enough?"

Governor Gailesh coughed, tugging at the collar of his robes. "They are friends of my son's, Loya," he said, a quiet warning.

"There is risk, surely," Loya replied, "but I'm certain we could make the reward handsome enough, I dare say. This is the heir to the throne. You would agree, of course, that finding him is paramount to the safety and security of the realm."

Loya looked pointedly at Steward Venhil. He nodded in Governor Gailesh's direction and said, "The purse would be supplied by the crown, Lord-Governor."

Gailesh mumbled something indistinguishable, but nodded his assent.

"Excellent," Loya said enthusiastically. "The information will be supplied in two days' time, after which these hunters can begin the journey to the Jaguar Hills and supply us with regular reports."

The meeting was adjourned, and the governors, steward and commander all stood and began moving towards the doors. Loya glanced across the room at Governor Gailesh, whose face was red and cheeks were puffed in a disgruntled fashion. When her gaze landed on Governor Nial, he quickly looked away, but she had caught his defiant expression before it passed into a blank mask.

She could sense the tide turning in this room. She considered the many ways in which she would need to ensure that the governors could be made pliant when the time came for her to unfold her plans. She'd need to make it theatrical, but perhaps not so... permanent as the disappearances of Parliament had been. Venhil would need to be dealt with, as well, but his fate could wait. Her colleagues needed to be put to heel, and she was nearly ready to set them beneath her boot.

Chapter Thirty-Two

Morvian

The task you've accepted,
You will rue it in the end;
But snakes have no shame,
Only fangs.

Morvian's eyes ran across the parchment again, hoping that reading the message a fifth time would provide more meaning than the first four attempts.

Not only had the Fayn taken his voice—his best tool with which to lead and his best defense against the naïve opinions of his king—but now they were taunting him with cryptic riddles. The last had come from a page no more than ten years old. When he had realized from where the message had originated, he tried to find the page to question him on how the Fayn had delivered it, but he had never seen the boy again. This new message had come with no messenger, but had been left on top of his desk while he had been out of his office.

Morvian no longer wished to try deciphering the riddles, the 'Secrets of the Wood,' which the Fayn had been so gracious to share with him. Perhaps they imagined they were being helpful in posing such obscurities, but they only made Morvian seethe with rage at their audacity to continue interfering.

The real puzzle that Morvian had thus far failed to piece together was who the "Agent of Change" was, the one he was meant to stop.

Change does not mind the seeker's path.
The depth of its desires finds purchase in the legend's mirror.
Three lures there are to quell the tyrant, just enough for blood to sing.

Goosebumps rose across the flesh of Morvian's forearms as he remembered the sinister voice of the Queen of the Fayn.

Three lures. Quelling the tyrant. An agent of change. The legend's mirror.

It was infuriating.

The only thing Morvian was certain of was that he was the 'seeker,' for his silence would keep him on his path, but by all the gods dead and alive, what possible benefit could his silence grant him in any way?

There was a knock on his office door.

He rolled his eyes, not deigning to move from the seat behind his desk. Everyone in the castle should have known by now that Morvian could not grant them entrance.

The door opened, and Sergeant Oren entered, his hands behind his back.

"It's a polite gesture, regardless, Commander," he said, the smallest of grins on his lips.

Morvian grunted in response. Whenever Oren was within the commander's range of hearing, their magickal mind link was activated. He had likely heard everything Morvian had been thinking for the past few minutes.

"Another message," he said carefully, his grin fading as he looked down at the piece of worn parchment in Morvian's hands.

Not a welcome one, I assure you, Morvian thought.

Oren nodded, letting him know that he was no longer suspicious of Morvian's involvement—only of the contents and originators of the messages themselves.

The sergeant sat in the armchair on the other side of Morvian's desk. His shoulder-length hair was dark brown, matching his stubble. He reminded the commander of his nephew: young, slightly arrogant, but with an ego that did not present problems—only solutions. He was resourceful, cunning. Oren's bright blue eyes stared across the desk at him, the only part of his appearance that stood out. Hyglenians rarely had such distinctive eyes.

"Do you suppose, Commander," Oren said, gracefully ignoring Morvian assessment of him, "that the Fayn call you a 'seeker' for a reason? Perhaps they expect you to find something for them."

Whether they do or not, I am not their puppet.

"No," Oren said thoughtfully, "but perhaps once you discover what it is they expect you to find, you'll find the other answers you seek."

A shrewd assessment. And the outcome of uncovering the Fayn's intentions?

Oren shrugged. "You would know better than I how that would aid your current designs."

The battle had not gone according to plan, with Sycil's magicks failing utterly. There were rumors that Sycil would be allying with Krashkin. With this latest catastrophe, they should have been assured victory; instead, they were left to believe that Sycil's involvement in the war with Creet was superficial at best. Hyglen could not afford a war with Krashkin—especially one aided by Sycillian magicks. Their allies were turning into enemies all around them. Their involvement in Creetian politics had seemed to be a worthy cause at the time, but now it seemed utter folly.

"You could not have known," Oren reassured him.

Morvian cast him a withering look. He did not need a lowly sergeant granting him leniency for his mistakes. Oren's gaze fell to the floor.

It was Morvian who had assured King Eusol that this war would come to a swift and satisfying conclusion, and their coffers would be doubled for their troubles. It had now become an infinitely more complex endeavor, and he knew himself to be a fool for expecting he could trust in a victorious outcome.

Tell the captains to reconvene and advise me of their next plans of attack. I want a constant watch on the Creetian camp from every direction, and keep a unit of scouts on the northern borders of the forest. Cut off any communication going back to Turivaun. If we can keep their army isolated, they'll run out of supplies given enough time. If all else fails, we will at least send them home starving.

Oren nodded curtly, stood from his seat, and made for the door.

And Oren…

The sergeant turned back, watching Morvian's face carefully.

I am not their puppet.

"No, Commander," he said, his face hard, "but that doesn't mean they aren't using you."

When Oren had closed the door behind him, Morvian pounded his fist on the desk, causing a bottle of ink to tumble over, spilling across the parchment he held. His mouth formed a curse, but no sound escaped him.

CHAPTER THIRTY-THREE

DANIA

Dania heard the rustling tent flaps and shot up from her place on the bed, a knife held in her right hand. When she watched Brudais appear in the entrance, she lowered the knife to the bedsheets, releasing the hilt.

His expression was pleasantly amused, but as she took in his full frame, she saw the cuts and bruises coloring the skin of his arms; there were many. He had the belt of the harness that held Ardent and Ire in one hand and his uniform in the other.

She swung her legs off the bed and stood facing him.

Brudais placed the harness alongside the weapons rack.

"Are you all right?" he asked, his voice gentle.

"Am I?" she replied, her incredulity showing plainly on her face. "What of you?"

"I'll be fine." Brudais twisted his shoulder, placing his hand to the joint and grimacing in pain. "Just a little sore."

The commander placed his cuirass against the chest at the end of the bed, still rubbing his shoulder joint.

"It took longer than I expected," she said quietly.

"Thousands of men killing each other usually takes some time."

Dania motioned for him to sit on the side of the bed, and he did so stiffly. She rounded the bed, asking, "Were those cuts cleaned?"

"Yes." He said it gently enough, but she heard the command in it. *Back off, Dania.*

"Perhaps you should rest while you can. I can fend for myself."

Brudais looked mildly surprised and opened his mouth to say something. He shut it quickly, perhaps thinking better of it. After a moment, he said, "Where would you go?"

"I could get us something to eat."

He nodded, falling back onto the bed, closing his eyes, and placing his hands over his stomach. Dania turned away as a smile lit her face. He must have been exhausted to have trusted her so fully. She had anticipated a much more vehement argument.

Recalling her last sojourn through mid-camp, she turned a few corners before rediscovering the location of the mess tent. An army of cooks were serving double portions to weary and wounded soldiers. Double rations had been ordered upon the soldiers' return to camp to ensure that they kept up their strength.

Dania found the end of the line of grumbling infantrymen, who looked like they were ready to fall to the ground and sleep for a fortnight. During her stay in line, there were a few tussles, and Dania expected to be caught in the middle of a scrap, but they were quickly settled with a few curses. After such a long battle, no one was willing to put up much of a fight.

When she reached the front of the line after a half-turn, she motioned to one of the cooks, who leaned in to hear her. The tent had been eerily quiet, so even hushed words could be heard widely.

"I need a meal for Commander Brudais," she said.

The main cook a few stations down overheard her words and abandoned his cook pot, moving to the back of the tent. When he reappeared, he was carrying a large, metal plate. It was filled with brightly-colored vegetables, heaps of rice, and a beef roast the size of her fist. Silver utensils were wedged beneath the hunk of meat. She could be killed for this meal on her way to delivering it. The cook had his back to the rest of the mess tent, handing her the plate carefully, but the smell of the roast was wafting over the latent scents of the rice and potatoes that the infantry were being served. Dania turned to face a few of the men behind her who were giving her murderous glances.

"For Commander Brudais," the cook said to them sternly, then turned away.

"Wait," she implored, holding the commander's plate tightly with both hands. The cook turned. "And for me?"

The cook glared back at her, but grabbed a nearby wooden bowl with a scoop of bland rice and ladled a cup of pleasant-smelling broth over it. When he held it out to her, she placed it on top of the commander's food and walked away as quickly as she could manage without dropping both meals in the dirt.

Once she found her way back to the commander's tent, she went to move the tent flap aside, but heard voices from within and stopped.

"Commander, the war council has been called. You can't ignore a summons, and why would you want to?"

"I'm not ignoring it; I'm delaying my departure. Tell the king I will be there presently."

"Sir, what is more pressing than our next move?"

Brudais sighed heavily. "A promise. Now, go inform the king."

Captain Yurik stepped out of the tent, eyeing Dania and the plate of food she bore warily for a moment before walking off in the direction of the king's tent.

Dania entered carefully, holding out the plate to Brudais. He was standing next to the wooden table, looking absentmindedly across the tent. He took the plate and placed it on the table, sitting down and cutting his roast in half. He slid one of the halves into Dania's bowl. Her eyes widened and she stood frozen as he sat and began tearing into the remaining portion on his plate. After a moment, he must have realized she wasn't eating, because he looked up and motioned for her to sit in the chair opposite him.

"You may not have fought but you still need to eat."

She spooned a mouthful of wet rice into her mouth, thinking it not half-bad. She had no idea what she was to do with the roast. It looked like it might fall apart if she tried to use her spoon, but she wasn't about to embarrass herself in front of Commander Brudais by picking at it with her fingers. She may have been a soldier, but she wasn't an animal.

Brudais' eyes were distant, locked on the table's wooden surface. "We have to present you before the king. Right now."

Dania choked on a mouthful of rice, sputtering.

"This is the best way to ensure that he grants leniency. If you hide for much longer, it will be suspicious that you were not found."

She supposed he was right, although she desperately wished he weren't. Standing before the king privately was one embarrassment she could face, but before an entire war council? The shame of the thought sent redness to color her cheeks.

"This is the best way. Please believe me. The more witnesses Tarison has, the better it will be for you."

Dania swallowed hard, tasting the salty broth against her tongue. "I believe you," she said warily, "but that doesn't mean I have to like it."

Brudais didn't shift his gaze from the table, but his pensive expression turned into a small smile.

Chapter Thirty-Four

BRUDAIS

Brudais watched Dania as she walked before him towards the king's tent in mid-camp. His gaze took in her long blond hair, gently flowing in the light breeze, and then moved lower, to the curves of her waist. He watched the leather segments of her uniform's skirt swaying against the bare backs of her thighs. He shook his head, bringing his gaze back up to her hair.

He knew that this situation was less than ideal, but he stood by his decision. The more witnesses, the better off she would be. His jaw tightened at the thought of all the males at the war council ogling her, like he had just been doing. He hoped his pheromones alone would indicate his claim to her, but he doubted it. *Claim to her?* he thought to himself in surprise. When had Dania become a thing to be claimed? He had never imagined himself as a jealous man before now—least of all over a female.

Out of the corner of his eye, he spotted Dania catching his wandering eye. She smiled slyly and turned back to the path ahead. Brudais hoped she couldn't read his thoughts, but if she couldn't, and his admiration had made her smile, then he was hopeful that something could grow from this soil.

"Remember, I found you in one of the supply caches. You were dressed in uniform, you had your own sword, and you hid yourself away, spying on training sessions."

She slackened her pace so that they were walking side by side. "Spying?"

"You couldn't have trained with the Seasoned without being found out."

Dania furrowed her brow. "And when they test my sword skills?"

Brudais, smirking, didn't respond until she whacked him across the shoulder.

"I'm sure they'll find them satisfactory," he said, his grin widening, "but I doubt they'll test you. They will question you to understand why you're here."

"And if I tell them the truth?"

"The king will probably find your presence here his own fault. Loya's tendency to take him at his word has surprised him before, and his infatuation with the governor may save you from any punishment. However, unless you leave out the magick use, you will be arrested." They neared the entrance to the king's tent and Brudais lowered his voice. "Don't let that slip."

They passed by the Black Guard who were standing watch on either side of the entrance. They were menacing-looking figures in black leather uniform, their sword hands placed tensely on the hilts at their sides as Brudais and Dania approached.

"You're late, Commander," one of them said offhandedly. "You best hurry if you don't wish to incur the same wrath as before."

Brudais bit his cheek to keep from replying, moving swiftly through the tent's entrance.

Dania turned to him with one eyebrow raised. "What did he mean?"

"I was thrown out of the throne room this Spring… for ridiculing the king."

Dania's eyes widened. "To his face?" she asked.

Brudais shrugged, unconcerned, then caught her arm before she could move any farther into the tent. They were in a kind of antechamber between the king's makeshift receiving room and the entrance. They were alone, but beyond this chamber, he could see two Black Guard at the receiving room entrance from within.

Bending down to whisper in her ear, he said, "I'm going to reveal your magick to all. You'll be visible the instant I utter this counter-spell. Are you ready?"

She turned her head, and their faces were mere inches from each other. Brudais stared into her eyes; she looked nervous, but determined not to be.

"*Quel vyn foreth veya rus.*"

He waited a moment for the spell to break, watching her eyes carefully, as the last remnants of her purple irises faded away to reveal her true hazel.

Grabbing her arm by the bicep, he hauled her through the receiving room entrance.

"Look who I happened upon in our supply tent," he said casually, moving past the Black Guard, dragging Dania with him. He felt her initial resistance, the light tugging against his grip. He released her and pushed her gently with one hand deeper into the tent.

Twenty pairs of eyes shifted to the entrance, and upon taking in Dania's form, they all widened in shock. Even Rydril—who had been privy to their schemes—was surprised to see that Brudais had decided to speed up the process. Brudais' gaze shifted from commanders to captains to Black Guard, finally settling on the king. Tarison was peering at Dania, his eyes calculating.

"Who is she?" Tarison asked, his voice devoid of emotion.

"Let her tell you herself," Brudais said, pushing her forward to stand before the king, who was sitting idly on his blackthorn throne. He watched in amusement as she began to curtsey, then switched to a kneel and head bow, arms out in reverence. Tarison's eyebrows drew together in confusion at this display.

"What is your name?"

"Dania, daughter of Riven the Black."

Brudais was surprised to see an incredulous expression on his king's face for an instant before a mask of indifference swept across his features to hide it.

"And what is your business in the encampment, Dania?"

Dania straightened her posture and stood at attention.

"I am here on behalf of Lady-Governor Loya of Drens," she said confidently. "She has sent me to follow the troops and prove my worth in battle, so that Your Majesty might reconsider her proposal to introduce women into the military."

Angry murmurs erupted throughout the room. Tarison raised a hand to silence them. "And why is it that you were chosen by Loya to represent the females of Creet?"

"I have taken the place of my sickly brother in Commander Rydril's Seasoned ranks. I believe Governor Loya's exact words were, 'You have the balls it'll take to prove yourself to the men in charge.'"

Dania's face reddened slightly, contrasting her point, as Tarison's eyebrows rose at her words, but she stood firm. Brudais could barely contain a grin.

There was a long moment of silence following these words until Tarison broke it.

"Loya may have made you believe your determination was enough to assuage our fears, but she is cunning enough to discover the whereabouts of Grandis' last living kin."

Shock swept across the tent again and an eerie silence followed. Brudais was not immune. Could that really be true? Dania—daughter of Grandis the Great? He looked over at her. Dania's lips had parted in astonishment, her eyes searching the king's for any sign of amusement or jest.

"Your father never told you?" asked the king. Dania shook her head slowly in disbelief. "'Riven' means 'peace' in the Old Tongue. King Reynold, my father, gave Grandis sanctuary after he was exiled from Krashkin. Regent Cavison knew of his settlement and new name, but he refused to divulge it to us before his death. We only ever knew that he went by the moniker the 'Black Peace.'"

Cavison had been right not to divulge such information, as having it meant an easy alliance with Krashkin and the certainty of war in the east. The inevitability of the confrontation with Hyglen had simmered for the last two decades, but Cavison had no desire to speed up fate—unlike his nephew.

Dania's face slid into a carefully calculated mask. Brudais wondered whether she finally understood the implications of saving her brother. She was the final spoke in a complex wheel, and she had been played by Loya into believing she was no one. Loya was sly to have taken Brudais' advice to present her to the king, but what she hadn't imagined was that instead of aiding her proposal for female inclusion, the king would be more likely to use her for his own political gain. Brudais clenched his fists at the thought of what Tarison could gain from Dania's cooperation.

"Considering your lineage, I am tempted to indulge Loya's fancies and allow you to be trained in combat. I still have my doubts that women can fight sufficiently."

"That is what I am here to allay, Your Majesty."

Tarison eyed her skeptically. "Have you been trained with weapons?"

"No, Your Majesty. Though I have watched the Seasoned training sessions and have been practicing on my own."

"It's a wonder to me that a beauty like you could have been overlooked—even were you using magick."

Brudais stiffened, waiting for Dania to give something away, but she held fast and didn't even twitch a muscle. To change the subject quickly, Brudais said, "She wasn't overlooked by everyone."

Tarison glanced at him with a venomous look. Brudais smiled back at him innocently.

"How did you come across her, Brudais, when she's remained hidden for so long?"

"Vanity," Brudais said. Dania turned her head to look at him, incredulous, and he smiled back at her wickedly. "She stole a uniform, thinking she could hide her gender behind conformity. She was mistaken."

Dania glowered at him, then turned back to the king. "A formality we did not anticipate."

Brudais realized what Dania was doing. Her feigned disdain for Brudais was for the king's benefit, to get on his good side. A shared dispassion for Brudais was one of the easiest ways into the king's good graces. At least, he hoped that was what she was doing. His throat went dry at the possibility that her disdain was genuine.

"Well, we are glad you have presented yourself—despite your misguided beginnings. We will outfit you with quarters, a privy, and a sword—"

"She already has a sword," said Brudais at the same time Dania pronounced, "I already have a sword."

Again, Dania turned her head to look at Brudais, but behind her annoyed expression, she failed to conceal the smallest of grins. When she turned back around to the king, they began speaking of further arrangements for her in the encampment, but Brudais had stopped listening. He pictured that grin on her lips, the realization of her intent, and the minutiae of her mind games, and a warm feeling filled his chest. He didn't know what it was like to fall in love, but he was fairly certain he just had.

BOOK III

THE WAX SEAL

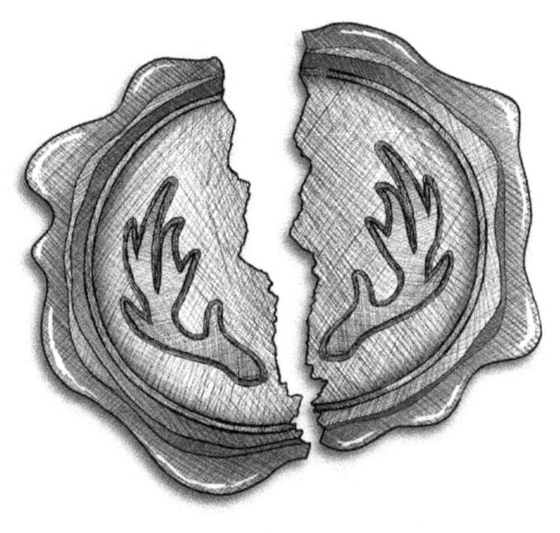

Chapter Thirty-Five

Morvian

Pexix's face faded from the bowl of water as Morvian stared down into it, wishing that what he had just heard was a lie.

Grandis the Great's only daughter… in Creetian hands.

Morvian grabbed the bowl, hurling it across the room. Water exploded from the raining ceramic shards, spraying Morvian and Oren lightly across their faces with the backlash and dripping down the wall. Oren stepped back a few paces, uncertain whether he was still welcome to witness the commander's fury.

Morvian stood there, breathing heavily for a moment, before he turned to his Mouth.

King Tarison will try to use this girl for political advantage. As none of us are aware of Krashkin's full strength, he could easily turn and offer the girl to them, creating an alliance against us.

Oren contemplated whether he should respond, but his curiosity won out over his caution. "Why is this girl so important to Krashkin, sir?"

Morvian sighed, exasperated. Did no one take history into account any longer? *Krashkin's involvement in this war will rest solely on Tarison's willingness to unveil her. She is the daughter of Grandis the Great—Krashkin's beloved hero of the Crescent Moon Wars. He was favored above all others as their legend and favorite son. You recall he was banished?*

Oren's frown deepened. "I'm sorry, sir, but my education was not that thorough."

Morvian placed his hand on his forehead, his thumb rubbing his right temple. *Hyglen was at the height of the eastern power in that age. King Eusol's father told Krashkin to exile Grandis. They had to, or else they would face the wrath of Hyglen—but they have been bitter about the exchange ever since and have shunned our attempts to reconcile. If they learned that Creet had been harboring their beloved champion and his family these many decades, they might pick up the sword again.*

"But the girl herself… why is she of any consequence?"

Blood, Oren, Morvian thought. *The blood of a legend tied to the Krashkin royal line. I can smell the scent of that lust a hundred leagues away on a light breeze. They considered marrying Princess Izal to Grandis' son before he was killed in the arena by Brudais. A daughter would be much easier, considering the Krashkin line has so many sons to boast of.*

Oren's eyes moved from left to right, calculating.

"If Krashkin were to enter the war, it would give Creet the greater advantage. They could attack us from two fronts, and with our full strength camped to the west, Bentixt and the surrounding cities would be vulnerable."

Morvian's eyebrows rose at Oren's suggestions. He didn't realize he had such a mastermind of military strategy speaking for him.

"I have many talents," Oren said, smiling mischievously. "Only one of them is shoveling horse shit."

Morvian grunted a laugh. *You're correct, of course. Bentixt is vulnerable with our army encamped. Had our only adversary been the Creetian army, we could have easily withstood their advances, but if Krashkin were to enter the fray, we would be surrounded. We'll need assurances that this will not happen.*

"And how do you propose we see to those assurances?"

Morvian's mind spun in a frayed tapestry of possibilities, each thread coming to its end with a snap—save one. It certainly wasn't the honorable thing to do, but if they were to end this war, they would need to fight dirty.

Morvian turned to Oren, whose eyes had glazed over slightly. Morvian took the soldier's shoulder and shook him once, hard. Oren came to and blinked.

What is the matter with you?

"Apologies, Commander. It can be difficult to follow your thoughts. You think so rapidly it can be mesmerizing at times."

Morvian waved him off. *The solution is simple. You'll need to get your cloak dirty.*

"I'm to go to the Bentixt slums, Commander?"

I'll need some mercenaries who are good at hiding in plain sight and aren't opposed to hurting a woman.

"I imagine that'll be the whole of the slums, sir."

Well, then I expect you back quickly.

Chapter Thirty-Six

ELDEVA

Eldeva grabbed a few more ungfey berries off the vine, setting them carefully in her other hand. She had collected a fair amount already, but they needed to be perfectly ripe for the spell to work. She picked one out that was a little too green, dropped it onto the cobblestone where the birds could get at it, then put her handful of berries to her mouth. She chewed them, allowing the pleasant tartness to spread across her tongue. When her mouth was full of the crushed berries, she swallowed them in one gulp, and with her next inhale, she muttered the spellverse.

She looked up into the glass window before her, peering into the solar of an unused suite in the east wing of the palace. She wasn't looking within but rather at her reflection in the tinted glass. Her face was grotesque. She had a dark purple bruise the size of a fist covering her right cheekbone, a bloody lower lip swollen to thrice its normal size, and a deep gash from the middle of her eyebrow down her eyelid. Painful warmth spread across her entire face, and she winced. Watching her reflection carefully, the cuts and bruises healed themselves, seamlessly sewing together and evening out the flesh, as if invisible hands were mending it.

The ungfey berries were known for their magickal properties, and aided by spellverse, they were most effective in healing remedies. She had been forced to parade her injuries at court for two days before King Ulden was satisfied. If she healed herself too quickly, no one would learn the lesson he meant to teach. So, she had gritted her teeth and bore the humiliation, while easing the pain with other means—a potion that took away sensation in localized areas. She detested giving in to her father's whims—particularly after such a violent, childish outburst as he had displayed—but she was always cognizant of the consequences of his displeasure.

Eldeva smiled weakly at her reflection, her face now just as beautiful as it had always been. In the corner of her eye, she saw Mayora picking more ungfey berries down the garden path. Her twin popped a berry into her mouth, smiling with delight at the unusual taste.

Had Eldeva ever been so young? Her sister was still a child, with all the lighthearted vigor of someone untroubled by the woes of the world. Eldeva had not been so naïve and carefree since her initiation into the Old Order—since her maidenhood had been taken at the tender age of thirteen so that she could access her full powers. This had been her wish at the time, and the ritual had been necessary if she were to continue surpassing the other students in her cohort. She didn't rue the choices she had made to get to where she now was, but every so often, when she looked at her sister, she wondered what a normal childhood would have felt like.

Eldeva walked toward Mayora, placing her hand on her sister's forearm and drawing her attention. Mayora's eyes lit with joy at the sight of Eldeva's bright, healed face.

"They worked!" she exclaimed, delighted.

A ghost of a smile met the remark. Mayora's expression wavered.

"Sister," Eldeva said. "My marriage to the prince is mere days away. I'll need your help to escape it."

Mayora's eyebrows drew together.

"Eldeva, it will be too dangerous. Surely, you can survive the prince in marriage. Maybe you don't have to see him very often. Perhaps it's just a marriage of convenience… "

Eldeva rolled her eyes in an immature gesture of disbelief. Her naivety was astounding at times.

"I am escaping this place. Father will never lay a hand on me again, Prince Ahnvil will never lay a hand on me to begin with, and you will be safely away from this madness. You can be sure that if I leave by myself, you will be my replacement."

"Me?" Mayora said, her eyes widening in shock. "I'm only sixteen."

Eldeva fought the urge to roll her eyes again. *So am I.* That was the difficulty with looking thrice one's age. People often forgot how old one actually was.

"He does not seem like the type of lover who is gentle and kind, my sweet. He will require you every night, and you will beg him to stop, and it will only make him more ravenous for your touch. You will crawl out of his bed, exhausted, sore, and unsatisfied every night, wishing that you had come away with me. I promise you that is your fate, unless you decide otherwise."

Was it true? Possibly, but Eldeva couldn't chance leaving Mayora there, regardless. Her sister knew too much about Ithiador for the secret to be safe once Mayora was the only outlet for King Ulden's rage at Eldeva's sudden departure. Besides, it was safer not to travel alone as a female.

Mayora's eyes filled with tears. She opened her fist, having crushed the berries she held in her hand. The dark purple liquid now ran down her forearm, dripping onto the dusty earth below.

"Please," Eldeva said, her eyes shining with impatience. "Come with me."

A tear fell from Mayora's eye, streaking her cheek.

"Can you promise me things will be better?"

Eldeva took her sister's hands in her own, not caring that the dark juice of the ungfey berries now stained her own hands as well. "Anywhere is better than here."

The spell that Eldeva planned to use for their escape from the palace was very complex and required a particular catalyst—the use of a tricky ingredient by the name of 'veyl seeds.' With the proper incantation, they would create a mirror image, a Shadow with substance, one that didn't need to be controlled by the Keeper but could act on its own. Eldeva had researched the spell in depth in the corners of the Old Order's library and understood the mechanics, but she had never procured veyl seeds for her own private ingredient stores. However, she knew that Ealdor Gunmai kept a case of these rare seeds in the student storeroom.

The Old Order had a strict policy of transparency with spellwork, and any ingredients that were taken from the storeroom were to be reported to an ealdor with the name and use of the spell being worked. Eldeva had pocketed the case of veyl seeds when she had gathered six thistles under the pretense of a lesser spell for a moontime remedy. When she only reported the thistle to Ealdor Ishva upon her retreat from the storeroom, the sorceress nodded solemnly and handed her a small vial of snake scales.

"For the pain, princess," she said. "Five scales should do the trick."

Eldeva thanked her graciously and retreated swiftly from the Order's quarters. As she made her way down the corridor to the royal suites, she rounded a corner and saw Prince Ahnvil walking with purpose towards her. She cursed under her breath. He had quite clearly seen her. She couldn't turn in the opposite direction without causing a scene.

"Princess," Ahnvil called, stopping her in her tracks. "What are you doing out of bed at such a late hour? Restless?"

The prince caught up to her, and when he was within a few feet, Eldeva stepped back several paces. When he advanced, she side-stepped and swept her skirts away from his reach.

"Prince," she said, a bite to her tone which she attempted to keep out. She knew it would only invigorate him. "I couldn't sleep. I went to get a book from the Order's library."

Ahnvil backed away a step, looking her up and down in a very undignified fashion. "Where is it? The book?"

Eldeva glared, pushing the case of veyl seeds, the vial of snake scales, and the thistles further into the folds of her skirts. The case and vial clanked softly together, causing Ahnvil's eyes to fall on their place in her pockets. She cleared her throat, and he looked up at her again. "I decided I had better try to sleep, so I left it behind."

Ahnvil grinned. "Just like a female; constantly changing your mind. I hope, Princess, that you do not decide to change your mind on your… acquiescence to this marriage. Sycil and Krashkin have been in conference to align for ten years. It would be a shame to jeopardize all that hard work simply because you don't like my… spirit."

Eldeva's eyes flashed. "Spirit?"

Ahnvil's grin widened at her display of anger. "I know I can come across as—"

"A pigheaded lout?" she offered.

Ahnvil laughed, taking a step forward. Eldeva stood her ground. "I am very much looking forward to having you in my bed. I won't deny that, but I am dedicated to an alliance between our countries. I would hope that you, Princess, have the same determination to avoid unnecessary bloodshed."

Eldeva played with the bracelets on her left wrist, causing them to jingle slightly. She had never considered that before. If peace between Krashkin and Sycil would end the raids and skirmishes on their borders, Sycil might be able to build a large enough army to support their allies—and perhaps even conquer. It would be a great aid to her people.

My people? she thought bitterly. Sycil was no more her home than any other place. She was trapped here by birth and circumstance and had only ever wanted to escape. The only advantage of her time here had been her education at the hands of the Old Order—and even that had scarred her beyond repair. Her only freedom was what little she could beg for, and she was tired of begging. Once she and Mayora were well away from this place, she would care for it as little as she cared for the abhorrent man standing before her.

"You are right, of course," Eldeva said gently. She stepped up to him, whispering in his ear, "but you may wish you entangled another princess in your schemes, my good prince. My bedroom games are notoriously… unorthodox."

She hated the smirk that lit his face. "Oh, Eldeva," he said, huskily. "I've been counting on it."

She slid past him, her breasts brushing against his bicep. He grunted. *Pigheaded lout, indeed.* As she made her way down the corridor, her suites within view, she smiled to herself, thinking about the face he would make when he found her gone.

Her hands placed the veyl seeds carefully in a line on the vanity's surface. It had to be exactly thirty-two seeds. She counted again, a little nervously, then started the second line a little further down. She counted again. Sixty-four seeds.

"Are you sure?" Mayora said anxiously from behind her. "This is such a complex spell, Eldeva."

"I'm sure," she replied, straightening up and looking at her sister with a withering expression, "that this is our only chance to escape. Now watch me closely."

Eldeva lowered her head to the first line of seeds, covering one of her nostrils with a long-nailed finger and inhaling the seeds up the other nostril, feeling them pass through her nose and settle like little lead weights in her lungs.

"*Viro fen veryl nos dreykil mek.*"

She opened her mouth wide, watching in the vanity mirror as the seeds came pouring out, flying and circling around each other until they moved with grace to Eldeva's right side. They fanned out, spreading with purpose, copying the shape of Eldeva's body.

"*Xec criss.*"

Eldeva blinked, and while her eyes were shut, a perfect replica of herself had formed from the seeds. It faced her and Eldeva held out her hand. The Shadow mirrored her movements, and their hands touched. It was solid.

"*Pherro fin.*"

The Shadow's hand fell to its side, and it stood next to the vanity bench, moving into the center of the room. Eldeva watched with enthusiasm as it grabbed a dress from the back of the chaise and began folding it. Then her vision swerved recklessly, and she slid off the side of the bench and onto the floor. Her vision went black.

"Eldeva!" Mayora called, grabbing her arm and shaking it hard.

Eldeva came to, her vision returning suddenly.

"I'm fine," she said, trying to sit up. "It happens sometimes after complicated spellwork."

"Perhaps you should not do it again."

"No," she replied, getting to her feet, making her way to the edge of bed and sitting down. "If they think you are missing, we won't get as far as Jherka before they find us. We need this to be convincing. Now, go, and do as I have done."

Mayora looked at her sister warily. "Do you need a moment?"

"Go."

The princess stepped towards the vanity, sat on the bench, and lowered her head to the seeds, snorting them up her nose. Eldeva repeated the spellverse and watched as the seeds vacated Mayora's mouth and formed a perfect copy of her sister's body. When she was done, Mayora's Shadow joined Eldeva's at the center of the room, where they both sat on the chaises and began speaking in hushed tones to each other.

Eldeva swayed again, but this time Mayora caught her before she could fall and lowered her to a prone position on the bed.

"I'm all right," she said, but she didn't get up. She lay on the bed, breathing heavily. The warmth was gradually leaving her body as the magick deserted her.

"Can they speak if asked a question?" Mayora asked.

"Indeed," she replied, "but they will reply simply and with little emotion. If no one heeds us, we should be able to get a decent head start. We'll be taking horses from the servants' stables, instead of our own—or else we'll be discovered immediately."

"I cannot ride Hectur?" Mayora's eyes welled with sudden tears.

"No," Eldeva said sternly. "If we take our own steeds, they'll know we've escaped and send men after us. Mayora, we must be careful."

Despite her sister's foolishness, Eldeva cared deeply about her. She was just so *young.* Eldeva could never have afforded to be so very naïve.

"Once I release the Shadows, they will go about our daily routines. We must leave now so that the stable hands will be asleep and not watching the horses."

Mayora looked at her Shadow pensively for a moment. "El… will we ever come back here?"

Eldeva wrinkled her nose, letting the absurdity of the question sink in. "Why would you want to?"

Chapter Thirty-Seven

DANIA

The Blood Guard overseeing their training session was looking lazily out at the pairs of sparring partners as they moved through the motions of their defensive sequences. Dania's eyes kept flitting back to him expectantly, but it seemed as though he were pointedly ignoring her presence, not to mention the shameful antics that were happening in her sparring session.

Her opponent was a thin young man who couldn't have been more than eighteen. His wide grin when he had been paired with "the girl" had been telling enough for Dania. She knew from the off that he would exhibit impropriety, but she had expected that Vus would take care of the situation, as the Blood Guard had been instructed to see to that recently.

In the last few days since Dania had been 'discovered,' she had trained with the men as a woman, and their demeanors were maddeningly different than when they had believed her to be a man. Some of the men went too easy on her, lessening their attacks and giving her more room for error than was typically allotted to the young men her own age. Others, like her current opponent, were typical, hedonistic males who attempted to grope her at every opportunity. Needless to say, their attentions were met with swift rebuttals, and the Blood Guard normally saw to it that she was reassigned to a more accommodating partner. Admittedly, she almost preferred the lewd partners to the meek; at least they presented a challenge.

Once the men in her Seasoned unit began to test her skills with hand-to-hand combat and weapons, they had been rather impressed with her abilities—especially given the blatant lie that she had only been spying on training sessions. That news had spread around the camp, and when she was having a quiet breakfast in the mess tent the next morning, a pompous male decided to stand up and shout, "You like watching? Watch this!" He proceeded to pull down the front flap of his trousers, revealing his flaccid cock, swaying his hips from side to side tauntingly. She gave him a look of utmost indifference and replied, "Watch what?" His fellows and the men who were near enough to hear the exchange roared with laughter. She had turned back to her plate, ignoring them all. *Males,* she thought with disdain. *There has never been a more obnoxious breed.*

She had been provided her own tent away from the barracks—'for propriety,' the king had explained, but was there any such thing amongst the animals she now trained with?

Her sparring partner lunged at her, grasping for her right breast, but Dania deftly moved out of the way so that his hand passed beyond her and her closed fist landed in the soft spot between his shoulder and arm. He grunted, and the grin was wiped from his face. She supposed that in a real battle, males would naturally aim blows at her breasts, as it was a frontal target, and a sensitive area, but the expression on her partner's face did not boast of tactics, but rather of lust. She backed up a few paces, providing distance so that his next attack would fall short, but he stepped forward hurriedly, thrusting his hands between her legs. She grasped his forearm, twisted it upside down and grabbed his wrist with her other hand, pulling down hard. Dania smiled, satisfied, when he made an unusual squealing sound in his throat.

"Attention!"

Dania's body went rigid at the shout, and she released her grasp on her opponent's wrist, backing up a few steps. Looking up, she saw Commander Brudais moving swiftly towards Vus, who was standing with his back erect, his gaze unmoving against the horizon.

When he was in front of Vus, Brudais raised his voice so that the entire practice field could hear. "Sergeant Vus, what just happened here?" he said, pointing his left hand out directly at Dania. She had never heard a more serious tone from him. Her eyes widened and she shrunk back, unsure whether she had just performed some criminal act.

Vus' mouth tightened. "The lad got a little spirited with the girl, Commander. Nothing I couldn't handle."

Brudais scoffed, his arm lowering to his side. "The only thing you *handled* was your own cock while you watched this unfold. You're relieved of your duties here. Go and find me a guard who wants *all* their soldiers to succeed."

Vus' face reddened as he pounded his chest with a formal salute and slunk away, cowed.

"At ease," Brudais said, moving his gaze around the practice field across each of the pairs in turn. "Mill about for a moment, while Vus finds his replacement."

The tension on the field immediately relaxed as the Seasoned realized they would not be reprimanded, and their straight posture slackened. Brudais moved slowly through the pairs until he reached Dania's side. His eyes fell on her sparring partner, who shrunk visibly under the commander's intense gaze.

"If you're that eager, boy, there are some goats in the supply wagon who might have you."

A quiet chuckle sounded throughout the company, and the soldier's face reddened in embarrassment. Served him right, the lecherous little blighter.

Dania looked up to see that Brudais was staring at her. "You're needed," he said, and he motioned to the outskirts of the practice field in the direction of mid-camp. She tensed at the seriousness in his voice, but she began walking as she was bid.

Brudais walked behind her, and she felt his gaze on the square of her back. It felt like a roaring fire singeing her skin. A shudder ran through her shoulder blades, where she imagined his eyes watching her. She was cognizant of other eyes watching as they moved across the field, as well, and the heat of embarrassment washed over her cheeks.

Once they were out of earshot of the Seasoned and had walked past Rydril's tent, Brudais quickened his pace and met her stride, walking at her side.

"You knew this wouldn't be a simple assignment," he said, his tone evening so that the seriousness began to fade from it, "but you've done a good job of it. Word will spread through the camp that you can handle yourself in a tussle and they'll think twice about getting... *spirited*... with you again."

Pride flooded her body, washing away the embarrassment. A small smile appeared on her face as she glanced sidelong at him.

"Only doing as I was trained, Commander," she replied, trying to keep her voice as even as his.

"Let's keep that quiet for now, if you please," he said. "We don't need anyone asking questions about how you came to be here. I already had to re-assign Lieutenant Lyvon because he had a close look at your sword when you were… not you."

She hadn't remembered that. Her training schedule over the last three days had been so busy that she had scarcely spared a thought for any of the consequences of her magick use, but Brudais had seen to them without being asked, and it seemed he didn't require gratitude for his intervention.

She watched him from the corner of her eye as he fought to keep his expression pleasant. She wondered about the formality. Throughout their previous encounters, he had remained natural, his speech relaxed. It had never seemed like he needed to mask his emotions before. In fact, she had been astonished at the ease of his honesty, as she had anticipated that evasion was inevitable in a male of his position and station. That he was now showing signs of insincerity caused her concern.

She had seen him only a few times since he had revealed her to the king and never long enough or in close enough proximity to speak forthrightly. She wondered if she was sensing avoidance in him.

"Did you just come to watch me train?" There was an intentional sliver of hopefulness in her voice in an attempt to gauge his reaction.

His head lifted from where it watched the ground before his feet. "No," he said, clearing his throat. "I was asked to summon you to the king. He has some questions."

"The king," she said with a palpable disappointment that she hoped he heard. His concentrated expression on the ground didn't change. "Questions about Loya?"

"I doubt that's the case. I have a feeling he's more interested in your lineage."

The subtle way Brudais said the word, as if it were difficult to say aloud, made her question his response. Had this been the reason for his apparent avoidance? If he truly thought that their fathers' duel in the Crescent Moon Wars affected anything, he was desperately mistaken.

The news that her father was Grandis the Great had been a shock, but the surprise had ebbed after her first night in the camp as a woman. She had stayed up the entire night, staring at the ceiling of her tent, realizing that her father—Riven, Grandis—had given her clues to her heritage. The stories he told were ones that were filled with so much detail she had thought he had missed his ultimate calling of becoming a bard. The details had been memories; the excitement in his voice had been genuine, remembered. It was like the king's words had allowed her to round the final turn in a maze which she had been navigating her entire life. When she stepped through it, it had felt… fitting, as if she had been waiting her whole life to be recognized for who she was.

Her head shook slightly at the memory. It had been like stepping out of a fog into a life she didn't recognize but felt was merited… was *right*.

Dania looked up at Brudais, who caught her gaze and held it. A deep sadness had filled his eyes. Coming to a halt in the middle of the path, she turned to face him.

"I am sorry," he said softly, still watching her intently, "for your brother."

Dania was confused at first and her eyebrows drew together. She had forgotten—because her life had merged into fables. Grandis had a son, as well as a daughter, when he had been exiled. Halvian had stayed in Krashkin when his father was banished. He was to marry a Krashkin princess, but when Brudais, Leifius' own son, had entered the Kresha Cup for the first time, Halvian could not have passed at the chance to prove himself. Brudais and Halvian had faced off at the head of the sword competition. It had been the most anticipated event in the history of the Cup, and Brudais had cut him down.

"He fought bravely," he said, his shoulders hunched, as if he were carrying a great weight. "Ardently."

Dania's head snapped up. Brudais' eyes fell to the ground, a look of shame and remorse spreading across his features.

He had not wished to kill him; that was plain enough. He clearly rued the act to this day. Dania swallowed and found a heavy lump in her throat. Had he named his second sword after her brother?

Brudais cleared his throat once more, straightening his stance. "The king awaits," he said, his tone no longer hushed but severe. "If you need me, I won't be far off. I can give you a spell to summon me if you wish. It's simple and won't draw attention."

Dania tried to swallow again with difficulty, nodding solemnly.

Suddenly, she felt a tug at the corner of her mind, as if someone were gently nudging her to open a barrier that she hadn't known was there. She was uncertain of what she was supposed to do but decided to relax into the feeling. The barrier opened of its own accord. The words in the Old Tongue floated before her, as if they were scribbled across a page in a hasty hand. Brudais' voice pronounced them for her, the words sliding over his tongue like smooth silk. Then the connection broke, and Dania's eyes opened to find Brudais walking away from her.

Tears welled in her eyes as she watched his retreating form. Before the connection had broken, a deep swell of regret had washed over her, enveloping her in a mirroring sadness.

She didn't know what had happened in that duel, but the result had consumed him with guilt for the last twelve years. Someone needed to forgive him for it, but she wasn't sure that person was her. She may have been Halvian's kin, but she had never known him. No, Brudais would need to forgive himself. After so many years of carrying that burden, she wondered if that were possible.

Dania walked briskly along the path until she saw the king's tent. It was a grand structure, and its highest point was well over twenty feet tall, dwarfing its surroundings. The entrance was flanked by two Black Guard, who stood in their unique uniforms like dark reflections of the imposing tent.

The Black Guard were the king's private wardens and were notorious throughout Creet for their particularly cruel methods of gleaning information. No one was foolish enough to admit aloud that torture was their forte, but everyone from the lowliest peasants knew to steer well clear of them. They had a saying in Creet that the unnecessary death of a commoner was often known as a "Black Guard's Question."

Dania hesitated before them, not sure how to introduce herself and make it known that she was expected within, but she didn't have a chance to form the words before the Guards acknowledged her presence.

"Well, if it ain't the legend's daughter," one of the guards said, spitting on the ground beside Dania's boot. "We best ensure she don't got no weapons on her person."

Dania's posture stiffened, defiance shrinking into submission. She did not need to anger these guards—no matter their uncouth demeanor.

"You're to be treated as any other soldier. King's orders," the other one rasped, leering at her wickedly. "So, spread your legs, soldier."

Dania's nose wrinkled at their behavior, but she obeyed. She placed one of her feet in line with but farther out from the other, then lifted her arms.

The first guard cackled. "Does as she's told, this one. Better than the last whore I had."

She kept her mouth shut, but couldn't keep the hatred from showing on her face. This only seemed to provoke their lewdness further. The second guard stepped up to her and began pawing at her uniform. His hands felt the leather of her jerkin, pushing at her stomach and sides, grazing over her breasts. Then he moved down to her sandals, checking her greaves, and his fingers glided up the sides of her legs and began working their way under her skirt. Gooseflesh erupted over her skin in revulsion, and she snarled unintentionally, like an animal.

The first guard said, "Now, none of that! You could be carrying a knife on that thigh of yours. We must protect His Majesty from any threats."

Dania ground her teeth as she endured the guard's hands on her upper thighs, but his fingers started to glide inward towards her sex.

She lost all control. She grabbed the offending wrist, twisting it back, and the sound of the bone snapping was *oh* so satisfying. The guard cried out in pain, holding his wrist with his other hand. "Oi!" The first guard rushed her, bringing her tumbling to the ground.

She rolled when she hit the soft earth, jumping up to stand a few feet from both guards. The second was still cradling his wrist, tears streaming down his cheeks, while the first was splayed in the dirt before her. She rushed towards the tent entrance and ducked inside before the guards could right themselves to chase after her. She knew that if she got to the king before them, they would be forced to retreat. They wouldn't embarrass themselves in front of their liege by admitting a female had outwitted them.

She walked swiftly down the antechamber and came to the king's receiving room. Trying to calm her heartbeat and the pulsing in her ears, she took several deep breaths before entering.

"Dania," said the king from his rustic throne, which seemed to have been fashioned from one of the blackthorn trees of the Fayn Forest. During her last visit here, she had considered that to be an ill omen, given the merciless welcome they had endured at the hands of that forest. The king, no doubt, thought it a symbol of triumph. "Welcome."

Dania focused on the throne, willing herself to be calm. "Your Majesty," she replied, moving into an elaborate bow. Her first encounter with the king had been clumsy at best, and her bow then had been uncertain and confused. She was now well-versed in a proper royal introduction in the male fashion and was determined to use it, instead of the feminine curtsey. It would be easier on all those concerned if she were treated like any other soldier.

The king once again displayed a lack of enthusiasm for this concept. His expression was one of distaste—although he decided against chastising her for the unusual display. Perhaps he realized the necessity of it, as well. She hid a triumphant smile from the royal gaze.

"We have asked you here to pose a question, but first we must ascertain your… well, my dear, your allegiance, to put things bluntly."

Dania's eyebrows rose involuntarily. She supposed that if anyone had the right to ask that question, it was the king himself, but she was still injured by the insinuation that she could somehow be allied with any country but Creet. She had been raised there since she was old enough to remember. It may not have been the land of her birth, but it was the land she had known best all her life. She had only just been made aware of her ties to Krashkin by the king himself. Could he truly think she had any allegiance to the place? Clearly so, if he was making such efforts to question it.

"My king," Dania said slowly, knowing she was on uneven ground. "My loyalty has always been to Creet. My birth in Krashkin was a circumstance beyond my control; my Krashkin blood a surprise, certainly, but no more than an intriguing history. My life in Creet has endeared me to the realm, and I think of no other country as my homeland. I owe no loyalty elsewhere."

The king raised his chin, looking down at her with penetrating, dark eyes. In his calculation of her trustworthiness, he seemed to be undressing her with those eyes, his gaze relentless as it stripped her down to her bare skin in its attempt to uncover her fully. She squirmed beneath that gaze, embarrassed she wasn't doing more to escape the situation—the assault—but he was the king. What else was she to do but obey?

After an uncomfortably long time, Tarison made a move to his guards on either side of the throne, who shifted and began moving toward Dania. She stiffened, readying herself into a fighting stance, but the guards passed her by, smirking, as they moved to the back of the receiving room, out of earshot. Dania straightened her posture, placing her hands behind her back again.

"We are glad you think so highly of Creet," the king said as he brought his hand to his chin, running it along the stubble of his jawline. "It should make our next question easier to answer. We are well aware of Lady-Governor Loya's efforts on behalf of introducing women into the military. It was not your situation which brought you to her attentions, that can be assured. Your bloodline was known to her well before she singled you out for this… enterprise. It was her ticket to surety. A legend's blood is not easily overlooked."

The king's face filled with contempt at these words, and she was distinctly reminded of the way he looked at Brudais during her introduction. She was aware of their abhorrence for one another, but she had hoped to use that to her advantage.

"Not all legends' children are so… " Dania caught the king's eye and held it boldly. "Vainglorious."

"We have yet to be proven wrong on that point," said King Tarison carefully, raising one eyebrow.

"How can I prove it to you?" She said it before she could stop herself, but suddenly realized that she had meant it. She had no love for the king, but she wanted to prove herself to Creet. She would not be made an outcast because of her birth.

Tarison smiled coolly. "Marriage."

Dania's eyes widened in panic. Surely he didn't mean… "To whom?"

"A Krashkin prince."

Confusion colored her response. "Would that not prove the opposite?"

"Not if it solidified a treaty between our realms."

A bargaining chip. That was all she was to him. It was little wonder that the king took any interest in her after he had unveiled her lineage. The burden of being a legend's daughter was only beginning to weigh on her, and already it was changing the course of her entire future—a future she had been looking forward to, a future in which she could prove herself on a battlefield.

Now, she was being asked to prove herself in another way, and she was loath to admit that it was a goal more far-reaching and admirable than her own. With Krashkin as an ally, Creet would be certain to overpower Hyglen. Her marriage might save thousands of lives by putting an end to an evenly matched war. All she had to do was give up her every desire.

Her brother's face came to her mind, followed by her home in Kevilly, the friends she had made in Turivaun, training with the men over the last few days, and suddenly Brudais' face appeared in her mind's eye. She blinked, and her posture slackened. Dania wouldn't deny that feelings had begun to grow between them, and there were moments when she thought... but they had not known each other long enough for her to consider him a reason to—

"It's sudden, we are aware, but will you consider it?"

The king's voice interrupted her thoughts. She cleared her throat.

"I will consider it, Your Majesty. The thought that my marriage could matter to the realm is baffling me still."

Tarison peered down at her, a small smile on his lips. "Your upbringing undoubtedly taught you that you were of little consequence, but you are paramount, Dania. Creet may not need to swell its ranks with women as Loya wishes, but an alliance of this magnitude could mean a victorious end to this war."

Dania was unused to her decisions holding such sway. The king of Creet was asking her to change her life for the good of her country, to bring balance and peace. Was that not a worthy cause? Were her desires so dear that she could afford to deny him?

Chapter Thirty-Eight

MORVIAN

A row of six mercenaries stood before Morvian, their stench palpable. They looked like some of the worst and dirtiest men Bentixt had ever belched out of its slums. Oren had done well, but their lack of hygiene may alert the Creetian scouts to their arrival. They would need to bathe before they set out.

Morvian began his inner monologue, and Oren, who stood beside him with a look of disgust on his face, began voicing the stream of consciousness running through his mind from his commander.

"You are here because you've agreed to apprehend two Creetians within their encampment. We are less concerned with your methods than with the expediency and secrecy of the task. You will dress as Creetians, which will mean slaying some scouts for their attire. Once you've secured your positions, you will find your queries and extract them from the encampment—*quietly*. Gagging them may do little, so you're to take them unawares and knock them unconscious. Carrying them out, you'll use the Veiling Spell you were taught by the ealdors. Once you reach Bentixt, you'll give the guards the passwords required and bring the prisoners straight to the Tower of Lyes. Your reward will be waiting for you there."

One of the mercenaries spat on the floor. He croaked, "You expect us to set foot in that place? You're as likely to throw all our skins in those cells as to release us with coin in pocket."

Morvian caught Oren's concerned glance. He looked back at the sergeant with a bored expression, nodding.

"All right, you'll deposit the prisoners at the southern gatehouse. You can collect your reward from the commander's office."

"And we can't just pick up our reward at the southern gatehouse?"

These were hard men, wary and muscular to the point of intimidation, but the mere thought of entering the office of Morvian the Mute was too much for them. The Tower of Lyes he could understand, for it was filled with men like them who had disobeyed the law and come to terms with those consequences, but his office? He had cultivated quite the reputation if that were the case.

The corner of Morvian's mouth twitched.

"We are at war, gentlemen. I don't have men to spare, or whom I trust, with that amount of coin," Oren said smoothly.

The mercenaries looked at each other, grinning stupidly. The idea of too much coin to carry easily spoke to their innate greed and silenced the concerns. *Any fear can be quelled,* Morvian mused, *given enough incentive.*

"Yes, sir," said one and the others chorused his words.

As they filed out of the guardroom, Morvian thought, *You chose a fine rabble, Oren. As long as Pexix's directions are correct, we'll have them in the dungeons by dawn tomorrow.*

Oren cleared his throat. "And the king, Commander?"

He need not know of these exploits until they are accomplished, Morvian thought. Better to present news—whether good or bad—after the efforts had already been made. Besides… Morvian felt a surge of pride at the possibility that this endeavor might end the war in its entirety. A good strategy should not be tempered by a king's naivety.

Chapter Thirty-Nine

Loya

Loya was forty-two years old and still considered to be an adolescent compared to some of her race, and yet she was breaking into the home of an eighty-five-year-old man to blackmail him. She felt like a child playing a prank, but this situation could not have been more serious.

The governors of Turivaun had finally made their displeasure with their female colleague known. They usually met every fortnight to discuss the goings-on of the city, and the country at large—meetings which Loya had been integral to since her appointment as a governor by the people of Drens District. Loya had tried to enter High Hall to retrieve a book in her office that she needed to consult, and found that her key no longer fit in the lock.

The way that Loya had taken charge at their last meeting with Steward Venhil had unnerved the other governors. They had always taken her appointment to the position with contempt, but her boldness since befriending Countess Staliva had strengthened their distrust. They had finally shut her out, doing so in the most cowardly way imaginable.

But Loya was not deterred. Not in the slightest. She had dealt with all sorts of males in her time as governor—the king not the least domineering—and she wouldn't allow a slight like this to go unanswered.

Hoisting herself up onto the ledge, Loya pried the lock of Governor Nial's river-front window ajar.

She had been sure to wear suitable attire for the occasion, so her light leather trousers, thick woolen tunic and ox hide boots looked more like a peasant's garb than an extorting governor's. She doubted Nial would care what she wore, so long as she kept her mouth shut.

She slipped in through the window and landed on an armoire that was just a touch too high for her comfort. She steeled herself, leapt off it with a gentle *thud!* and made her way through the dark townhouse.

Governor Nial of Litos District had been chosen for his unusually unique proclivities, but also because he did not employ a butler. She found this intriguing for a few reasons: a man who couldn't even trust a butler in his service was a man she could easily coerce, and having no butler meant that the house would be much easier to enter without being detected.

Walking through the house was difficult, given the lack of proper lighting, aside from the moonlight shining through the overly large windows of his living room. When she finally found her way to the parlor off the mudroom, she made herself comfortable in one of the armchairs, crossed her legs, and waited.

A quarter turn had passed when the door of the townhouse flung open, revealing a half-shadowed and maturing gentleman, a light rain following him in. He closed the door and hung up his coat, but then he reached for the flint at the edge of the drawing table to light the candle there, and he froze. He couldn't see her, but she was certain he could feel her presence.

"Shy, Governor Nial?" Loya said silkily, tapping her fingers on the wooden arm of the chair where she sat. "I hear that's not the case when you're with your grandson."

Nial sputtered instead of arguing his defense.

"You're correct, of course, Lord-Governor. We should be more discreet. Ears everywhere. Take a seat."

Loya motioned towards the big armchair across from her. Nial walked over and slid into it like a defeated child after his mother had called him to bed.

"You and the other governors have locked me out of High Hall. This would vex me if I didn't have so much dirt on you all that I could build a hutch for every Creetian who lives in Turivaun. All I want is the key, and you can go about your merry way, fucking whosoever you please.

"If, however, I don't get what I came for tonight, I will let all of Litos District know that their governor is a kin-petter, and tomorrow by midday, your seat will be vacant. I know how much Creetians value the sanctity of familial bonds, but you, Lord-Governor, being half Geldivinian, perhaps haven't realized that. You will."

Loya couldn't see the look on Nial's face, but she could sense the fear in the room, the panic. Nial shifted in his seat, deciding: his pride or his governorship?

"The keys are all you want?"

The latter, then.

"And a promise that you will tell no one of this conversation," she replied.

As Loya heard the keys to High Hall—and her deliverance—jangle as Nial dragged them out of his trouser pocket, she allowed herself a small smile of victory.

The echoes in the chamber rose as Loya stepped into the room and glided to her seat across from Governor Gailesh. She remained standing, ignoring the indignant remarks and expressions directed at her. Loya simply smiled in reply, tapping her fingertips lightly against the back of her chair.

"Lord-Governors of the districts of Turivaun," she began, and a hush fell over the chamber as her voice rose above the irascible murmuring. "I have placed before your seat an envelope inscribed with your name and title. Please do me the honor of opening it now."

It took a moment or two for each of them to open their envelope. It was a moment more before the collective gasps escaped their mouths, and they stood up from their seats, furious at her audacity. Loya glanced over at Governor Nial, who placed the card back in his envelope and used magick—before everyone in the chamber—to incinerate it. She smiled pleasantly at him.

"You must be curious to know how I've collected such a vast wealth of information on your persons, but for now, that is not the point. The point, my lords, is that I have it and that I've shared it with a select few people who—should something unfortunate happen to me—will release it to the districts of this fine city immediately."

There was silence for a moment before Governor Ilym of Quies said, "What do you want?"

Loya's smile turned sinister. "I have a list of demands. First, I must never be kept from a governor's moot—unless my seat has been filled by another. Second, moots must be held every week, instead of every fortnight—there are too many concerns that need to be addressed for this listlessness to continue. Third, you will use your influence to assign a marriage contract for Prince Ithiador with the Countess Staliva."

"That is beyond the governors' purview!" shouted Governor Gailesh of Kelvs.

"I have faith that you will accomplish the task with your vast connections, Lord Gailesh. And lastly, elections will be held while the king is away."

The last demand was a point of great contention; every voice in the chamber was raised in outrage.

"The steward will never allow it!" Governor Ilym said vehemently.

The voices quieted, expecting Loya to falter under the remark.

Loya's smile widened, showing her teeth. "I will take care of Steward Venhil."

As she walked out of the room, her shoes quietly tapping against the marble and her skirts dragging on the floor were the only noises that could be heard.

Chapter Forty

BRUDAIS

Brudais paced the inside of his tent, a constant movement from weapons rack to his chest of armour.

His thoughts were a myriad stream of discontent and confusion. He had thought that his interest in Dania had been simple—lust had been the prevailing answer, as Rydril had suspected. He had expected it to pass, not to consume his every thought. Her fiery hazel eyes when she was riled flooded his groin with need. Thinking about the curve of her backside, the smooth skin of her thighs. The way her hair fell almost to her backside, glistening bright against the sun. Imagining her breasts pressed tight against her tunic and jerkin all day, sweat running down her sides from the exertion of training...

He growled in frustration as his cock throbbed, hard now.

But he had more than carnal feelings for her. He had seen the fascinating way her mind worked, almost paralleling his own. Her trick against the king as she pretended to work against Brudais to gain favor with the monarch was cunning, and she had contrived the idea on her own.

Her tactics in the practice field today had also been calculated. She had been deliberate in her dispatch of her boy opponent after he had made his sexual advance, and instead of allowing it to happen again, she had let every man in that practice circle know that she was not one to be trifled with, and the word had spread throughout the encampment already. There were whispers of 'Don't lay a hand on Dania, daughter of Grandis—you might lose it.' He had heard the rumors circulating, smiled fondly at the fear in the messenger's eyes as they relayed them. She had a lot to learn about swordplay and battle, but in the tactics of self-preservation and security, her mind was constantly working, avoiding the harder fights by issuing challenges and igniting the fires of discontent which caused her to be feared and respected.

She had only known of her lineage for a few days, and yet she was proving that she could withstand the legend's weight. She had already begun to outwit Brudais with her scheming mind. She was a rival.

His cock pulsed harder, aching for release. He sat down on the side of his cot, willing himself into a calm state. He breathed heavily, exhaling and inhaling in even rhythms for several minutes, leaving his mind empty. The throbbing began to subside.

Once he and his cock had calmed down, his breathing returned to a normal rhythm and the thoughts began to pour through him again.

What did any of this matter if Dania was not of the same mind? Of course, there had been a few glances—moments of closeness in which he had thought she might move towards him, brush her lips against his, but they had always ended almost as soon as they had begun. He knew that she did not despise him; that was certain from her pretense to the king. He had seen the grin on her face—the one that she had allowed only him to witness, to make him aware of the games she played—but that was only an admittance to familiarity, to friendship. *Masiya above*, Brudais prayed, grinding his teeth together painfully, *don't let it be only friendship she desires from me. I couldn't bear it.*

He balled his fists into the sheets of his cot. Then an image of his mother's tear-streaked face swam before his vision, the agony of it biting his insides with guilt. She held the lifeless body of his father in her arms, utter hopelessness etched onto her features, like a stone statue.

Love makes you weak… senseless… powerless. Perhaps it was best not to love at all. His mind told him that this was the safer route, but another part of him stirred, stretching out with a tentative reach. His heart, perhaps.

His previous relationships with women had been merely a means to an end. Protection from overzealous noblewomen during public affairs. He had never truly expected to find a rival in the opposite sex, one that made his skin burn and mind reel. He had nearly given up hope that she existed. But there she was. Dania's face came into his mind's eye, a devious smile lighting her lips. Those lips…

He couldn't talk himself out of it. He would go to her tent. The only way to know for certain that she felt the same was to test the theory. He imagined his lips brushing hers, his fingers gliding along her neck to cup the back of her head. Yes, that would do. And if she reviled the act, he would succor his wounds alone in dashed hopes and disappointment… but if she kissed him back… perhaps he wouldn't be alone tonight.

The excited thought propelled him out of his tent and along the path to Dania's. He had barely realized he had made the journey by the time he arrived. There were no lights on in her tent against the darkness of the night. She may already have gone to sleep, expectant for another rigorous day of training tomorrow. He stepped toward her tent, clearing his throat loudly.

"Dania?" he called, his voice low.

There was no answer.

"Dania, are you there?"

He waited.

A sudden panic caught him off-guard, and he threw the tent flaps back to reveal the inside of her tent. A cot stood at one end of the tent, but the mattress was askew, the front laying against the grass while the back was wedged into the cot's frame. A small weapon's rack lay on the ground as if someone had kicked it across the tent, the sword Aurelius had given her lay underneath it, halfway out of its sheath.

Brudais turned around and sprinted for Rydril's tent. He had to get to a war horn to wake Rydril's battalion. Something was not right, and until Dania was found, she was in danger.

Brudais skidded to a halt in front of Rydril's tent. There was blood on the edge of the weaving on the tent flap. He pushed through and a sight met his eyes that made his stomach plummet into his guts. Rydril's tent was in the same state of disarray as Dania's, with fallen furnishings. The table at the center with the map had been knocked over, causing figurines to be scattered across the ground.

Searching the tent frantically, he grabbed Rydril's war horn and put it to his lips, blowing a long note. He ran out of the tent, blowing the horn again, twice. Three blows meant infiltration.

It wasn't long before the majority of Rydril's Blood Guard surrounded him, calling questions of concern and confusion.

"Rydril and Dania have been taken," he said, his heart thumping against his chest painfully. There were cries of anguish and despair around him, but he silenced them with a move of his hand. "Ten scouting parties. Search the borders of the camp from here to the north and east. Don't come back until you find out what happened. Go!"

The Blood Guard moved swiftly around him, getting into formations and selecting leaders, moving in all directions to search for their commander.

Brudais stood rooted to the spot. He knew men were asking him questions, but he didn't hear them. The only thing he could hear was the sound of his heart against his chest, the blood rushing in his ears.

He didn't know how much time had passed before he saw two guards carrying a wounded scout before him. The sound rushed back into his ears, flooding them with noise.

"I'm sorry, Commander," the scout said. His jerkin was soaked with blood, and some trickled down the side of his mouth. "They were dressed in Creetian uniform. I didn't know their true intent until—" He coughed, blood spurting from his mouth.

"I know, lad. Get him to a mender!" he said sharply to the Blood Guard who had him by the shoulders. They carried him off in the direction of the mender's tent.

"Commander!" He looked to his right and Captain Peric was running towards him. "It looks like they were on horseback and came in through the northeastern edge of the camp. There was a skirmish and five guards were slain, but one man in civilian garb was found there as well. He looks Hyglenian by his features and he carried a crude knife."

Brudais' mind raced. They had been kidnapped—not killed outright—which meant there was a possibility Brudais could treat with Morvian for their lives. There would be no heroic rescue; Bentixt was situated on the side of the mountain and fortified heavily. Unless… if he could find a way to infiltrate the lower level of the city and sneak into the castle the same way the Hyglenians had infiltrated the camp. There was a chance, but he would have to attempt it alone. Too many men would draw too much attention.

Drawing attention, he thought. *Yes, that would do nicely.*

Brudais looked up, glancing along the lines of Blood Guard who had returned to hear orders from a commanding officer.

"Who here has played The Hunt?"

Uncertainly, everyone raised their hands. Brudais gave them a reassuring smile that didn't reach his eyes.

"Well, friends, looks like we're going hunting."

Love may have made some weak, but it sharpened Brudais' mind to the point of a single focus—a clarity so intense, it felt like the rest of the world shone only through a red haze. He didn't doubt blood would be shed because of this, but he knew love had not made him powerless. He would see all of Hyglen in ash before he let anything happen to Rydril and Dania.

Chapter Forty-One

DANIA

Dania's head pounded.

She groaned with pain, but then her eyes suddenly shot open. The blurry images she saw made her head spin. She blinked a few times, trying to focus. Her hand raised to cup the back of her head and came away wet. She held out her hand in front of her, focusing on the red blurs she saw. Blood.

"Decided to rejoin the living?"

It was Commander Rydril's voice. Her eyes moved in the direction it had come from, and her eyes slowly focused on his outline. He was leaning against the wall, sitting with his hands on his knees.

Dania tried to sit up, positioning herself against the adjacent wall. She was wearing her nightclothes, which consisted of a baggy pair of trousers and a linen shirt that hugged her torso.

Clasping the back of her head with her hand again, examining the damage, she grimaced in pain as her fingers touched the wound.

"They gave you a good whack, I see," came Rydril's deep voice again. "Me, as well." He held out his palm to show her the dried blood caked on it. With amusement, he said, "Never thought going to sleep early could be so perilous."

Dania glanced around at her surroundings, taking in the thick iron cell bars. There was a bench in the middle which Rydril had avoided sitting on—probably for fear that it would collapse from the termites burrowing their way through the wood. The ground was littered with dirt, muck, and what Dania guessed was blood. Her gorge rose as the smell enveloped her nostrils. The only comparison she had was horse dung and animal entrails, but she knew that these smells were Human, not animal. There was a bucket in the corner, flies buzzing along the edges; that was where she supposed the putrid stench was coming from. *Our chamber pot*, she thought. *Prisoners—but to whom, and where are we?*

Rydril chuckled darkly. "Welcome to the Tower of Lyes, Dania. Hyglen just obtained two very interesting chess pieces. I wonder what they'll do with them."

Dania looked across at Rydril, her eyes still blurring slightly.

"Your apathy towards the situation is astounding, Commander. I thought you would be devising a plan of escape or a clever way to outwit our host."

Rydril scoffed, a sour look on his face. "The cat is riled, I see, but you'd do well to remember to whom you speak. I don't take kindly to criticism from common foot soldiers."

Dania looked around her for a moment, then back to Rydril. "Common, am I? If I were so common, why was I captured?"

Rydril wrinkled his nose, but she knew she had won her argument. "So, you know what the king had planned for you?"

Dania shrugged and immediately regretted the action. A fresh wave of pain rolled through the back of her head and nausea hit her like a boulder. Grimacing, she said, "I'm female. I'm used to males trying to use me for their own gains."

"Marriage to a wealthy prince is a better option than dying on a battlefield."

"That depends on who you are, I think."

She had looked to the ground, focusing on the bricks beneath her to steady her nausea, so she didn't see her commander's reaction to her words, but when she looked up again, his eyes were assessing her.

"You would rather perish?"

"No, Commander," Dania said, her eyes boring into his own. She felt a trickle of blood run down the back of her neck. "I would rather *live*."

The last word held a double meaning. Her life didn't just depend upon survival. Now that she had been amongst the men, fought them in training, worn their clothes, and been treated with a modicum of respect, she had started to get accustomed to the idea that this would become her life. Her conversation with King Tarison had, in a few moments, crumbled that prospect, shattering her hopes. She was to be traded off like a prize of war for the security of foreign aid, and the worst part was that she was leaning towards agreeing to it. What were her desires against the security of a kingdom?

She glanced back up at Rydril, who seemed to be deep in contemplation. Abruptly, he asked, "How are you faring in training?"

It was an odd question, given their circumstances, but she embraced the change of subject. "Very well. The Blood Guard has been most instructive. I think my parry has improved considerably, and my footwork has benefited from the direction."

"And your fellow soldiers? How have they adjusted?"

Dania winced slightly, her face growing a little warm. "I'm sure you've heard the rumors."

Rydril cracked a small smile. "If you're referring to you 'taking the hand,' yes, I have. I'd like to know what led to such a catchy phrase coming from my battalion. They aren't the most creative lot."

Dania hesitated, but the earnest look on Rydril's face made her continue. She told him about the encounters with men from his battalion, men who were little older than boys, trying to overpower her, to cross the line. She told him of several instances when those men had gotten too riled, and their hands had wandered where they should not have. She described how she had gotten quite adept at twisting wrists.

"And this works on any man?"

"Common foot soldier to Black Guard."

"Black Guard?" Rydril said disbelievingly.

Dania shifted uncomfortably under his gaze. Rydril must have noticed, because he cleared his throat and said, "What brought out the fighter in you, Dania?"

That was a strange question, but she pondered it while she wiped at the trickle of blood that was running down her neck. It was beginning to tickle.

"I suppose it's the feeling of being trapped, Commander. A cornered animal will thrash out in defiance—even when they know they are overpowered. I have been overpowered all my life—by circumstance, by caste, by coin—and I have been waiting for a chance to prove my worth to all who have ever doubted it—including myself. When Loya came to me to save my brother, I knew I could die in the attempt, but I realized that I wanted this chance more than anything I've ever wanted before. An opportunity to become more than I was born into, more than I was allotted. I resent that my father was a legend, for now I have an idea of what it's like to live in the shadow of greatness, to need to prove your own, like Brudais."

Rydril cleared his throat warningly.

"Like *Commander* Brudais," she corrected quickly, her cheeks flushing with heat.

"You already wanted to prove yourself, before you learned of your lineage."

"Yes, and now there is an expectation of greatness to live up to that I can barely conceive of achieving. I want to live my life with sword in hand, fighting for what I believe is right, but I will now forever assume the shadow of Grandis the Great—renowned warrior, fiercest fighter in the east, a man whose morals were questioned by many and considered reprehensible by most. I only knew him as Riven the Black, loving father, talented sailor. I want to show my strength is in my will. How do I step out of my father's black shadow when I feel consumed by it? My will cannot compare to the darkness his shadow has cast."

Rydril had been frowning throughout her impassioned speech, but his frown deepened at her last words.

"Brudais has struggled with that question his entire life. He has never considered the answer lies in himself, not in what others perceive."

Dania's eyebrows furrowed. "What do you mean?"

Rydril smiled warmly, the first time he had ever done so for her. It was so comforting that she almost forgot where they were. "I can give you the answers, but you will never see them. Not until you've discovered them on your own. You children of legends are so... needy."

A smile formed on Dania's face, and it turned into a quiet laugh. "Yes, I suppose we are."

It was quiet for a few moments before Rydril turned to her. "Have you told Brudais about the marriage proposal?"

"Doesn't he already know?"

"He suspects, surely, just as I did before you confirmed it, but what I meant to ask was, have you told him your thoughts on it?"

Warmth clawed at Dania's cheeks again. "He—I... " she fumbled to a halt, at a loss for words.

Rydril chuckled. "Brudais may appear... roguish... to others, but it is his own way of keeping a palatable distance from those who might consider him... well, a prize. I doubted, before this campaign, that he was capable of love outside the bonds of friendship and family. I imagined he had quenched the flames of those fires—that his desire was chiefly confined to the bedroom—but I can see it in his eyes, Dania. The way he looks at you is as if you're the only thing on this earth. It kindles hope in me that I forgot I had."

Dania went pale at his words.

"You seem distressed by the news," he said, surprised and concerned.

Dania clawed at the wall behind her, struggling to stand. Her head spun violently, and she grasped the wall for support. Rydril got up to help her, reaching out in case she needed a hand. She grasped for her next words.

"How could I ever compete with him? The Kresha Cup champion, the hero of The Fennon, commander of legions of men, proven hearty in battle. How could I ever be anything more than the woman on his arm?"

Rydril looked at her, stunned, his wide eyes searching hers for a sign of falsehood or jest. She had nothing but sincerity to give him in return. Her eyes were just as wide—although she brought a hand up to her head to steady her bobbing vision at the sudden movement.

"You're worried about being overlooked?"

Dania ground her teeth, her eyebrows drawn together.

"And that is fine for you to sneer at, isn't it? A man of accomplishment, looking down on the ex-governess for wanting to make a name for herself, for not wanting to be overshadowed, overpowered, yet again. If I were to entertain the notion that you are right and that Brudais has feelings for me, I demand that I have the same opportunities that he had to prove my worth, prove that I am at least his equal. I could not live with less."

Rydril blinked, the hand that he had been reaching out to assist her suddenly contracted back to his side, as if a snake had lunged for it.

"This is your true desire, and yet you would entertain subjecting yourself to marriage to a Krashkin prince, who may never allow you to hold a sword again? To what point and purpose?"

Dania settled, moving so that her back was against the wall. She slid down its length, the grit and grime covering the back of her shirt and trousers, but she didn't care. She bit at her chapped lower lip, sighing. "Peace."

Rydril backed into his own corner of the cell, sliding down to the floor. There was a long silence between them in which only dripping water somewhere in the cells could be heard.

Finally, Rydril cursed, then a laugh escaped him.

"Dania," he said, his voice dark with humor. She looked up at him warily. "You may not think you can measure up to Brudais, but I think *he* may not measure up to *you*."

Chapter Forty-Two

Loya

They had to go to a place outside the castle walls, so they would not be spotted, and they could not use Loya's villa for fear of the magick being traced back to her. Loya had gotten word from her contact in the Zethland court that magick could be read within the walls of a structure, and if a true Seer were to be brought to her villa, they would see the magick used within. Ironically, Tarison had several Seers in his employ for such purposes. He called them his Inquisition so that he could determine if magick were being used by his subjects, but no one ever thought to question that the Seers used magick to inquire into the king's matters. It was frequently this way since Regent Cavison's execution. The commoners were not allowed the use of magick, but it was overlooked in the royal family. Nobles might get away with it here and there, but with Loya's head already so close to the chopping block—especially with that little spat with the other Turivaun governors—she needed to keep her nose clean. A spell like the one they were about to use would not be looked upon favorably by any Inquisitors who might come knocking.

They had situated themselves in a hovel in Quies District, vacated by its current occupants with a few coin and honeyed words. Staliva looked mightily uncomfortable in the squalor that surrounded her, but Loya had stayed in worse places before. She wasn't bothered by the filth.

The hovel was cozy enough for their purposes, dark and dank, except for a few furnishings. Two cots with molding blankets lined the walls, and a cauldron sat in the center of the room. A few bottles of salt and sand were positioned at Loya's feet, while she and Staliva sat cross-legged on the damp floor.

"Are you certain that you are equipped to perform this spell?" Loya asked for the second time, eyeing Staliva carefully. Staliva had been nervous when Loya had brought the idea to her. The Spell of Rudiment was advanced magick, according to her Zethland contact. The Order of Estol did not condone the use of it—unless in extreme circumstances—as it was more of a curse than the benign magicks they practiced. It caused the subject of the spell to revert back to a state of need, the mind transitioning from adulthood to infancy wherein motor functions—and, most especially, their ability to form complete thoughts—were entirely diminished. Loya had frequented some of the houses of elderly subjects of the crown and imagined that this spell would cast the subject into a similar state of dependency. No one would allow Venhil to remain as the king's appointed steward in such a state.

They would cast him out and appoint the next in line, Commander Okriad. It was a shame for the king that his wife had never conceived an heir. He had more than a few bastards wandering the realm, but none that had the legitimacy and favor of the people. The only heirs to the throne were hundreds of miles away, or lost to the winds. Prince Ithiador's claim was undisputed. He was the sole heir to the throne, but his disappearance left the realm unstable. Loya's plans had been designed around his triumphant return to Turivaun after securing their victory in Hyglen with help from the Jaguar Hills, but those plans were teetering on the abyss now that his whereabouts were unknown—and with the uncouth treatment of the Hillpeople after Ithiador's disappearance, they could easily assume their help was now out of the question.

In lieu of any other legitimate options, the closest heir to the throne was Brudais. His claim was in contention, however, due to his murky lineage. Olvar the Bastard had been well known and favored by the Creetian people, so much so that his sire King Reynold II had legitimized him. Olvar had never vied for the throne, even being the firstborn son of the king, but his brother Soville the Heartless had never forgiven his father for his kindness to his half-brother and had tolerated him at court about as much as Tarison did Brudais. Olvar's son, Leifius, had produced the only living male heir after Ithiador—not that Brudais had ever made designs upon the throne. In fact, he had shown outright contempt at the mere suggestion. He was happy to pursue his greatness elsewhere, like his sire and grandsire before him. The line of legends was well-known and expected, but that didn't mean the people forgot where it had originated—in royalty.

The people only believed in the legitimacy of the royal line so long as they benefited from it, and that had not happened since Reynold himself had sat the throne. Ithiador had been a glimmer of hope for the people, thinking that the reign of terror that Tarison now instituted might perhaps come to an end with his rule. This was the campaign that Loya clung to and was now propagating throughout the city within her net of spies. If Ithiador did not return, it would be easy enough to set up Brudais in his place, having come from the Reynold line, as well. If he fought her on it, she would remind him of his sworn duty to his country. The most reluctant rulers were often more suited to it than those who sought power, regardless.

Staliva would marry whichever of the two deigned to seize on Loya's designs and solidify the love of the people. Regent Cavison had been well-loved by all, and Tarison's treatment of him and his family had stood an abhorrent stain on his first days as king. People pitied the outcast child of Cavison, and their pity would provide fruitful retribution; her elevation of status would be like a balm to the unjustified conduct of Tarison in his greed. Loya's eyes brightened at the thought of the look on Tarison's face when the people he had failed to win over in favor of his own desires cast him aside. Triumph swelled in her chest.

Not yet, she reminded herself. Her plans had not fully hatched, and she still needed to knock a few pieces down before the stage could be set for that triumph.

Staliva had been quiet, letting Loya run away with her thoughts, which suddenly made the governor wary. "Staliva, my dear, you must be sure you can do it. I've been told that if the spell is rejected, it may backfire."

"I know," Staliva whispered, staring into space. "I'm readying myself… but I can do it."

"What do you need from me?"

The countess' gaze traveled vacantly from the other end of the tent to meet Loya's eyes. Her lips twitched. "Passion. It would calm the nerves."

Loya leaned forward without hesitation, her lips locking over Staliva's with vigor. Her tongue glided along Staliva's in a frantic dance, hunger igniting between them. It was necessary, yes, but Loya could not help but admit to herself that sometimes necessity and desire were harmonious. Loya's hands locked on Staliva's waist, trailing down to her hips. Staliva jerked away suddenly, and when Loya released her and sat back, she watched as purple flames danced in her lover's eyes.

"*Uhn veya fel reqial pale.*" Staliva's voice was lower than usual, as if she were forcing herself to appear more confident and powerful than she normally felt. She supposed this was necessary to entice the magick that she was calling.

Loya grabbed the bottle of pink salts before her and poured it into the cauldron. It hissed, the oil at the bottom of the basin sizzling as the two ingredients met.

"*Veya fel paq.*"

Heeding the words, Loya poured the sand into the cauldron. The sizzling stopped, and a sudden pop caused Loya to flinch.

"*Reqial pale joh fan Venhil, blesa von Creet.*"

A pale pink cloud of smoke erupted from the cauldron, causing Loya to shrink back. She and Staliva began coughing as the smoke consumed the entire hovel. It swirled around the confines of the room, creating a slow tornado, which began to levitate objects in its wake. The blankets on the cots lifted from their stagnant positions and caught in the twirling air. Loya ducked as one of them nearly struck her, but the other encased Staliva in its tattered fabrics. She flailed her arms, but the blanket seized her, bringing her to the floor.

Loya jumped up, rounded the cauldron, and fumbled past Staliva's thrashing body. Coughing and spitting, Loya reached the door of the hovel, opened it, and the smoke poured out into the night. One of the blankets trailed past Loya with the force of the maelstrom and swept slowly to the ground once it was released into the heavy night air.

Loya turned around, rushing back into the hovel and grabbing the blanket off Staliva, who had gone still. Loya's heart pounded in her ears as she knelt beside the countess, her hand to Staliva's pale face.

"Staliva," she said, coughing and wheezing as she forced herself to speak. "Staliva, look at me."

There was no motion from her, and Loya shook her shoulder. She tore at the blanket, wondering whether it had taken on a life of its own and was now crushing Staliva's torso. Once the blanket was torn off and lay on the ground, Loya placed her hand back on Staliva's cheek.

"Staliva, look at me!"

Suddenly, her eyes opened, and she looked panicked. She began hacking, her chest racking with the effort of getting the smoke out of her lungs. She tried to sit up, and Loya helped her, putting a hand on her back to steady her movements.

"Masiya, save us," Loya whispered.

After a few minutes of coughing, Staliva sat with her elbows on her knees and her hands in her hair, exhausted by the ordeal. She looked sideways at Loya, who had sat herself down beside her, watching her carefully.

"I forgot how to speak," Staliva said, her eyes wet with tears. "I forgot how to breathe."

Loya's eyebrow furrowed at her words. "But you can now."

Staliva's began to shake in violent tremors from the exhaustion. Loya laid a hand on her, rubbing her back in a repetitive rhythm.

"Yes," Staliva said quietly, turning away from Loya and coughing, "but Venhil won't recover so easily."

Loya's hand stopped its motion, feeling the shaking beneath it still. "You're certain?"

"I can feel it working," she replied softly. She turned her head, and Loya watched in fascination as several hairs on Staliva's head turned white, contrasting starkly against the dark brown of the rest of her tresses. Her face was flushed bright red from the effort of coughing, but no other markers seemed to indicate that the spell had done more damage.

"You seem unharmed otherwise."

Staliva groaned into her forearms. "I am spent."

Loya nodded solemnly. "Arrik is outside with the horses. We'll get you back to the villa as quickly as we can, and you can rest for the next three days if needed."

Shaking, Staliva began to stand, and Loya put a hand underneath her armpit and elbow to help her.

"Three days will not be enough, I fear."

"We have time," Loya said encouragingly. She just wished she knew how much.

Chapter Forty-Three

BRUDAIS

"Commander, The Hunt is a children's game. How will it help us get Commander Rydril back?"

Brudais' mind was racing as he considered the nuances of infiltrating Bentixt. It would take a great deal of distraction from the Hyglenian forces to clear away the entry points. Brudais had only visited Bentixt once in his life, and he had never anticipated needing to sneak in. A good commander would have anticipated that eventuality, but he had not been a commander yet. He had been a cocky youth who had just won his first Kresha Cup. The idea of one day being required to scale the Tower of Lyes had not even crossed his arrogant mind, but the memories of the place were still with him, and he did recall an awful stink coming from the western mountain gate. A sewer, perhaps? It would be less guarded than the gate itself. He wouldn't risk any of his soldiers' lives for the possibility that it wasn't.

He was going on this mission alone, but the distraction his men could cause would keep Morvian busy enough not to suspect his quiet entrance into the city. The Hyglenian commander was likely betting on Brudais to make a bold move—or a stupid one.

He had to play this game out very carefully. The boldness of the move would be a feign. The real puzzle would be Brudais' lack of involvement—until he was standing over Morvian with a knife.

Brudais stood still in the midst of Rydril's Blood Guard, his muscles quivering with the effort not to jump into action. They had surrounded him as if he were their second in command, a loyalty that Rydril carried for him which had clearly rubbed off on his battalion.

"The shepherd has taken your commander. How will you get him back?" Brudais posed, his voice carrying against the breeze whipping through the grasses of the encampment.

"We fight!" someone yelled from the group, and a chorus of agreement met the simple statement.

"How will fighting get your commander back?" Brudais looked around at the men, whose expressions were concerned but devoid of deeper thought. "If you want to fight for Commander Rydril's life, you will need more stealth than outright bloodlust. Think about the game. The *children's game*, as Peric pointed out. We must needs a distraction—and one arrogant pup to sneak behind the shepherd's gaze."

Brudais watched with increasing pride as the Blood Guard's eyes lit up with interest and understanding.

"I am going to infiltrate Bentixt, climb the Tower of Lyes, and get Rydril and Dania out. You are Rydril's finest and truest soldiers. If you want to help with his rescue, you will mobilize your unit and march on Hyglen's forces."

Murmuring broke out in the group, but it seemed to be of acquiescence instead of dissent.

"Alone, sir?" Peric's voice said, his voice clipped. "We'll be slaughtered."

"I said 'mobilize.' I did not say 'engage.'"

"Will that be enough of a distraction?"

Brudais began to pace. The Blood Guard nearest him backed away to allow him room to do so. "It must be. We can't afford to lose any of you to stupidity. Besides, the shepherd's forces are stationed an hour's march from here. If they know you're likely to advance, they may intercede, and we may force a counterattack, which the king will have no choice but to meet. Whether or not there is a battle, Morvian will be too distracted to care if a few tower guards go missing from their posts."

"How do you plan to infiltrate the capital?"

Brudais watched Peric out of the corner of his eye. Rydril had trained him well as his second in command. It was inspiring to see a soldier who had a knack for strategic planning.

"My last stay in Bentixt was long ago, but I have an idea of where their sewers empty. If I ride to the capital with a fresh steed, I'll be there in a few turns. You can begin mobilizing once I reach the city. By the time I find my way to the tower, Morvian should be well aware of your plans to attack. The tower is guarded heavily at night, but if I can get there by early morning, the guards may be more concerned with their breakfasts than with keeping their eyes and ears alert. Besides, a morning attack is less obvious. They'll only expect trouble in the dark hours."

"And if you get lost in the sewers? If they're anything like Turivaun's, it may be a labyrinth."

Brudais faltered in his steps for a moment, then continued pacing. "I have an uncanny sense of direction, Captain." *Or rather*, he thought wryly, *I know a spell.* He trusted his own Blood Guard and *veritas* to see the common sense of using magick in such an instance—despite its illegality—but he didn't know Rydril's well enough. He had to be careful with his candor.

Brudais stopped pacing, giving each man in his view a look of the utmost sincerity. "You won't be sacrificial lambs, lads," Brudais said. "My *veritas* are with you."

The relief on their faces was reassuring and the tension much less palpable. Slowly, a smile came to his face.

"Commander Rydril will be back with us in a day's time."

It was a promise that the Blood Guard would hold him to. He steeled himself for the next twenty-four turns. It would be a long fucking night.

"Commander Brudais!" a voice yelled against the murmuring that had broken out. The crowd cleared, and a messenger pushed his way through the throng of Blood Guard, his eyes wide as he took in the scene around him. When he made it to the edge where Brudais stood, he gulped visibly. "You're summoned to the king's tent."

Brudais grunted and shooed the boy away. Once the messenger was past the point of hearing, Brudais' muscles relaxed slightly.

"This changes nothing," Brudais said, his tone clipped. "Captain Peric, get word to the *veritas* of the plan. Speak with Captain Yurik. Begin preparations, but don't mobilize until nightfall, and ensure that the Hyglenian scouts spot you."

"Aye, sir." The group chorused the words like a choir of baritones.

They dispersed from the practice field, and Brudais walked briskly toward mid-camp. He didn't have time for a royal summons, and he didn't have patience for any cautions the king would make against this endeavor. Brudais would not divulge his plans, and the king could hang himself with his caution. Whether Tarison liked it or not, Rydril and Dania's capture was provocation. Wariness was no longer an option.

Brudais stood uneasily in the king's tent with his hands clasped behind his back in a respectful military fashion. His stance was erect, and every muscle in his body was tensed at the awareness of the six Black Guards who surrounded him. They were far enough away so as not to assume menace, but their very presence in the tent at an informal meeting with the king suggested malign intent.

"A kidnapping of the most grievous kind has befallen our camp." Tarison's voice was almost bored, if not for the hint of outrage that suffused his words. He was a clever actor, and almost convincing in his charade. "We are most distressed. Commander Rydril was a vital asset to our cause."

"Is," Brudais corrected sharply.

Tarison looked down his nose at Brudais from his blackthorn throne, a familiar look of contempt on his face. "Yes, of course, but you must realize that there is no hope for the commander now. He is surely in the Tower of Lyes, Bentixt's most heavily guarded prison."

"Hope is a matter of perspective," Brudais said stiffly, "not circumstance."

Tarison ignored him. "And Dania," he said, his voice changing to a purposefully calculated yearning. "We had so wished that we could use her. Her lineage is as impressive as yours, and Krashkin would have slavered for a taste of her. It would have meant an end to the war."

And an end to her life as she knew it, thought Brudais bitterly.

"Again, you say, 'would have' and 'wished.' It appears that the great Tarison King of Creet has given up on one of his most loyal servants and the leverage he needs to end the atrocities he started… because the alternative would be difficult."

The sneer in Brudais' voice did not escape the king's notice. Tarison's nose wrinkled, and he grew angry. "Difficult? Or rather impossible. We know that your feelings for the girl were growing, and your friendship with Rydril is unrivaled, but you cannot possibly imagine a favorable outcome from intervention."

Brudais released his clasped hands and let them fall to his side. His hand was now close enough to his knife hilt to make the Black Guard collectively take a step forward. Tarison held up a hand lazily to stop them.

"I have quite the imagination, Your Majesty."

Tarison looked into his eyes for a moment. Brudais felt the weight of the stare, and the calculation behind it. He knew the moment the king made a choice, for his gaze left the commander abruptly, and he sighed theatrically.

"Go, then," he said, bored again. A faint whisper of resignation and amusement traced his tone. "Do as you will, Commander, but you will leave your *veritas* under my command."

Brudais scoffed loudly, causing Tarison to glare at him.

"My *veritas*, king?" he said with genuine mirth. "My *veritas* will do as they please in my absence. You can recall them at your pleasure, but I make no promises of their loyalty beyond its place behind my sword."

Tarison glowered. "And if you are dead?"

Brudais grinned. "May the gods have mercy on you, Your Majesty, and on all of Hyglen." He placed his right palm on the hilt of his knife, causing the Black Guard around him to tense and do the same, but Brudais walked in the opposite direction, leaving a disgruntled king and disappointed guards in his wake.

He needed to get Ælon and two other horses saddled. If he could get to the Rayshiel Forest on the outskirts of the mountain pass to Hyglen by midnight, his plans would not go amiss—although he did wonder why the king had acquiesced so easily. Alas, he didn't have time to ponder what it meant.

He began running through the encampment to the northern borders, not even allowing himself the dignity of a brisk walk. His muscles ached by the time he reached the northern stables. When he found Ælon, he grabbed his saddle from the rack and flung it over the stallion's back.

"We're in for a rough night, my friend," he said softly. The horse's head bobbed up and down agitatedly in response.

Brudais prepared two other horses from the stables: a blue roan and a chestnut mare, who looked fresh and fleet footed. The walk from the forest to the western mountain gate would take close to two hours, but he couldn't afford to leave the horses closer to his destination—even if he could fashion a post with some cover. He assumed the guards scouted the mountainside. Besides, the forest offered enough cover that once they escaped, they could rest for a while in the shade of the trees before setting off again for the camp.

His mind wandered towards Rydril and Dania's welfare, and whether they had been tortured or maimed. He grit his teeth, imagining a thousand ways they could have been harmed already.

I will get them back, Brudais promised himself.

Now, he had several hours of riding to uncover the reason that they were kidnapped in the first place, and once he unveiled the truth of it, he promised his Ire.

Brudais blinked suddenly as he situated himself on Ælon's back. A conversation with his mother came back to him, a choice between passion and fury. He had made her a different promise, one that might save his life from the hands of his liege lord.

His brow furrowed, and he clasped Ælon's reins in his hands, urging the horse forward, the reins of the other two horses at his hip. He had time to think on the road, but he had aught else to spare. Ælon eased into a trot as they made their way out of the stables, then Brudais gave him his head. He would need the horses' stamina if he were to make it to the sewers by morning.

The plan was fraught with faults, but it was the best he had. And if he died trying to free them? Oh, Pallina would kill him. And that would be the least of his problems.

Chapter Forty-Four

Morvian

A putrid stench wafted up Morvian's nostrils and he gagged. The Tower of Lyes was notorious for its treatment of prisoners, but he hadn't ever had cause to visit the place until now, and the smell alone was punishment enough for such an endeavor. As he made his way up the steps, Oren trailing behind him with a handkerchief to his nose, the stench grew worse and worse.

The guards at each section's entrances must have been immune to the smell by now. He pitied them as he passed them by, their grimaces plainly showing their enthusiasm for holding such an esteemed guard post. Oren's soft chuckle behind him reminded him that their minds were linked. He often forgot because of Oren's lack of reciprocation. His mind was eerily mute most of the time, a deep contrast to Morvian's. A spark of annoyance floated through the link. Perhaps he had struck a nerve with his Mouth. He was never certain when Oren would separate the string of thoughts Morvian had at any given moment enough to be offended by one. Cursing the scholars for not having found a more permanent solution to his affliction, he moved up the stairs.

The prisoners he sought were being held in one of the top chambers. Once they had found the entrance to the cells, the guards motioned them into the chamber. It was dank and murky, as if they were so high that the midnight mists were seeping into the walls of the tower. Morvian peered through the darkness, motioning at Oren.

"Light the torches at the end of the chamber," he said to the guards, who quickly obeyed.

When the flames of the torches ignited, the chamber was flooded with a pale light, and two figures beyond the cell doors came into focus. A dark-skinned man leaned against the cell, his muscled forearms resting lazily against the horizontal bars. The stubble on his face was dark, which cast an eerie brightness to his chestnut eyes against the torch flame.

"Morvian the Mute," Commander Rydril said, his tone casual. "A pleasure to see that the man behind the master plan cares enough to make an appearance—although I must say, your accommodations have been better… or so I've heard."

Morvian sneered.

Oren cleared his throat and read Morvian's mind to find the exact words his commander sought to convey. "Commander Rydril, the pleasure is mine. If the accommodations are not to your liking, we would be happy to find you a shallow grave instead."

A broad smile appeared on Rydril's face. "Your Mouth is about as intimidating as one of the tower's rats."

"A rat," Oren said through gritted teeth, clearly offended at the metaphor, "has its uses, and its bite may be more fatal than a sword wound."

Rydril scoffed. "What is it you want, Commander?"

Morvian took a step to the right and peered into the darkness beyond Rydril's form. A female was standing against the opposite wall, one knee pulled up, while her bare foot balanced on the bricks behind her. She was wearing a tattered pair of trousers and a tight linen shirt which accentuated her breasts. If not for this feature—and the dirty blond hair that nearly touched her backside—he mightn't have known she was female at all. Her left arm was smeared with mud—or what Morvian *hoped* was mud—but she held her hands behind her back in a mockery of military fashion. Could this truly be a legend's spawn?

"Are you the daughter of Grandis?" Oren asked gently. *Too gently*, Morvian thought, flashing a look of warning at Oren. His Mouth's sentiments had no place here. Oren stiffened at the look.

The female shifted her stance, putting her foot on the floor and her hands to her sides. Now Morvian could see the fire behind the ruffled exterior. Something in those piercing hazel eyes told him she was dangerous.

"I am Dania," she said, a little hoarse. The muscles on Rydril's arms and upper back stiffened, as if anticipating a blow. "My father was Grandis the Great."

Morvian's shoulder relaxed a little, finally having received a straight answer, but he had expected the need to torture this information out of her. Suddenly, he came to the realization that if his expectations had proved wrong, he didn't trust the results.

"How can I know for certain?"

Dania smiled, an act which caused a shiver to pass down both Morvian and Oren's spines. "Why don't you open this door, and I'll give you a demonstration?"

Rydril chuckled softly at Oren's look of panic which he could not conceal. "You could ask the guard who tried to hold her down earlier. I think you'll find him in the corner of the guard tower still holding his jewels and moaning."

Dania's smile widened. "That was foreplay," said Dania, balling her fists at her sides. "Give me a weapon and I promise you'll be impressed."

Morvian watched her, trying to determine whether that was a jest or a feign, but her expression seemed genuine. She wasn't just a pawn that King Tarison had planned to use to turn Krashkin against them. She was a danger to him, personally, now that he had given her cause to hate him.

Oren turned to him, shock in his eyes, as he read Morvian's next thought. The commander nodded grimly at Oren, who grudgingly stepped back to grab a crossbow from the nearest guard. Rydril sprang into action, moving backwards and to the right to cover Dania's frame. Oren handed the crossbow to Morvian. He loaded it and growled at Oren, who reluctantly said, "Stand aside, Commander Rydril. You are of great value, and Commander Brudais' attempted rescue will bring him right into the city, where we can dispose of him quietly. The girl, on the other hand, was a Creetian bargaining chip to bring the war to a swift conclusion. I have no use for her."

"You might, if you understood her worth."

Morvian scowled. Oren said, "I understand vengeance, Commander. Krashkin's as well as her own. There is nothing that can be gained from keeping her alive."

"There is, however, something to be prevented by keeping her alive," Rydril said smoothly, as if he already knew he had won the argument. Morvian's interest piqued.

"And what would that be?" Oren asked slowly, his eyes darting from Morvian to Rydril in an attempt to keep up with the conversation.

Rydril watched the end of the bolt in the crossbow carefully as he moved towards Morvian, hands raised in a placating gesture, the cell bars their only separation. The Creetian commander's eyes shone bright against the torch flame. "Brudais is in love with her."

Morvian could not control the astonishment on his face. If he were to murder this girl, Brudais would sweep through Bentixt with a vengeance so deadly that he shivered at the thought of the blood that would be spilt. He had not planned to harm Commander Rydril for fear that he would provoke Brudais' wrath. If Morvian had the blood of Brudais' beloved on his hands, all his carefully laid plans would collapse into piles of ash. Unless Brudais fell perfectly into the trap Morvian had set, he would be at the mercy of a renowned killer. Could he afford to take the chance that his trap might fail?

Morvian knew Brudais and had made it a point to follow the commander throughout his military career. He was loath to admit that Brudais might have been the cleverer of them. The risk might have been too great to ignore—although the risk of Grandis' daughter's sanctuary in Creet ever coming to light for their Krashkin neighbors was likewise a terrifying risk. The crossbow wavered in his hand.

Morvian smiled suddenly. The hand that held the crossbow dropped to his side. A new plan began to form in Morvian's mind.

The look on Oren's face was surprised and confused, but there was a hint of respect there, too.

"All right, Commander," Oren said slowly. Morvian watched as the expressions on Rydril and Dania's faces turned from haughty to concerned. "You win this round, but I promise you, I shall win the next. I'm looking forward to Commander Brudais' visit."

Stepping back, he pivoted on his feet and strode out of the chamber. On Morvian's way past the guards, with his Mouth at his heels, Oren commanded the guards not to touch the prisoners and to get them more appropriate attire. They would be having a guest soon.

Chapter Forty-Five

Loya

It hadn't taken longer than a few days for Staliva's spell to show signs of fruition. At first, Steward Venhil had been forgetful, his speech slurring, and many of the dignitaries who dealt with him regularly were beginning to think he had been imbibing in his favorite extracurricular activity of drinking himself into a stupor during his working hours. Then it became obvious that he was no longer fit for duty when, one morning, he had failed to remember how to step out of his bed. Menders had been called to see to the steward's health, but no one could account for the sudden change. Everyone had been adamant that Commander Okriad take over the royal duties while he… recovered.

It was Loya's luck that, when the Inquisitors were called to investigate, they were lackluster in their attempts to find a magickal culprit. Okriad was too busy with his new post to consider following up with them, and the matter was quickly determined to be an 'unfortunate turn of the steward's health'—likely brought on by his unhealthy lifestyle. Once the rumors—circulated not only from Loya's spies, but also from the common folk themselves—began to spread that Venhil had gone mad from something he had picked up in the brothels he frequented, the people no longer seemed to suspect a hex, but rather a justified and fitting fate. Since the steward had never deemed it appropriate to cultivate a good reputation amongst the people, it was no surprise to anyone that he had already been forgotten by the time Okriad took his seat of office.

Loya mused at the wonderful potential that this new order of power presented for her. Okriad was one of the newest to his station of command, and he was more concerned with advancement and praise than actually ruling the country in the king's absence. Since he had no true friends at court, Loya had made herself available to him for counsel at every opportunity. He accepted her aid for lack of an alternative; his 'lowly' station as commander and ignoble background made him an outsider to the nobles at court, and Tarison's advisors deemed him an inappropriate alternative to the drooling, immobile Venhil. Loya had taken advantage of this ostracism, frequenting the castle more in the last fortnight than in the whole of her first term as governor.

"But Lady-Governor, what of the supplies being requested by the army in Hyglen? Can we afford to provide them, and what protection can we afford to spare for their transit?"

"Lady-Governor, there have been stirrings of riots in Kelvs District over the food rationing. How can we abate such tendencies during wartime?"

"My dear Lady-Governor, the people are crying for the return of their prince. What more can be done to discover his whereabouts?"

Loya had a solution for every problem Okriad brought to her—save Ithiador. She had assured the new steward that the prince would be discovered, given enough time and resources, which her allies in Phesius were willing to provide, but even she was having difficulty coming to terms with no one hearing even a whisper of Ithiador's whereabouts since his disappearance. The people were beginning to think that with the king and his heir absent, Creet was ripe for a foreign adversary to attempt to seize power. Little did they know that Loya was already ensuring that power would be seized from within.

The only kink in her carefully laid plans was that her two assurances of securing the throne were across the continent, either waging war or lost to the winds. It would have been much easier to secure this coup with a corporeal figurehead whom the people could turn to during this uncertain time. Alas, there was only Loya and the blubbering fool who was hanging on her every word.

Things could have been worse.

"Governor."

Arrik's voice was hesitant as he spoke from the doorway of the library, where Loya lounged on a chaise, her book propped against her knee, open to a page on the Krashkin Raids. She had been deep in concentration on the history of the subject—especially the Creetian people's abhorrence for Grandis the Great, who had propagated a great deal of the raids in his time. It was incredible how a figure such as him could be so revered by one class of Humans only to be reviled by another. Legends were complicated beings. She didn't want to raise her head from her page until she had finished the sentence, but the quaver in the boy's voice merited her attention.

When her gaze shifted from the text to the doorway, Arrik stood there, rigid and unmoving, a knife positioned in the crook of his neck. A thin line of blood ran down the skin. Loya peered into the darkness of the corridor to see a woman, clothed in a plain beige burka which sunk to the floor in folds and crossed over her shoulder in an eastern fashion. The hand on the knife must have belonged to this woman, whose head and face were obscured by her garments, but her eyes were alight with magick. Loya saw the gleam of purple in her irises even from a distance. They sparkled threateningly in the dim light.

Slowly, Loya closed her book and slid it onto the table in front of her, taking extra care with her movements.

"Good 'morrow, my lady," she said, trying to keep the quaver from her voice. The knife on Arrik's neck pricked his skin again, a renewed stream of blood rolling down the boy's neck. "How can I be of assistance to you?"

The woman's eyes narrowed. Her trust in others must have been minimal, at best, for an offer of assistance in this situation to be considered hostile.

"I welcome you into my home," Loya said with more confidence, "and hope that my page has not given offense in his ignorance to your customs."

There were a few seconds between her words and the gradual lowering of the knife where Loya studied the woman's expression. Her eyebrows had drawn together, and then slowly relaxed, the creases between her eyes softening. Arrik gulped, his eyes pleading with his mistress.

"Will you let him go, my lady? He's just a boy."

The woman considered this for a moment. "Boys can be just as cruel as men… perhaps more so."

Loya stood slowly, hands outstretched in a sign of surrender. The woman's hand twitched.

"Indeed they can be," she said, choosing her words carefully, "but this one means you no harm, and I am rather fond of him."

After a moment of contemplation, the woman released her grip on Arrik's shoulder and held the knife away, pushing him gently forward into the room and away from her. Arrik tripped over the rug and stumbled his way to Loya's side, breathing heavily.

Loya breathed a sigh of relief, putting a calming hand on Arrik's shoulder.

"Now, my lady, what can I do for you?"

Now that the intruder was free of her captive, her eyes glided around the inside of the library, undoubtedly looking for more threats. While she considered her next words, Loya spotted another figure hovering in the shadows behind her. She was a young girl—perhaps no more than fifteen—wearing a scarf around her head but nothing to cover her face. Her expression was one of terror, with her dark eyebrows scrunched together, fear in her wide eyes.

"We are in need of sanctuary," said the woman, whose voice was smooth but held a deep and menacing undertone.

Loya had supposed as much. Raids were not common anymore, and she doubted very much that her guards would have failed to report intruders in the city before she could make the proper preparations to prevent her manor from being invaded. She doubted still further that two young women would have been part of such a raid. It was not often that peoples from the east traveled into Creetian lands—unless they were traders. Somehow, Loya did not anticipate that they were here to trade goods with her.

Her initial inspection of the two had caused her to believe they hailed either from Hoefke or Sycil. Their tattered appearance—as if they had been on the road for many leagues—tended to indicate the former, but the woman had a presence about her that lent itself to royalty. Her shoulders had never relaxed and she stood tall, as one of noble birth. Even the girl, in her terror, gave the impression of nobility. Hoefkians were vagabonds, their dwellings in huts amongst desert plains, and even their highest of office were raiders and thieves. These two females gave off an air of nobility with their posture, which meant that they were Sycillians. Only King Ulden's spawn would show such inherent traits in their demeanor.

Princesses, she thought, surprised. Princesses in need of sanctuary. Her mind began spinning with the possibilities and consequences of such action. Ulden would be furious. Tarison would never agree for fear of magickal retribution. Things would need to be kept quiet. As long as Okriad heeded her advice, she could sneak them off to a corner of their allied lands, but did she dare?

She was fully aware of Princess Eldeva's alleged power from her Sycillian spies. Her education in the Old Order was well-known, and Loya didn't need an angered sorceress on her list of enemies—not at such a crucial time. It might even be to her advantage to aid them. Calling for a favor in the future from one so powerful might prove the difference between success in her schemes and utter failure. *Look at how useful Staliva has been*, she reminded herself, gazing at Eldeva with a renewed sense of certainty.

Loya smiled pleasantly, squeezing Arrik's shoulder to remind herself that the boy was still present. She needed to take care with her every word.

"Princess," Loya said, watching those purple eyes light with surprise to hear the title, "I am happy to assist you however I can, but tell me, if you will, why you came to me, of all people, with such a request."

Eldeva clasped the edge of her face-covering, pulling it down so that Loya could see her features clearly. She was beautiful beyond compare, and her delicate features contrasted with the hard expression she wore. She looked to be in her fifties—the prime of her Human life—but Loya knew that the girl was only sixteen, like the twin sister standing at her back. Amazing, how magick could rob one of youth and innocence. If Loya had come across Eldeva without knowing her, she might have suspected she was Mayora's mother.

"Prince Ithiador spoke highly of you," said the princess, her voice softening as it said the prince's name. "He said you could be trusted."

A foolish concept, trust, she thought, but didn't allow the sentiment to show on her face. She smiled warmly instead. "I am always happy to help a friend of the prince."

The purple hue in Eldeva's eyes was fading, but the light in them at the mention of Ithiador grew. "Has he returned to the city?" she asked.

Loya analyzed the tenor of her voice and the light in her eyes and came to a sudden, shocking conclusion. Ithiador was more than a mere acquaintance to this Sycillian princess. She was surprised that her spies had not unveiled the truth sooner than she herself had—especially given the princess' own transparency. What good was a spy who could not even inform her of a foreign love affair between two such important figures?

"I'm afraid the prince has still not been found," she replied. "We are employing all our efforts to ensure his safe return to Creet."

Eldeva's face hardened at the news. "He has passed beyond my Sight—I fear he is in the clutches of an enemy whose magicks are far more powerful than ours."

The Old Order was known to be one of the most formidable magickal orders created by Humans. The only rival to its authority was the Order of Estol, which had originated in Zethland. If the magicks veiling Ithiador's whereabouts were beyond their power to uncover, she wondered about the other possibilities. Non-Human races like the Crendor and Lowens were well-versed in their magickal abilities, but they were far-removed from Kreshan affairs, and their isolation on their respective continents of Firdesh and Madidus gave Loya the impression that they couldn't care less what happened in the Ten Kingdoms. But there might have been a race on Kresha which would despise Humans for their intervention and conquest of the Kreshan continent. *Although*, Loya thought uneasily, *it is just a myth*. The Fayn had not been seen or heard from in centuries. Could they really have played any part in these insignificant Human affairs?

"Perhaps you would like to take a seat?" Loya asked, motioning to the couch and armchair across from her. At least she would have enough separation from the princesses to feel at ease during their conversation. Eldeva and Mayora moved slowly to the proffered seats and slunk gracefully into the cushions. Mayora's expression was beginning to soften.

"Arrik, bring us a pot of tea, will you?"

The boy had been ready to bolt regardless, so she thought she might as well give him an excuse to run while keeping his dignity intact. He rushed from the room, holding a hand to his bloodied neck.

"So, you have tried to contact Ithiador with magick, I take it," she said, keeping the conversation on the prince, as this seemed to be a safe topic for the princess—though not so safe that it could be openly admitted to. If the Creetian people knew that Ithiador had been bedding a sixteen-year-old Sycillian princess, they would be furious. Not only were Sycil and Creet on rocky terms, but the prince was nearly thrice her age.

"I have, but to no avail," said Eldeva despondently. "He was meant to contact me after his venture to the Jaguar Hills, but I have not heard from him since."

Loya swallowed, a lump forming in her throat. She wondered absently what activities their last encounter had entailed. Trying not to envision such a thing, she said, "If he were in any mortal danger, I feel that it would have been discovered."

Ithiador's prone body came to Loya's mind suddenly, and she imagined him buried deep in the Fayn Forest, his pale skin stark against the red leaves that covered him. She blinked. Thank the gods she had a secondary solution to her coup's lack of leadership. She could not imagine Brudais shirking this duty if the choice were between him and Tarison. The good of the people demanded it, and Staliva was a beautiful woman. Despite their familial relationship, he would marry her for the good of the realm.

Eldeva blanched, as if she had read Loya's thoughts. "Who is she?" the princess said, her expression hardening and her voice leaking with venom.

The tone and subject had changed so suddenly that Loya realized she must truly have been reading her thoughts. "Who, Princess?"

"The bitch you intend to wed to Ithiador," Eldeva said, her eyes narrow and hostile. "You are planning a coup with him at its head."

Loya's gaze fell on Mayora, whose eyes were wide in panic, looking at her sister in shock and fear.

Eldeva stood from her seat in the armchair, her burka skirts pooling onto the floor. Her eyes flashed violently, and Loya slid further back on her chaise.

"The Countess Staliva," she said slowly, so as not to provoke Eldeva further. "They are to wed as soon as he returns."

A tense silence hung between them. The expression on Eldeva's face did not change, but the purple of her irises shone with an eerie light against her sun-kissed skin. A heaviness filled the air as she breathed in. Loya closed her eyes and covered her head with her arms as every window in the manor shattered.

Loya pulled the blanket over her; the cup of steaming tea in her hands was not enough to warm her bones after what had happened, and the lack of windows was creating a cooling effect on the entire manor. The chill was harsh, surely, but what was more chilling was the look in Princess Eldeva's eyes when she had unleashed her rage. Loya had never seen anything like it.

She suppressed a shiver, glancing across the table at Mayora. The girl was staring into her cup of tea, unblinking. It had been her suggestion that Eldeva take a calming bath following her… outburst. The sisters had held hands and conversed in low tones away from Loya, but the governor had the impression that of the two princesses, Mayora showed the majority of the emotional maturity. She at least knew how to calm her sister after Eldeva had called too much magick to her, allowing it to consume her.

Loya had led Eldeva to the bathroom on unsteady legs, expecting the princess and her excess of power to eviscerate her if she made a wrong step. Her body was rigid with fear when she returned to the library after drawing Eldeva her bath. Loya had servants who could have done these things, but she had warned them away with her wide-eyed stares as they approached, imploring them to flee, which they had gladly done. She was surprised at their resilience and willingness to help—even after the windows had shattered. She might have fled herself if she didn't think it would get her killed.

Mayora blinked suddenly, her gaze slowly meeting Loya's. "I apologize for my sister's reaction," she said quietly. "Her response to any threat is to call the magicks to her. She doesn't know another way."

Loya wondered at the idea that Eldeva considered Ithiador and Staliva's marriage to be a threat. She didn't know how long Ithiador had been bedding the girl, but it must have been serious for her to take such offense to his future plans. *Although,* she thought, *she is only a girl.* A girl whose emotional stability was in question. Just what had Ithiador gotten himself entangled in?

"The windows are no matter," Loya said gingerly. "I can have someone here to see to them tomorrow. It may be a few days of discomforting chill before they can be replaced, but we will make do. I am more concerned with Princess Eldeva's… mood."

Mayora flinched at the word. "She has talked of nothing but your prince since we left Vorsai. I'm surprised she was able to control her magick as well as she did at your… distressing news."

Control her magick? Loya wanted to scoff, but stopped herself, gulping instead to find her throat had suddenly gone very dry.

"Is there any chance that Prince Ithiador might wed my sister, instead of this… countess?" Mayora's voice quavered as she said the words. "She *is* a princess, after all."

Loya almost choked at the look of hope and sincerity in the girl's eyes. She may have been more emotionally mature than her sister, but that said nothing of her naivety of political alliances. Enemies did not wed unless they were trying to broker peace treaties. Sycil and Creet had not been in talks to do so for over two decades. With the contention between them regarding the rightful possession of the Jaguar Hills, she doubted they ever would again.

"I'm afraid," Loya said slowly and evenly, "that is not possible. Princess though she may be, your sister is also a well-known sorceress—not to mention she is only sixteen, like yourself. Creetians do not marry until they are twenty."

"Sycillians can marry at thirteen."

Just one of the many practices Creetians found abhorrent in their errant neighbors.

"When Ithiador returns, he will need to make a strong match with a well-known and beloved figure. Eldeva is a foreigner with no ties to this land. She will be treated as an outcast, and Ithiador's claim may be challenged."

Besides, Ithiador may not return. This was all conjecture until he resurfaced.

"Despite this turn of events, I still wish to help you." Loya licked her lips and took a sip from her teacup. The hot liquid soothed her dry throat. "I can offer you sanctuary, but it cannot be in Creet. If your father were to discover that Creet had knowingly hid you from him, we would be inviting war. I have many connections throughout the Ten Kingdoms. I think if you must hide from King Ulden, you will need to go as far as possible. Nesliarc or Zethland should do. You will be safe there."

Mayora sipped her tea. "Eldeva will not like that option."

"Your wish was for sanctuary," Loya reminded her. "They are your only options."

A nagging feeling settled in Loya's gut as they continued to sip their tea, the chill wind swirling through the library from the shattered glass windows. It was better to aid a dangerous person than to thwart them. Loya was playing a dangerous game by doing both.

Chapter Forty-Six

BRUDAIS

His hands fumbled with the horses' reins as he tied them hastily to the tree. He loosened Ælon's reins slightly, knowing that if he weren't back when he expected to be, the horse would simply untie himself and find food.

He crossed the mountain footpath swiftly, as the deepening night settled. The noises of crickets and wind around him were isolated and eerie, but the lack of guards told him he still had a ways to go before he reached the mountain gate.

Why had Morvian resorted to kidnapping? Dania was likely a means to stop the alliance with Krashkin—that much was easily perceived—but how he knew of her existence was not so simple. Regardless, to Morvian, it would be more prudent to kill her than to keep her alive. This thought caused his pace to quicken along the foothills. Rydril's predicament seemed like the most obvious trap in the world. By capturing his best friend, he would draw Brudais out, separating him from his Blood Guard. Morvian had always seen him as a rival, and perhaps he meant to kill Brudais to ensure Hyglen's best chance of winning the war. The other commanders had their uses, but even Brudais had to admit, they were more a liability than an aid to strategy. So many voices in one ear only led to confusion. Better to have a single voice speaking clearly and confidently to keep the doubt at bay. That is what all the kings before Tarison had understood, and what he suspected Tarison did understand but ignored in favor of loyalty at the cost of chaos. If Brudais fell, and Rydril was not there to lead the *veritas*, he wondered who they might turn to… or against.

If Tarison expected their loyalty, he was sadly mistaken. The Creetian troops would be divided, and the *veritas* would perhaps abandon the campaign outright. Creet would challenge Hyglen with even numbers and possibly fall within a few weeks, running back to Turivaun with their tail between their legs. The War That Never Should Have Been, ending in spectacular failure, all because the camp had been infiltrated by a half dozen men with stolen Creetian armor. *Tricks and lies*, he thought, cursing softly. Morvian was cunning, but… so was Rydril. If they met face to face, perhaps his friend would convince the commander to spare Dania, for his sake. He had made it clear enough to Rydril how he felt about her. He wouldn't let them kill her without using a few tricks of his own. Brudais smiled, hoping he was right. Sweet Masiya, please let him be right.

After a few hours on foot, the forest thinned and the mountains came into view. It was too dark to tell where the mountain gate was, but he quietly scanned the area with his eyes until he spotted the torchlight. He moved towards it but at a good enough distance where the guards would not spot him in the pale light. He had decided to check the area to the right of the gate first. It would have been easier for them to situate a sewer on that side, given the city was up the right side of the mountain.

He heard the murmuring of the guards at the gate as he slipped around to the right. It didn't take him long to find the small culvert where a mountain stream ran through Bentixt's walls. He discovered that not far from this culvert was an open sewer tunnel, and the foul stench filled his nostrils. He gagged as he walked closer, the smell making his eyes water, but he didn't have a choice. This was the only way he would not alert the guards to his whereabouts. There were no Hyglenians guarding the sewer, so he moved through it, careful not to make any noise as his boots gently came in contact with the water flowing from its base.

Once within, he saddled up close to the edge of the sewer, upon a ledge which was elevated from the rest of the tunnel and the muck that was slowly seeping down the mountainside. He was careful not to step in it; he didn't need the guards smelling him before he slit their throats.

It took him a half turn to move through the tunnels, but he did not encounter another living soul. He wondered why the open sewer passage wasn't more heavily guarded, but then... perhaps there was a reason why his passage wasn't being blocked.

When he emerged from the labyrinth of tunnels, he found a stone staircase leading up to a metal grate. He was slow to push it open, but it creaked loudly regardless. Brudais had his dagger out in a matter of moments, anticipating some resistance. He expected a host of guards to come pouring down the passageway, armed to the teeth... but there was no one to guard the grate, either.

Brudais' stomach tightened. This was too easy.

Suddenly, he heard footsteps echoing along the corridor, and he pushed himself to the side of the wall, waiting. When the footsteps rounded the corner and a form moved in front of him against the darkness, Brudais sprang forward, grasping the guard by the arm and pressing his dagger to the figure's throat. Instead of slicing through his windpipe, Brudais decided he needed answers more than a Hyglenian corpse to hide.

"Answer my questions, or your body feeds the rats."

There was no response besides a quavering breath and the smell of urine.

"Why are these tunnels abandoned?"

The guard gulped, his skin pricking the blade. "By order of Commander Morvian, the sewers were to be unmanned for the next two nights."

"Why?"

"Haven't a clue. No reason was given."

"Where are we?"

"Under the city barracks."

That accounted for the smell, at least. "How do I get to the Tower of Lyes from here?"

The guard hesitated a little too long, likely trying to determine whether a lie would get him killed. Brudais grabbed his arm, twisting it behind his back harder, then drawing his attention back to the knife at his neck. "The barracks buttress the tower on the western side. Take the tunnel to the right and follow it until you meet a fork, then take the stairs on the left... but there has been a double guard posted on the tower since last night. You won't make it up those stairs."

He had expected as much. His solution had been to bloody his sword with Hyglenians until he reached the summit, but he now realized his chances of success were lessened, lacking the element of surprise. Morvian knew he was coming, wanted him to come, to get himself killed in this attempted rescue.

If he were to surprise Commander Morvian, he would have to make a personal visit.

"Where is the commander's office?"

Brudais felt the guard flinch. "Down the left corridor, east. Past two corridors, up the stairs on the left. His office is the first set of doors you'll come to."

"And you wouldn't be lying to me, would you, my good man?"

The guard shivered. "No, sir."

Brudais moved his hand, pulling the dagger away from the man's neck. The guard breathed a sigh of relief, but Brudais brought the hilt of the dagger down on the back of the guard's skull, and he crumpled to the ground in a heap. It was a mercy he couldn't really afford at a time like this, but the guard wouldn't come to until Brudais had reached Morvian, and by then it wouldn't matter if he raised an alarm. Besides, he had made a promise. Passion over fury.

He followed the guard's directions until he reached the staircase. Torchlight lit the corridor before him. He heard several guards speaking, their voices trailing down the stairway. Surprise meant blood or stealth, and he couldn't afford to make the noise that blood would require—especially with two guards.

"G*hove hei sheen*," Brudais whispered into the thick air. Holding out his hand before him, he watched it disappear before his eyes. The spell was called the Degrees of Nightshade. Depending on its strength, it caused the Keeper to become invisible to the naked eye. He could sneak up the stairs, past the guards, and into Morvian's office, without a single drop of blood spilled. His mother had taught him the spell when he was sixteen, but he never had occasion to use it—until now. The magick within him warmed his bones, reminding him that it was present and willing. He quietly ascended the steps, his light footsteps barely audible against the guards' echoed conversation.

He was nearly to the top, watching the two guards argue quietly amongst themselves.

"The Creetians are about to attack," one of them said. "We should be preparing our reserve troops."

"Do you trust the commander or not?" the other whispered fiercely. "He's got a plan. Men like him always have a plan."

"Well, I hope his 'plan' can save our troops from the *veritas*."

Brudais' heart thudded in his chest, preparing himself to walk between them.

"It will," the other guard said. "You'll see. He didn't capture the two in the tower for no reason."

Slowing his breathing, Brudais slipped lightly between the guards, passing by them with no resistance, but when he reached the edge of the torchlight, one of the guard's glanced in his direction.

"Wha' was that?" he asked, panicked.

Brudais halted, not wanting them to overhear his footsteps.

After a long moment of silence in which the guards looked around the corridor, the other said, "You seeing ghosts again?"

"Shove off. I thought I saw something over there."

"Expect it was your imagination again."

"If you were on guard duty here more often, you'd see ghosts, too."

Brudais stepped across the corridor while they continued to bicker, his footsteps once again lost against their prattle. He passed the two corridors the guard had told him about, then came upon a set of giant oaken doors. He grabbed the iron knob on the right and pulled. The door opened into a circular foyer, leading to a great staircase which wound up along the edge of the wall. Brudais mounted the steps, climbing them until he reached a wide chamber. The room had a dank, musty feel to it. It was lined with bookshelves. There were no windows, just stark stone walls hung with a few tapestries. A long oak desk stood at one end, and behind it sat Commander Morvian.

His face was drawn with concern as he scribbled furiously over the parchment laid before him on the desk. Brudais' gaze shifted to a chair to the left of the desk where a young soldier with dark stubble sat idly, his piercing blue eyes scanning the room without interest.

Morvian looked up, giving the young man a scathing look, and he immediately stopped tapping his foot against the stone floor. When Morvian moved his gaze back to his parchment, he must have caught a glimpse of Brudais in the corner of his eye. The Degrees of Nightshade faded without constant reinforcement, so his guise may have been wavering in the torchlight. It was no matter. Brudais released the magick and watched the look in Morvian's eyes turn from curiosity to surprise.

The young man jumped out of his chair, spinning around to look at Brudais in alarm and terror.

"Commander," he said hoarsely, clearing his throat. "We did not expect you… here."

Brudais smiled, glancing from the man who had spoken to Morvian, whose eyes were calculating. This was the Mouth, Brudais presumed. He'd heard Morvian had found a way around his… predicament. "But you expected me elsewhere, I'm sure."

"Indeed," said the Mouth.

Brudais stared at Morvian, whose shock had all but disappeared.

"Would you care to sit down? You must be exhausted."

"I prefer to stand in the presence of enemies. More room for maneuvering."

The Mouth gulped. "As you wish," he said shakily. "Do you know why you are here, Commander?"

"It was either kill my way to the top of the Tower of Lyes, or hold you hostage until you bring me what I came for."

Morvian had the audacity to smirk. His Mouth was not so bold, and the look of terror persisted. He said, "You are here because I have managed to take the only two things you'd be willing to die for. Your friend was easy enough to target, but I had no idea what I instigated when I kidnapped the girl."

Brudais clenched his jaw.

"Friendship and love. So banal, yet so powerful."

An involuntary growl came from deep in Brudais' throat. "Is there a point you're intending to reach?"

"I have something you want," the Mouth said, becoming increasingly confident. "You can have them back… for a price."

Brudais stepped forward, and immediately the Mouth took three frightened steps back, nearly knocking over the chair in his haste to vacate the area within reach of Brudais' sword point. Ignoring this display, Morvian watched Brudais intently as he took a seat in another chair across from the desk, lowering himself slowly onto the cushion.

"As long as we're negotiating terms," he said, his gaze moving from the Mouth to Morvian, "I might as well get comfortable."

The Mouth's quivering breath was all that could be heard in the chamber before Morvian reached down to open a desk drawer, drawing out a bottle of Nexvin's Finest and two snifters.

If the choice is between blood and whiskey, Brudais thought, watching Morvian pour two glasses and slide one across the wooden desk, *I suppose amber is more palatable than crimson.*

Chapter Forty-Seven

ELDEVA

Eldeva shifted in her seat, the horse below her snorting uncomfortably. She had never warmed to animals. She wondered whether it was her magick that caused them to always be discontented in her presence, or her nature to make things flee.

An image of Ithiador came to her mind, and she snarled, pushing it aside. It had not been any fault of hers that Ithiador was to marry that harlot. She understood the political ramifications and reasoning, but that didn't mean that her heart didn't ache at the thought of his hands on the countess, tenderly exploring her perfect Creetian curves. Eldeva hissed, and her horse stomped its foot into the ground warningly. The heat was rising in her at these thoughts, and she had to calm herself before it consumed her again. She was embarrassed by her reaction in Governor Loya's manor, but she had been taken by complete surprise.

She had not really expected Ithiador to have returned to the city, but she certainly hadn't expected him to be caught up in a coup attempt upon her arrival. Plans that he didn't even know about, entangling him in betrayal of kin and seizure of the throne. After all his rhetoric about keeping to the royal line of succession, he would be placed in an impossible situation. Tarison would be ousted, his heir would ascend in his place, and she supposed the Creetians would rejoice in their change of fortune. Eldeva refused to care for their plight. Her only thoughts circulated around Ithiador's wandering hands, his betrayal of her.

They had never had a real chance of happiness together. Sycil and Creet were bitter enemies, always feuding over something, but Eldeva had thought that perhaps if she were to forsake her Sycillian roots, the Creetians might open their arms to her. *Foolish girl*, she thought bitterly. She was a sorceress of the Old Order. Creetians were conservative in their culture, and primordial in their refusal of magick. Loya had been right. She would have been an outcast, and Ithiador's judgment would have been questioned.

Mayora's voice interrupted her thoughts. "Sister," she said softly. "Can I help?"

Eldeva's lip curled in a sneer. "Not unless you can change the past."

Her sister sighed. "If I knew how, I would… for you."

The princess looked up, gazing out onto the horizon. They were riding through the fields of Phesius with an escort of Creetian guards. They had made good time since they had set out from Turivaun two days prior. Their escort was leading them over allied lands to the Recluos River, where they were to board a vessel that would take them upriver to Zethland's capital, Lolaith. There, they were to be succored and taken under the wing of a prominent priestess of the Order of Estol named Xenia. She had agreed to help them for Loya's sake. She now owed a lot to Loya, and this priestess, for their goodwill. She wondered how they intended her to repay them.

A thought occurred to Eldeva as she gazed out on the grassy plains before her, the sunlight dancing on the blades of grass, moving peacefully with the winds. *I don't need to change the past,* she thought, giving way to a smile. *I just need to change the present.* And that *was* within her control.

When Eldeva had stayed with Loya for those short few days before they had set out for Zethland, she had sensed that the governor had recently used magick. It was how she picked up the scent of that Creetian bitch who was to wed Ithiador. It was a psychic scent which, with enough practice, Keepers could distinguish and analyze, uncovering a fellow Keeper's last spells. Loya gave off only a whiff of spellwork, but it was enough for Eldeva to determine which spell she had helped the countess with last. The Spell of Rudiment. It was complicated spellwork for an amateur like Staliva. She was surprised it had worked with such expediency. Eldeva herself had only performed it once on a goat. It had regressed so much that it no longer had the ability to see or walk, and they had slaughtered it before Ghavole's altar not long after.

Eldeva and Mayora had a tent pitched for them in the Phesian wilderness. It was their third night on the road, but it was a great improvement upon their previous travels. They had rode for long miles from Vorsai to Turivaun over treacherous desert. When they had come upon the Recluos River on the Creetian borders, they had bathed in the waters fully clothed. Their travels had left them worn and exhausted, and they were fortunate that the last leg of their journey was in the boat of a fisherman, who had happened upon them bathing in the river. This journey had been much smoother with four guards to keep them safe from vagabonds on the road, acting as servants when they made camp to rest each night, setting up their tents for them and cooking them food. Tonight they had settled on the bank of a deserted lake a days' ride from the river.

It was well past midnight now, and Eldeva lay awake, staring at the roof of their tent. If not for the Creetian people and their prosaic ways, Eldeva might have stood a chance marrying their prince. Creetians… with their conservative ideals. They needed to be taught a lesson; they could refuse to use magick, but that did not mean others would even the playing field to better suit them. The world was an unfair place. Eldeva was distinctly aware of this. Perhaps the Creetians would think twice about their magick ban and abhorrence of sorcery if they saw what their folly unleashed.

She pushed her blankets aside quietly, so as not to wake her sister, and left the tent. The guards were asleep in their own tents, but the fire was still crackling. One of the small pots they used to cook their meals was lying beside the fire, and she positioned it over the embers, pouring a bit of water from one of the guard's canteens into it. It sizzled against the sides of the warm pot.

She placed both hands on the cold earth before her.

"*Veeola, sheeru fa,*" she whispered, and raised her hands, palms up. Flecks of salt separated themselves from the ground under her hands and rose into their air, settling into her palms. It was enough.

"*Uhn veya fel requial pale.*"

She flung the salt into the pot. It hissed as it mixed and dissolved into the liquid. Warmth began to lick her toes, trailing slowly up her legs.

"*Veya fel paq.*"

Heat flooded her pelvis, blossoming in her chest. She grabbed a handful of sand from the ground, sprinkling it into the pot.

"*Requial pale joh fan sorhail von Creetian hal.*"

A blinding light filled Eldeva's eyes, and she gasped in surprise—only to find that smoke filled her lungs. She coughed until she tasted blood filling her mouth. Then she felt the pain, seizing her like two hands grasping both sides of her head and squeezing until her skull cracked. Between the coughing and the pain, she suddenly couldn't breathe. She fell to her side, grasping desperately at her throat. She gasped, feeling a swift air fill her lungs. Her eyes were wide in terror, but all she saw were blurred shapes through the tears and she could hear nothing over the sound of her own screams.

Chapter Forty-Eight

BRUDAIS

Brudais raised the glass to his lips, but waited for Morvian to take the first sip.

"You don't trust me?" the Mouth asked, his voice a little weak.

"Would you?" Brudais countered, watching the smirk return to Morvian's face. "Your deceptions have landed us in this mess in the first place. Poison is the last way I wish to leave this world."

Morvian's expression was thoughtful. "What about magick?" the Mouth said shakily. "It was good enough for your father."

Brudais stiffened, his entire body rigid. The glass slid from his hand, shattering against the stone floor.

"What did you say?" His voice was menacing, and the Mouth shrank back a few paces farther.

"Leifius of Creet, murdered by a sorcerer's spell. It's a well-known story in the east."

"It's a well-known *lie*," Brudais replied, his fists clenched on the arms of his chair.

"If you say so. I've never heard of an illness that can spread through the body in only two days, devouring muscle like acid. I do know a spell, though. It's called Vorshayth's Rite. It was all the rage a few decades ago—particularly among assassins. So common, in fact, that people suspected the spreading of an unknown illness. The Rite is known to have... *protective* qualities, ensuring that healing magicks fail."

His mother's image came to his mind—Xenia, crouched over his father's still body, her face drawn and pale, years older than it had been before she had tried to heal him—and to no avail.

"Who gave the order?" he asked quietly, teeth clenched.

"No one knows for certain," the Mouth replied, "but his king was suspected."

Tarison. Brudais' blood ran cold. No clever thoughts came to him, no witty remarks. His mind was blank and his body still. He could feel pure rage coursing through his veins, pumping anew with every heartbeat.

"Why are you telling me this?"

Morvian's face was carefully devoid of emotion. "Because I need to tell you another story. One about his son."

Brudais' pulse quickened.

"Leifius' son was destined for greatness from a young age. All knew him to be a kind and just young man. He got along well with everyone he met—save for one acquaintance. His king. This king was starved for power, so he murdered his regent-uncle and claimed the throne at a young age. Too young. He made many grabs for more power, dismantling Parliament, taking governors under his thumb. He had only one opposing force, who had made a name for himself under the regent's instruction. Leifius' son was becoming famous, a legend in his own right, collecting loyalty from the soldiers he commanded. The king could not touch him—not even with all the power he had procured.

"So, he came to me. He devised an elaborate strategy, a charade in which our two countries would go to war, but it was all a ruse so that this commander—this nuisance, who had amassed too much loyalty—could be put to the sword, without anyone suspecting their king had been behind it. He paid me handsomely for the privilege.

"But the king got impatient and greedy. He pulled a bargaining chip he shouldn't have, and threatened me with it, and now I'd like to bargain with you, instead."

Brudais was shaking with rage—pure, unadulterated rage. He looked at Morvian, whose eyes were shrewd, staring back at him.

"Would you like to hear my bargain, Commander?"

He didn't trust himself to speak. He didn't trust himself to move without lunging over the desk and grabbing Morvian by the throat.

"I will give you back the commander and the girl, so long as you make good on your unspoken promise, the wish that you've been dying to carry out ever since your demotion."

Through clenched teeth, Brudais said, "And what wish would that be?"

"Tarison's head… parted from his shoulders."

The ice in his veins warmed at the thought. Justice for his father. Vengeance for himself. The release of his best friend and the woman he loved. It was too good to be true.

"I should tell you," the Mouth said shakily, backing away another step, "that per Tarison's instruction, if we could not kill you in battle, he would pay double for us to use the spell that killed your father. He said it would be… poetic."

Brudais lunged around the desk. He grabbed Morvian by the neck and hauled him to the stone wall, unsheathing his dagger and laying it against the commander's neck.

"No. Tearing out a mute man's throat—*that* is poetry."

Chapter Forty-Nine

DANIA

Dania watched the guards carefully as they opened the cell door, tossing a few garments on the floor and backing away quickly. They must have heard from the guard whose balls she'd bruised. *Don't lay a hand on Dania, daughter of Grandis; you might lose it.* A small smile came to her lips. She was beginning to make a reputation for herself.

"You're to put these on and clean yourselves up."

A bucket of water and a clean cloth were brought into the cell. Once the guards had gone, locking the cell firmly behind them, Rydril stood from his corner and walked over to the garments, picking them up to examine them.

"A dress," he said, moving the fabric in his hands. "I don't think it would suit me." He held it out to Dania, amused.

She stood and joined him in the center of the cell, smiling back at him. She slid the dress out of Rydril's hands. "What are we supposed to be cleaning up for, do you wonder?"

"I think we have a visitor," he said, leaning down to grab the clean tunic and trousers still lying on the floor. He grabbed the back of his dirty tunic and brought it over his head. Dania quickly turned away, giving him some privacy.

"Gods, you *are* modest. Brudais was right."

Dania turned her head back to glare at Rydril, whose muscles gleamed against the sunlight streaming in through the cell window.

"How would *he* know?" she asked as she faced the other end of the cell, and pulled her own tunic over her head. In the corner of her eye, she saw Rydril turn in the opposite direction. A gentleman.

"My wife would kill me if she knew I was undressing in the same room as a maid," Rydril mumbled under his breath, but the air was so still in the cell that Dania heard every word.

Dania removed her trousers and slipped into the dress.

"You can tell her I was a friend, not a maid."

"To Palli, it wouldn't much matter."

She heard the smile in his voice when he said her name. It was uplifting to hear. It made her wish someone would say her name with so much love. *'Dania.'* She heard the memory of her name on Brudais' lips, full of passion. Shivering, she slipped the dress over her shoulders.

Hearing an end to the rustling of clothes, she turned, hoping Rydril had finished dressing. He stood there, tall and proud, in a clean, gray silk tunic and linen trousers. The expression on his face as he looked at her was…

"What?" she said, surprised. "Is my nose bleeding again?" Her fingers shot to her lip.

"No, no," he said, bemused. "You look lovely."

Dania rolled her eyes. "I'm sure you say that to all the girls you get captured with."

Rydril chuckled. "I do, in fact."

"Flirtatious scoundrel," she said, reaching for the clean cloth. "What would your Palli say?"

"She would beat me within an inch of my life, I'm sure."

"Our secret, then."

"You are gracious, my lady."

"Anything for you, Commander."

After they cleaned themselves of the dirt and grime of the past twenty-four turns, they sat back in their cell and waited. It didn't take long for a few guards to return, but they looked furious, their faces contorted in rage. Rydril stood quickly, blocking Dania from view.

"We just got word from Morvian's Mouth that your friend ain't cooperating with the Commander," he said, and Dania recognized him at once as the guard who had tried to rape her. His eyes were on her, staring with hatred behind them. "He needs to be reminded that you're prisoners here. A few of the girl's fingers should do the trick."

He pulled a knife from his belt, and another of the guards fumbled for the keys to the cell.

Dania's eyes widened, moving her fingers reflexively. She had never considered just how much she used her fingers until she was faced with the prospect of losing them.

"Now, hold on," Rydril said, his hands up in surrender. "You don't want to do something you're going to regret. Whichever of you lays a hand on this girl is going to have Brudais to answer to, and seeing as he's already… uncooperative, I'd say you'll be dead before the sun sets tonight."

The guard opened the cell door, advancing on them.

"Morvian wouldn't have ordered this. Do you take orders from his Mouth?"

The guard spat, moving towards Rydril with the knife extended. "Only the ones I like."

Rydril lunged forward, his arms outstretched to knock the knife away. It dislodged from the guard's hand and flung across the cell to the opposite wall, hitting it with a *clang!* Rydril and the guard grappled, with Rydril pushing him to his knees. Dania placed herself against the wall, watching as the second guard advanced on her. He had no knife in his hands, but he was much larger than her. She would have to dodge and parry, tire him out like she had with Wren. His fist swept through the air heading straight for her face; she ducked just in time, his fist slamming into the stone behind her. He let out a strangled howl of pain, and Dania took the opportunity to slam her full body weight against one of his legs, knocking him to the ground.

In the corner of her eye, she saw Rydril wrestling the guard on the ground. They were getting closer to the knife lying in the corner by the wall. Her guard grunted as he hit the stone, and Dania grabbed the hilt of the knife at his belt and yanked it free of its sheath.

"Rydril!" she called, placing the knife on the ground and shoving it towards him. He grabbed for it, but so did the guard, and they struggled for the hilt.

Suddenly, a boot kicked her in the stomach, knocking the wind out of her. She coughed and sputtered, unused to such a sensitive area being targeted in a fight. Her opponent clasped her shoulder, and his forehead collided with hers. White light spread across her vision, and a splitting pain enveloped her, along with a wave of nausea.

When the light disappeared and her vision returned to her, she grabbed the side of the guard's face and tore with all her might. A cry of agony echoed across the cell walls. Dania's hand came away bloody.

"You bitch!" he yelled, and she tried to twist away from him as he clutched the side of his face, but the skirts of her dress were pinned under the guard's knees. He reached back his balled fist, ready to punch her again. If he had, her head would have knocked against the stone ground, the back of her skull splitting open—but instead she heard a soft grunt and saw a knife sticking out from the man's chest. He crumpled over, nearly pinning Dania under his dead weight before she spun around to escape. Her eyes fell on Rydril, who was watching her with his arm still outstretched after having thrown the knife at her guard. He smiled, but it faltered as he saw Dania's expression. The guard beneath Rydril had reached the knife by the wall and grasped the hilt.

"Look out!" she yelled, pointing at the guard. Before Rydril looked down to see what she meant, the guard had lodged the blade deep into Rydril's leg. A fountain of blood spurted from the wound. Rydril toppled over, holding his leg wound tightly, but it was gushing blood. Dania tried to move towards them, but her skirts were lodged underneath the massive corpse. She tore at the dress, but Rydril held out a hand to her. The guard stood over his opponent, watching as Rydril struggled to stop the bleeding.

"Any clever last words, Commander?" he asked, laughing.

Dania cried, "Don't you dare, you fucking scum!"

Rydril's face was calm, not in pain. He almost looked peaceful. He knew. It was a mortal wound.

"It don't matter, bitch," the guard replied, stepping towards her and grabbing her by the hair. She flinched, pain ripping through her scalp as he lifted her up. She tried to grab at his hands, tear at his uniform, but she was weak now, weak with the realization that Rydril could do nothing to save her, that she was alone. "He'll be dead any minute."

He tore at her skirts, causing them to rip, and as soon as she was free of the weight of the dead guard, she pushed her feet against the corpse and lunged at the guard. He grappled with her, but she was no match for him this time. All the will to fight had poured out of her the moment she had seen the peaceful look on Rydril's face.

The guard gathered her around the waist, lifting her up and moving out of the cell. She screamed, tears streaming down her cheeks as she was carried away. She watched Rydril as he let himself fall to the floor with exaggerated slowness, releasing the wound and letting himself bleed out. She screamed until her voice was hoarse, in defiance of reality. *This is not happening. This can't be happening.* But the tears in her eyes told the truth.

Chapter Fifty

BRUDAIS

"Do you want me to cut your throat, Morvian, or will you stop inching your hand towards the dagger at your belt?"

Morvian went still.

Brudais' best position was to hold the commander hostage until he got what he came for. He wasn't certain the plan would work, but it was better than submitting to his bargain. Were he to murder Tarison, with Ithiador still in the wind, no one would be left to take Creet's throne—save Brudais. If he ascended the throne after killing the current occupant, the people would turn on him, saying he did it for his own designs. His reputation would be smeared beyond repair. He'd be labeled a kinslayer, a kingslayer, and worse—another Grandis the Great—a legend whose avarice propelled him into the spotlight. No one would ever trust him again.

Screams came from outside the corridor. The hairs on Brudais' forearms stood on end. Morvian looked worried.

"Can your Mouth speak for you or has it run off?"

The screams turned to sobs, but became louder as the door to Morvian's downstairs chamber opened.

"Yes, he's just there," the Mouth said, his voice quivering as he popped his head above the downturned chair he was hiding behind.

The wailing reverberated off the staircase walls and when it reached the top of the stairs, it ceased. Only a few sniffles could now be heard. Brudais couldn't turn his head from Morvian, or he might go for his dagger again.

"Dania?" he called without looking.

A shifting of movement, a swift curse and a light scuffle.

"Tell your guard to let her go," he said loudly, "or I'll push this blade so far into your throat, it'll hit bone."

"Do as he says!" called the Mouth from behind the chair.

The guard must have backed off, for he heard a sharp intake of breath, as if he'd been holding Dania by the throat.

"Come to me," he said softly, taking his left hand from Morvian's shoulder and reaching backwards towards her. He heard the shifting of feet and skirts—was that a dress?—across the floor as she slowly obeyed, grasping his hand firmly. She was just far enough away that Morvian couldn't maneuver to grab her if he got past him.

"Brudais," she said, hoarse and breathless.

"What happened?"

He heard shuffling feet, like the guard was getting ready to bolt.

"Tell your man to stay exactly where he is."

Dania's hand was trembling.

The Mouth said, "You have not been dismissed, Sergeant Gorril."

"What happened?" he said again to Dania, this time more urgently.

"Rydril—he—there was so much blood."

Brudais' eyes bore into Morvian's. "Send your healers to help Rydril."

The chair the Mouth cowered behind slid across the floor, making a violent scraping sound. "Our guards are in the cell now. They brought the mender, but… he was already…"

Brudais' heart stopped. "You can bring him back." He looked pleadingly into Morvian's eyes, who were filled with concern and anger. He had not meant for this to happen. An accident.

"He won't be the same," said the Mouth. "He won't be the Rydril you remember. They never are."

Another sob escaped Dania at his back.

A red haze filled Brudais' vision. He wanted to unleash Ire upon them all—every last Hyglenian he could get his hands on. He tore his gaze away from Morvian, whose concern had turned to anticipation, and he looked back at Dania. Her eyes were brimming with tears, her beautiful blond hair askew, as if someone had grabbed her by it, and her nose was bleeding. A welt was forming on her temple.

Passion over fury. He had made a promise… but justice did not necessitate fury.

Put the sword where it belongs. A voice that hadn't come from the Mouth, or Dania. He remembered it from years before. It was Rydril's deep voice, coaxing him to make the right choice.

Brudais tugged on Dania's hand, drawing her closer. He dropped the dagger from Morvian's neck, sliding it back into its sheath. He pulled out Ire and handed it to Dania.

"If he makes a move to run, cut off a foot. That'll slow him down. She's sharp enough."

He watched as Dania moved into a fighting stance, holding the sword tip out to Morvian as Brudais stepped away, pulling Ardent from its sheath.

"Him?" he asked Dania, who nodded fervently.

His gaze left hers and caught the guard's, who went rigid.

"Commander, you won't let him… surely, I was just doing my job…"

Morvian's Mouth spat, "*Your job?* You jeopardized this entire operation with your need for revenge. Sergeant Gorril, you were tasked with bringing the girl here, not threatening to dismember her. You will pay for your indiscretions, whether they are at the end of Commander Brudais' blade, or mine."

Good. They were in agreement.

Brudais moved toward the guard with Ardent at his side. He was not a small man, but Brudais would have him in three moves, if it came to a fight. He had no sword, only a rusty-looking knife.

"I can execute you like a sow or like a man," Brudais said evenly. "I'll give you the choice."

The guard's expression turned to dismay as he realized his situation. He turned to run, tripping over his own feet as he tried to make it down the stairs. Brudais pulled out his dagger again and flung it at the guard's knee. A howl of pain echoed along the walls as the knife wedged between his cartilage, and he fell down five stairs, holding the wound.

"I'm not done with you yet," he said quietly, almost to himself.

He stalked to the top of the stairs, then proceeded down them, grasping the dagger from the man's knee and pulling it out without mercy. The guard howled some more. He tried to grasp the stairs below him, to crawl away, but Brudais grabbed him by the shoulder of his uniform and hauled him up the stairs. When he got to the top, he placed the guard on his knees, and he sat on his legs, whimpering in pain.

"If you're to be a sow, I might as well dedicate your sacrifice to Hevalior in memory of my best friend, who you murdered in cold blood. May his winds carry you to Culveil, where your cowardly soul can burn for all eternity."

He positioned himself behind the guard, sliding Ardent cleanly across his neck with one fluid motion. The guard choked as blood filled his mouth. His hands went up to his neck, as if the wound could be closed with a bit of pressure. He collapsed on his side, spewing blood across the stone floor. Brudais watched as his eyes rolled up into the back of his head, watched the blood pouring over the floor. He didn't feel better. He felt an emptiness that seemed to pervade his entire being.

He didn't know how long he stood there, watching the blood drip down the stairs behind him, but he didn't hear a single sound from the rest of the room. Not until the door creaked open below, and a hesitant voice called, "Commander?"

"What is it?" the Mouth called, his voice cracking.

The voice hesitated. "The Creetian troops disengaged from battle and fell back to their encampment, but before they made it fully to cover, they seem to have been placed under some sort of spell. They are wandering aimlessly across the camp's borders. None of the captains can make sense of it. This seems like the perfect time to re-engage. Should we attack?"

Brudais' gaze swam around the room until it landed on Morvian. "Commander—if you let Dania go and don't attack the Creetian troops, I'll take your bargain."

Dania looked back at him, a fervent question in her eyes. He didn't have time to tell her. It was her life and the lives of every Creetian soldier… or their king. A worthy sacrifice if ever he saw one.

A pregnant silence lingered.

"All right, Brudais," came a rasping voice from Morvian's lips. "Let's see if you're as good in the shadows as you are in the glaring sun."

The Mouth choked from behind his overturned chair, realizing his master had just spoken with his own voice.

Chapter Fifty-One

Loya

Loya sat cross-legged on the throne of the receiving room, her skirts pooled around her regally. This was the closest she would ever get to real power, she supposed, so she might as well enjoy it while it lasted.

Commander Okriad was under her thumb now. With Venhil dispatched, drooling under Staliva's spell, she was the real power in Creet, and no one had even realized her ascent. All she needed now was a pliant co-conspirator to whom she could offer this power. She certainly couldn't keep it for herself, but she was wise enough to know that her scheming would merit some reward. Perhaps a stewardship—if the people of Creet could stand to see a woman so elevated. At the very least, her designs for introducing women into the military would be awarded the proper accolades and financial assistance. The war had been good for one thing, at least.

Staliva was getting anxious, though, with Ithiador's whereabouts still unknown. Loya may have been concerned, but she had another option that seemed slightly more enticing now regardless. Brudais, at least, had never knowingly bedded a child and a sorceress. She would need to keep such affairs quiet, which meant paying people for the privilege of their silence. It was a nuisance she could have done without.

Besides, Ithiador had now been missing for several moons. Was there really any hope in finding him after such a prolonged absence? Loya's foot began to bob, causing her skirts to sway against the metal foot of the throne.

She would continue her schemes until he was found or Brudais was guilted into the position. Things would have just been easier if one of them arrived before the king returned.

What good was a coup without a figurehead?

Chapter Fifty-Two

ELDEVA

Eldeva could feel the horse beneath her, but she couldn't see it. Her eyes had glazed over, and she saw a mirage of ghostly shapes in millions of shades of gray, vying for her attention. Some were wisps of smoke, barely there, while others were more solid. She reached out to grasp at one of them, one that looked like a man, but nothing was there. She drew her hand inward, hugging herself.

They were moving slowly toward something dark and ominous in her ghost-vision, a large black splotch against the pale gray expanse. She wished they would turn around, head back to where they had come from, but she didn't remember where that was. She didn't even remember where they were going.

When she looked up again, a spot of blue was coming out of the black splotch. It was an amorphous mass against the backdrop of a painting, but it was the most real thing that Eldeva had seen in what felt like three lifecycles.

She reached out for it, grasping for it in the distance, but when she heard men begin to shout, she covered her ears with both hands, pushing inward, holding her breath. The noise felt like agony. She shut herself out completely from the world as her teachers of the

Old Order had taught her to do in her training. Slowly, gradually, she slipped into an unconscious state where she could hear, see and feel nothing of the outside world, only the thoughts in her own mind.

That is when she began to panic.

Sounds beget troubles where troubles beget sound guidance.

When a jackrabbit catches the rat, it doesn't stop to sing.

What advice would a mule give to its cart driver if he were a prince?

The mule or the cart driver?

'Prince' is just a clever name for someone who would destroy you.

Eldeva began keening softly. Even her very thoughts were not making sense—at least she realized this fact. She shut out her thoughts, too, which left her with one last option.

She drifted aimlessly into the black oblivion of sleep.

Eldeva opened her eyes to a frowning Ithiador hovering over her. She smiled. A gentle dream. What could it hurt to act on selfish inclination? She began to get up from the ground where she lay and she was about to kiss him when he pulled back suddenly, realizing her intention.

Not a dream. She looked around quickly. All the Creetian guards were standing on one side of her, with Mayora among them, and on Ithiador's side were a race of people unknown to Eldeva. They were beautiful to behold, but their expressions were grim. They had a dangerous aura. They were clad in dark green and black armor and their skin was palest white. Fayn, she surmised.

"Prince Ithiador," she said, her voice sounding a little muffled from sleep.

"Princess Eldeva," he said, equally formal. He offered her his hand, which she took, and hauled her to her feet. She heard Mayora breathe a sigh of relief. "You were mumbling nonsense. You called me a mule."

"An honest mistake," she snapped. He looked at her with chagrin, then motioned for one of the Fayn to come forward. She wondered if he were commanding them since the Fayn did as he requested.

"V'pnor, make sure the princess is purged of the chaos within."

Ithiador's voice held all the authority of a king, but Eldeva didn't have time to dwell on it before the Fayn's hand was on her forehead and the magick from within him was filling her entire body, scooping out everything that wasn't supposed to be there and leaving everything else in place. Instead of a heat that usually coursed through her when magick took hold, there was an icy chill as she felt her bones strengthen, her skin tighten, her eyes clear, her hair grow, and her heart race. She assumed that she had looked like an old crone after casting the Spell of Rudiment on so many people at one time, but the Fayn was bringing her back from old age and—she assumed—from madness, as well. She owed these creatures her life and her mind... and the debt rankled.

The magick left her as the Fayn took his hand off her forehead. She breathed in deeply, looking down at her hands, then she gasped. She looked up at Ithiador in horror. They had not just brought her back from old age; they had brought her back to her body's natural state. She now inhabited a sixteen-year-old body once again.

"What have you *done*?"

Ithiador's smile was a little woeful. "Would you rather have been a mad crone, ready to die with the use of one more spell? We've given you your mind and your life back, Eldeva. You should be grateful."

She was shorter than she remembered, so it was difficult for her to maneuver at first, but she trudged up to Ithiador and grabbed his elbow, dragging him away from the watchful eyes and eavesdropping ears of the Creetian guards and Fayn.

"You did this on purpose, because you know about Loya's coup," she said, a single tear rolling down her cheek.

"Yes," he replied simply, making it easy for her to hate him.

"And you wanted me out of the way."

"No, Eldeva. I want you to take your own path. Our tryst can no longer continue. You may have been physically mature, but your mind is not yet. You proved that when you thrashed out at the entire Creetian army—though it was me who you were really angry with. You could have killed yourself. You nearly did."

Eldeva shrugged. "Perhaps I should have."

"Eldeva," Ithiador chided. "You do not love me. You love to fuck me. Do not pretend not to know the difference."

"Do you even know her, your future bitch queen?" Eldeva said with a bit of venom.

"She's my cousin. I've met her several times. I don't claim to know her, but she is Creetian, and the people know her well enough through her father. If it were another way, in another time, and you another age, perhaps we might be together, Eldeva."

"Don't treat with me as you would a child," she bit back. "You never thought of our relationship as anything more than convenience and pleasure."

Ithiador's frown deepened. "You say you are not a child, but your actions speak volumes to the contrary."

Eldeva scoffed. "Anyone who was betrayed as I have been would have acted the same."

"Betrayed?" Ithiador reached for her arm, but she backed away quickly. "I wish you happiness and peace, Princess. Nothing more."

"Nothing more," she said through clenched teeth. "That is abundantly clear."

There was silence between them for a few moments while Eldeva straightened her spine and crossed her arms over her chest.

"Where will you go now? To the capital?"

"No," said Ithiador firmly. "I need to undo what you have done. The spell must be reversed. We ride for Hyglen, and the Creetian war camp, and I must ensure a certain investment is… equipped."

She saw a strange gleam in his eye as he said the latter, and she looked away before he could see the curiosity on her face. He had always been a little distant. It hadn't caused her alarm, as it had added a little mystery to their relationship. Regardless, it was no longer a dilemma for her to parcel out. Ithiador was riding southeast, and she was riding north.

The distance between them couldn't get much greater.

Chapter Fifty-Three

Dania

"In there," a guard told them, opening the door in the servants quarters and motioning inside. Dania looked at him dumbly for a moment before making her way into the room. She didn't admit to herself she no longer cared whether Morvian's ultimatum was a trap. She just wanted to sit quietly and not think. Brudais moved behind her, close enough for her to feel the heat of his body on her back.

"Where is Commander Rydril's body?" he asked hoarsely.

"It's been taken to the catacombs. It will be housed there until the morning. Commander Morvian has specified a pyre to be built just outside the city walls. You can rest here until the morning, and we'll supply a wagon for transport."

Brudais nodded. "Thank you."

Dania eyed Brudais as the door shut behind them. "Did you just thank him?"

Brudais put a hand on her shoulder and pushed her gently, farther into the room.

"He didn't murder my best friend."

He clearly knew what she had been thinking, and she couldn't disagree, but she wasn't ready to start thanking the men who had kidnapped and imprisoned her. Brudais moved to her side so that they were face to face.

"They showed me a kindness I didn't deserve, and they let you live. I can't be grateful and grieve at the same time?"

Dania's cheeks flushed in shame, highlighting the pale tear streaks on her skin. She looked around the dimly lit room. It was sparsely furnished with two shallow beds lined with woolen sheets and a wide table in the corner with some herbs, a bowl of water and a few washcloths. The walls were bare and illuminated only by two candles placed on either side of the table.

Dania held out her hand. Brudais looked down at it for a moment before taking it, and she led him to the bed closest to the table. He stood by the edge, looking at the opposite wall with a blankness in his blue eyes that unnerved her. Dania went to unbuckle the straps of his cuirass. Brudais' gaze met hers with a question, but Dania furrowed her brow and nodded once, looking back down at the straps. He allowed her to remove his armour, greaves, and bracers and place them on the ground gingerly.

She went to the table and soaked a washcloth in the bowl of water. She didn't know what herbs were on the table, but she assumed they were for healing minor cuts and bruises. She twirled a few of the stems in the water with the cloth and wrung it out over the bowl. The trickling of the water falling back into the bowl was louder than a hurricane in the quiet room.

She brought the cloth back to where Brudais stood. His stance had not changed, but he now stood in only a tunic, red with speckled blood. His face was covered in blood, but she had a feeling none of it was his own. She drew the washcloth up to his face and touched it to his upper jawline. He blinked suddenly, looking down at her. She nodded again, and continued to stroke his jaw, cheeks, and forehead with the cloth. Then she drew it across his neck, and he let out a quiet hiss. Dania moved the cloth away and saw a thin scratch from his jaw down the length of his throat to the nape of his neck. Someone had almost torn his throat wide open.

"You've been distracted," she said, clucking her tongue in a gentle tease.

The ghost of a smile lit Brudais' lips. "Rydril would be ashamed."

Dania went back to the table and placed the cloth back in the bowl, wringing it out again. The water droplets were deafening.

She was about to turn around when she felt Brudais move towards her, hearing his muted footsteps across the stone floor. He moved behind her, their bodies close, before he placed his hand on her forearm, guiding her around so that they were facing one another. Taking the cloth from her hands, he wiped her face lightly, washing away the blood from her lip, and the dirt and tears that streaked her face, making her feel renewed. When he trailed the cloth against her lips, she tasted lavender and comfrey. Brudais' fingers just lightly touched her hair.

Dania licked her lips as he leaned in, their faces so close, she could feel his breath against her skin. Her heartbeat was pounding in her ears as they stared into each other's eyes, trying to read each other's thoughts. Dania didn't have a single thought in her mind—except what he would taste like.

Her eyes fluttered closed as his lips brushed against hers. It was gentle at first, and she savored the salty-sweet tang of his lips. Then, as if the world had shifted, Brudais' fingers slid into her hair, and he grabbed the back of her neck. His mouth opened, and he slid his tongue past her lips. She allowed him to take her over, placing her hands on his sides and grasping his tight muscles. His other hand had dropped the cloth and was now on her hip, moving lower as the kiss deepened. His fingers moved over the curve of her backside, squeezing her tight enough to propel her forward into the curve of his body. She felt his hard cock against her stomach, and only a few layers of clothing separated them.

Dania's head swam, unable to think of anything but the musky smell of him, the taste of his tongue, the feel of his muscles beneath her fingers. His passion was intoxicating. His need was invigorating.

Dania walked towards the bed, leading Brudais in front of her. He backed to the edge of the bed, and she pulled at his tunic, needing to feel his skin against hers. Their lips broke apart only long enough for Brudais to lift his tunic over his head and throw it onto the floor. Dania's hands were on his chest in an instant, exploring his body, slick with sweat. He began undoing the laces of her bodice as his tongue explored her mouth hungrily. His lips now tasted faintly of the comfrey from her own.

They broke apart again so that Dania could slip out of her dress, and Brudais sat on the bed, reaching out to grab Dania's hips and moving her forward, on top of him. She obeyed, straddling him between her thighs. As soon as she did, Brudais' mouth closed around her left nipple, his tongue swirling around until it peaked. Dania moaned, arching her back and lifting her hips. He slid into her, anchoring them together. Nothing had ever felt this way before—the rawness and rapture.

Dania gazed into his eyes, the warm darkness swallowing her in their depths. She shivered, goosebumps rising on the flesh of her arms and upper thighs. Brudais held her closer, thinking her cold, no doubt, but Dania's body wasn't what was chilled. In losing herself to the slow rhythm of their warm bodies pressing against each other, Dania realized that she was at risk of losing herself in him.

"Dania," Brudais whispered, his voice a husky mixture of desire and desperation. Of love.

A sudden dread filled her.

Chapter Fifty-Four

BRUDAIS

The flames of Rydril's pyre had grown high, billowing into clouds of smoke as they drifted into the red-orange sky. They had waited until the fire had died down, to cool enough for Brudais to scoop some of the ashes into a satchel for Pallina and the children. He could see their anguished faces as they spread the ashes in the courtyard gardens, saying farewell to the best of husbands and fathers. Tears welled in his eyes at the thought.

He knelt in the grass beside the pyre, hands on his thighs.

"You bastard," he said quietly. "What did you always tell me about getting distracted? All you had to do was hold your fucking wound closed until the menders came."

He held back his fist and punched one of the timbers of the pyre, which crumbled beneath his hand and sent a cascade of sparks across the ground before him. Two of the crumbling timbers collided and burst into a haze of ash and embers.

Dania was at his side in an instant, a hand on his shoulder.

"Don't blame the dead," she whispered. "They cannot defend themselves."

"He would need to defend a lot of his actions to satisfy me."

He heard a gentle sigh, almost amused, escape her. "As he is not here to do so… he did his best to protect something very dear to his best friend. After his rough treatment, he didn't have the strength to fight his wounds. He succumbed to them in peace, Brudais, knowing he did the right thing. That is the best any of us can hope for in the end."

Brudais looked up at her, surprised. "Did he come to you in a dream and tell you to say that? It sounds just like him."

Dania forced a sad smile. "We had an understanding, he and I."

Brudais' curiosity was not as strong as his grief. He did not press her, and she did not offer more.

It was midday before they found their way back to the horses. Ælon had untied himself from the tree and was wandering not far off-lead, grazing in a sunlit glade. When they had mounted, Brudais' eyes fell on the third horse, riderless, and anger grew in him again. His gaze shifted to Dania, who looked serene and comforting. The rage cooled seeing her so calm. Her strength kept him tethered.

They rode for hours across Pelosia Field in silence, giving the hills to the north a wide berth so as to avoid Hyglenian scouts. When they reached the outskirts of their encampment, a Creetian scout came to greet them. It was one of Aiylus' boys.

"The entire army was under a spell, Commander. We had been retreating from Hyglen's forces when… well, it was like we were struck dumb. We were all confused, unsure what we were doing. Some of us forgot how to walk. We all forgot how to speak. Hyglen could have easily surrounded and slaughtered us if they'd had a mind. No one seems to know what stopped them."

Dania looked at Brudais, her gaze penetrating. He had told her of Morvian's bargain and had expected her to at least understand that he had no other choice. Instead, she had given him a look of deepest disappointment. She had not explained why, but he assumed he would hear her side of things before he completed his end of the bargain. He didn't have enough strength to listen to it now.

"How were you cured of the spell?" Brudais asked.

The scout looked surprised, as if realizing he had only told half of a story. "Prince Ithiador returned!" Brudais' entire body stiffened at his words. "He was traveling with the Fayn, who reversed the spell. It took the entire day, as every soldier had to be… what did they call it? Purged?"

The Fayn? Ithiador had been traveling with them?

He sent the scout back to report to Aiylus and spread the word throughout camp that Commander Brudais had returned. When they reached the edges of the eastern camp, Captain Peric and the rest of Rydril's Blood Guard had gathered to meet them. When they saw the empty saddle on the third horse, a few cries of dismay went up throughout the group.

"Commander Rydril is with the gods," Brudais said, his voice sounding stronger than he felt. He waited for the commotion to die down before he continued. "His last breath was used to protect the daughter of Grandis. Do not treat her unkindly for the act. She would have done the same for him, just as he would have done the same for any of his men, for any one of you."

Brudais and Dania dismounted their horses and led them through the crowd of Blood Guard, who stood in disbelief of the news of their commander's death. Even so, when they passed by, hands clapped Dania's shoulders, a sign of respect and solidarity. They did not know what had happened in the tower, but they had accepted that Dania was not to blame for it. Rydril's sacrifice for her had made them see her in a new light—as one of them. When Brudais looked at her, her eyes were filled with tears. Rydril had given her a gift upon his departure from this life, and she showed her appreciation of it openly.

Dania stood at the tent's entrance, her arms folded across her chest, staring into the fabric of the tent wall as if seeing through it. Brudais watched her, studying her expression from his corner of the room. She looked pensive but somehow disconcerted, like she wanted to say something but was too afraid to put the matter forward.

He moved towards her, stepping behind her and placing his hands below her shoulders, feeling goosebumps rise at his touch. She sighed contentedly, leaning back into him, and he bent down to kiss her neck. Before his lips met her skin, she turned around, looking deep into his eyes.

"Brudais..."

There was hesitation in her tone, but even so hearing his name on her lips sent a shiver of pleasure down his spine.

"How can you think to do this?"

His eyes closed and he grimaced. So, now he was to discover the reason for that look of disappointment he had witnessed earlier. When he opened his eyes, they met expectant hazel counterparts.

"Dania... the situation merited a certain course of action. I had no choice."

"But you do now," she replied, her arms dropping to her sides.

"Does my word mean nothing?" His tone held a bit of an edge to it, daring her to argue. Dania must have noticed, for she took one step back.

"Does breaking a pledge to an enemy constitute a broken word?"

"It does," Brudais replied, his temper beginning to rise. She had not been in his position when Morvian had come to him with his bargain, when the entire Creetian army could have been put to the sword. His choice was sound. One life for thousands. "Besides, Tarison brought this fate upon himself. He wanted a war. Now he will be the one to end it."

Dania's expression hardened. Brudais turned away from her, beginning to pace. He could not stand the look in her eyes, the accusation.

"Have you heard of the Creed of Legends?" he asked, not waiting to hear her answer. "Legends do not concern themselves with the opinions of others. They live their lives based on a creed known only to them. They live and breathe this creed and no matter what, they never break it. That is what makes someone a legend. Not their fame, power or lineage—but their conviction in the face of trials and misfortune. Their unwillingness to accept fate."

Out of the corner of his eye, he saw Dania's pensive expression return. He continued pacing.

"I don't expect anyone to understand, not even another legend. My creed is my own. Just as yours is."

Dania lifted her head to stare at him, her eyes wide in confusion.

"*My* creed?" Her voice shook as she said the words, and the weight of their meaning hung heavy in the air between them.

"You will discover it," he said, slowing his pace to a halt, facing her. "When you're ready."

"I am no legend," she said, her arms folding over her chest to hug herself. "I couldn't even save my commander in that cell."

"You said yourself there was nothing Rydril could have done—neither could you." A sudden sadness swept over him, remembering. When he glanced up at Dania's face, he saw the same sadness washing over her features. "And you cannot know your strength until you are tested."

Her frown deepened, and she looked down at the ground. Brudais could not leave her with that feeling. He moved quickly to her side, his hand gently lifting her chin. "Look inward. You'll find your creed and follow it faithfully."

Dania looked into his eyes, and he watched as something shifted in them, watched as some decision was made. He did not ask her what it was. He recognized the conviction in them—no matter what internal debate she had just won—or lost—it was her own victory or defeat.

"Now I must follow mine," he said gently. She blinked back tears as they began to form in her eyes. "Will you let me go?"

Her lip quivered as she realized that he was giving her an opportunity—not only to argue her point but to *persuade* him. Every fiber of Brudais' being fought against the admission that he might allow someone else to dictate not only his fate but his very creed. He hoped he was not wrong to place his trust in her hands, to allow her to decide. Dania's calculated gaze bore into him, causing his heart to beat faster, his palms sweating. Then a beautiful smile lit her lips, not amused or vindictive, but *knowing*.

"Your creed is your own, Commander."

Brudais exhaled, realizing he had been holding his breath for her answer. He smiled at her in return, relaxing his tensed muscles.

"I should go," he said, turning toward the weapons rack and picking up his harness, putting his arms through the straps so that Ardent and Ire were positioned on his back. He felt Dania's hands moving to tighten the straps. Her help felt like permission, like a promise.

They were silent as he buckled his dagger's sheath to his waist, and he didn't look back as he pushed back the tent flap, moving into the darkness.

The night was black before him, but the moon didn't even cast his shadow on the ground. He felt the warmth in his extremities as the magick from the Degrees of Nightshade filled him while he stalked through the camp. If anyone saw him moving towards the king's tent, fully armed, they may suspect that something was amiss.

Brudais walked right past the Black Guard who stood outside the king's tent and their searching eyes passed over him as if he weren't even there. He moved down the antechamber. It was silent and still until he entered the receiving room, and at the other end was the opening to the king's chambers. Torchlight flooded onto the otherwise dark ground of the receiving room and quiet voices could be heard arguing.

"I tell you, brother"—Brudais knew that voice well; it belonged to Ithiador—"if Morvian didn't tell him, there cannot possibly be an infiltrator in our camp."

"But how did the bastard know to take the girl?" Tarison's voice was low and urgent.

"A fluke? Perhaps—"

Brudais had moved closer so that he was just outside the entrance, hugging the tent's interior. Then someone within the chamber stood up, walking towards the entrance. Brudais' entire body froze as Ithiador folded back one of the flaps.

"Brudais," he said smoothly, staring directly at him. The sight shield had not dropped. How could he know—? "Please come in."

He immediately released the magick, and his form became visible again, but he reformed the spell over his weapons so that Ardent and Ire were hidden to the naked eye. Ithiador didn't seem to notice the change, and he motioned for Brudais to enter the chamber. The prince's expression was pleasant, but something was... *off*. Despite the pleasantness, Brudais sensed something unfamiliar beneath his gaze. He entered the chamber, distinctly aware of Ithiador's eyes following his movements.

Tarison sat in an armchair on the other side of the room. He barely acknowledged Brudais as he entered, giving a perfunctory nod in his direction.

"Please sit, Brudais," Ithiador motioned to the chair to Tarison's left, as the prince reclaimed his seat facing the king.

Brudais slowly sunk down into the chair. "Were you speaking of Dania?" he asked carefully, looking from Tarison's bored expression to Ithiador, whose face was alight with polite interest. He needed time, time to consider his next move. With Ithiador as witness, he could not very well perform the murder he had come there to do, but then Ithiador's mind brushed against his, a gentle touch, but one filled with urgency. He rode the cord to its end, opening his mind just enough to hear...

I know why you're here.

"The girl?" Tarison said, snapping Brudais' attention back to the present conversation. "You're quite fond of her, aren't you, Commander?"

You're here to kill my brother.

"Perhaps," Brudais replied, trying to snap the cord. It refused to be severed. "We've been through a great deal together."

What was he to do? If Ithiador knew, then he needed to get out—to run. The thoughts tumbled out of him and down the cord like a bramble of burning questions and commands, but he sat frozen, unable to move.

Then a silence lingered along the cord before Ithiador's words echoed like a thousand voices at once.

I would see it done.

"Krashkin has too long been in isolation, I think," said Tarison, his eyes shone with mirth. "I have asked her to enter a marriage pact with them. She seems... amenable."

Brudais' jaw tightened. He couldn't let his jealousy over Dania be the reason for this. He wouldn't let his rage overtake him. He had made a promise.

Brudais, remember what he has done. Save our people from this monster.

Would Leifius have saved the people from this fate if he had lived to see it—even if it meant giving up his renown? Xenia's words swam before him from moons past. *You don't have to live in his shadow. Make your own.*

Even if Brudais were considered an outcast for the act—even if everyone who had ever called him a legend reviled him for it… even Dania—his creed told him this was the right thing to do.

Brudais stood from his seat, and in one smooth movement, grabbed the hilts of Ardent and Ire and slid the short swords out of their sheaths. He took a step forward, dropping the sight shields that hid them, and laid them against Tarison's neck in an X. The king's eyes bulged in outrage.

"How dare you?!" Tarison exclaimed hoarsely.

"How dare *I*?" asked Brudais. "I've often wondered how you *dared* to kill your uncle to ascend to the throne you sit on today, how you ordered thousands butchered for your own gains, started wars so that you could eliminate officers you found unworthy, how you murdered Creet's legend because he threatened your claim."

All the color drained out of Tarison's face. His eyes glanced toward Ithiador, who sat watching with a keen interest, but no hint of empathy or remorse stained his features. He was still and silent as the night.

"You are a plague, *my king*, and if no one else has the will to dirty their hands with your blood, I will gladly do it—not because you have been a pestilence on my life, but because you are a revolting creature, and by the gods, this world needs less of your ilk."

Before Tarison could let out a cry for help, Ardent and Ire were slicing through his windpipe, through the skin, sinew, and muscle of his neck and blood was spurting in every direction. Brudais watched as the life drained out of his king's eyes, making certain that he was dead before Brudais closed his own, feeling the hot blood on his skin. Ithiador's hand was on his shoulder. He let his swords fall to the ground on either side of him and dropped to his knees, kneeling before the dead king.

BOOK IV
CONTRIVANCES

Chapter Fifty-Five

Morvian

Morvian looked out onto Pelosia Field, his vision blurring slightly as he gazed into the smoke. The grasses were scorched, and charred bodies littered the ground as far as he could see. His perception shifted, and he could see beyond Pelosia to the Jaguar Hills, to the Creetian and Phesian midlands. It was all the same: the fields burned, smoke rose from every corner of the continent, and the bodies… so many corpses strewn across the earth like locusts after the harvest.

One of the bodies before him was holding out its hand, as if to plead with the skies. He reached out to touch it, and the charred flesh suddenly lunged forward, grasping his wrist and singeing his skin. The blistering heat moved up his arm and through his body, engulfing him in flames. His eyes moved west, along the borders of the Fayn Forest, expecting to find the red leaves up in flames… but it was untouched by the chaos that affected the rest of the realms.

Morvian jerked awake, breathing heavily. Sweat saturated his nightclothes.

Oren was at his side in an instant, a hand on his shoulder. "Commander," he said cautiously.

Morvian shook his head. Thank the gods Oren could no longer read his thoughts. To have admitted such a dream on the eve of a peace treaty signing would have been quite the ill omen. Now that his thoughts were his own again, he could simply ignore the portents. There were bound to be nerves when one considered trusting one's enemies. That was all it was—anxiety manifesting as grotesque and frightening images. It meant nothing.

If it meant nothing, then why were his palms still sweating?

He looked up at Oren's concerned face. There was no longer a need for the sergeant to be by his side day and night. Morvian had regained the use of his voice, but he had become used to Oren's persistent presence and had decided to name him his personal man-at-arms—a glorified bodyguard who had proven himself useful. He was a foil for Morvian's mind to voice his ideas, a willing servant who had not yet disappointed and, Morvian admitted grudgingly, a welcome companion. The commander had lived in isolation for most of his career, keeping everyone at a polite distance for fear of betrayal.

Oren's mind had been laid bare before him. There had not been a single thought of betrayal—or even of desertion.

The irony was not lost on Morvian that the only person he saw fit to trust was a man who could not lie to him.

Morvian waved Oren's hand off his shoulder, standing up shakily. He still felt the heat of the flames under his skin.

"I'm fine, Sergeant," he said, his voice raspy. Ever since he had regained his speech, his voice sounded as though he had not used it in years. "We need to get ready. What time is it?"

"Just past dawn," Oren replied, straightening his stance.

Morvian moved to his chest of drawers. His lodgings were small but had all the accommodations he required. The large windows that looked out onto The Lady and The Moon, two picturesque lakes nestled in the western reaches of Creet, spanned nearly the entire length of the southern wall. The villa where the treaty was to be signed now housed every king and ambassador in the Ten Kingdoms. It was a gem in the middle of nowhere. King Ithiador had insisted on hosting the dignitaries and had spared no expense to house and feed the amassed assembly of royals. Their tastes were expensive, and having enemies housed under one roof was a feat of political savvy that even Morvian could scarcely have accomplished without battle erupting in the corridors.

He pulled open the chest and pulled out his ceremonial uniform.

"Am I to accompany you to the moot, sir?"

"Of course," he replied. "I need you to keep an eye on the other ambassadors—particularly, Commander Brudais."

"He has still not arrived, Commander."

Morvian turned to Oren, placing his uniform on the back of the armchair that stood to his right. "Is that so?"

"It was mentioned that Commander Nezaun is to sit with King Ithiador as counsel."

"And Steward Loya, I suppose, will want her say." Morvian rubbed the back of his neck, his face tightening. "Why is Brudais absent?"

"Would you like me to inquire, sir, or would you like my opinion?"

"Both."

"Perhaps," Oren said slowly, "he refused, but I will ask… discreetly."

"Do that," Morvian replied. "I'll meet you in the entrance hall in half a turn."

Oren nodded, moving to the door. He turned for the briefest of moments, glancing sidelong at his commander before opening the door and sliding into the hallway.

Morvian didn't like the thought that Brudais was not there. He did not anticipate subterfuge from the commander, but his presence at this moot had been expected by every royal who had made the journey. It would be considered an insult to many, but perhaps it was a political decision. Brudais had slain a king. Perhaps Ithiador or Loya had simply suggested his presence would concern the assembled dignitaries.

If that was their aim, they were off the mark. Morvian knew every royal there. Brudais was a stabilizing force, and a legend whose reputation and personable nature would be a boon to such a tumultuous situation. It also would have assuaged the doubts that he had acted alone in Tarison's fate and put an end to the rumors that they had covered up the blood on his sword with a patchwork coup. Despite the good-natured assurances that Loya had begun those workings well in advance of their king's demise, Hyglen, Sycil, and Hoefke were hesitant to sign a treaty with known kingslayers. Their hesitancy, however, didn't count for much against the pressures Creet was putting on their coffers as a conflict deterrent.

Creetian forces now patrolled all waterways in the midlands and had placed an embargo on trade between the east and western Kreshan realms. Their presence at this moot seemed their only way to pacify their new oppressors, so they had grudgingly accepted the invitation. Now it was time to fight for their freedom, thus ensuring peace throughout the continent as the price.

Morvian grit his teeth. Freedom under duress was better than direct oppression. It was a new order, now that Ithiador sat the throne, with his Fayn allies whispering their secrets in his ear. He had been introduced to the new Creetian ambassador, Prince V'pnor of the Fayn, and his skin had crawled for hours following their encounter.

Suddenly, Morvian's dreamscape came back to his mind and the taste of ash filled his mouth.

It meant nothing, he was certain, but his hands shook slightly as he lifted his uniform from the back of the armchair.

"And the embargo will be lifted?" King Ulden of Sycil asked.

"I assure you, I will pull the Creetian guard back to the city and leave the waterways open for trade once again." Ithiador's voice was even, but there was an undertone of warning. "I want only the peace we enjoyed before my brother's misguided warmongering. Now, can we come to terms?"

"What you're asking for, King Ithiador, is a reinstatement of the treaties implemented following the Crescent Moon Wars," said King Heqvelt of Zethland, "but those treaties were proposed and signed by a legend. I see no reason why we should not have the same assurances now. Where is my nephew?"

"Yes," Morvian said, trying to make his rasping voice heard across the chamber. "Where is Commander Brudais? He is the reason we are here treating at all—instead of slaughtering each other on a blood-soaked battlefield."

Beside him, King Eusol cleared his throat. "Agreed."

A murmur of assent swept through the chamber at Morvian's words, but when he glanced at the Creetians, V'pnor showed his teeth in a menacing smile, which caused a tremor of shivers to run down the commander's spine. King Ithiador looked perturbed, but when the voices died down, he said, "Brudais is under trial and stripped of his rank until such time—"

A roar of outrage erupted from the Creetian allies. King Heqvelt's eyes were wide, but his words of protest were drowned out by the rest of the commotion that had arisen from Ithiador's words.

"Until such time," Ithiador said, raising his voice to a dignified shout, "as he is exonerated of all charges!"

After the voices hushed, Heqvelt said in a low tone, "You begin your rule in an odd way—by shunning your allies, taking up with foreigners, and insulting your legend."

"I will rule how I see fit, King Heqvelt, just as you do in your own realm."

Ithiador was young for a king, but older than his brother had been when he had begun his reign of terror. Morvian wondered whether the Fayn's secrets had poisoned the prince he had once known. His voice didn't even have the same lighthearted quality it once had. It was now harsh and serious, and he was not entirely convinced that the weight of the crown was what had altered it.

"Since our ambassador speaks for the Fayn as well as Creet on these matters, I will let Prince V'pnor speak regarding the additional precautions to be taken should this treaty be broken."

Silence swept over the assembly as V'pnor rose slowly from his seat. He was an imposing figure, with long black hair that reached his elbows, sharp nails that resembled a cat's claws more than a Human's fingers, and pointed features across his pale face. His lips were mauve and stood out in a sinister way against his alabaster skin.

Morvian felt Oren's muscles tense behind him where he stood, quietly surveying the scene. Oren's abhorrence for the Fayn had not lessened with time.

"To ensure this treaty is followed by all those gathered here, we feel that it is necessary to sign in blood."

Another murmur broke out amongst the royals, for this was not a simple request. The use of blood on a contract of this magnitude… ink left them the choice of breaking such promises. Blood was binding. A spell was cast in its creation which could hold them to their word. The consequences of breaking the contract would be dire for their entire kingdom.

"Peace comes at a cost, Your Majesties," said Ithiador, his expression expectant.

Morvian looked around the room. Royal masks of indifference had slipped into concern and anxiety. Not one of the kings before him looked pleased with the arrangement, but neither did they desire the wrath of the Fayn.

Ashes and dust against a cold expanse. It didn't mean anything, he assured himself, but as he looked into V'pnor's piercing eyes, he was beginning to feel the weight of prophecy about him.

Chapter Fifty-Six

BRUDAIS

Brudais breathed in the scent of her as he nestled up to her bare back. His nose touched the spot on her shoulder blade where she was particularly sensitive and goosebumps rose across her entire right side. He smiled as Dania sighed contentedly. Waking up to her touch had been a blessing the last few moons, but he had seen how she had grown distant in the last fortnight. Hearing her sigh like that, bleary and unaware on the cusp of sleep, gave him hope that perhaps he had imagined her distance, but that hope skittered away when her muscles contracted as he laid a hand on her hip.

She sat up in bed, turning to him and giving him a polite smile. Polite. He imagined grabbing her by the back of the neck and kissing her hard, driving any thought of politeness from her mind. She had enjoyed it when he had done it before, willingly submitting to his touch and the pleasure that it promised, but things had shifted. His touch now seemed to bring uncertainty—even guilt. It had always been this way with his paramours in the past. At some point, they had left him for one selfish reason or another. He had hoped that Dania would be different—that she would recognize the need in him with a need of her own—but it was clear now that her needs differed, despite the undeniable chemistry between them.

He had waited for thirteen nights to uncover her reason. He would not wait longer. The urgency and vigor with which they had made love last night told him she planned to tell him today, regardless.

"Is this it, then?" he said, leaning back into the pillows, his hands behind his head. He did not bother to cover his nakedness with the sheets, but Dania seemed of a different mind. She grabbed her nightclothes and hurriedly dressed. He watched her every move, then his eyes took in the look of shame and the pinkness in her cheeks. "You're finished with me."

"That is not—" she began, turning to him as she secured the last button of her shirt in place, but she struggled to find the words.

"Not polite enough?" he offered, growing angry. "I don't care for the formalities. Just tell me why so that I can put my mind at ease."

Dania turned her body to face him, the pinkness in her cheeks growing a more pronounced red, mirroring his anger. "I'm engaged."

Brudais' hands moved from behind his head to beside him on the mattress so quickly he didn't even know he had done it. He sat up, peering at Dania with a calculating stare.

"You said you understood my reasons. Killing Tarison was necessary."

"I did," she replied, folding her arms across her chest. "Can you understand *my* reasons?"

Ithiador had offered Dania a marriage contract with Krashkin, one of many marriage proposals that had sprung up in the wake of the treaty. They were a way to ensure that the peace treaty they had signed was not broken frivolously. The blood oath they had taken held serious ramifications. The Kreshan royals were adamant that peace must be held at all costs, so they had decided the best way to ensure this was to crossbreed all the royal lines. It had worked in the past. Princes and princesses from far and wide were displaced from their homelands and forced to live in foreign countries with forced arrangements, all because kings could not be trusted to keep their promises.

Brudais thought that Dania had agreed to the arranged marriage proposal because she had, all along, reviled him for his part in the Creetian coup, but her face was resolute. Her needs were not selfish in the least. Peace was her desire, to make a difference for Creet's benefit. His face fell. How could he fault her for such a desire?

"Prince Ahnvil is a lecherous wretch," Brudais said, his anger returning.

"I have known the touch of other lecherous wretches before," she said, blushing as she held out a hand as if to say, '*Such as the naked man lying before me.*'

Grudgingly, a smirk formed on Brudais' lips. "You have a stronger constitution than I, Dania daughter of Grandis. I would give up my title and reputation if I could spend the rest of my life ravaging you."

A laugh escaped her, and it was the most beautiful sound Brudais had ever heard. Then she must have had an unpleasant thought because she sobered, and her eyes darkened. "Things between us would never have… we were not meant to be, Brudais."

"How could you know that?" he asked, crestfallen.

"You are Brudais son of Leifius, a legend of Kresha. Your path is carved in stone. Mine is still being written. I know it sounds selfish to want to carve my own path, but your fame would outweigh mine at every turn. You would overshadow me without even trying to do so. How could I become a legend if I were with you?"

Brudais stared at her, his expression pained. He moved to her side of the bed, stood beside her and grabbed her shoulders. She shrank from his intense gaze, but he laid his hand on her neck, turning her head to face him. Their eyes locked, and her hazel irises shone against the sunlight streaming through the windows.

"You are a lion, Dania. If you have a mind to use your teeth, nothing can keep you caged."

Her smile was worth every ounce of pain he could endure at her departure.

Then she glanced down and brought a hand up, placing it against her belly.

"Not even a child?"

Every muscle in Brudais' body tensed until it felt like his sinew would snap with the faintest touch, but then he relaxed just as suddenly, and pleasure flooded through him.

"You're with child?" he asked, full of joy.

A tear slid down Dania's cheek. "I cannot keep it." The emotions washed over him in waves, drowning him. He had barely had time to surface from this latest undertow when he heard her say, "But perhaps you can?"

Brudais brought both his hands up to cup the sides of her face. "You are a woman of conviction, and I will never be able to repay you for your kindness."

As his thumb wiped the tear from her cheek, she said, "Oh, I'm sure I'll find some form of repayment suitable to my needs."

"Commander," King Ithiador said, his tone a mockery of the lightheartedness that he once had. "It is good to have you with us again."

Brudais stood in the king's private solar, his hands behind his back in military fashion. He had never been invited to the king's quarters when Tarison worn the crown, but he had been there many times when Cavison had been regent. He had found his body over by the fireplace, drenched in blood from collar to knees. The images that formed in his mind made him grimace. Cavison had been as good as a father to Brudais after Leifius had died. He made it a point not to dredge up such memories, but something in the air had filled him with quiet dread.

He glanced over at the Fayn, who stood positioned on either side of Ithiador. Perhaps it was the magick that leaked from their very pores, saturating the room and filling it with memories of blood and death. He wondered how the prince whom he had known for most of his life could ally with such monsters, but Ithiador did not seem to be the prince he had known. Not anymore.

Yesterday, Brudais had been acquitted of all charges against him upon his return to Creet. There had been no trial, as had been expected, for Ithiador had made a proclamation in his defense and had his rank reinstated. Loya had told him that they could not have allowed him to go without punishment of some sort after having slain King Tarison, but she had spread the word throughout the realm that Brudais had saved the Creetian forces from slaughter. In doing so, any animosity or doubt that had arisen at his sworn allegiance to King Ithiador had disappeared in the wake of such news.

His reputation had been restored, and it had left Ithiador free to pardon him. Mind, he could have done so without the consent of the people, but Ithiador had always been able to see the larger scale of things. Waiting on the people's consent made them feel as if their opinions mattered, and starting off his rule with their approval was paramount to his future aims—whatever those aims might be.

"It is my intention to reinstate your previous position as sole military commander, effective immediately. Your expertise is needed in the coming years, and Kresha has need of a good sword and sharp mind to see it into the new age."

Brudais' face remained indifferent to the king's words, but sweat began to pool at the base of his spine. What did he mean, the 'new age'? He glanced around at the Fayn, whose sinister smiles gave him further pause.

"You desire to conquer?" he asked evenly.

"Conquer is such a coarse term," Ithiador said, rising from his seat and stepping forward so that he stood in front of Brudais, a pleasant smile on his face. "I mean only to ensure the peace that we are now blessed with."

There was a reason Ithiador would need Brudais at the head of his army, instead of heeding to Tarison's fractured mess of a command. Brudais studied Ithiador's eyes. His irises had been a warm blue before he had crossed paths with the Fayn. They were now a chill near-white. It was not Ithiador who had allied with the Fayn. Perhaps it was the Fayn who had overtaken their prince.

"Nothing would bring me greater shame," said Brudais slowly, "than to break such peace."

Ithiador's gaze flicked to Brudais' tattoo which swathed the length of his left arm, then quickly settled back on the commander. Brudais waited for his friend to respond to his jest, to say the words back to him that he longed to hear, to be reassured of his autonomy. *You have no shame.* Say it, damn it!

"Yes, well," Ithiador said, turning his back on Brudais and returning to his seat. "Our aims are aligned. For now."

Brudais' heart plummeted.

"Do you accept my offer, Commander?"

His gaze fell to the floor, devising a way to respond that would not sound like a refusal.

"Would you give me a day to consider, Your Majesty?"

Ithiador glanced to his right where Prince V'pnor stood. The prince gave him a curt nod.

"I will have your answer by midday tomorrow, Commander."

Brudais nodded, bowing formally and turning on his heels.

His pulse raced as he stepped through the chamber doors. What had he done? He had killed one tyrant, only to set up another in his place. Ithiador meant to conquer the Ten Kingdoms with Brudais at the head of his army. Whether Ithiador had been seduced or enthralled by the Fayn at his side, the blood treaty had simply been a way to infuse magick into every decision that would be made from that point on. If Ithiador had already been under the Fayn's spell when he signed, then he would be immune to the consequences of the spellbinding, but none of the other royals would have that luxury. Ithiador could conquer with impunity, while a single defensive move against him would wreak havoc on the other realms.

It was not lost on Brudais that Ithiador might be able to accomplish such a task without him, but with him, he would have the *veritas'* support, and with them, the entire army. The Fayn had not attempted to ensnare him yet, but they only needed to wait until he had agreed to their ruse. He needed to get as far away from Creet as possible. His presence here only made the likelihood of Ithiador's plans succeeding even greater.

Brudais clenched his fists. Dania, and the child… he could not leave them here, while Kresha rumbled like a volcano ready to erupt. His pace quickened as he made his way through the castle corridors to the stables.

Dania would not go willingly, and he knew he could not make her, but the child was his, and he was devising a plan that would ensure its safety… well away from the grasping magicks of the Fayn.

Chapter Fifty-Seven

DANIA

Dania was used to the stares and whispers as she walked down the street now. She was a female dressed in male clothing; it wasn't something they saw every day, and it singled her out as the daughter of Grandis, who had trained with the Seasoned and survived the Tower of Lyes. Her trousers and tunic had been fitted by a tailor recommended by Brudais, though the attire had been feminized somewhat. Her curves were pronounced against the luxurious fabric. She didn't look like a commoner, but she certainly didn't look like a noble. She was forever in between, and so she thought her attire should accentuate this difference. Now, everywhere she went, she heard the gossips follow her, and saw the confused looks turn to recognition. No one else would have the guts to appear at court in such a scandalized fashion. It must be the daughter of Grandis who walked among them.

King Ithiador thought her display intriguing when she had appeared at her required audiences. He had given her a smile and commented on the design of the fabrics, failing to mention that she should have been in a corseted dress before the monarch. She had appreciated the leniency, but knew it was for the sake of her father, not her own deeds, that she had merited it.

The shadow of Grandis lay heavily on her. Everywhere she went, she heard his name in her wake. She had spoken to Brudais about how he had survived living in the shadows of such greatness. His response had been simple: "Do everything in your power to overcome it… or submit to the inevitability."

She would make a name for herself. Inevitability could hang, as could submission.

She had walked down High Street until she came to the blacksmith's shoppe. Moving past the sign that read 'Aurelius',' she entered the shoppe. The proprietors' back was turned as he stoked the fires of the forge, but he must have felt her presence, for he turned immediately, holding out the hot poker to his side.

"What can I do fer you—" He clearly didn't know what to make of her attire, seeing the long blond hair in contrast.

Dania offered a warm smile, which caught his eye. Recognition dawned upon him, and he threw the poker onto the ground and stepped forward, grabbing her around the shoulders and lifting her up in a bear hug. Dania grunted and laughed at the same time, but the rest of the air vanished from her lungs as Aurelius hugged her tightly.

"Awreyleeose," came her muffled reply, as her face was buried in his jacket.

"Apologies, lass," he said, releasing his grasp, setting her down, and holding her at arm's length. "You look a bit… odd… like that. Didn't recognize you."

"Odd?" she said, regaining her breath.

"Different, is all. You look… like a right lord. Only prettier."

"I'll take the compliment you meant, sir," she said, her smile widening. Her expression suddenly sobered. "Is he here?"

Aurelius smiled broadly. "He is, and without his parents, mind. The governor—steward—she set it up special for you."

Relief consumed her, and all the tenseness she had felt over the last few days melted away.

"In the house, lass. Go on, then."

When Dania entered the cottage next to the forge, she looked around the kitchen and saw the back of his golden-haired head as he held out a tentative hand to the fireplace. His governess swatted it away with a stern hand of her own.

"No, Lord Adrian; it's much too hot to be pokin' about the coals."

"Ah, but Lord Adrian is fireproof, my dear," Dania said, her voice shaking with anticipation. "Didn't you know?"

His head turned and he let out an excited squeal of surprise. His boyish grin was a balm to her heart.

"Day!" he called, jumping up from where he knelt on the ground. She squatted down so that she was level with him as he ran into her arms. She felt the world snap into place as she squeezed him, and a few tears slid down the sides of her cheeks.

"My Addie."

When she returned to the townhouse that evening, her spirits were high. Loya had promised her that she would smuggle her correspondence to Addie—regardless of his parents' wishes. She was a legend's daughter, and Okriad had just been demoted to company lieutenant. His standing was lower than her own in terms of reputation, which made her a bit giddy at the thought.

When she had shut the door, Brudais rushed to her in the foyer.

"You have to leave," he said urgently.

"What?" she replied, taken aback. "Why?"

He launched into an explanation of his audience with Ithiador, describing his suspicions in precise detail.

"I have a plan. Loya has consented to look after you until you come to term. She will put off the questions as to why the engagement with Ahnvil is being delayed, so long as you stay hidden."

"Where am I to go?"

Brudais faltered, and as he held her hands in his own, she felt them shaking. "That is up to you," he said quietly, hesitantly. "I'm to barter passage to Madidus."

"Madidus?" Another continent, but she understood why immediately. It was the Land of a Thousand Isles. No matter how long Ithiador and the Fayn looked for him, they would never find him, and their jurisdiction ended at Zevida Bay. To enter Madidus with an army would be considered an act of war against the Lowens. They would never risk such a venture for the capture of one man—even if that one man were Brudais.

The kennings on Leifius' sword came to her mind. '*World-breaker*,' '*anarchy-granter*.' If Brudais were to lead the Creetian armies, his fate would be sealed. She understood his urgency and need, but her heart ached all the same.

"Come with me."

Brudais' tone and eyes were pleading. She was reminded of his words before the wolf attack on the encampment. He had held her hand then, too, but the confidence that he had exuded was not present now. He looked utterly shaken.

"I can't," she said, her voice wavering. She would have loved to spend the next seven months lounging on an island in the middle of nowhere, slipping into bed with the man who stood before her, but what she wanted no longer mattered. "Loya and Staliva found me once using magick. What's to stop Ithiador from using the same spells to uncover my whereabouts were I with you? Besides… my place is in Krashkin. If what you say is true and Ithiador intends to break the treaty, I have to do my part to keep the peace and stability in the realms for as long as I can manage."

Brudais brushed a stray strand of hair out of her face, hooking it behind her ear. His expression was… proud. "As do I," he said.

His hand slid to the nape of her neck, and he pulled her forward, his lips locking with hers in a desperate kiss. *So, this is goodbye*, she thought, and a sob escaped her. He pulled her closer, his arm wrapping around her waist. She never wanted to let go of his embrace… but what she wanted no longer mattered.

Chapter Fifty-Eight

Loya

It had been a fortnight since Brudais, legend of Kresha, had been declared a war criminal and had been exiled. Loya still had difficulty believing it, that Ithiador had the balls to do such a thing. After two days of seething in the barracks, the *veritas* had packed their bags and headed to whatever corners of Creet they called home, with a promise that they would not return until their commander did. The better part of their army had disbanded, but the king's response was that they would not be needed in these times of peace. That was his official response, anyway. Loya had had an earful of Ithiador's true feelings on that matter behind closed doors.

When Brudais had come to her with a favor several weeks ago, she had been eager to help. The commander had been instrumental in her rise to power. Dania was with child, and although Loya was disappointed that Dania had neglected her advice not to get too attached, she understood the girl's reasoning. If Brudais had ever looked at Loya the way he looked at Dania, she might have forgone her ambitions in favor of a comfortable life tucked away with him. Love made one wholly irrational to one's own needs.

Now, it was Loya's task to prolong Dania's engagement to the Krashkin prince and hide her presence until after the birth of her child. She didn't anticipate much resistance on this front, but the most difficult part would be getting the babe to Brudais after. She would have to facilitate a nursemaid and a guard on a journey down the Recluos and across the sea to Madidus, where Brudais had assured her he would be waiting.

He was taking a great chance, trusting Loya with this much information. Once his status as criminal had been secured, Loya could simply have gone to the king and told him where he could find Brudais eight months from now, but something held her back… and that something was Brudais' silence when she had asked him why he was going to Madidus. Why would the commander abandon his country, his army, and the love of his life? The riddle had been eating at her every night since his departure.

Loya moved her skirts surreptitiously under the table. She sat in the king's private dining quarters with a plate of morsels before her: ripe cherry tomatoes, bright green leeks, and the moist breast of a pheasant, slathered in cream sauce. She had barely touched her food, and the king had noticed.

"What is it you wished to discuss, Loya? Clearly, the food doesn't suit."

"The food looks enticing, Your Majesty," she replied, "but I have no stomach for it today."

King Ithiador sat up straight in his high-backed chair, putting down his fork and knife on opposite sides of his plate. "Your moontime?"

Loya tried not to let her surprise show on her face. How could he have known that? Could he now smell weakness enough to exploit it? She shifted in her seat uncomfortably, but soldiered on.

"The subject matter I wished to bring forth regards our Creetian-Krashkin alliance."

"Is that so?"

"I think it would be wise to postpone their marriage until the Summer. The restoration of our realms' relationship should be more thoroughly celebrated. I think a royal wedding in Creet would have the people abuzz with excitement, a welcome diversion."

"Why would we wait so long?"

"I think Dania daughter of Grandis deserves a Creetian honor guard of female warriors. They would need to be trained, of course, and with Rydril's battalion on leave, and the *veritas*—well, they will need some time to be accepted by the people. Just as Dania was required to prove herself."

"And you think it wise to postpone such an important union for this endeavor?"

Loya straightened her back. "It would be a statement that would ensure the support of the people in the introduction of females in the military to replace—" She stopped herself before saying *'veritas'* again, as the look on Ithiador's face at their previous mention was approaching livid. "—our lost forces."

Ithiador sat unmoving for a moment, then looked up with a cold smile. "Yes. As ever, your mind is of great assistance in navigating these waters, Loya." Then he leaned forward. "I appreciate the part you have played in my ascension to the throne, but you should know that I won't forget the lengths you've gone to in order to sit where you now sit."

A threat and a thank you. She would celebrate and heed it. Loya bowed her head.

"Were I to persuade Your Majesty of these measures, Dania has insisted that she journey to the Naythic Temple in the Ohnville Mountains… for cleansing. It's a Krashkin tradition for the bride to live in isolation for a time before the wedding. She wants to show she respects their customs."

"How clever of her," the king said. "Although I had wished to use her to divert the realm's attentions from… a certain legend."

Loya smiled. "This act of selflessness in favor of Creetian-Krashkin relations *will* divert the realm's attentions. I assure you, his name will be lost to the winds within a few moons. A new legend has arisen in his stead."

"Am I unwise to give her to the Krashkins, then?"

"Not," Loya said slowly, "if we prolong the engagement, thus securing her place in our people's hearts."

Ithiador's lips curled once again into that cold smile.

Why had Brudais left? Loya was certain that smile had something to do with it, but she was now the Steward of Creet. She would hold her office with dignity and cunning, no matter what vipers lurked beneath the sheets.

Chapter Fifty-Nine

ELDEVA

Eldeva grabbed at her fur-lined cloak, tucking it in frustration against her frozen skin. These harsh winter climates of Zethland were about as different from the blistering heat of Sycil as could be, and her body still had much adjusting to acclimate to them.

It had been a while since she had played with fire magick, so her hesitancy nearly caused the spell to fail, but the flames flickered to life in the palm of her hand. The flame warmed only her hand, but the magick that spread through her extremities warmed her still further.

She looked around her as she stood on the terrace, the wind whipping through the snow-capped trees of the forest that surrounded the castle and all of Lolaith, Zethland's capital. The lake was frozen, and thick mounds of ice and snow covered its surface.

With a particularly powerful gust of wind, her magickal flame was snuffed out, and the heat of the magick within her dissipated, leaving a chilling emptiness in its wake.

She had been exiled to this barren place of ever-winter, and the worst of it was that she had come willingly. Given the choice, she would have chosen a kingdom which reveled in the education of magicks, so she could not truly complain about her lot. The Order of Estol was similar in many ways to The Old Order, but they refused to use magick through others. They called Eldeva a Reaper for her past sacrifices and said they would endeavor to stamp out the 'evil' practices that she had considered to be quite normal when living in Sycil.

She was lucky to be in a realm that had the magickal lore she required to seek her vengeance, but this time, Eldeva assured herself that she would not make the same mistakes as before, and she would bide her time carefully.

Ithiador had taught her an important lesson. She imagined she had loved him once, but he had made it clear that their 'tryst' was no more than that—lust and need. His betrayal by marrying that outcast bitch and choosing to make her queen, instead of a princess who was born to it… even if love had never flourished in their relationship, he still should have considered Eldeva to be a prize, whose royalty and dignity belonged on a throne. Instead, he had banished her to the winter wastelands of Zethland. An outcast. A pauper, dependent on the goodwill of others.

Eldeva's fists clenched at her thick fur cloak, both to increase the warmth and alleviate her anger.

Suddenly, she heard a sob from the other end of the vista. She turned to see Princess Xenia, sitting on a bench, gazing into the depths of the dark green forest before her. Her cloak had fallen from her shoulders and was draped around her waist, and her wracking sobs were almost silenced against the gales of wind carrying the drifting snow.

"Princess?" Eldeva said. As she moved closer, she could see tears falling from the woman's face, freezing to her skin as they slid down her cheeks. "Are you all right?"

Xenia looked up, wiping furiously at her face to hide the evidence of her distress. "I'm fine, Princess Eldeva."

"You don't look it," she replied, wiping off the snow that had accumulated on the bench next to her and sitting down. She instantly regretted it, as the cold seeped through her layers of clothes and into her body.

Xenia nodded vacantly. "No, I don't suppose I do." After a long moment of silence between them, Xenia looked up. "My son…"

Oh yes. Eldeva had heard what had happened to Brudais son of Leifius. After ridding his people of a tyrant king, he had been demoted from his station, exonerated, and then reviled as a war criminal—all within the span of a few weeks. She and the rest of Kresha had assumed his exile had meant that he would come to Zethland to spend his remaining days with his mother and her relatives—perhaps even lead their armies, as King Heqvelt was enamored with him. However, he had fled not to the north, but to the south, down the Recluos. He had been spotted in Sceryl, bartering passage on a ship whose heading had been Madidus. It was a riddle that the entire continent would be puzzling about for the next six moons.

Eldeva knew that this much was true: Ithiador's vacillation pointed to his guilt. Perhaps he had let something of his plans slip to Brudais—plans which involved the blood oath treaty and his Fayn friends. The magicks they possessed were beyond anything Eldeva could ever dream of, but it frightened her to her core that those beings held so much power in their pale palms.

She draped Xenia's fur cloak over the woman's shoulders, allowing her to continue her blubbering without freezing to death. Xenia was a powerful Keeper, and she could use friends like her in the coming years.

Friends like her son, too, would be a most auspicious boon to her cause. Brudais and Eldeva had both been spurned by Ithiador, their reputation in shreds since he had his way with them. They owed him for the troubles he had caused, the exile he had forced on them.

The world had been cruel to her, but for each slight she had suffered, Eldeva promised to be crueler.

www.ingramcontent.com/pod-product-compliance
Lightning Source LLC
Chambersburg PA
CBHW071335020826
48982CB00024B/770
9798992362329